IT WAS TIME TO CALL A HALT BEFORE IT WAS TOO LATE

"Honoria," he gasped, reaching behind his neck to unlace her fingers and bring her arms down to her side. "You really don't know what you're doing."

"Don't I?" Her blue eyes were glazed with passion, but her voice was even and clear.

Jack reached up and untied the fastenings at the back of her gown. "No, you don't," he said hoarsely.

She stood silent while he pushed the dress off her shoulders, down her arms, and onto the floor. She stood before him, clad only in her chemise, her swollen breasts jutting against the thin fabric. His hands ached to reach out and touch them, his mouth wanted to taste their sweetness.

Jack swallowed hard. If he was smart, he'd race out the door to the safety of his room. He was in as great a danger as he'd been in ever since he met her.

Wasn't this what I wanted? Didn't I plan to seduce her? He had done his work too well. She was ready and willing, and on

Jack reached out and to
made it a point never to

Prince of

Prince of Thieves

by

Melinda McRae

A TOPAZ BOOK

TOPAZ
Published by the Penguin Group
Penguin Books USA Inc., 375 Hudson Street,
New York, New York 10014, U.S.A.
Penguin Books Ltd, 27 Wrights Lane,
London W8 5TZ, England
Penguin Books Australia Ltd, Ringwood,
Victoria, Australia
Penguin Books Canada Ltd, 10 Alcorn Avenue,
Toronto, Ontario, Canada M4V 3B2
Penguin Books (N.Z.) Ltd, 182-190 Wairau Road,
Auckland 10, New Zealand

Penguin Books Ltd, Registered Offices:
Harmondsworth, Middlesex, England

First published by Topaz,
an imprint of Dutton Signet,
a division of Penguin Books USA Inc.

First Printing, May, 1994
10 9 8 7 6 5 4 3 2

Topaz is a trademark of New American Library,
a division of Penguin Books USA Inc.

Printed in Canada

To twist Churchill's words, never has one person owed so much to so many:

To Hilary, for keeping faith.

To Ruth, for her unflinching editing and constant encouragement.

To Megan, Jen, Kristin, and Liz, for their helpful voices at the other end of the phone. You pulled me through.

And to Eddie and the boys for the music.

The world is full of orphans: firstly those
    Who are so in the strict sense of the phrase;
But many a lonely tree the loftier grows
    Than others crowded in the forest's maze—
The next are such as are not doomed to lose
    Their tender parents, in their budding days,
But, merely, their parental tenderness,
Which leaves them orphans of the heart no less.

—Byron, *Don Juan*

Chapter 1

Shropshire, 1814

It was as good a day as any to die.

The man known as Jack Derry stared down from the gallows cart at the crowd gathering on the town common in Gorton. A soft summer breeze rifled his long, dark hair and the strands tickled his cheek.

He took a deep breath, then nearly choked on the fresh, sweet-smelling air, so different from the fetid miasma of prison. How long had it been . . . ?

Don't think about that now, he told himself. These last few moments were too precious to spend remembering the miserable hellhole that had been his home for the last five months.

His gaze drifted across the common. A fair turnout, Jack judged. Nothing like what a hanging in the city or any of the provincial capitals would bring, but it was a decent crowd for this part of the country. He should be flattered at "Gentleman Jack's" last success.

Feeling a light tap on his shoulder, he glanced back into the sad, weary eyes of the minister. A grin leaped to Jack's lips. "Still trying for one last chance?"

"It is never too late to save your soul, my son."

Jack laughed, a rich, ripe sound that sounded strangely foreign to his ears. When had he last laughed? At his trial, when they had pronounced the verdict of guilty? At the sentencing, when the order was death?

Oh, yes, he had laughed, finding the entire proceeding an amusing farce.

Now, he didn't find it so amusing. Yet Jack no longer cared. He only wanted the whole thing to be over and done with, so that he could . . . could what?

Be at peace with himself? He'd had plenty of time in jail to reflect on his wasted life, realizing it was only a matter of time before he came to some bitter end. There were worse ways to die than this. At least it would be quick

"Are you ready, Mr. Derry?"

He nodded curtly to the minister, who began to read from a worn prayer book. Jack concentrated on blotting out the words and focused his attention on the throng assembled on the green. A few of the onlookers met his challenging gaze; most looked away. He caught the eye of a fetching young lady and winked boldly, smiling at the blush it brought to her cheeks.

"Mr. Derry?"

The minister's soft voice brought Jack back to attention.

"We be ready," said the tall man standing next to him.

For one fleeting moment, Jack wished he had followed the advice of the men in the lockup and had drunk himself senseless this morning. His throat tightened in dread, making the simple act of swallowing nearly impossible; his fists clenched and unclenched spasmodically.

It was time.

Jack glanced down at his bound hands, then lifted his gaze to meet that of his jailer. And nodded.

It was time.

He focused his eyes on the lovely lass in the crowd and a brief smile flitted across his face. A woman had been his downfall; treacherous Rachel, who'd lied to save her own skin. Ironic justice that the last thing—

The black hood came down over his head, blotting out all light, and Jack sucked in his breath. Despite his resolve, rising panic bubbled up within him. He lifted his hands as if to tear the cloth from his face, then dropped them limply.

It was better this way, he reminded himself for the hundredth time. *Better for them and better for me. This way, no one will ever know.*

The cart rocked gently as the minister stepped down. Jack tensed, waiting for the hangman who'd been brought all the way from London for the occasion. He would fasten the rope around Jack's neck, the minister would utter a last prayer, then the horses would be whipped up and—

Please let it be quick.

In the ominous silence, the sound of thundering hooves and the noisy rattle of an approaching carriage rang in Jack's ears. A last-minute spectator? Jack's lips curled in derision. They had better hurry or they would miss the show.

"Stop, oh stop!" A woman's voice cried out above the din.

"Wot's going on?" the jailer asked.

"I say there, hangman, stop these proceedings!"

Jack froze at the words.

The voices in the crowd rose to an angry murmur, and Jack strained to hear what they were saying. He caught the words "judge" and "mistake" and "disgrace," but nothing else made any sense.

By some miracle was he going to be saved from this fate? Had Rachel recanted her story and absolved him of guilt?

Suddenly, someone tore the hood from his head, and Jack blinked at the bright glare of the summer sunshine.

He saw the judge—the same judge who had presided over the trial—standing in stern conversation with the deputy. A diminutive lady stood at his side, staring up at Jack with tear-filled eyes.

The judge took her by the arm. "Is it he?"

She nodded her head, dabbing at her eyes with a white handkerchief. "Thank God, we arrived in time."

She looked directly at Jack and spoke slowly, deliberately, as if talking to a young child. "Samuel, dear, it is I, Melissa. Do you recognize me?"

Jack examined the woman. Her huge poke bonnet hid most of her face, but he noted the creamy skin, tip-tilted nose, and wisps of reddish hair straggling from their pins. His eyes scanned her slender form for some sign of familiarity, then he sighed. Jack knew two things for certain: his name wasn't Samuel, and he had never set eyes on this woman before.

Yet her mistake might prove to be his salvation. What should he say? His words could mean the difference between life or death and he hadn't the foggiest notion what to do. Did he acknowledge her, or admit that he didn't know her?

"I say, man, do you recognize this woman?" the judge demanded.

Jack glanced at her again, as if hoping she would tell him what to say. She lifted her chin slightly and he caught a brief glimpse of those blue, tearstained eyes before she dropped her gaze again. Yet perhaps because he so badly wanted a sign, he thought he saw the faintest shake of her head.

His luck had been bad for so long, he shouldn't count on it turning now. But with a gambler's innate optimism, he had to give it a try. "No." Jack shook his head. "I don't know this woman."

The judge nodded and clasped the woman's hand. "It is as you say, ma'am. A sad case."

She dabbed at her eyes again, then directed a pleading look at the judge. "Would it be possible . . . ?"

"Of course. Hangman, release the prisoner."

Jack's legs nearly collapsed under him at the words. The crowd gasped and Jack heard the young woman release an audible sigh of relief. He had done the right thing, but what did it mean?

"You, there"—the judge pointed to the sheriff's deputy—"help the prisoner down from the cart."

"Ain't he to be hanged?"

"Not this day," said the judge. "And not at all, if the King be merciful." He turned to the crowd, whose angry murmurings over the cancellation of the day's entertainment grew louder. "Go home. There's to be no hanging today! There has been a gross miscarriage of justice in this case. Go home."

Jack could hardly believe his ears, but he wasn't going

to protest. The mercy of the king? Miscarriage of justice? Was he to be pardoned at the last moment? It seemed far too good to be true, particularly since his rescuer thought he was someone named Samuel.

He looked down at the strange woman again. She caught his eye for a moment and gave him a tremulous smile before she averted her gaze.

The deputy reluctantly helped Jack from the cart, scowling at the judge the entire time.

"Let's retire to the inn," the judge said. "There are papers to be signed before this matter is complete. I'm certain Mrs. Harding would like to rest out of the sun."

A hundred questions rushed through Jack's brain but he dared not utter any of them, for fear he would make a mess of things. He didn't know how the hand of providence had come to his aid, but he wasn't going to do anything that would put him back on that cart.

"My poor Samuel," whispered the woman, resting her gloved hand on his arm. "I am so sorry this happened. If only I had known . . . Come with us to the inn. We can get you a nice cup of ale there. You like ale."

Jack thought he would much rather have a glass of madeira, but he would willingly drink horse piss if it meant he wasn't going to hang today.

The inside of the small taproom was dark and cool, smelling of stale beer, roasted meat, and baking bread. Jack's mouth watered in anticipation.

"Now, Mrs. Harding, if I could trouble you . . ." The judge pulled out a chair and she sat down.

"Oh, sir, I am so grateful that we saved him in time." She sniffed audibly. "To think that my poor Samuel . . ."

The judge patted her shoulder in a fatherly manner. "There, there. All is well now. Only the formalities are left. I'll send the papers to London and release your poor husband into your care."

Jack tried to hide his amazement. First, this woman called him Samuel and now she claimed to be his wife. He might have done any number of foolish things in his life, but he knew he had not married this woman.

God, he needed that ale.

As if answering his wishes, a serving girl hastened in, bringing a tray with foaming mugs, hot bread, and cheese. Jack reached to grab the mug, forgetting that his hands were still bound. He looked to the judge and held out his hands.

"Please?"

The judge cast a wary glance at the woman. "Are you quite certain . . . ?"

"Oh, yes, please untie his hands. He won't cause any trouble, I know it."

"Very well." The judge slit the ropes that bound Jack's wrists together.

"My poor Samuel," the woman murmured soothingly, as she rubbed at the red, chafed marks. "Everything will be better now, I promise. I'll take you home and you'll be happy again."

"The ale?" Jack asked hoarsely. He would enjoy this charade more once he had a drink.

She handed him the mug and Jack drank half of its contents in one gulp. Had any country ale ever tasted so wonderful?

The judge cleared his throat. "There is the matter of the recognizance, ma'am."

"Of course."

Jack watched as the woman drew some notes from her reticule and handed them to the judge. She signed the papers, which the judge separated into two piles.

"Are you certain you can manage him by yourself?" The judge cast an apprehensive glance at Jack.

"Of course I'll be perfectly safe with him! He's my husband, after all." She smiled in a conciliatory way. "I do have my coachman, you remember. I am not completely alone."

"But what will you do when you get him home?"

"Even if his mind is impaired, he is still an able worker." Her eyes grew sorrowful. "At least he *will* be after he has been properly fed and tended. Do all prisoners fare so poorly in this town?"

The judge coughed. "We do what we can for the indigent men, Mrs. Harding."

"It appears that is not enough."

"Perhaps not, Mrs. Harding. But you may be on your way. I will write to you if any other questions arise. However, I feel confident that this matter will be dealt with in an expeditious manner."

"Good." She extended her hand. "I very much appreciate your assistance, sir. My prayers have been answered, thanks to you."

The judge beamed. "All in a day's work, my lady, all in a day's work. I never thought he was such a wrong'un as they claimed. But with Sir Charles so determined . . .

That is neither here, nor there. I wish you well, Mrs. Harding, and you too, Mr. Harding." He nodded at Jack.

Jack politely nodded back.

"Samuel." The woman touched Jack's arm lightly. "We are going home now."

Jack didn't hesitate further; he followed her out to the dust-covered traveling coach and climbed in. She took the opposite seat, the judge shut the door with a resounding slam, and the carriage lurched forward.

Perching gingerly on the edge of the seat, Jack stared at the woman who sat facing him. "Who in the hell are you?"

"Hush!" she hissed, looking around as if they could be overheard. "Do you wish to spoil everything?"

Jack reached out and clamped his hand around her wrist. "Don't mistake me. I am grateful beyond words for what you did. But I think you should tell me why you are calling me Samuel and masquerading as my wife."

"It was the only way I could think of to rescue you," the woman said. "If you are really Samuel Harding, the warrant for Jack Derry is invalid. And since poor Samuel is mentally defective, he cannot be tried for his crimes."

"Why are you rescuing *me*?" he asked.

"Because I need your help."

Jack's laugh was incredulous. "Do go on, Mrs. Harding—or is that even your real name?"

"Of course it isn't. But perhaps you should listen to my proposal before you find out more about me."

Jack settled back against the cushions. "I'm all ears."

"I need the services of a thief."

Jack stifled the urge to laugh again. Of course! It had

to be that. Never mind that he had nearly been hung for that crime. "Why me?"

"I was told that you're willing to help a lady in distress. I need you for two reasons. First, I want you to help me find something that is . . . misplaced. Then—"

Jack interrupted. "I'm not interested."

The woman opened her blue eyes wide in dismay. "What do you mean, you're not interested? They say Gentleman Jack never turns down a lady's request."

"By all rights, I'm supposed to be dead now. Since I'm not, I would like to stay alive for a while. And retrieving 'misplaced' objects for ladies will not insure that."

"There is no way you'll be caught."

Easy for her to say, when it was his life at stake. "How do you propose to guarantee that?"

"You need not concern yourself with the details. I'll take care of them. Are you willing?"

He fixed her with a curious glance. "What is it you want me to take?"

"A necklace."

"A necklace? You arranged this elaborate charade for a mere necklace?"

"It isn't a 'mere' necklace." Her chin rose haughtily. "It has been in my family since the time of Queen Elizabeth and is worth a fortune."

"If it's in your family, why are you taking it? Or dare I ask?"

"My uncle stole it from me and I want it back."

"Why not go to the authorities?"

"Because they wouldn't believe me." She bristled with indignation. "That necklace should have been *mine.* My father left it to me in his will. I *know* he did. Somehow, my uncle destroyed that will and put another in its place. He took everything. *Everything.*"

Jack folded his arms across his chest, eyeing her with weary interest. "How do I know this isn't an elaborate trap?"

Her brow puckered with exasperation. "I told you there is no way you can be caught. That is the other reason I need you—there are two necklaces. One is a very clever copy. I need you to tell me which one is real. Uncle plans to sell the fake one and cheat his buyer. When I take the real one, he won't be able to object else he'll have to admit that he sold the paste."

"What do I get out of it?"

"Besides your life? I will pay you for your trouble."

"I want half the proceeds."

"Half? That is ridiculous. I was told that you would only take a small percentage."

Jack grinned. "But you are asking me to do two things. My price goes up accordingly."

"I can only pay you five hundred pounds."

"Five hundred?"

"Where else can you get that much money so easily?"

"Do you have a buyer for this necklace?"

She flushed. "I thought you might be able to help me with that, as well."

"Hmm. Now it's three things you want me to do. My price is rising steadily."

"Six hundred."

"Eight."

"Six, and all your expenses."

Jack sighed. She was right: six hundred pounds looked like an enormous sum of money to him right now. He could live well on that amount. "Where is this necklace?"

"At my uncle's house—at least it will be, by the time we arrive there."

"How do you intend to manage the theft? Will you unlock the doors every night so I can search the house?"

"Don't be silly. You will be there as a guest."

Jack snorted derisively, plucking at his tattered shirt. "And how do you propose to accomplish that? You see me with everything I possess. I will look a bit out of place."

"I'll supply you with new clothes, of course. You are said to be quite the gentleman and this is not London society after all. I imagine you will fit in well enough."

"How gracious of you to say so."

"Don't sound so churlish. If I hadn't arrived in time, you would be dead now. Try not to forget that."

She had a point. She had saved his life. And if he hadn't thought his life worth saving an hour ago, now that he had it back, he wanted to hang on to it.

The whole plan might not be as bad as it first looked. If he had free run of the house, it should be easy to find this necklace. And once he had arranged for the sale, he would have money, clothes, and his freedom.

"I'll do it," he said.

"Good." She held out her hand. "Shall we shake on the matter, Mr. Derry?"

With a rueful grin, Jack offered his hand. "A thieves' bargain, miss."

"A thieves' bargain."

Jack leaned back against the cushions and watched her

through half-closed eyes. Half-hidden beneath that enormous bonnet, her features were rather pretty. Her traveling dress was a subdued gray, but Jack knew enough about women's clothes to recognize the fashionable cut. Obviously, she came from a family with money.

She certainly had nerve, and an impressive single-mindedness of purpose for one who looked so young. She couldn't be much over twenty.

"Dare I ask your name?"

"Honoria. Honoria Sterling."

"Miss?"

"Of course," she retorted. "If I had a husband, I wouldn't be in this fix."

"How old are you?"

"That is none of your concern."

"I like to know a bit about the person I'm working for."

"In due time, I'll tell you everything you need to know."

Closing his eyes again, Jack realized he was tired. Exhausted. Sleep had only come in brief snatches last night. Every time he had drifted off, he had awakened to the feeling of the rope tightening around his neck, the lurch of the cart, the feel of his legs dangling—

He took a deep breath to clear the horrifying images from his mind. *Forget them,* he told himself. Forget the past, and everything that had happened. Remember only that he was alive, and safe.

Chapter 2

Watching him sleep, Honoria sank back against the seat, limp with relief. She had succeeded. Jack Derry wasn't dead; he was sleeping across from her and had agreed to help. Now she must set the rest of her plan into motion.

For a moment, she felt a twinge of doubt. She hadn't told him *everything* yet. How would he react then?

Better to worry about the next step. Right now, Gentleman Jack did not look like much of a gentleman. It might take more time than she had thought to get him ready to play his role. And time was one thing she didn't have much of.

But she would do whatever she must to make sure he succeeded. She needed that necklace with an all-encompassing desperation. The money it would bring would give her the future she longed for. And Jack Derry was an integral part of that goal.

When she first learned that her uncle intended to sell the necklace, she'd been consumed with fury—until she realized what she must do. Uncle had taken her necklace; she would take it back. But she had to make certain she had the real one; the paste copy would do her no good.

Gentleman Jack would be her accomplice—a thief who specialized in retrieving "lost" trinkets, a thief with manners, charm, and nothing to lose.

The enormity of what she planned almost overwhelmed her. If only her father had not died. . . . But that carriage accident had robbed her of more than a father. Uncle Richard's treachery left her with nothing—no home to call her own, no money, and an uncertain future.

She'd left Norcross as soon as she'd discovered her uncle's treachery, seeking refuge with her old nurse. Honoria didn't care what people thought or said about that. But now, her limited funds were almost gone. She'd have to throw herself on the mercy of her mother's family—or go back to her Uncle Richard.

She yearned for the freedom to live as she wanted, without being dependent or subservient to anyone. The money from the necklace would allow her to regain control over her own life. That was worth all the risks she took now.

And Jack Derry was the key to her success.

Never having met a thief before, she had not known what to expect. Surely a thief who was called "gentleman" would be able to play his role without arousing suspicion.

Yet as she examined him carefully, Honoria's initial confidence wavered. His dark, lank hair brushed against his shoulders, a ragged stubble covered his face, and his months in prison had left him thin and pale.

Still . . . asleep he looked younger than when she had first glimpsed him in Gorton. He was good-looking, despite his rough appearance and the weary lines on his face. He had a strong, determined jaw, and the hint of a cleft in his chin. Yet it was his hands that intrigued her the most. Those long, lean fingers looked like the hands of a gentleman, rather than those of a common thief. She could understand why he was known as *Gentleman* Jack and how he managed to fit into society.

As she watched him sleep, Honoria gradually grew aware of something else. She wrinkled her nose in distaste.

After hesitating for a moment, she shook him gently. "Mr. Derry?"

His eyes flickered open.

"Could I ask you to lower your window, please?"

Blinking sleepily, Jack stretched his cramped muscles. "The air is a bit heavy in here."

"It isn't the air, Mr. Derry." Honoria pressed her handkerchief to her nose. "I fear you are the source of that unpleasant smell."

Jack grinned mischievously. "That is the price you pay for consorting with common thieves, Miss Sterling. Had I known you were going to come calling, I would have taken pains to pretty myself up."

"Well, we will soon take care of that."

"A good thing, too." Jack scratched his head. "A bath, new clothes, a hot meal. That would suit me just fine, Miss Sterling."

As he scratched again, Honoria pursed her lips but did not speak.

She watched warily as he leaned back and closed his eyes again. In moments, his gentle snoring filled the coach and she relaxed again. Honoria did not think he was a dangerous man, but she was glad her pistol was within easy reach. Dirty and ragged as he was, she still sensed a strength in him that made her uneasy.

Yet she had gone too far to turn back now. One way or another, she would make sure he played his part to perfection.

Jack's eyes snapped open at a sudden noise and he looked around in sleepy confusion. The carriage was not moving. In the dim light, he saw that Miss Sterling was gone. Cautiously, Jack peered out the window.

They were in the courtyard of a busy inn. For a brief moment, he thought of jumping from the carriage and running. Then reality pressed upon him. He didn't have anything beyond what he wore, no money, and no means of obtaining any. His clothes were rags, his appearance unkempt; he would not get far.

Honoria peered into the carriage. "Oh good. You are awake. I brought you something to eat."

The tantalizing aroma of the meat pies she carried wafted through the window and set up an unpleasant rumbling in his stomach. He grabbed a pie from her hand and greedily bit into it. Never had simple food tasted so good.

She climbed inside and sat facing him again. "I hope you do not mind eating here. I thought it best if you didn't leave the carriage."

"Afraid I might bolt for it?" Jack asked bluntly.

"No, I feared the other patrons would run from you."

He laughed and swallowed the last of the first pie and reached for another.

"Goodness, you are hungry," she said. "I would have stopped earlier, had I known. I thought you needed the sleep."

"I did." Jack looked at her blandly. "And there is another thing I need, now that we've stopped. The privy . . ."

"Of course. I will have my coachman accompany you."

Jack understood. She was still unsure of him and her caution pleased him. Jack did not want her doing anything foolish; there was more than a necklace at stake here—there was his life.

Jack dozed off again in the afternoon heat. He didn't know where she was taking him, and he really didn't care. There would be a soft bed and a hot bath at the end of the day, and that was all he cared about right now. That, and getting as far away from Gorton and the gallows rope as possible.

The summer shadows were lengthening when the carriage pulled off the main road and onto a narrow, rutted lane. The jouncing woke Jack and he peered about him anxiously.

"Are we at your uncle's?"

"Good gracious, no." Honoria laughed. "He lives at Norcross, in Gloucester. I am taking you to Nursey's today."

"Nursey?"

"My old nurse. Miss Redford. I needed someplace to hide you while I prepared you for your role."

"Wonderful." Jack sank back into his seat. An innocent girl and an old nursemaid. His ideal companions.

"Don't worry." Honoria's voice sounded soothing. "It will only be until I can get you some clothes."

"Won't your uncle wonder why I'm with you?"

A delicate tinge of pink spread across her cheeks. "I have developed a plausible tale."

"Oh?"

She swallowed nervously. "You will pose as my betrothed."

"Your what?"

"It was the easiest thing I could think of."

"How can you be engaged without your uncle's permission?"

"He is not my guardian," she answered vehemently. "In fact, he will be enormously relieved to think that I am to be wed."

"The last I heard, young unmarried ladies didn't travel about without a chaperone—particularly with their intended."

"That is where my cousin Edmond comes in. We will meet him on the way to Norcross and he'll accompany us there."

The situation looked more and more complicated by the moment. Jack glared at her with suspicion. "What else haven't you told me?"

"That is all. Except that you will be posing as Cousin Edmond's friend—to explain how I met you, you see."

"What does your cousin Edmond do?"

"Edmond doesn't 'do' anything," Honoria explained. "He lives in Yorkshire with my aunt. He is a sportsman; he lives to hunt and shoot." She looked anxiously at him. "You do know how to ride, don't you."

Jack nodded.

"Good."

He eyed her with an assessing look. "Does your old nurse know about your plan?"

She shook her head. "I told her that I am bringing Edmond for a visit."

"How do you propose to fool her—by keeping her blindfolded during the entire time?"

"Nursey's never met Edmond. And even if she had, I don't think it would matter much. Her hearing isn't very good and she doesn't see as well as she used to."

In other words, anything short of a Hottentot would pass as Edmond under her eyes.

The coach rolled to a stop in front of a rambling stone cottage, half-buried under ivy and some flowering vines. Honoria grabbed for the door and jumped out, and Jack followed her.

"It's small," Honoria said. "Norcross is far grander."

Jack grinned. "After the Gorton jail, a pigsty would look like a palace."

As he followed her into the house, Jack's eyes widened at the sight of her gently swaying hips, her shapely and softly rounded bottom. He thanked God she was easy on the eyes. He would hate to lower his standards out of desperation.

"Nursey?" Honoria called as she stepped through the cottage door.

"I'm coming, I'm coming." In a few moments a wizened, stooped lady stumped into the flagged hall. Dressed in black from head to toe, she wore an outrageously ornate cap of black lace that trailed ribbons in every direction.

She peered nearsightedly at Jack. "That you, Norry?"

Honoria reached out and clasped her hand. "I am back, Nursey, and I've brought Cousin Edmond with me, as I promised."

The old lady squinted at Jack through her spectacles. "Tall, ain't he? Must get that from his father. None of the Durhams were ever tall." She shook her head. "Saw a great, gawking girl in the village t'other day. Good thing you will never be tall, Norry, dear."

Jack glanced at his rescuer. The top of her head barely reached his shoulder. In his experience, short women tended to be bossy, and so far Honoria had done nothing to disprove that impression.

"Well, well." Nursey turned and shuffled down the hall. "I shall need to get you two settled. I will put Desmond in the room at the back. Hope he finds it good enough for him."

"Edmond," Honoria said, correcting her gently. "I think he will be pleased to sleep anywhere, Nursey. But first, he needs a bath."

Nursey sniffed the air. "Is that Desmond? Thought the dogs had got in again. Tore up the garden last week, they did. Water's heating in the kitchen, like you asked."

"Thank you." Honoria looked at Jack. "Edmond, do you mind bathing in the kitchen? That way, you won't have to haul everything up and down the stairs."

Jack would willingly have bathed in the front drive. He could barely remember the last time he had experienced a hot bath.

In the kitchen, pots of water steamed on the stove. The bathing tub in the middle of the floor would be cramped for his tall frame, but he didn't mind. It was a *bath*.

"There are soap and towels." Honoria pointed to the table. "I bought the strongest lye soap I could find, and there is oil of hyssop in the jug."

"Hyssop?"

Honoria looked uncomfortable. "The coachman suggested it. He says it . . . it helps to cleanse the body of unwelcome visitors."

Jack grinned at her discomfort. He'd had lice for so long in prison that they seemed like old friends.

"I have some clean clothes for you to wear." Honoria looked at him closely and frowned. "I had to guess your size, of course, but they will do for now. We can get you some proper clothing tomorrow in the village." She pointed to a box by the table. "Put your old clothes in there and Hawkins will burn them."

"You leave now, Norry dear," Nursey said. "I'll take care of Desmond here."

Jack stared at her indignantly. "You will not."

"Oh, bosh. I've bathed every manner of man-child in my life. Grown man's no different."

"Out!" shouted Jack. "Out, out, out!"

Honoria took the elderly lady by the arm. "Come with me, Nursey. Edmond is a trifle shy, you know. I am certain he can manage on his own."

Nursey peered at Jack doubtfully but allowed Honoria to lead her from the room.

Lugging the heavy pots of water from the stove, he poured them into the tub. When he had adjusted the water to a temperature barely below scalding, he stripped off his rags and tossed them in the box. He sniffed at the decoction in the jug and then bent over one of the empty buckets while he poured it onto his hair. He worked it in well until his scalp was thoroughly wet.

How long should he leave the stuff on? The cool liquid running down his back persuaded him that enough was enough. He plunged his head into a bucket of water and then shook his wet mop like a dog. At last, he lowered himself into the steaming water. His skin protested against the heat, but he gritted his teeth and endured the pain. It might scald a few more unwanted guests off his body.

Jack shut his eyes, his head lolling back against the metal rim. The tub was far too small, forcing his knees up to his chest. But this was heaven. Miss Sterling could leave him here forever and he wouldn't utter one word of protest.

Scant hours earlier he had stood on the gallows, almost welcoming the end of five months of hell. Now, he was free—or as free as he could be without a penny to his name—and he had an unexpected future stretching out before him.

A future that would be a damn sight more comfortable with his proceeds from that necklace. If she was willing to pay him six hundred pounds, what must the thing be really worth? It amused him that her uncle had swindled her; it only showed that all families were a nuisance. Jack had walked away from his own family eleven years ago, but they had turned their backs on him long before that. Jack, the incorrigible younger son. Jack, who refused to follow the path laid out for him by tradition and family desire. Jack, who had finally had enough and left at sixteen.

He'd spent most of the intervening years in a perverse attempt to prove that all their dire predictions were right—winning and losing at cards, dice, horses, and women.

He never intended to become a thief. He had retrieved Sarah's brooch from her lover's house as a favor. Even when grateful ladies began paying him for his efforts, he had not considered it his calling. But when money became tight, he had deliberately sought out clients. It had not bothered him to be called "thief"; it was only a convenient label he could hang on himself. And as long as ladies—and some not-so-ladylike females—acted with indiscretion, there would be a need for his services. He was paid handsomely for his efforts—in cash, and in other, more delightful ways.

It had all gone well until Rachel. She had hired him to help her "steal" some of her jewelry, in order to pay her gambling debts. But when her husband caught them, she denied it all and sent Jack on the path leading to the gallows in Gorton.

Until Honoria Sterling arrived just in time to set him free.

When the water cooled to the point where he could move without wincing, he grabbed the soap and scrubbed himself with fierce energy, wanting to scrape every last memory of prison off his skin. At that moment, he vowed that whatever the future held, he would never, ever, go to jail again. He would do everything, and anything, to make sure it did not happen again.

It would be easy enough to leave England when the job was done. The Continent was now open after years of war, and the young United States was across the ocean. Maybe he'd buy some land and become a wealthy Virginia planter.

When he finally realized that the water was cooler than the surrounding air, Jack left the tub and stepped gingerly across the flagstone floor. Grabbing the towel from the chair, he rubbed his body vigorously. He grimaced at the sight of the rope burns on his wrist. A shiver ran through him when he thought of just how close he'd come to death.

But he was alive. And he had every intention of staying that way.

He didn't believe in God, or providence, or even luck. But something had been working in his favor this morning, and he wasn't going to question the why of it. He would only make the best use of this new opportunity.

"I've brought you your clothes. I hope they are a reasonable— Oh!"

Jack gathered the towel around his torso and lunged behind the chair, glowering at Honoria in the doorway. "Do you always walk in on your guests, Miss Sterling?"

"I thought you were still in the tub." Her cheeks were scarlet, yet she continued to stare at him until Jack felt like a freak at a country fair.

"Have you seen enough?" he demanded harshly.

"Your clothes." She dropped the bundle from her arms and scurried from the room.

Horror wasn't the reaction Jack usually elicited from women, but he doubted that any female would vie for his attentions now. He looked down at his pasty skin and protuberant ribs—five months in prison hadn't done much for his appearance.

He inspected Miss Sterling's choice of clothing. The shirt was fine lawn—a little frayed about the collar and cuffs, but nicer than anything he had worn in a while. When he pulled it over his head he discovered the sleeves were short and the body too wide, but it was clean.

Apparently she was ignorant of all the components of a man's dress, for there weren't any drawers. Shrugging, he pulled on the socks, and breeches.

His wet hair dripped down the back of his shirt, reminding him that he needed to do something about that mess.

"Miss Sterling?" he called. "Cousin Honoria?"

"Yes?"

"I need a comb and brush for my hair."

"You need more than that," she said sternly, entering the kitchen. She pointed to a chair. "Sit."

He looked at her doubtfully. "What are you going to do?"

"Cut your hair." She pulled a pair of scissors from her pocket. "Unless you are trying to bring back the styles of Charles II?"

Jack sat.

"Did you rinse it thoroughly with the hyssop?"

"And I scrubbed it with the soap till my scalp was raw. Believe me, I don't enjoy lice any more than you would."

She tugged and pulled at his hair, untangling the snarls

without regard for his pain. All the while she hummed a disastrously off-key tune.

As she pulled and cut his hair, Jack gritted his teeth and tried to think of pleasant things—a nice glass of madeira, a warm, soft bed, a warm, willing woman in that bed . . .

"There." Honoria put down the shears. "You're a bit more presentable."

Jack brushed a damp clump of hair from the bridge of his nose. "I don't suppose you have shaving gear?" *That* would make him feel more presentable.

Honoria left, to return moments later with a small leather case. A silver-handled razor, brushes, and shaving soap fitted neatly inside.

"I'll need a mirror," Jack told her.

"Oh, I'll shave you."

"Like hell you will."

"Don't be foolish, Mr. Derry. I shaved my father for many years."

"And he's dead now."

Honoria glared at him. "I did not kill my father and I have no intention of killing you."

Jack moved as if to comply, and then whirled toward her. Grabbing her tiny wrist, he carefully extricated the razor from her fingers.

"A mirror, Miss Sterling?"

Her expression showed surprise but not fear. She was a game one.

"You needn't worry that I will use the razor against you." He grinned. "You have your pistol, after all."

"It isn't that . . ."

Suddenly, Jack realized she was more worried about him than herself. "My dear lady, if I had any intention of doing myself in, I would have cheated the hangman long ago. No"—he rubbed his hand across his stubbled cheek—"I only want to feel completely clean again. And I will be damned if I'll let a woman shave me."

She nodded and retreated from the room again, returning a short while later with a small mirror.

When he finally left the kitchen, Jack felt like a new man. He needed only a good pair of boots and a glass of fine wine to make his life complete.

Honoria wasn't in the parlor, but Jack saw the ancient nurse sitting near the window, a pile of mending in her lap.

"Is that you, Desmond?" she demanded.

"Yes! Where is Miss—Cousin Honoria?"

The old woman peered at him over the rims of her spectacles. "I know you think you are fooling her, and me too. But I wasn't born yesterday, no indeed. I know what you are up to."

"You do?"

"Yes, indeed. And I will not have it, do you hear me? Thinking you can dance in here, claiming cousinship as the reason to take my Norry away. I know your game."

He eyed the old lady cautiously. "What game is that?"

"Game? 'Tis no game, you young rascal. Norry deserves a good life and I mean to see that she gets it. Living on some isolated farm is not for my baby, no indeed. She was born the daughter of a lady and she deserves to be a lady."

"I wish you both luck in *that* quest," Jack muttered.

"What's that? Speak up, young man."

"I said Honoria certainly is a lady."

Nursey nodded her agreement. "That's why she has no business with you up in Yorkshire. You will have to take your fancy plans elsewhere, Desmond. Find another girl."

Comprehension dawned. Nursey thought that he was after Honoria's hand in marriage. He smothered a laugh.

"I have no intention of taking Cousin Honoria to Yorkshire," he said firmly.

"Tsst," hissed the old lady. "Do not think to turn me up pretty. Someone has to look after that girl."

Honoria stepped into the room. "What girl?"

"You, Cousin Honoria. Nursey believes I have designs upon your fortune."

"Now, Nursey, I told you Edmond was here for a visit. He is going to escort me to Uncle's."

"And then take himself back to Yorkshire." Nursey looked darkly at Jack.

"Whatever you wish," he said, looking doubtfully at Miss Sterling. "Why does she dislike Edmond so?"

Honoria laughed. "Nursey is firmly convinced that I shouldn't marry anyone below the rank of earl. You are not elevated enough to suit her."

"Thank God." Jack looked down at his stockinged feet and wiggled his toes. "I don't suppose you have another pair of boots for me."

She licked her lips nervously. "We'll have to get them in town, with the rest of your clothes."

Jack stifled a grin. Did she think he'd flee in the middle of the night? He had no intention of leaving, but she didn't need to know that. Let her think that she was treating "Gentleman Jack" with proper caution.

Chapter 3

Dinner was a simple meal, prepared by Nursey's serving girl, but it tasted wonderful to Jack. He ate until he knew he couldn't swallow another bite.

"We sit in the parlor in the evening," Honoria told him, when they'd finished eating. "Nursey likes me to read to her."

The room was stifling hot, with a small fire burning in the grate to keep Nursey warm. To Jack's relief, she fell asleep almost at once. If she called him "Desmond" one more time . . . Jack dragged his chair as far from the fire as he could and slouched down in it. He tried to mask his boredom while he listened with half an ear to Honoria read from Milton.

From under lowered lids, Jack examined her closely. He wouldn't characterize her as beautiful. Her features were average: her nose a little too tipped, her lips a bit too thin for his taste. Still, she had an innocent prettiness about her that he liked.

Innocent was certainly the right word. Innocent and naive as hell. He shuddered to think what could have befallen her if she had chosen one of the other prisoners in

Gorton to carry out her scheme. Pistol or no pistol, men like Eddy Muldoon or Roger Hart would have stripped her of every item of value—including her undoubted virginity—and left her in a ditch without so much as a by-your-leave.

Honoria prepared for bed that night with an aching weariness. She had been on edge all day, from her first fear in the morning that she might arrive too late to rescue Jack Derry from the gallows, to the strain of bringing him to Nursey's and getting him settled. Now, she needed to buy him clothes, fill his head full of the things he needed to know, and then make the journey to Norcross.

In truth, she couldn't complain too much about Gentleman Jack. Although she deplored his mocking manner, his speech held a hint of refinement that matched those gentlemanly hands. But was he enough of a gentleman to carry on the elaborate charade that she planned? Would he be able to pass as Edmond's friend—and as the kind of man she would marry?

He had to, she thought with fierce determination. This was her one chance to free herself forever from her uncle. If she failed—if Jack Derry failed—there was no future for her. She would be dependent on Uncle Richard forever. It was a fate she couldn't endure.

Bitter anger flooded her as she considered her predicament. This was all her Uncle Richard's fault for stealing her inheritance. She would show him that there was more to Honoria Sterling than he thought. She would steal the necklace out from under his nose and then she would travel to the places she and her father had talked about.

Italy. Egypt. Turkey. And when she tired of traveling, she would find a place to call home, until the urge to travel came upon her again.

And maybe she would find the one thing she wanted most of all—a family of her own. A husband, and children to gather around her in the evening, and make her feel needed, and wanted, and alive.

Jack stretched lazily. He'd slept like a baby; exhaustion and a soft bed conspired to give him one of the best nights he'd had in months. Once again he thanked the luck that had brought him here. He was out of prison and facing the future once again.

This job might even prove to be a more pleasant experience than he had first anticipated. At least he'd be able to eat and sleep in comfort. At best, he would find himself amid a convivial gathering at a country house. It had been a long time since he'd enjoyed that life and he was eager to enjoy it again—good food, excellent wines, amusing conversation, and an army of servants to take care of all his needs.

He dressed quickly and made his way to the kitchen.

Honoria greeted him. "Good morning. Or should I say, 'good afternoon'?"

"What time is it?"

"Half past twelve."

"I slept fourteen hours?"

Nursey waggled a warning finger. "Always said traveling at these modern speeds was a danger. Better in the old days, when people knew enough not to task themselves unduly. Bad for the liver, it is."

Honoria quickly set some bread, cheese, and sliced ham on the table. Jack ate hastily, with enthusiasm.

When he glanced up, he found Honoria watching him intently. "Is something wrong?"

She pointed to the napkin beside his plate. "Do you know what to do with that?"

Jack grabbed the cloth.

"How, exactly, did you earn the nickname 'Gentleman Jack'?" she asked.

"It had nothing to do with my table manners." He winked broadly.

"Oh." A prim expression settled on her face.

"But I assure you, Miss Sterling, I will have no problem posing as a guest. I merely forgot myself in the face of the best food I've seen in months."

Honoria rose. "After you have eaten, shall—"

"I want to go outside."

"Really, Mr. Derry, it is most important that you—"

"I've been in prison for five months, Miss Sterling. Locked in a room with only the briefest glimpse of the outside world. You can't keep me locked up in this house as well."

Honoria acquiesced reluctantly. "You may take a turn around the garden."

"You have my boots."

She looked flustered at the reminder. "I'll get them."

As if she'd forgotten she had taken them, Jack thought wryly. He was surprised she hadn't locked him in his room last night.

Then again, maybe she had.

Honoria set his boots before him with an apologetic

smile. "Hawkins tried to do his best, but I'm afraid there wasn't much to work with."

Jack's boots still looked old and battered, but every decent patch of leather shone with a shine many valets would envy. "The man must be a wizard."

"He has his talents," Honoria said, fastening her pelisse.

Jack followed her outside into the small, overgrown garden behind the cottage. He unlatched the gate and stepped into the lane outside. Nothing but open fields stood between him and the tall trees that marked the nearest cottage. It was more space than he had seen in months.

Despite the hot afternoon sun, Jack wanted to break into a run, just for the sheer enjoyment of his freedom. He plunged a hand through his hair and looked around, marveling at everything he saw and heard. The guinea-gold hue of ripening grain on the far hill. Birds twittering across the sky. The faint bleating of sheep somewhere in the field and the lowing of a distant cow. The sweet smell of the very air around him.

God, it was good to be alive.

Honoria took her own delight in watching him. For a grown man, he was most childlike in his enthusiasm. Still, she could understand his joy. She couldn't begrudge him his sense of freedom.

Jack headed across the field in long, loping strides, moving so fast that Honoria was hard-pressed to keep up. "Slow down, please," she gasped.

He halted and turned, arms akimbo, with that wicked,

unsettling grin on his face. "I'm surprised at you, Miss Sterling. I thought you had more pluck."

"You put on skirts and see how fast you can tromp across a field." Honoria felt a mote of satisfaction at the fact that he was breathing hard himself.

"I've made a list of all the guests who are to be at Uncle Richard's." She handed him a folded piece of paper. "Perhaps you should look at it, to make certain you do not recognize anyone."

"Do any of the guests know about the necklace?"

"*Everyone* knows about it. It's the talk of the town." She saw the look of dismay in his eyes.

"Why is it the talk of the town?"

"A German prince is buying it," she explained. "That's why it will be at the house. He's coming to get it."

Jack stared at her open-mouthed. "You plan to steal this necklace from under the nose not only of your uncle but also some prince?" He pointed an accusing finger at her. "Miss Sterling, you are quite insane."

"I am not," Honoria said, calmly picking a daisy from the clump at the side of the path. "How else am I to get my hands on it? Usually it's in the vault at the bank in London."

"It's hard to believe that your uncle would try to swindle the prince with a paste copy. Isn't that dangerous?"

"Not at all. It is so excellent a copy that only an expert jeweler could tell the difference. Or you."

He shook his head. "Pardon me if I'm a bit skeptical of this plan."

Honoria ignored his doubts. "You are free to depart at

any time, Mr. Derry. It's your decision whether or not you wish to have six hundred pounds with you when you do."

Jack opened his mouth as if to add something, then closed it suddenly.

Honoria watched him carefully as they continued walking at a slower pace. He moved with a careless, easy assurance, looking relaxed and comfortable. She found him far more intimidating than the desperate prisoner she had rescued yesterday.

"I would like to review the family history with you," she said as they reentered the house.

"I want a bath."

Honoria glared at him. "You had a bath yesterday."

"I did. And I'll probably have one again tomorrow, and the day after that, and the day after that too. And if I'm lucky, in a month or so I'll feel clean again."

"You can bathe every hour if you wish once we reach Norcross, but here you must concentrate on what I have to tell you."

"I can't concentrate if I'm uncomfortable." Jack scratched behind his ear. "One bath isn't enough to get rid of all the creatures."

Honoria took an involuntary step backward and considered. It wouldn't do any good to take a vermin-infested man to Norcross. "You'll have to heat your own water." She pointed to the buckets in the corner.

He bowed. "As you wish."

Jack behaved as a perfect gentleman at dinner, to show her that her confidence in him wasn't misplaced. Why had she decided to take such drastic steps? Jack had once prided himself on how well he knew women—until Rachel came along. Now he wasn't certain whether he knew anything about them. Once again, they seemed as mysterious and inscrutable as they had all those years ago when he first felt the fascination of their siren's call. And Honoria Sterling puzzled him more than most.

In the parlor after dinner, he sank into his chair with a sigh. Another dull, boring evening. Jack began to look forward to visiting the wicked uncle.

While Honoria read *The Times*, Jack evaluated her form. She was quite short. The tips of her toes barely touched the floor when she sat back in the chair. Yet short as she was, she was all in proportion. He remembered the tempting sway of her hips that he'd admired yesterday. She was well-rounded in all the right places. Beneath the cloth of her dress, her breasts would be soft, warm, inviting, her skin smooth and silken . . .

In the glow from the fire, her hair shone. He tried to find the words to describe the exact shade of her hair. Red sounded harsh, auburn too tame; it wasn't copper-bright, but a softer hue. More of a pale chestnut. Like the color of his first pony.

He stifled a laugh. He *had* been in jail too long. He never would have compared the color of a woman's hair to a horse's coat before. He'd have used a more flattering, seductive comparison.

"What's that you say?" Nursey's voice grated in his ears. "The Russians are invading? What happened to Bonaparte?"

"The Tsar was visiting London, Nursey," Honoria explained. "For the celebration of the Allied victory."

"The world has been saved for autocracy," Jack noted dryly.

"You hold republican sentiments?" Honoria asked him.

"Oh, not at all. The rule of the common man would be the ruin of us all."

"Eh? What's that? We're to be ruined?" Nursey demanded.

"We have been saved from ruin," Jack shouted back. "Now, if only someone will save us from the victors."

"Do be quiet, both of you, and listen." Honoria turned back to the paper.

"Do you honestly think I care what's going on in London?" Jack asked. "Tell me something I need to know."

"What would you like to hear?" she asked sarcastically. "The criminal reports?"

Jack jumped up, and grabbed the paper from her hands and sat down again.

Opening the paper, he scanned the page. "See? Now here is something of value." He read an account of the elaborate celebrations in Hyde Park.

Honoria stared at him. "You can read."

"Of course I can read."

"I assumed . . . I wasn't sure you could."

Jack's lips twisted in a cynical smile. "It's useful in my line of work. I pay particular attention to the social notices."

Honoria colored.

Nursey glanced at him sharply. "What's that you say, Desmond? Work? Pah! You've never done a lick of work in your life, I'd wager."

"Of course not," Jack retorted. "I live a life of slothful idleness."

"Cousin Edmond has a nice estate in Yorkshire." Honoria directed a pointed glance at Jack. "He only has to work at being a gentleman."

Ignoring her, Jack scanned the advertising in *The Times*. Gloves, carriages, horses, and wines of every quantity and description. All for sale. If one had the money.

Remembrances of his life in London came back in a rush. Wild gallops through the park in the morning fog. Dawn peeking through the curtained windows of some gambling hell, when the next turn of a card meant success, or ruin. Life pushed to the limits every day, without a thought for the next. Only in the last months had he realized just how stupid he had been.

While Jack read to himself, Honoria stole several glances at him. She now suspected that he was of higher birth than she first thought. Had cards been his downfall? Or perhaps he'd had an indulgent mother, who spoiled and petted him, and made him unwilling to follow his father's trade. And when he had lost his money, he had no talents.

Except good looks and charm. He had those two things in abundance. Even Honoria, who had little experience with men outside her family, was forced to admit he had appeal. Those large, expressive brown eyes were his best feature, particularly when combined with that devastating smile.

Honoria smiled. "You've worked hard today. Nursey always has a glass of sherry before she retires. Would you like some?"

Jack grimaced. "I detest sherry." He pushed himself out of the chair. "I think I'll go to bed."

"Good riddance," Nursey mumbled.

He hastily pulled off one boot and tossed it to the floor at her feet. Honoria looked at him with a puzzled expression.

"Just so you know I'm not planning my escape," he said with a wide grin. He pulled off the other boot and padded off to bed in his stockings. Halting at the door, he turned back, giving her a broad wink.

"Don't forget to lock my door as well."

Chapter 4

Over the rim of her upraised teacup, Honoria glanced at Jack as he entered the kitchen. "Good morning, Cousin."

He growled a greeting as he took his seat. "What exciting activity do you have planned for today?" he asked, unable to keep the sarcasm out of his voice.

"Today we'll get you new clothes."

"And boots." Jack sat down, shaking out his napkin with a flourish.

Honoria brandished a sheet of paper. "Everything you need is on my list."

"May I see it?" She'd probably left off half the things he needed.

"Later," she said airily. "Eat, so we can get started."

After breakfast, he dutifully followed her out to the carriage. As it jounced down the lane, Jack glanced out the windows with growing curiosity. He had been too exhausted to pay attention to his surroundings when he'd arrived, but now he found it a treat to examine the verdant countryside. He wondered idly what county they were in.

Having slept for most of the journey, he had no idea how far from Shropshire they'd traveled.

Glancing down at his ill-fitting shirt, he hoped that he'd be able to find some decent clothing—something that fit properly.

His eyes widened with surprise when the coach reached the outskirts of Manchester. It wasn't London by any means, but it was a far cry from the market town he'd expected. There was bound to be a decent tailor here.

Jack could already envision his new wardrobe: fine lawn shirts, of course, and crisply starched neckcloths. Vests in subdued colors—perhaps with some elegant embroidery—breeches of the softest buckskin, and a pair or two of pantaloons. There would riding coats, morning jackets, nightshirts, robe, stockings, shoes, boots . . .

"Where are we going?" he demanded after the carriage drove past the second tailor's shop he spotted.

"To a merchant who won't take all my money," Honoria retorted. "Did you think I was going to buy you a fancy new wardrobe? I have better uses for my money. You will be able to buy whatever you want *after* you retrieve my necklace."

The carriage finally stopped before a shabby storefront on one of the side streets.

"This is a dealer in secondhand clothing!" Jack protested.

"Yes, Mr. Derry, it is. And if you want to have anything to wear, you had better come inside with me now." Honoria climbed down from the coach and entered the shop.

The proprietor greeted her with enthusiasm.

"My poor cousin had his trunk stolen." She motioned for Jack to come closer. "Do you have some clothing that might fit him?"

"He is rather tall." The man looked at Jack with a doubtful expression. "Still . . . I'll see what I can do."

He bustled around the shop, snatching items of clothing from the towering heaps scattered atop every surface. At last he plopped down a great armload of clothing on the counter in front of Honoria.

She inspected each item with a critical eye, tossing aside a well-worn shirt. This was going to be more of a problem than she had thought, Honoria realized. Not only did the clothes have to fit Jack, they also had to be of the right quality.

"Jack, come help me."

Honoria pulled a pair of dark green breeches from the pile and handed them to him. "These look like they will work."

A disdainful look crossed his face. "You expect me to wear these?"

"What's wrong with them?"

"They're so . . . provincial."

"I hate to tell you this, Jack, but we *are* in the country. You won't be wearing black satin knee breeches to dinner." She shoved a pile of shirts into his arms. "See if these fit as well."

Grumbling under his breath, Jack ducked into the curtained alcove to change.

He reappeared a short time later, striking a dandified pose before her. "Will this do, Cousin dear?"

Honoria glanced at him briefly, nodding in approval at

the fit of the clothes, then pointed to a stack of waistcoats. "Look for something suitable there."

She bent to look at the shopkeeper's new offerings, then turned as Jack tapped her on the shoulder.

"What do you think?"

He held out his arms and slowly circled around, giving her a full view of the vivid green-and-pink striped atrocity he wore.

"That has to be the ugliest waistcoat I have ever seen!"

He grinned. "There is this other"—he held up one embroidered with gaudy pink roses—"which do you like best?"

She darted him an appalled glance, then realized he was teasing her, and laughed. "I think you should keep both. You will be the most stylish man at Norcross."

Until that moment, Jack had not realized just how enchanting his rescuer was. When she smiled, there was a dimple in her right cheek, and her eyes brightened with delight.

"Do that again."

"Do what?"

"Smile. I want to see that dimple again."

Blushing, Honoria looked away. "I beg you, *Cousin*, do be serious."

Jack held up a vest of plain gray silk. "Is this better?" He slipped it on and buttoned the front. "See, it even fits."

"Much better. Did all the shirts fit?"

"As if they were made for me."

"Good." She turned to the hovering shopkeeper. "We'll take the shirts and that vest. Plus the breeches."

"Don't forget stockings," Jack said as he slipped behind the curtain. "And handkerchiefs. And drawers, Cousin Honoria. A man must have drawers."

At the next shop, they found a riding coat, and evening wear for the country. Jack thought longingly of the grand clothes he'd owned in better days—tailor-made coats that were so snug he could barely swing his arms, shirts of the finest lawn, stockings in pristine white silk, and boots of highly polished leather. All were gone now, sold ages ago to keep him alive in prison. He shrugged. He could think of worse uses for them.

At last, they found everything he needed—even boots and shoes. Honoria settled amid the packages in the coach with a sense of satisfaction.

"We can find the other items you need among my father's things." She glanced at Jack. "We need to think of a new name for you to use."

"Jack's safe enough," he said slowly. "You can't hang a man for being named Jack. How about . . . Barnhill? I knew a fellow with that name up in Gorton."

"Will he mind if you use it?"

"Probably not. He's dead now." He lay back against the cushions and closed his eyes.

Honoria watched him. She knew a few more things about Jack Derry now. He liked expensive things—no doubt he would have spent all her money if she had let him. As it was, she had laid out more than she'd planned, but his new wardrobe was necessary if he was to play his role. His success was far more important than a few extra shillings.

She still didn't know what to think about him. She'd expected a more deferential attitude from him—after all, hadn't she saved his life? But he seemed more intent on teasing her than thanking her. Teasing her! What kind of thief was he?

A *gentleman* thief, she reminded herself.

His easy assurance both attracted and repelled her. It was like the fascination of a candle flame—one wanted to touch, but knew one's fingers would burn if they got too close. And she did not doubt she would be burned by this man.

She and Jack were two very different people. She could no more adopt his easygoing ways than he could see her need for a stable future. A man like Jack Derry didn't care a whit for things like safety, and security.

Maybe he'd never had them, or didn't realize their value. But for her, who'd known both and had them rudely pulled out from under her when her father died, they were the most important thing of all. More important than legalities and society's rules. Important enough that she'd plotted and lied to rescue a thief from the gallows and planned to fool her uncle and all his guests in order to take back her necklace.

"I hate to see a woman thinking so hard. It leads to wrinkles."

Honoria was startled and annoyed by Jack's devil-may-care attitude. "One of us has to plan ahead," she told him.

"But not to that extent. There is very little you can do about your problems while you're in this carriage."

"Then what do you suggest I do?"

Jack grinned. "Why not enjoy the scenery?" He gave her

a searing head-to-toe look that left her feeling hot and flushed. "*I* am."

Her cheeks flaming, Honoria averted her gaze.

"I want to start packing right away," she informed him when they reached Nursey's. "I don't want to discover I've forgotten something at the last moment."

Jack found it hard to believe that the efficient Miss Sterling could forget anything.

"We're leaving soon, then?"

She nodded. "Tomorrow. My cousin is expecting us."

"Packing's a monumental task," Jack said with a grin. "Would you like me to help you?"

Honoria smiled. "I can pack my own things, thank you. There's a small trunk in the nook under the stairs. You can put your clothes in it. I'll have Hawkins bring the rest of your things in."

Jack grunted.

Hauling the small trunk back to the room, he gathered his clothes and flung them onto the bed. Shirts, cravats, waistcoats. He grinned. Drawers, stockings. Scooping up an armload, he tossed them into the trunk and reached for more.

"Here's the rest of your shirts." Honoria stepped into the room and halted abruptly, staring aghast at the jumble of clothes in the trunk. "What are you doing?"

"Packing," Jack replied, dropping the next pile of clothes into the trunk.

Setting the shirts on the bed, Honoria plucked Jack's clothes from the trunk. "This isn't packing. You've just tossed things in here willy-nilly."

"How else does one pack?" Jack asked innocently.

"You fold them," she said. "Neatly and place them inside the trunk in an orderly fashion. Otherwise things are so crumpled it can take hours to iron the wrinkles out."

Jack shrugged. "I didn't think a few wrinkles mattered."

"They may not in your circles, but they will at Norcross."

Jack picked up a waistcoat and folded it into a tiny bundle. "Is this better?"

"Give me that!" Honoria snatched it out of his hands. "I'll do your packing. Go entertain Nursey, so she won't try to help me."

"Afraid my shirts will end up in your trunk?"

Honoria laughed lightly. "Or worse." She waved him off and turned to pack his trunk.

When she finished, she found him in the parlor. Nursey slept in her chair and Jack was reading *The Times*.

Honoria drew a slip of paper out of her pocket. "I made a list of everything I put in your trunk. Did I forget anything?"

Jack glanced quickly at the list and shook his head. She was incorrigible with her lists. His mother would adore her.

He instantly recoiled at the thought. He hadn't thought of his mother in an age—well, maybe briefly on that day at Gorton. But not in such a specific way.

Honoria Sterling was just the sort of respectable female his entire family would like. And that realization was strong enough to dampen any interest he might feel for her. Jack would walk over hot coals before he'd do anything to please his family.

After all, hadn't he nearly hung for that very reason?

Then he laughed. He doubted he could ever do anything good enough to suit them. He'd always be rebellious Jack, obstinate Jack, imperfect Jack, the family black sheep. The youngest child, who, instead of being cosseted and cherished, had been ignored. Younger sons were a nuisance, and the youngest was the biggest nuisance of all.

And he'd lived up to the label. Terrorizing the nursemaids, tormenting his tutors, openly battling his father over every point of contention. Until they'd given up and washed their hands of him.

He could live with their disapproval. It was their indifference that was killing. So he'd run, and was running still. And would keep running, until he found something he cared about more than himself.

If he ever did.

He tossed and turned on his bed for what seemed like hours before he finally gave up the attempt to sleep. Pulling on his clothes, Jack slipped out of his room and headed toward the parlor. Maybe reading the papers would put him to sleep.

He grabbed *The Times* and settled into a chair. What would he not give for a nice glass of brandy! But only Nursey's detestable sherry was available.

A sound caught his ear and he lowered the paper. Honoria stood in the doorway, a pistol pointed directly at him.

Jack raised his hands in a defensive gesture. "I couldn't sleep."

"Neither could I," she replied in a low voice.

His eyes met hers. "Would you mind lowering the pistol?"

Flushing, Honoria lowered the weapon. "I thought it was a housebreaker."

Jack laughed. "Didn't you think I'd protect you? Or did you think I was the guilty one?"

She stepped into the room and set the pistol on the table. "I wasn't sure what I would find."

"You really don't have anything worth stealing. It'd take a desperate man to be interested in a cottage like this. I'm not depraved enough to steal from an old lady."

"A rather high-minded notion from a convicted thief," she observed.

"Morality has nothing to do with one's social status—or criminal record," Jack retorted. "Some of the most amoral people hold the highest titles."

"There is honor among thieves, then?"

"A damn sight more honor than you'll find in some of the houses of the high-and-mighty." Jack's eyes glittered dangerously. "As you should well know, Miss Sterling. From what you've said, there's little honor in your home."

Honoria admitted there was truth in what he said. An outsider would never believe her uncle had acted so treacherously.

"Besides," he continued, "why would I want to give up the fine life you're providing me with? It's not an easy thing to support oneself by stealing. I'm 'Gentleman Jack,' after all, not a common highwayman."

"I imagine if it were necessary, you would lower yourself."

"Ah, but you've given me such a tantalizing glimpse of the higher life awaiting me at Norcross." Jack's voice was soft and cajoling. "Why would I want to sleep in a ditch when I could feast at your uncle's table?"

"I suppose you're right." She sat down in the opposite chair. "I am only nervous about being able to find the necklace once we reach Norcross."

"Why does your uncle want to sell it?"

"For the same reason I do," she replied. "Money."

"If he inherited the estate, doesn't he have enough already?"

Norry shook her head. "It's really a small farm. It was plenty for Papa and me, but Uncle Richard has greater ambitions."

"Political?"

"Personal, I think. He thinks that 'baronet' is far too modest a title."

"And money spread about the right places might bring something better." Jack nodded his head. "The way of the world. Money will buy almost anything." He grinned. "Except happiness, they say."

"You believe that about as much as I do," she said, her voice tinged with bitterness.

"All I know is that life is a great deal easier if you have money," said Jack. "Once I find the necklace, we'll test the adage."

She darted him a curious glance. "What was it like for you, being in prison?"

"Thoroughly unpleasant, I assure you." Jack's tone was mocking. "I highly recommend it."

"Were you . . . were you frightened before the hanging?"

He shrugged. "By then, I didn't care much one way or the other."

"Did you ever wish you hadn't done it?"

"I wished I hadn't been caught," he said. "But if I had it to do all over again, I certainly wouldn't have pulled that particular job."

"Was that the only time you were ever caught?"

He raised a mocking brow. "You read the papers. Gentleman Jack's successes were legendary."

"Or exaggerated," she replied. "You'd have to be in ten places at once to have done all they claimed of you."

"My talents know no bounds."

"Did you make a lot of money at . . . at your trade?"

"Sometimes yes, sometimes no." Jack's lips curved into a cynical smile. "I had a deplorable tendency to spend it rather freely."

"What will you do with your share of the money from the necklace?"

"I'm off to Paris."

"What, nothing more exotic than that?" Her tone was teasing. "I would have thought you'd prefer the Levantine, or the mysterious Orient."

"I might like excitement, but I don't like deprivation. I had enough of that in prison. Paris has all the amenities I need."

"What about the language?"

He shrugged. "I can speak enough French to get by."

"I suppose it's too much to hope that you plan to live a respectable life there."

Jack laughed. "Nicely put! What you really want to know is if I plan to continue my life of crime." He darted her an amused glance. "That all depends on how long my money lasts. I always walk straight until it runs out."

"You'll have enough that you could become respectable."

He place a hand over his heart. "Me? Respectable? The very word sends a chill through me."

"It'd keep you from the gallows!"

His expression grew solemn. "I assure you, I have no intention of being in that position again. I learned my lesson."

"Then you should live an honest life," Honoria replied with a weak smile.

"No, I'm just going to be very careful not to get caught again."

Honoria shook her head. "You're hopeless."

"Don't think that you can reform me, Honoria. Believe me, others have tried and failed."

Honoria stood and shook out her skirts. She stopped at the door and looked back at him. "The question is, Mr. Derry, have *you* tried?"

Damn her, Jack thought as he watched her leave. He could take care of himself. He didn't need another woman trying to make him into something he wasn't. Lord knows, enough of them had tried over the years.

But as his family discovered long ago, Jack did what he damn well pleased, no matter what anyone else thought or did. Honoria Sterling would find that out eventually. He wasn't going to change his ways for her—or anyone.

Chapter 5

It was barely light when Hawkins rolled the coach in front of the cottage. Honoria looked flustered and discomposed—probably at the prospect of putting her plan into action. Jack sympathized; he was edgy himself.

The trunks were loaded, Hawkins jumped onto the box, and Nursey whispered last-minute instructions to Honoria. Jack shooed her out of the way and climbed inside, firmly shutting the door behind him, and the coach moved down the rutted lane.

"Where are we meeting your cousin?"

"In Gloucester. There's a quiet inn there."

"How much further is it to Norcross?"

"Thirty miles. I intend for us to spend the night in Gloucester, and travel on in the morning."

"So the grand drama begins."

She nodded. "Is there anything you still wish to know? You are clear on the history of the family?"

Jack sighed wearily. "Intimately."

"Can I tell you more about Uncle Richard?"

"I believe you didn't mention the color of his bed-hangings."

"Don't be silly. This is a serious matter. I can't be whispering last-minute instructions in your ear once you arrive at Norcross."

"I doubt even your cousin knows more about the family than I do."

Honoria took a deep breath. "I expect you to do your best."

"Relax," he advised her. "You've planned everything. All that's left is for your little scheme to play itself out." He smiled his encouragement and she responded with a wan smile of her own.

"I have no qualms about my performance—you're the one I'm worried about," Jack said. "Both your cousin and your uncle are going to know that something is afoot if you keep fiddling with your hands like that."

Honoria jerked her intertwined fingers apart. "I can't help it. I *am* worried. If we don't find the necklace, I am lost."

"What if we trap your cousin in a compromising situation? He'll be forced to marry you then."

"That would be rather difficult to explain if I'm already engaged to you," she said.

"I could graciously bow out, nursing a broken heart, of course."

"Thank you for the suggestion, but I'd rather not marry Cousin Edmond."

"Then you will have to rely on me to see this thing through. Perhaps we could work out some signals, in advance. That might ease your worries."

"Signals?"

"So that if I veer into dangerous territory, you can warn

me. For example, if I'm about to pick up the wrong fork, you can wink your left eye. Or tug at your right ear if I'm talking about unsuitable things."

"A swift kick under the table might be more effective," Honoria said with a deceptively innocent smile.

"Not if I yelp in pain. That would cause comment."

"If things grow too dangerous, I shall swoon. Will that reassure you?"

"Can you do that?" Jack asked. "Swoon at will? I've always admired that talent."

"I don't know; I've never tried. But how difficult can it be? The heroines in books do it all the time."

"Is that what you see yourself as—a heroine in a book? Going to do battle with the wicked uncle?"

"I only want what is mine," Honoria said before lapsing into silence.

Jack looked out the window, hoping her determination would carry them both.

It was late afternoon when the carriage rolled into Gloucester and pulled in front of the Stag & Pheasant. Jack helped Honoria from the carriage and escorted her into the inn.

"We're meeting Mr. Edmond Stephenson," he told the innkeeper. "Has he arrived yet?"

"No, sir."

"Then we will take a private parlor," Honoria said. "And two rooms for the night."

"Only two rooms?" Jack arched a brow. "Surely you don't intend—?"

"For you and Edmond to share? I didn't think it would be a terrible imposition for one night."

"Oh," said Jack, trying to look crestfallen. "I thought you meant for you and me . . ."

As they entered the parlor, she caught the teasing look in his eyes and she laughed. "You thought no such thing and you know it!"

"I can always hope . . ."

"Just remember—I am not one of your immoral society ladies."

"I would never confuse you with one." Jack winked broadly. "I never knew them to steal from their uncles. Usually it was their husband or lover, sometimes a brother . . ."

"Remember, don't say anything to Edmond about your past," she reminded him.

"Afraid that he will be shocked to find you consorting with a common criminal?"

"It's not that," she said quickly. "I don't want to have to worry about him, too. The less he knows the better."

"Does he know why I'm here?"

"Of course not." She examined her toes. "Actually, he doesn't know anything about you."

Angrily, Jack yelled, "What? I am growing damn tired of you springing these 'little' surprises on me, Honoria."

"I didn't want to tell him about my plan before I rescued you, in case things went wrong."

"Or in case he tried to talk you out of it?"

"Well," she admitted, "there was that, too."

"And what if he decides not to cooperate? You want to

label me as his friend; if he doesn't agree, what are you going to do then?"

"Edmond will agree. Otherwise he will never get back all the money I borrowed from him."

"Just how much did you borrow?"

"More than I'd hoped, actually. It was your clothes, you see. I hadn't planned on that expense when I first talked with him, and I spent all my travel money. I will have to wait until you sell the necklace."

Jack shook his head. If this plan worked, he suspected Wellington might give Honoria a job on his staff. She showed a very impressive knack for intricate planning.

"I am going to change," Honoria announced. "You stay here in case Edmond arrives. And don't tell him anything! Wait for me."

Saluting deeply, Jack rang for the barmaid. He ordered a mug of ale and when it arrived, he sat back in his chair to enjoy a few minutes of peace and quiet.

Honoria's faith in his ability to help her made him nervous. No one had shown that kind of trust in him for a long time, and he didn't think he was ready for it now. Long ago, he'd decided not to rely on anyone, and not to allow anyone to rely on him either. It was the easiest way to avoid feeling guilty if he ultimately disappointed them.

But Jack didn't delude himself—Honoria was helping him only so he'd help her. Tit for tat. She gambled on him because she needed his help. And as a gambler himself, he also knew that she had calculated the odds, and decided he was likely to do just as she wished.

Usually, Jack liked to go against the odds; the winnings were fewer, but the payoffs higher. His recent experience made him more cautious. Honoria Sterling just might have made the right choice in picking him.

What did he have to lose?

A short man, with thinning blond hair, peeked into the room.

"Oh, excuse me. I was looking for someone. I must have the wrong room."

The man was smartly dressed in buckskins and top boots, with a coat that indicated a London tailor.

"Are you Stephenson?" Jack asked.

"Yes, I am." His expression grew puzzled.

Rising lazily to his feet, Jack motioned the man into the room. "You're in the right place." He set down the mug and extended his hand. "I'm Barnhill. Jack Barnhill. Your cousin will be down shortly."

Edmond's gaze turned wary. "You're with Honoria?"

"It's an interesting story—and one which your cousin should tell. Do you want some ale while we wait?"

Edmond rang for the innkeeper, then paced back and forth across the room in short, jerky steps while he waited. "Where the devil is that girl? We'll lose the light if we don't depart soon."

"I think your cousin intends to spend the night here."

"What do you know of her plans?" Edmond demanded.

"Let's say I play a major role in them. Your cousin certainly has a head for plotting. Should have turned her loose on Boney's empire years ago."

"Edmond!" Honoria stood in the doorway, a warm smile on her face. "You're here at last." She raced toward him and enveloped him in a warm hug. "You've met Jack?"

"Barely." Edmond examined Jack with obvious suspicion. "Who is he? What is he doing with you?"

"He's the final piece of the puzzle," she said. "Remember how I told you there's a copy of the necklace? And I feared I would have to take both to make sure I had the right one?" She pointed at Jack. "Jack is going to solve that problem."

"You are a jeweler, Mr. Barnhill?"

"In a manner of speaking. I know enough about the trade to tell real from fake. You might say it's my specialty."

Edmond's gaze darted back to his cousin. "Is this wise, Honoria? To bring another person in? It will only increase the danger."

"On the contrary, it will reduce the danger. This way, Uncle can sell the paste while I take the real one."

"Have you examined his credentials?"

"He came highly recommended," Honoria replied calmly. Jack smothered a laugh and she shot him a quelling look.

"Well, I suppose it makes sense." Edmond sat down. "Where do you plan to hide him?"

"He's coming to Norcross with us."

Edmond jumped to his feet. "What?"

"It's a much more efficient use of his time. He will help with the search as well."

Shaking his head, Edmond began to pace the room again. "Your uncle isn't going to like it."

"He doesn't want me there in the first place. He only wants to maintain a facade of family closeness. He will let

Jack stay." She grinned smugly. "Besides, he'll be rather pleased when he hears the tale I've concocted for Jack."

"What tale?"

"We are engaged."

"You're jesting."

Laughing, Honoria patted Jack's hand. "Won't Uncle Richard be pleased to think he will be rid of me forever?"

"How can you pretend to be marrying this fellow? You don't even know him." Edmond's voice rose to an agitated pitch. "No one is going to belive you agreed to wed a total stranger."

"That's where you come in—I plan to say that he is your friend."

"Are you mad? I don't even know the man."

Honoria shook her head at his obstinacy. "That's why we're spending the night here. You two can get your stories straight."

"Honoria, I thought you were being foolish when you first came to me with this scheme of yours. Now I know you are."

"Come with me for a minute." Honoria smiled at Jack as she dragged Edmond out into the corridor. "We won't be a minute."

"Where did you find that man?" Edmond whispered in a loud voice.

"Never mind. The important thing is that we need him."

"You are going to trust a complete stranger?"

"Believe me, he has as vested an interest in my scheme as you do." She tapped her foot impatiently. "Now, are you going to help me or not?"

"I still don't like it."

"I didn't ask you to like it; I only ask you to cooperate. Please?"

Sighing deeply, Edmond nodded. "I still think you're taking an enormous chance. But I know how important this is to you. If you think this man is crucial to your success, I will go along with whatever you want."

Honoria kissed him on the cheek. "Thank you, Edmond."

Back in the parlor, she greeted Jack with the news. "Edmond has agreed to cooperate, Jack."

"Oh, good," Jack said, with barely concealed sarcasm.

"Jack, you fill Edmond in on the story we came up with and make sure he knows it backwards and forwards. I don't want either of you to make any mistakes once we get to Norcross."

Honoria watched the two men carefully during dinner. She feared Edmond would remain cool toward Jack, but her cousin thawed completely and they chatted like old friends. Thank goodness they shared a common interest in horse racing. This was the last major hurdle before arriving at Norcross. Honoria chose to take the success as an omen for the future. Everything had gone perfectly so far; her luck would continue to run good.

Exhausted as she was, sleep still would not come when she finally climbed into bed. Surprisingly, she felt pleased that Jack would be with her at Norcross. He was annoying and provoking, but she enjoyed exchanging barbs with him. Jack Derry might irritate her to the point of screaming, but he also made her laugh. And it had been a long time since she laughed.

Honoria thought sleepily about the sunny cottage in Italy or the south of France that she would buy once this was over. The garden would be filled with lilacs and roses and honeysuckle. In the summer afternoons, she would take a chair and sit outside and read, her peace disturbed only by the buzzing of bees and the chirping of birds. There would be no demands, no responsibilities; she would do only what she wanted, when she wanted. The idea was heaven.

And in the garden she could dream of other places she wanted to go and other things she wanted to see. And perhaps, sometime, when she deemed it safe, she would come back to England. There were places she wanted to see on this very island. The seashore. The Lake District. She still carried dim memories of a family excursion there, before her mother died. When she was seven, Honoria had been allowed to tag after her parents as they roamed the paths along the lakes. She would like to go back there.

But first, she must get her hands on the necklace. Jack Derry was the man to help her do that. She trusted him as she did no other. He was the only one with the skill, courage, and daring to carry out her plan successfully. Honoria didn't want to consider the consequences of what she was asking him to do, but she knew what would happen if he were caught. It was harder to think of sending Jack to his death, rather than a faceless convict she had only read about in the papers. Now that she knew him better, with his teasing smiles and his mocking laughter, she cared what happened to him.

Still, Jack was an experienced thief; he could take care of himself.

Already she doubted that the judge who had escorted him from the gallows would even recognize him. It was not merely the new clothes; Jack's whole demeanor had changed. He was confident, assured, and very different from the confused and exhausted man she had freed in Gorton.

Goodness knows, he cut a better figure than Cousin Edmond. She smothered a giggle. If she had to pretend an engagement, at least she could be paired with the handsomest man in the house. She nestled back against the pillows with a self-satisfied smile. Yes, she had made a wise choice. She was fully confident that Jack Derry would be able to carry out the imposture.

Honoria fell asleep with a faint smile on her lips.

The company sat around the long table in the dining room. Honoria could not tear her eyes away from Jack, who was doing everything wrong. He tucked his napkin into his collar, and tore off chunks of meat with his bare hands before stuffing the food into his mouth. The first gasps of shock from the other diners changed to titters, then to audible laughter. Honoria wanted to bury her face in her hands, but she couldn't look away from the embarrassing scene.

The man on her left leaped up. "This man is not who he claims! He is not a real gentleman!"

"Imposter! Imposter!" the voices chorused.

Honoria pressed her hands over her ears but she couldn't stop the voices.

"She's the imposter!" Jack cried, pointing to her.

"Imposter! Imposter!" the others cried, turning their hate-distorted faces toward her. "Imposter! Imposter!"

Honoria sat bolt upright in bed, her heart pounding painfully. Then she lay back against the pillows, trying to still the panic that threatened to overwhelm her. It was a nightmare. Only a nightmare.

But a nightmare that had seemed all too real for comfort. She had placed her entire future into the hands of a thief. Everything depended on his success. If he failed . . .

Honoria tried to quell her doubts. No one would suspect that Jack was anything but what he pretended—a friend of Edmond's and the man she intended to marry. No one would look beyond those explanations, not even her uncle.

Edmond lay still, listening to the muffled snores coming from his roommate. His first reaction to this new development had been dismay. What could Honoria have been thinking of, to involve this stranger? Her actions threatened to disrupt his own carefully laid plans.

But the more Edmond considered matters, the more he favored the inclusion of this stranger. He wouldn't explain Jack's role to Richard Sterling when they reached Norcross; Sir Richard didn't need to know *everything*. It was enough that Edmond had told him of Honoria's plans to steal the necklace.

A deep excitement crept over him as he considered things further. Sir Richard had promised him a reward for helping to thwart Honoria's plans. Now, Edmond accompanied her to Norcross for the express purpose of keeping an eye on her. Since Honoria thought he was on her side, Edmond would be in a position to put a stop to her thieving when the moment arose.

But what if he did not? Sir Richard had offered him a tidy sum to interfere with Honoria—enough money so Edmond could pay off some of his most pressing debts. But should he really settle for such a trifling sum when he could have more? What if he took the necklace?

Jack Barnhill provided him with the perfect opportunity. Richard Sterling thought Edmond was working for him; Honoria thought Edmond was helping her. By playing the two against each other, Edmond could put himself in the position of getting his own fingers on the necklace—and making it disappear.

And who would people blame? Jack Barnhill. The one stranger among them, the perfect scapegoat. It would be easy enough to plant a few clues to heighten suspicion. Even if Sir Richard didn't find the necklace on Barnhill, he would always think that Jack was the thief.

Edmond laughed silently at the thought. Honoria thought she was so clever, when in reality *he* was the clever one. Only a foolish, sentimental female would think that family ties meant anything. Edmond owed her no more than he did a casual acquaintance; he wasn't responsible for her simply because their mothers had been sisters. His first obligation was to himself, and with the necklace in his possession, all his money worries would be resolved.

Barnhill would tell him which necklace was real, then Edmond would take it and damn them all.

Chapter 6

It was early afternoon when the coach approached Norcross. The lane opened up onto a wide green lawn which surrounded a many-gabled country house, fashioned from gray Cotswold stone.

As they halted in front of the modest entry, Edmond climbed down and went to ring for a footman, leaving Jack to help Honoria from the carriage.

"So this is your real home," he said, scanning the windowed facade with a critical eye. "It's a good-size house for just two people."

"And now Uncle has it all to himself," she said, bitterly. "I hope he finds it lonely."

"Even the most crowded house can seem lonely if one doesn't belong."

Honoria darted him a sidelong glance. "Do you come from a large family?"

"No," said Jack, turning to help Hawkins with the luggage.

Hoarse barking interrupted the silence. Jack swung around and saw a pack of dogs race around the corner of the house, heading straight for him.

Jack froze. Dogs. He had hated them from the moment he was two years old and pulled the tail of his father's huge mastiff. The beast had sunk his teeth into Jack's calf and he still carried the marks. The very sight of the pack made the scar on his leg throb. Frantically, he sought an escape. He could make a dash for the door, but would he reach it in time? Grabbing the nearest valise, he held it up like a shield and started to run, but he was too late.

The pack of slavering, yapping dogs surrounded him, jumping up and pawing at his thighs. Jack whirled to his right and tripped over Edmond's portmanteau, landing on his rear with a jarring thud. Instantly the dogs swarmed around him, poking wet noses into his face, nudging his back, sniffing his hair.

Jack buried his face in his arms. A wet tongue lapped against his hand. "Get these beasts out of here!"

"Jep! Joss! Jim! Hey, up!"

Immediately, the dogs darted away.

Jack lowered his arms cautiously. The dogs, tails wagging and tongues lolling, circled a tall, gray-haired man who moved forward with long, loping strides.

"Sit," he commanded and the dogs obeyed. He hurried over to Jack and helped him up.

"Are you hurt, sir?" He smiled apologetically. "The lads are a trifle energetic today, I'm afraid. Too many visitors. They feel it's their duty to welcome each and every one."

"I've had worse greetings." Jack brushed off his mud-stained breeches and tried to appear at ease although his heart still pounded in his chest. The largest dog grinned at him, as if sensing his discomfort.

Honoria approached, a tight smile on her face. "Hello, Uncle Richard."

Jack struggled to keep his expression impassive. So this was the wicked uncle. The man before him looked like a harmless country squire in his shapeless jacket, faded buckskins, and scuffed top boots.

Richard bent down and gave Honoria a modest peck on the cheek. "I'm pleased that you've arrived." He glanced with open curiosity at Jack. "I thought you were bringing your cousin Edmond?"

"I brought him. He's getting someone to help with the luggage." Honoria stepped closer to Jack and took his arm in hers. "I did not write because I wanted to tell you the news in person. Uncle, this is Jack Barnhill. We are to be married."

"Married?"

To Jack's ears, Sir Richard sounded more alarmed than relieved.

Honoria cast an adoring glance at Jack. "Yes."

"But when . . . ? How . . . ? Where did you meet him?"

"I told you that we should have written your uncle first," Jack said in a loud whisper to Honoria. He patted her hand and gave her an indulgent smile. "It was love at first sight, I'm afraid, Sir Richard. I hope you are not angry with our little surprise."

"Jack is a friend of Edmond's," Honoria said hastily, as Edmond drew near. "A very old and dear friend."

"I see." Richard's face brightened at the sight of Edmond. "Ah, there you are, Stephenson. I hear you've been playing matchmaker."

Edmond smiled weakly. "Can't say I had much to do with it—other than introducing them, of course."

Sir Richard took Jack's hand. "Well, I'm pleased to meet you, Barnhill. It will give me great pleasure to announce such happy news during our little gathering." He glanced at Honoria. "That is what you wish me to do, isn't it?"

"There is no hurry, Uncle. I do not want to disrupt any of your plans. I know you wish this to be a special visit for your important guest."

"Yes, yes. It's not often that we get to see a real foreign prince in Gloucester, is it?"

"No."

Sir Richard nodded, then glanced at the dogs, who frolicked at his feet with barely suppressed excitement. "I had best see these rascals back to the kennels." Sir Richard turned to Jack and Edmond. "Come along, my man can see to your luggage. I'll show you the kennels."

Jack hesitated. "I really don't think—"

"Come on, come on," Richard said, grabbing his arm. "Do you know I've got some of the finest hunting dogs in this part of the country? Why, you should hear what the Beaufort says of them."

Honoria stepped forward. "Good grief, Uncle, we just arrived. I am sure Edmond and Jack would like to unpack first."

"Oh, I don't mind," said Edmond.

"Is Aunt Sophia here yet?" Honoria asked.

Sir Richard nodded.

"Then I should like her to meet Jack. He can see the dogs later."

"That's fine with me. Just make sure she understands

what is going on. I don't want her thinking this young man is a long-lost brother of yours." Richard gave a nasty smile and struck out across the lawn. The dogs leaped to their feet and followed.

"Your brother?" Jack asked Honoria.

"Aunt Sophia tends to be a bit . . . confused, at times."

"Why didn't you tell me about those damn dogs?" he demanded as they walked toward the house.

"How was I supposed to know you didn't like dogs?"

"You could have said something."

"What would you have done—refused to help me?"

Jack frowned. Of course he would have accepted her offer, dogs or no dogs. But he still wished she'd told him. "Just don't expect me to show an interest in them. I don't care how important they are to your uncle—they don't have anything to do with the necklace."

"Uncle might change his mind about approving of you," she teased.

"I don't give a damn what your uncle thinks about me. I'm here to help you find that necklace." Jack dropped her arm and stalked up the stairs.

"Oh, Jack, dear," Honoria called after him.

He turned to look at her.

"We are supposed to be engaged, remember?" She held out her hand. "Try to display a few tender feelings."

Immediately, Jack dropped to his knee. "Forgive me, darling," he pleaded.

"Stop that."

Jack stood and brushed off his knee. "You really need to make up your mind, Honoria. Am I to court you, or treat you like my sister?"

"Just try not to make a spectacle of yourself," she said as the front door opened before them. A broad smile lit the face of the black-suited man who stood in the entry.

"Plummer!" Honoria took his hand. "It is so good to see you."

"I'm pleased to see you, miss."

"Plummer, this is Jack Barnhill. He is a friend of Cousin Edmond, and a *special* friend of mine. Can we find a nice room for him?"

"I believe so. I have arranged for you to have your old room, miss."

"Oh, thank you. Is the room at the top of the rear stairs free? Perhaps Jack could stay there."

The butler agreed. "I will have the luggage taken up."

"Thank you, Plummer." Honoria turned to Jack. "Do you wish to see your room before we beard the lions in their den—or meet the guests, if you prefer?"

"You don't expect me to present myself in company while still in my traveling clothes?"

"Heavens, no. What could I have been thinking?"

Honoria led Jack up the mahogany staircase. "Uncle's rooms are to the right," she said, when they reached the landing. "That's the oldest part of the house, while most of the guest bedrooms are in the new wing."

He followed her down the corridor to his room. "The servant stairs are here. I thought you could use them to come and go without being noticed."

"So thoughtful."

Jack surveyed his room. The chamber was small, but well-furnished; the old-fashioned bed even sported curtains.

"Meet me in the drawing room when you are ready—it's to the left as you go down the stairs. I want you to meet Great-Aunt Sophia—she's a dear."

"I can't wait."

After she left, Jack walked to the window and looked out. The stable blocked the view to his right; trees pressed in on either side. A hedged garden occupied the land immediately behind the house. A nice, cozy setting, Jack thought, and a damn sight better than the gallows.

Honoria couldn't control the pounding of her heart as she approached her old room. It had only been three months since she had left Norcross, but it seemed like an eternity.

Her room looked much the same—yet it wasn't. Her old furniture was here, but with her personal things gone the room appeared bare, stark. A stranger walking in would never know a thing about its former resident.

Honoria thought she would enjoy being at Norcross again, but coming back here, now, as a guest, only served to remind her that this was no longer her home, that she no longer belonged. Here. Or anywhere.

Angrily, Honoria wiped her eyes. Crying was not going to solve anything. The only thing that would help was the necklace. She would never be able to call Norcross her own, but the necklace would enable her to have a home of her own again. Uncle would rue the day that he had decided to cheat her.

After changing from her traveling clothes, she ventured downstairs to the drawing room. She nodded a greeting at the two ladies who sat chatting, then gave a cry of delight when she spotted her great-aunt Sophia, Dowager Lady Hampton.

Honoria gave the elderly lady a hug. "Aunt Sophia! I'm so glad you are here."

"Hmph? Why wouldn't I be? You were the one who insisted I come." Sophia lifted her quizzing glass and inspected Honoria. "Stand up straight, gel, and let me have a look at you."

Meekly, Honoria complied under the stern gaze of her favorite relative.

"You've been working too hard, my dear." Sophia sighed and patted Honoria's hand. "You shall come home with me this time. I will see that you're taken care of."

Honoria did not want to offend Sophia by reminding her that "home" consisted of a room in the house of her grandson, who would never agree to support another indigent relative.

Sophia leaned closer and spoke in a loud whisper. "What sort of boring mushrooms has your uncle invited this time? Not the woman with that pesky dog again?"

Honoria laughed at that memory—one of her few good ones of Uncle's reign at Norcross. "She won't be back—the sight of that ball of fluff chasing Uncle's prize pups guaranteed that."

"Any nice young men?"

Honoria took a deep breath, hating the lies she must tell. "My cousin, Edmond, from Yorkshire, is here. Mama's sister's son, you remember. And he has a friend—Mr. Barnhill."

Sophia's eyes twinkled. "Two young blades to court you! Well done, girl."

"I don't wish to be greedy. You may have Edmond for your own."

Sophia guffawed. "Like that, is it? Tell me about your Mr. Barnhill."

"You will meet him soon enough," Honoria said with an air of mystery.

"Tall? Handsome? Fair or dark?"

"Be patient."

"So your uncle has managed to snag himself a prince for his party, has he? This might be as interesting as my fiftieth birthday. Didn't we have a grand fete at Houghton? I am certain we did. Freddy was there."

"It was a wonderful party," Honoria assured her. She did not mention that the party had been held almost thirty years ago, and that Freddy had been dead for half of that. "Tea, Aunt Sophia?"

"I'd rather a drop of brandy," she whispered, "but I suppose all the ladies are having tea."

"I'll get the brandy from Uncle's study."

"That's a good girl." Sophia patted Honoria's hand.

Jack changed his shirt, dusted his boots, and decided he might as well brave the drawing room. He reminded himself of the money that would be his when this was over.

He found his way with only one small detour. Taking a deep breath, he pushed open the door. Three pairs of female eyes turned in his direction. Jack swallowed uneasily under their scrutiny, scanning the room for Honoria, but she wasn't there. Now what was he supposed to do?

Finally, he cleared his throat. "Do any of you know where Miss Sterling can be found?"

"Who wants to know?" an ancient crone demanded.

"I am her guest."

The woman raised a quizzing glass and studied him with irritating directness. Jack grew increasingly uncomfortable, but he could not very well sit without an invitation. Were they going to keep him standing all afternoon? And where the hell was Honoria?

"Here is your special tea, Aunt. Uncle sends his regards—oh!" Honoria stopped so quickly that liquid splashed out of the cup.

"Honoria!" Jack stepped forward, deftly taking the tray from her hands. "How pleasant to see you again."

"Jack." Honoria's voice quavered.

He set the tray on the table. "Your tea, my lady."

Sophia cackled. "Got a head on your shoulders, don't you, lad?"

"Jack, this is my Great-Aunt Sophia, Dowager Lady Hampton. Mr. Barnhill."

Jack bowed.

"And these ladies are guests of my uncle." She introduced him to Mrs. Mayflower and Lady Bolton.

"Sit here, young man." Sophia patted the chair next to her. She took up her quizzing glass and surveyed Jack head to toe.

"Amazing," she said at last. "You have the exact look of—but never mind, you wouldn't know him. Long before your time. You're from . . . where did you say you were from?"

"Yorkshire."

"I am pleased that you are here with my lovely girl. I want to see that you keep her entertained." She waved her hand at the room. "You see the type of people her uncle consorts with. Now if this were my house, t'would be filled with interesting people. Not these namby-pamby bores."

"Auntie!" Honoria hissed at her. "Do be quiet."

"What this place needs is more young people; they always liven up a room. Tell me why you didn't bring some of your friends, Mr. Barnhill."

"Because this is Uncle Richard's party," Honoria answered for him. "It was gracious enough of him to allow Edmond and Jack to come."

"You have just as much right to invite your friends." Sophia sniffed her disapproval and looked sternly at Jack. "See here, young man, I will hold you responsible for making sure this girl doesn't expire of boredom before the week's out."

Jack beamed. "I would be more than happy to entertain Miss Sterling."

"Miss Sterling, is it? What type of man have you found for yourself, Honoria?"

"A very polite one, Auntie."

Sophia pointed a bony finger at Jack. "If you expect to win my girl's heart, you will need to speak up. She's 'Norry' to those closest to her."

"May I call you Norry, then?" Jack asked with a grin.

"If you like."

With effort, Sophia rose and clutched her cane. "Now that you're here, I can take my nap." She held out her arm to Jack. "Walk with me to my room. I need my rest."

"As you wish, Lady Hampton."

After Jack and Honoria saw Sophia to her room, they paused in the corridor.

"Uncle observes country hours, so dinner will be at six tonight," she said. "The bell rings at a quarter of."

"Am I supposed to hide in my room until dinner?"

"You can have tea in the drawing room, if you like."

Jack remembered the stifling heat and the fact that he and Honoria were the only people under fifty.

"Never mind. I'll unpack my trunk. *That* should make an entertaining afternoon." He sauntered toward his room.

Honoria returned to the drawing room, her mood not eased by the appearance of new guests. Even Aunt Sophia's presence could not cheer her. Sophia was only a reminder of the fate that awaited Honoria. She did not want to end up as someone's elderly aunt, dependent upon the largesse of relatives and living on her memories of the past.

Honoria had too few memories to live on. Only dim remembrances of her mother, and the few years of happiness spent with her father before his death. She wanted to start accumulating more of the memories that warmed the hearts of old ladies in their declining years. The necklace was her only hope of escape, her only hope for a life of her own. She would forge a life for herself, away from those who wanted to put her into a tiny box and close the lid. It was her life, and she would make the decisions for it.

She was glad she had decided to pass Jack off as her intended. It would be natural for her to spend most of her time with him. And Honoria confessed to herself that she would like that. She wanted to know more about him—his family, his past, why he had become what he was. But she needed to remember that he was only a temporary gentleman. She must not forget that Jack Derry was a thief.

Guests continued to arrive throughout the day: Reginald Grose, a plump solicitor from Gloucester; Cyrus Latham, who often bought Uncle's dogs; Squire Norton and his wife, old friends of Uncle's. All nice, middle-aged couples.

Honoria thought her face would crack from smiling so much. She had enjoyed entertaining Papa's guests, playing hostess at his gatherings. His guests had been interesting people. They would gather in the drawing room and talk politics, literature, music, and whatnot until all hours of the night. Uncle Richard's dull friends indulged in trivial gossip and sporting talk.

Jack awoke with a start at the loud pounding on his door.

"Jack!" Honoria called. "Are you there?"

He took a deep breath as he remembered that he was safe, at Norcross. Or at least as safe as he could be under the circumstances of Honoria's convoluted deceptions.

"I'm here."

"Dinner is about to be served. Didn't you hear the bell?"

How long had he been asleep? Ages, if it was time for dinner. "I'll take my dinner on a tray."

"You will not." Her voice was determined. "I want you dressed for dinner and out here immediately."

Ten minutes later, Jack strolled out the door. "Will I do?"

Honoria evaluated his appearance with a critical eye. "Is that how I showed you to tie a neckcloth?"

"It is plain Yorkshire style. We don't bother with frills in the country."

"I shall have Edmond help you tomorrow. He will see that you're turned out properly."

"How thoughtful of you, my dear."

"Try to behave yourself at dinner," she warned. "I seated you next to Great-Aunt Sophia, since she seemed to take a liking to you. I will be across the table. Do pay attention and I shall signal you if you are doing anything wrong."

"You are so helpful."

"Tonight, I want you to observe," Honoria instructed. "Learn everyone's names. I marked their rooms on this plan."

Jack grinned at the paper she handed him. "Where is your room, beloved? I do not see your name here. Does your wicked uncle force you to sleep belowstairs? Or in the stable?"

"I am at the other end of the hall," she said crisply. "And don't call me 'beloved.' "

"I thought you wanted me to appear loverlike," said Jack, hastening down the stairs behind her.

"Only when we are in the company of others," she reminded him.

He grinned widely, opening the drawing room door for her. "I'll try to remember," he said. "But I'm sure you will remind me if I forget."

"I most certainly will."

Chapter 7

Honoria couldn't remember a single thing she ate that night. All her attention was riveted on Jack Derry. She watched with inheld breath while he cut his meat, passed a dish of creamed carrots, and signaled the footman for more wine.

She mumbled inconsequential replies to her partner's queries, who must have thought her a miserable conversationalist. But she couldn't concentrate on anything except the man who sat across from her. She prayed that he wouldn't do anything to give himself away.

Aunt Sophia seemed thoroughly charmed by him, but that was hardly a recommendation. In her present state of mind, Aunt Sophia might think he was anyone—a favored nephew, a long-dead son, or even one of her own husbands. Sophia was the only person who could denounce Jack as an imposter and no one would blink an eye.

It was clear that he had thoroughly charmed Sophia. She still thought of herself as a belle, and Jack played the role of fawning admirer to the hilt. He would earn Sophia's undying devotion—at least as long as she remembered his name.

Despite Honoria's apprehensions, he looked as if he belonged at the table. His secondhand evening clothes appeared to be tailor-made for his tall frame, and the casually knotted cravat made him look especially dashing.

If she had not known who he was, she would never guess that he was not a true gentleman. Uncle's guests would never suspect that he been released from prison less than a week ago.

As the dinner progressed, however, Honoria noticed that he looked increasingly ill at ease. Was he drinking too much wine? He still had to get through the after-dinner port with the men. What if his tongue grew loose? Honoria would not be there to watch him, and heaven knows if Edmond would react quickly enough to prevent any damage.

Recalling her frightening dream, Honoria clenched her fists in frustration. From the moment Jack had entered the house, the situation had been out of her hands. For better or worse, he was on his own. Honoria hated this feeling of helplessness. But it made her more determined than ever to have her plan succeed. She never wanted to be helpless—and penniless—again.

Jack found Honoria's scrutiny annoying. Couldn't she see that her intense interest drew attention to him? He fought back the urge to make a total fool of himself—and her—at dinner. He had nowhere else to go if he was thrown out of Norcross. After a week of decent meals, clean clothing, and a soft bed, he was growing fond of such luxuries again. He didn't relish being on his own without a shilling to his name.

He took another long swallow of wine. Jack rather liked that dotty old lady on his left. She was obviously as eccentric as her niece, but at least she didn't go about forcing her craziness upon others.

The whole situation would be amusing if both he and Honoria were not so desperate. Perhaps he could start a career on the stage when this masquerade was over; he would certainly have enough practice as an actor by then.

Whatever he did, it wouldn't be in London. He was tired of having to hide his real identity. If he could get to France, he would be just another Englishman, and in the chaos that followed Napoleon's defeat, opportunities would abound for an ambitious man.

Jack looked up from his musings, startled to see that the servants were removing the cloth for dessert. The ladies would soon be leaving and he would be able to breathe again. It wasn't easy to feel comfortable with Honoria's wary eyes on him every minute.

As soon as the ladies left, Jack let out a relieved sigh. Then he caught Edmond's eye and raised his glass in mocking salute.

"Port?" Richard Sterling handed Jack the bottle.

Jack gestured to his wineglass. "I'll stick to this, thank you."

"An excellent vintage. Laid down by my brother, bless his soul. I'll give him credit, he knew his wines." He winked at Jack. "Bet you don't get claret this fine in Yorkshire, now, do you?"

Jack laughed. "Not often."

Relaxing in his chair, Jack looked about the room with amusement. It was like old times, sitting around the table, savoring a glass of wine after dinner.

"Went up to Yorkshire last year for the bird shooting," Reginald Grose, the solicitor, announced. "Didn't think much of it. Shoot birds, do you, Barnhill?"

"I like to do my hunting from the back of a horse," Jack said.

"Ah, yes, that's the way." Sir Richard passed the port around again and Jack filled a glass this time. "Following a pack of hounds hot on the scent. A pity it's only August."

"Planning on having the new pups out on the field this year?" Latham asked.

Sir Richard nodded and began a long analysis of the merits and deficiencies of each and every one of the dogs. Jack stifled a yawn. The food and wine were making him sleepy and the conversation was not exactly riveting. Still, it would be worse out in the drawing room. Trading polite words with respectable, middle-aged ladies was not his style.

He grinned at the thought of Honoria sitting there, fretting. She would be wringing her hands, afraid he would make some foolish mistake that could bring the entire house down upon her head.

She did not know how good a judge of character she really was. Jack knew that he was one of the few men in the country who could make this escapade succeed. But he was not going to reassure her on that score. Let her worry.

He smothered another yawn. Richard Sterling seemed to be an arrogant ass, especially with his passion for dogs.

Dogs had their place—on the hunting field. But that was as close as Jack wanted to be to them. That earlier encounter had been most unpleasant.

Edmond nudged his arm and Jack's head snapped up.

"Never thought it'd be the young 'un falling asleep over his after-dinner port." Squire Mayflower laughed.

"Probably past his bedtime." The men roared.

"Long past." Jack grinned. "Morning's only a few hours off."

"Better get used to southern habits, old friend," Edmond warned him. "We'll be practicing town hours before long. Dinner at eight, supper at twelve, and dancing till dawn."

"Turn your days and nights topsy-turvy," added Mayflower.

"I'll try to manage," Jack said with a wry grin.

Sir Richard pushed back his chair. "Time we rejoined the ladies. We don't want to keep them waiting too long." He clapped a fatherly hand on Jack's shoulder as they left the room.

Sophia motioned for Honoria to sit beside her when the ladies retired to the drawing room. "The boy has pretty manners for a Yorkshireman."

"Yorkshire is not the end of the world, Aunt."

"No, but it's certainly not London either." Sophia took a sip of her tea. "Still, I can't but think that I have seen your Mr. Barnhill before. His face looks so familiar . . ."

"Did I tell you what a nice visit I had with Nursey? The dear is getting on, but doing well." Honoria didn't need Sophia puzzling about Jack's identity. She had a tendency to think everyone looked familiar, but the very thought of her connecting Jack with someone else made Honoria nervous.

She prayed nothing was going wrong in the dining room while the men drank their port. Honoria dreaded the thought of Jack being alone with her uncle, even if Edmond was there to keep an eye on him. With any luck, the men had been chatting about some masculine pursuit, and she assumed Jack would manage that well enough.

Honoria looked up when the men came into the room. Sophia signaled to Jack and he hastened to her side.

"Honoria tells me you're quite the huntsman, Mr. Barnhill. My dear departed husband did so love to hunt. Why, from the moment of the first huntsmen's horn in fall I would see nary a sight of him until the last covert was flushed."

"You didn't join him?"

"Me? Hunt? Goodness, no, you silly boy." Sophia patted her hair in a coquettish gesture. "I am not one of those modern women who think they should do everything the men do—and more. Although I did have a fine seat—many told me so."

"A pity I wasn't there to see it. I do so admire a lady with a fine seat."

Edmond joined them. "Hunting season's not too far away, eh? I wouldn't mind getting my hands on some of your uncle's pups this season."

"Shh," said Honoria. "Mrs. Bolton is going to play the piano."

Schooling his features into a pained smile, Jack stared

up at the ceiling. If he wasn't careful, he might fall asleep and tumble out of his chair. Which might not be a bad idea—it would certainly liven up the evening. This had to be the epitome of the worst of country life—cooped up in a house with a dull collection of guests, the prospects for entertainment dim, and no hope for a reprieve.

Suddenly, he caught his breath. There had been no hope of a reprieve in jail either, but it certainly hadn't been boring. No, prison had not been dull. Until his money ran out, he had food, wine, and an occasional woman. The company wasn't the best, but Jack had not minded that. There was a blunt honesty about most of his fellow prisoners that he came to appreciate.

Glancing at Honoria, Jack saw her lean over and whisper something to Sophia. How long must he remain before he could flee to his room? Honoria would probably insist he stay until the bitter end.

When the clock on the mantel chimed half past nine, Jack groaned. He was not going to endure this any longer. After casting a quick glance at Honoria, he rose to his feet.

"It's time for a game," he said. "How about some charades? Or forfeits?"

Honoria looked surprised. "I don't think—"

Jack waved her protest aside. "I know! We could try this—'Change Seats, The King's Come!' "

"Splendid idea, splendid." Sophia prodded Honoria with her cane. "Haven't played that games in ages."

"Good, good," said Jack. He took an empty chair and set it next to hers. "Quickly, everyone, arrange the chairs in a circle."

"What do you think you're doing?" Honoria whispered.

"Trying to liven up the evening. I've seen jollier funerals."

"These people don't want to play silly children's games."

He pointed toward the guests, who were laughing as they moved their chairs into a circle. "This is probably the most exciting thing that has happened at your uncle's in months."

Honoria looked unconvinced, but Jack refused to be deterred. "Now, make certain we have one fewer chair than there are people. Edmond, Honoria, you need to move your chairs. Don't dally!"

When everyone was seated, Jack stood in the middle of the circle, chanting "Change seats, change seats." He turned in a slow circle, eyeing each of the guests in turn. Suddenly he called out "The king's come" and everyone leaped up and scrambled for new chairs. Sir Richard found himself without a seat, and Sophia tittered at his discomfort.

"Change seats, change seats," Sir Richard intoned, after good-naturedly taking his place in the middle of the circle.

This time, Jack dashed across the room and took the seat Honoria vacated. She moved around the circle, trying to find another chair, but all were taken.

"You're in the center," Lady Hampton called, stamping her cane on the floor. "Get on with the game, girl."

After the next change, Jack caught a glimpse of Honoria—and marveled at the sight of her flushed cheeks, sparkling eyes, and joyful expression. She looked more relaxed—happy—then he'd ever seen her. And more beautiful.

To his surprise, the guests continued the game of Change Seats for almost half an hour; at last they declared themselves exhausted with such exertion.

Sophia announced that she was ready to retire and Jack stepped to her side and offered his arm. Honoria followed them.

"I can help Aunt Sophia," she told Jack at the foot of the stairs. "You can return to the drawing room."

"Oh pooh, let the boy feel useful." Sophia patted Jack's hand. "Nothing is better than a strong male arm to lean on." Sophia stared at him intently as they slowly went up the stairs. "Are you sure we haven't met before? You look exceedingly familiar."

"Perhaps we danced at a ball in London last spring."

"Oh, tosh." Sophia tapped him lightly on the arm with her fan. "I haven't been to town in ages. You've never been to my grandson's, have you?"

"Can't say that I have."

"Come in the spring," Sophia whispered conspiratorially. "The garden is best then."

They halted outside Sophia's door. Jack bowed low over her hand. "It's been a pleasure, Lady Hampton."

"I haven't had such an enjoyable evening in an age." She gave Honoria a knowing look. "I heartily approve, my dear."

Honoria turned pink and hastily guided Sophia into her room while Jack sprinted to the safety of his bedchamber. He was not going back to that drawing room for anything.

It had been worth the boredom to hear Honoria's laughter as she participated in the game. Usually, she worried so much about her necklace and her future and the money that she could not enjoy herself.

Oh well, she would learn soon enough not to worry about tomorrow, but to grab the enjoyment of today, as he had, finally. Yet he still paid the price for that knowledge. He was tried of playing Jack Derry, tired of being who he wasn't—and tired of people wanting him to be what *he* wasn't. Dutiful son, lighthearted wastrel, honorable thief. He was none of those. But it was what everyone expected him to be, and if he didn't fit the label, it became his problem, not theirs.

When this whole stupid adventure was over, he would never again try to pretend that he was something other than his real self. He would do exactly what he pleased and everyone else be damned.

Yet a nagging voice asked wasn't that what he had been doing all his life? Doing exactly what he wanted, without regard for the consequences—to himself or others? Wasn't it that very disregard that had brought him within minutes of his own death?

Maybe, Jack conceded reluctantly, but if he had learned anything from that experience, it was that he didn't want it repeated. If he began listening to himself, and not the warped expectations of others, he would be better off. He had his own best interests at heart, which was more than anyone else could say.

Honoria Sterling thought of him only as a thief and she congratulated herself for having picked such a gentlemanly one. She thought that *her* efforts brought about his transformation from thief to gentleman. In reality, she had taken a terrible chance, and never considered that such a change would be impossible.

Granted, he had played along with her, but she didn't have to be so blind. Couldn't she see that he had always been more than a common thief? Did she really think a genuine gallows bird could play the gentleman? How foolish. And demeaning. She expected him to be only what she wanted him to be.

Just like his father had.

Jack froze at the hateful memories. *Jack, I am disappointed in your studies. Jack, I have made a decision about your future. Jack, you will do as you are bid.*

Jack was nobody's puppet. Not his father's and certainly not Honoria's. If she didn't like it, let her find herself another thief.

Taking off his boots and coat, he lay down on the bed, but remained wary and alert for some time. The bustle in the corridor told him that the other guests were finally retiring for the night. It might be a good time to do some exploring.

He waited until all was quiet, then cracked his door and peered out. It was dark in the hall; only the night candle flickered at the far end of the corridor. Easing the door open farther, he stepped onto the narrow stairs and scanned the bedroom passage.

Jack was about to start down the back stairs when he heard the soft click of a door latch. He moved back into the shadows and watched Edmond step out of his room, and then tiptoe down the hall. He tapped lightly on a door; it opened and he slipped inside.

Just who was Edmond visiting at this hour of the night?

Somehow, Jack didn't think it was Lady Bolton or Mrs. Mayflower. Jack counted the doors and then ducked back into his room and pulled out the folded map Honoria had given him. He counted out the number of rooms, and frowned. Honoria.

They were cousins, after all, and they might be taking this opportunity to talk privately—something they hadn't had a chance to do today. They might be carrying out a financial transaction—hadn't she said she spent all the money she'd borrowed from Edmond? There were any number of reasons why they needed to be together.

But in Jack's experience, there was only one reason for nighttime visits to a lady's room. It would explain why Edmond was so willing to help her. In fact, the whole situation now made perfect sense. There was more than cousinly obligation operating here.

Jack did not like the idea that Edmond was alone with Honoria in her room. And he liked even less the thought that the two might be lovers. Not because he wanted Honoria for himself, but because it boded an attachment that could be dangerous to Jack. He was the odd man out. If the whole operation fell apart, Jack had no doubts that he would be the sacrificial goat and it would be his neck in the noose.

Chapter 8

Jack woke early—something he rarely did in the old days, but it became an ingrained habit in prison. How long would it take before he could sleep until noon again?

The morning room was deserted when he arrived, but the table was laden with food. Jack helped himself to a thick slab of bread, several slices of cold beef tongue, and a welcome cup of coffee. He looked up as the door opened, and he smiled as Honoria entered.

"Good morning," he said, standing to pull out her chair. "Tea or coffee?"

"Tea, please,"

"Did you sleep well?"

"I thought I would like being in my old room, but I found it uncomfortable. It was too strong a reminder that I do not belong here anymore."

Jack eyed her closely. "Is Edmond about?"

"He's probably still sleeping. He is not an early riser."

"A pity. I thought he might want to show me the estate."

Honoria's face brightened. "Would you like to ride? Uncle has a fine stable."

"I'll wait for Edmond."

"Then how would you like me to take you around the house?"

Jack shrugged. "It's as good a time as any."

"Do you want to get your map?"

"Why? I have you for a guide."

"I thought you might want to mark down anything that looks suspicious or catches your eye. For further investigation."

He tapped a finger to his temple. "My memory is excellent."

Honoria quickly finished her breakfast. "The two most likely hiding places for the necklaces are the study and Uncle's room, but we cannot look there now. He keeps both rooms locked."

"That is no problem," Jack said. "As long as you can find me the right tools."

"Do you know how to pick locks?"

Jack ducked his head modestly. "I have some skill in that direction."

"Good. We can try the study tonight, after Uncle Richard has gone to sleep."

Honoria led him across the hall to the library, but Jack halted in the middle of the floor.

"Not so fast." He knelt and rapped on the floor with his knuckles. "The necklace might be hidden under a loose board."

Honoria shot him a disbelieving glance. "Don't let your imagination get the better of you." She pushed open the door to the library and Jack followed behind her.

"This room isn't as private as the study, but it would be easy to hide something amid all these books."

Jack glanced at the overflowing bookshelves between each window. "It will take a long time to look through them all."

"Do you think it is possible that he hid the necklace here?"

"He might have done any number of things." Jack pulled a thick volume off the shelf and blew off the dust. "He could hollow out a book and hide almost anything between the covers."

Dismay crossed Honoria's face. "Do you mean we have to examine each and every one?"

"I think it is far more likely that he hid it somewhere else. I wouldn't spend time here until we have exhausted the other possibilities."

"I wish we could do that now. I want to find that necklace."

"You know the staff here. See if you can get hold of the keys to the study and his bedroom. It will save time if I don't have to play with the locks. And try to find a way to get your uncle out of the house so I can search those rooms."

"I'll try."

Jack ran his finger along a row of books, grimacing when he spotted the Latin titles. Lord, he hated Latin. Once, it had been the bane of his existence. The intervening years had only shown him how right he had been about its uselessness.

When he turned around, he saw Honoria standing in the middle of the room, looking at him with a thoughtful expression. He smiled disarmingly. "You are certain there's no hidden chamber beneath a stairway? No priest's hole behind a fireplace? It would make things a lot easier."

"There is nothing like that here."

Jack headed back into the hall. "Where to next, sweetling?"

Honoria ignored the endearment. "We may as well look at the rest of the ground floor. Unless you want to check the cellar?"

"I'll leave that for a later date." Jack turned and looked at her. "Haven't you forgotten to give me one important bit of information?"

Honoria paused in the doorway. "What's that?"

"What does the damn thing look like?"

She stared at him. "You mean to tell me you didn't notice last night?"

"Someone was wearing it? Who?"

Honoria threw up her hands in exasperation. "I am beginning to see why you were caught and jailed. You aren't the most observant man in the world, are you?" She crossed the hall again, Jack right on her heels. Flinging open the drawing room door, she marched over to the fireplace.

"Look." She pointed to the picture over the mantel.

The darkened portrait featured a lady in seventeenth-century dress, posed with her hand on the head of some mangy dog. Jack remembered glancing at the painting last night, then looking away when he noticed the dog. Now he looked closer.

And sucked in his breath.

He was no jeweler, but he knew that Honoria Sterling

had been right about one thing—the necklace around the woman's neck was worth a fortune. There were enough diamonds and rubies to buy half the countries in Europe. The central stone alone would keep a person in funds for decades. "Wherever did your family get this?"

"I believe it changed hands in a game of cards. Originally, it belonged to the mistress of a royal duke." She looked at him anxiously. "Will it be too difficult to sell?"

Jack doubted that there was a "fence" in the country who would touch it. It was too remarkable, too easily recognized. Unless they chose to take it apart and sell it, stone by stone.

And that would be a bigger crime than stealing it.

He turned away from the picture. This was not some lady's trinket, it was probably the most valuable piece of jewelry he had ever seen—and Jack was no stranger to expensive jewelry. No man, especially one as arrogant as Sir Richard, would stand aside and let the theft of something like that go unavenged.

"Let's see the rest of the house," he said curtly.

While they roamed up and down the corridors, he wondered again at her single-minded determination to achieve her goal. Jack admired that as much as he feared it, because if it came to a choice between her necklace and his safety, he knew what he would choose. And he knew that she wouldn't make the same choice. He must remember that.

Honoria needed the money to live on and she was a realist. She might be soft-hearted and tender in some areas, but he had already learned that she could be as tenacious as a bulldog at other times. The necklace might be a family heirloom, but it was useful only for the money it could bring.

And it would bring a great deal of that. Enough so that he began to think that her offer of six hundred pounds might not be enough. He just might want to renegotiate his agreement with Honoria.

By lunch, Jack was exhausted and short-tempered. He saw more of Norcross than he ever wanted to, from the wine cellars to the attic, and everywhere between. Honoria was as thorough a tour guide as old Mrs. Benson.

Mrs. Benson. Jack still shuddered at the memory. She had been the housekeeper while he was growing up, or the "wrath of God," as he'd often called her. Did she still lurk about the halls of his father's house, terrorizing small children by coming upon them at the height of their mischief? She must have been prescient to have caught him so often.

He frowned. Why was he thinking about the past so much these days? He had spent months in prison, facing death with little regard for what happened to him in the past. Now, he seemed dogged by memories that he would rather forget.

Ever since Honoria rescued him, he had been unable to push the memories away. It was as if the longer he played his role of Jack Derry, gentleman thief, the more his real self tried to jump to the fore. And that would never do. He was not who Honoria thought he was, but he wasn't the same person he had been before, either. That man had vanished long ago and Jack wanted it to remain that way; it was too painful otherwise.

Clenching and reclenching his fists, he damned Honoria for dragging him into this, for dragging out these memories he had tied so hard to suppress. In a few days, she had reversed what it had taken him years to achieve.

She should have let him die.

Right. Jack sneered at his own foolishness. Painful as memories were, they were a damn sight better than death. Having come so close to it, Jack valued life more than ever.

Only he didn't want the complications that life offered. Honoria wanted him to care about her quest and Jack did not want to care about anything except himself. The longer he stayed here, the harder it was going to be to free himself from her expectations. He almost felt silken chains wrapping themselves around him, and a chill of fear shot up his spine.

"I must sit with Aunt Sophia for a while," Honoria whispered to him as they left the dining room after lunch. "When she falls asleep, I will come and get you. You'll need those things of my father's I promised you."

Jack nodded. He would much rather hide in his room than spend an hour or two with Sir Richard's guests. Apart from the fact that they were all at least thirty years older, they were all sporting-mad. Horse racing, he would discuss, but hunting, hounds, and pheasants weren't among his favorite topics.

While he waited for Honoria, Jack reexamined her carefully drawn floor plans. Fewer than half the bedrooms were currently occupied, although more guests would arrive before the prince did.

Glancing out the window, he saw Honoria coming in from the garden. Was she dallying with her cousin? Jack still found it hard to believe, despite the evidence of that nocturnal visit. As near as he could tell, Honoria did not even know how to react properly to a man's advances.

There was something wrong with the picture of Honoria and Edmond together, although Jack could not quite put his finger on it. He hadn't seen much sign of closeness between them, although Lord knew, Honoria was an accomplished actress. She was certainly capable of pretending indifference to Edmond in public at the same time that she entertained him in her bed.

He must watch them closely. His life might depend on knowing what was going on.

A light tap sounded on his door. "Yes?"

Honoria whispered, "Come with me. The trunk is in my room."

Feigning shock, Jack halted. "You're asking me to attend you in your bedchamber?"

"Unless you would rather sit in the middle of the corridor, I think it is best. I assure you, no one will interrupt us."

A small, leather-bound trunk stood at the foot of her bed. Shutting the door behind her, Honoria locked it, then bent over the chest and opened the lid.

"This looks useful," Jack said, picking up a shiny, silver object. "A compass. Just the thing if I go riding."

"You don't have to go on your own. Edmond or I can come with you."

"Draw me a map. I like to ride alone." He peered over her at the other contents of the trunk. "Did your father have a quizzing glass? I would dearly love to be able to stare Lady Hampton up and down in that haughty manner she adopts."

He held an imaginary glass to his eye, tilting his nose into the air. "Is there some connection between our families?" he mocked in a dry, nasal tone. "Wasn't your father at school with my father?"

"Stop that," said Honoria, giggling.

Jack deigned to lower his gaze, glaring at her with mock disgust. "My dear girl, have you not heard that young ladies of good breeding ought to be *seen,* and not *heard*?"

"Oh, I'm so very sorry."

"Think nothing of it, my dear. Society is forgiving of those who have the proper connections. And I'm connected to just about everybody."

Honoria sat back on her heels, laughing still. "I wish Papa did have a glass. I would love to see the sight of you and Aunt Sophia together."

"I'll ask Lady Hampton to let me borrow hers." He reached into his coat pocket and pulled out an imaginary box of snuff. With a great flourish, he opened it, placed a pinch on his wrist, and sniffed audibly. He held out the invisible box to Honoria.

"Try some, my dear," he said, in the manner of Reginald Grose. "It's such a refined habit."

"Wherever did you learn how to imitate people so well? You must be a born mimic."

"Perhaps I've missed my true calling. I should have set my sights on the stage."

Honoria turned back to the trunk and pulled out a

heavy gold pocket watch, with a trailing chain. "Papa wore this every day. It was a gift from his own father."

Catching the sadness in her voice, Jack watched as she reverently handed it to him.

"How did your father die?"

"It was a stupid accident. The carriage overturned and his neck was broken."

He gently touched her arm. "I'm sorry, Norry."

"Thank you." Her voice broke. "It was such a shock; I thought we would be together forever."

"At least you regret his death. I used to pray for my father's."

"You didn't get along well with yours?"

Jack laughed harshly. "That is an understatement. We despised each other."

"That is a terrible thing to say."

"I don't think it bothered him much."

Honoria reached out and touched his hand. "How sad for you. No wonder you fell into evil ways. Your father should have dealt better with you."

"Oh, he tried, but I fought him every step of the way."

"Did he know about—about your trial?"

"I saw no need to inform my family. I suspect he would have been supremely indifferent to my fate, in any case."

"What an awful man!"

Jack's eyes lit with a roguish gleam. "Feeling sorry for me? Most ladies do."

Honoria shut the lid of the trunk with a thump. "I think you are feeling sorry for yourself."

"Not at all. I like being on my own. Families are a damned nuisance. I would rather take care of myself."

"Then you know why I want that necklace so badly." Honoria's expression hardened. "Find it for me."

After Jack left, Honoria thought about what he had said. What had his family done to alienate him so badly that he didn't even want them to know he was going to die? Not because it would cause them pain, but because their presence wouldn't have brought him comfort. And after what he said, she wondered if they would have come even if he had asked.

An ineffable sadness tugged at her. Jack was as alone as she was. *If* he was telling the truth. His tragic tale might be just that, a tale deliberately designed to win her sympathy.

Yet Honoria suspected that there was truth in it, however exaggerated. No one could feign the note of pain that lay beneath Jack's bitter words. There was no question that he was estranged from his family. Had they cast him out, forcing him into a life of crime? Or had his criminal activities shocked and appalled them?

Either way, it explained a great deal about him—his obvious education, his gentlemanly habits. However disreputable he was now, Honoria suspected that he came from a respectable background.

In the end, Honoria felt sorry for him. She had lost her father, but she had enjoyed his love until the day he died. Jack made it sound as if his father had never cared for him. No wonder he had gone astray.

She and Jack were less disparate than she'd first thought. He, too, needed caring for just as she desperately sought someone to care for her. It was what she had been searching for since her father died; what the money from the necklace would be a substitute for, but would never replace.

During the afternoon, Honoria went in search of the butler. She found Plummer in the dining room, putting away the silver.

"I hate to bother you, Plummer," she said, apologetically.

"Not at all, miss."

"Uncle Richard wants everything in order for the prince's arrival. I am perfectly confident that everyone is working very hard, and rather than pester you incessantly, I thought I could take charge of your keys for a few days."

The butler looked reluctant.

"I'll leave you the ones to the cellar and the silver, of course," she said hastily. "I know those areas are all in order. I am more concerned about some of the extra bedrooms and the closets."

Plummer's face relaxed. "I concur with that, miss. And you must tell me if you find anything awry. I want to know if anyone has been shirking in their duties." He took one of his key rings and handed it to her.

"Thank you very much, Plummer. I am sure I will have only glowing reports."

"Now you watch over those keys," he said. "It won't do to mislay them, not with all the guests that are coming."

"I will guard them with vigilance," she said and hastened up the stairs.

She slipped the ring of keys beneath Jack's mattress. Somewhere on the ring was the key to Uncle's study. Tonight, Jack would be able to search that room at his leisure.

It was a struggle to contain her excitement until after dinner, when she drew Jack aside in the drawing room.

"I have the keys—they're under your mattress. I had to take the whole ring from Plummer, but the study key is there. Come to my room an hour after everyone goes to bed."

"I would be glad to join you in your room anytime."

Honoria looked exasperated. "Do be serious. We are going to search for the necklace tonight."

"How could I forget? Is Edmond coming too?"

"Do you want him to help?"

"No," said Jack curtly. It would be bad enough having to work under Honoria's nose. He did not want Edmond hanging about, too.

"The key to my uncle's room is on the ring too. He's planning to take us all to Cirencester tomorrow, so you will be able to search his room while he's gone."

He grinned. "By tomorrow night, you could be a very wealthy lady."

"I hope so."

Two hours later, Jack tapped lightly on the door and slipped into her room.

"Ready?" he asked, with a conspiratorial wink.

Honoria picked up her candle and followed him out into the corridor. The house was silent and filled with shadows that seemed more comforting than ominous. At night, they wouldn't be disturbed in their searching. She followed Jack to the study.

It took a few moments before he found the right key, then he unlocked the door and they stepped inside.

At least it wouldn't take them long to search the room. Her uncle had rearranged the study to his tastes, replacing her father's possessions with his own. Pictures covered the walls—all dogs—and a large mahogany desk dominated the room.

"The desk is the most likely place to look," Jack said. He tried the first drawer but it was locked. "I don't suppose you have the key to that?"

Honoria shook her head. "I thought you said you could pick locks?"

"Some locks," Jack said as he knelt and examined the desk more carefully. "And if I have the right tools."

"What do you need?"

"Do you have a hairpin?"

Honoria pulled one from her hair and handed it to him.

"You look behind all the pictures," Jack said as he lit another candle. "I'll work on this lock."

Honoria was certain there weren't any hidden compartments behind the paintings, but followed Jack's orders. After all, this was "Gentleman Jack," whose reputation rested on any number of daring thefts. Who was she to argue with his suggestions?

"There's nothing here," she said emphatically after she'd struggled to realign the last picture. Jack still knelt before the desk, a look of growing frustration on his face.

He pointed to the curio cupboard on the east wall. "Look in there. I want to get this desk unlocked."

Norry peered into the glass-fronted cabinet. She didn't see anything big enough to even hold the necklace, but she opened the door and looked carefully at every object.

"Damn!"

Norry jumped at the sound of Jack's voice and she whirled about. "What's wrong?"

"A hairpin isn't going to do the job," he said, leaning back on his heels, his brow furrowed in thought. Then he emptied his pockets onto the carpet. Honoria spotted several nails, bits of wire, a fork, a penknife, and a few items she didn't even recognize.

"Where did you find all those things?"

"Oh, here and there." Jack picked up the penknife and stuck the quill splitter in the lock. "You'd be surprised what you can find lying around a house like this. Now hold the candle, so I can see what I'm doing."

Honoria leaned over his shoulder to watch, fascinated, as he tried a succession of tools in the lock.

"Do you think this is going to work?"

"It won't if you drop hot wax all over me."

She stepped back. "I didn't realize it was so difficult to open a lock."

"I could force the thing in a minute, but then your uncle *might* suspect something."

"I know you're trying."

Jack sighed. "Thanks."

It took a frustrating twenty minutes before he at last succeeded in opening the lock. Honoria eagerly pulled the top drawer open.

"It doesn't look promising," Jack said, scanning the contents.

Honoria rifled through the quills, paper, sealing wax, and pins, the common contents of a gentleman's desk. But there was no necklace. She knelt down and looked through the other drawers in quick succession.

"It's all papers," she said. "What do we do now?"

"Let's finish with the rest of the room."

Resuming the search, he lifted every picture and ran his fingers over the backing, looking for signs of tampering.

A muffled noise from the hall made him jump.

"What's that?" Honoria whispered fearfully.

Jack grabbed her wrist and sank into a chair, pulling her into his lap. "Now, let's see how good an actress you really are."

He cupped her head and drew her lips to his. Over her startled gasp he heard the clicking of the lock and the squeak of hinges as the door swung open.

Chapter 9

Stunned by Jack's sudden actions, Honoria did not resist but melted into his kiss without conscious thought. His lips were warm, insistent, enticing.

"What's going on?" a male voice demanded.

Jack looked up. "Oh, Edmond, it's you."

"What do you think you're doing?"

"I was afraid you were Sir Richard. I'd rather be caught stealing a few kisses than stealing a necklace."

"You may release me now," Honoria said quietly.

"Must I?" Jack asked.

She shivered at the intense feeling she saw in his warm brown eyes. "Jack . . ."

"All right." He dropped his arms and she sprang from his lap.

"What are you doing here?" Edmond demanded again.

"Don't be silly, Edmond," Honoria said. "We've been looking for the necklace."

"Why didn't you tell me?"

"I didn't think we needed to," Jack said. "It would only put you in a dangerous position."

"I don't suppose you thought about the danger you put

Honoria in, did you? I insist that you include me if you are going to do any searching. God knows what could happen."

"I think Jack can protect me from Uncle Richard," Honoria said dryly.

Jack put a possessive arm around her waist. "He wants to know who is going to protect you from me."

Honoria batted Jack's hand away and looked sternly at her cousin. "If I cannot trust Jack, why would I have brought him here?"

Edmond shrugged and turned away. "I suppose you know what's best."

"We will have to look again tomorrow," she said to Jack as she blew out the extra candles. "That is, if you don't find it in his room."

"Whose room?" Edmond asked in a suspicious tone.

"Uncle's."

"You think he hid the necklace there?"

Jack locked the study door behind them. "More likely there than in the kitchen."

"But won't it be dangerous? What if he catches you?"

Honoria smiled. "Really, Edmond, don't you think I've planned this? Richard will be at Cirencester. Jack will have plenty of time to search."

Edmond coughed. "How nice."

"Sweet dreams," said Jack as they reached Honoria's door. He took her hand and kissed it, then sauntered down the hall toward his room.

Edmond watched until Jack's door closed before he pushed Honoria into her room. He shuddered to think how close she'd come to ruining all his plans. If she had found the necklace tonight . . .

"What were you thinking of, searching without me?"

"I didn't think it was any concern of yours."

He strove to control his irritation. "I don't trust this Barnhill fellow."

"Are you afraid he's going to hit me over the head and steal the necklace? Or ravish me?"

"It looked as if he was trying."

"If you hadn't interrupted, he would not have needed to do such a thing. What were you doing there, anyway?"

"I went down to get a book from the library and saw the light beneath the door."

"Thank goodness Jack kept his wits. If it had been Uncle Richard even he could not blame two people in love for wanting to be alone."

"And if it had been your uncle, you might find yourself married to the fellow before you had a chance to say no."

"I doubt Richard would even care if he found Jack in my bed."

"Honoria! How can you talk like that?"

She grinned. "Edmond, I know what I am doing, both with Uncle Richard and Jack. If you are going to worry so much, I will send you home to Yorkshire until this is all over."

Edmond began to sweat. "No, no, I'll stay. And I'll try not to interfere. But you know I am concerned for you. You are my cousin, after all, and I want to look after you."

"I appreciate that. You've helped so much already."

"I despise what your uncle did. I only wish we could expose the whole scheme."

"As long as I get the necklace, I'll be content." Honoria yawned. "Now, let me sleep. Remember, we're going to Cirencester in the morning. Do you want to ride in Sophia's carriage?"

"I'm going with Mayflower to look over some horses instead."

"Let's cross our fingers that Jack is successful while we're gone."

Edmond pressed a light kiss to her forehead. "For your sake, I hope he is."

Honoria opened her door and looked out in the corridor. At her nod, Edmond left. When he heard her door close, he continued past his door and down the rear stairs. Crossing the ground floor, he climbed the main staircase and turned toward the original section of the house. At Sir Richard's bedroom door, he rapped softly.

"Who's there?"

"Stephenson."

Sir Richard opened the door and let him in.

"They searched your study tonight," Edmond told him.

Sir Richard's eyes gleamed. "So, she has enlisted him in her plan, eh? Probably the reason he wanted to marry her—she would have quite a dowry. Or maybe he wants the necklace for himself."

"I did find them in each other's arms."

"Hmm." Sir Richard paced back and forth. "Well, it would be easy enough for him to pretend, if that is his game. Are they lovers?"

"I hardly think so."

"What do they plan next?"

"Jack is going to search your room tomorrow while you're at Cirencester."

Sir Richard smiled. "Good, good. They're doing exactly as I intended. Fools, the both of them."

"Is there anything more I can do to help?"

"No, everything is well in hand. I'll toy with them for a bit longer, then allow them to 'discover' the copy."

"Honoria said something about searching again tomorrow."

Sir Richard clapped Edmond on the shoulder. "You're doing a good job, my boy. I can't tell you how much I appreciate your coming to me with this tale. We'll turn the tables on that little schemer."

Edmond smiled blandly. Sir Richard's overwhelming confidence would be his ultimate undoing. Edmond relished the sense of satisfaction he would feel when he pulled this off. He didn't care if he ever saw Honoria, Sir Richard, Yorkshire, or even England again. Once he had the necklace, he could live like a prince wherever he went.

•

Honoria dashed into the morning room just as Jack took a bite of his broiled kidneys.

"Uncle Richard and the others are getting ready to leave."

"I did so want to go with you. I love old churches."

Honoria rolled her eyes. 'Try to restrain your disappointment. We will take lunch, so don't expect us back until after four. You will have plenty of time to work undisturbed."

"What if someone asks me why I'm not going?"

"Tell them you have a bad headache or an upset stomach."

"What if I find the necklace while you are gone?"

"Stuff it under your pillow until I get back. Honestly, Jack, do I have to tell you every little detail? Use your head, for once."

Jack mumbled something under his breath, which Honoria was glad she couldn't hear.

"I need to get ready. I promised to ride with Aunt Sophia."

Jack waved her off. "Have a nice time."

Sophia looked up eagerly when Honoria entered the drawing room, then her eyes narrowed.

"Where's that nice young man of yours? I wanted him to ride with us."

"Jack? He wants to stay home. Said he had a touch of the headache."

Sophia frowned. "Then I'm staying, too. Don't want to spend the day with a bunch of gossiping magpies."

"But, Aunt," Honoria said quickly, "you were the one who wanted to see Cirencester. Jack will be fine."

Sophia set her mouth in a stubborn line. "If he stays, I stay. I didn't come up to Gloucester to be bored."

"You will have to speak with him yourself." Honoria knew it was pointless to argue with her aunt when her mind was fixed on something. "He is the one with the headache."

Sophia stomped off toward the morning room and Honoria dashed to follow.

"What's this Norry says about you not coming to Cirencester?" Sophia demanded.

Jack pressed a hand to his forehead. "I'm a trifle out of sorts today."

"Nonsense." Sophia tapped her cane for emphasis. "You're coming with us. I'll have my girl bring you a tisane. You'll feel much better."

"I feel a spasm coming on." He grimaced as if in pain. "I'd better lie down." Jack staggered out of the room.

Honoria barely suppressed a smile at his outrageous playacting.

Sophia snorted her derision. "Out of sorts or no, it's his duty to act as your escort. You march right after him and tell him he had better be in that carriage in ten minutes."

With resignation, Honoria headed up the stairs and pushed open the door to Jack's room. He lay on the bed, hands behind his head, eyes closed.

"Get up," she commanded.

Jack opened one eye. "I thought I had a headache."

"Aunt Sophia insists you accompany us to Cirencester or she won't go. You won't be able to search the house if she stays, so you might as well come along."

"A truly heartfelt invitation." Jack sat up, a wry grin on his face. "Don't blame me for this; I told her I didn't want to go."

"Obviously, you didn't do a convincing enough job. The carriage will be in front in a few minutes. Be there." Honoria slammed the door behind her.

Sophia insisted Jack sit beside her in the closed carriage, facing Honoria and Mrs. Grose.

"This was a lovely idea," Mrs. Grose said. "I do so love visiting old churches."

"I, too," said Jack. "Particularly Norman ones."

Sophia looked at him with interest. "I didn't realize you were interested in church architecture, Mr. Barnhill."

"A minor interest of mine. In my younger days, there was some talk of my studying for the church."

Honoria bit down hard on her lip to keep from laughing aloud at his outrageous lie. What Jack knew about religion could probably fit on the head of a pin—if it took that much space.

"My nephew is at Oxford now, preparing to take orders." Mrs. Grose preened with smug satisfaction. "We have hopes of a good parish."

Sophia looked at Jack with motherly concern. "Tell me, Mr. Barnhill, why didn't you take orders?"

"Alas, my father died young and I inherited the estate. With no younger brothers . . . I was disappointed at first, but now I'm content with life in Yorkshire."

Sophia and Mrs. Grose made soothing sounds.

"You can climb the tower with me, then," Honoria said. "I am sure you will be an informative guide."

"As you wish," Jack replied, with a twinkle in his eye.

Honoria regretted her blatant invitation, but she didn't want Jack spending too much time with Sophia. She might not recognize Jack, but she was perceptive enough to see through the false tale of their engagement.

At Cirencester, Jack helped the two older women from the carriage and guided them into the church. As soon as they were inside, Honoria grabbed Jack's arm and pulled him away.

"I want to climb the tower."

"I'm not stopping you."

"I need an escort."

He stared at her. "If you think I'm going to carry you up those stairs, you're crazy!"

"I don't expect you to carry me. I want you to *accompany* me. You are the only one agile enough to climb all those stairs. And I, for one, want to see the view."

"Fine. We will climb the tower."

By the time he was halfway to the top of the one-hundred-and-sixty-two-foot tower, his legs ached, his chest hurt, and Jack knew he should have stayed below. However, there was some compensation for his pain. Honoria went before him, and if he walked slowly enough, his eyes were at a level with her nicely shaped ankles. Even better, if he stayed only five paces below her on the steep stairs, he could admire the sight of her nicely rounded bottom. Watching its gentle sway as she proceeded up the stairs made this ridiculous climb endurable. That, and the remembrance of their hasty embrace the night before. Too bad Edmond had entered so quickly; Jack would not have minded stealing a few more kisses.

He was breathing heavily when they reached the top. Resting his arm against the ledge for a moment, Jack struggled to catch his breath. When he thought he could speak and breathe at the same time, Jack followed along the platform until he found Honoria.

"No doubt they used this in place of the stocks for recalcitrant parishioners. More than one trip up those stairs and a person would forswear all objectionable behavior."

"Is your life of indolence wearing on you?"

Jack laughed. "I doubt even a goat would enjoy scrambling up those steps."

She ran her hand over the pitted stonework of the wall. "Just think, they started building this around 1400. That's more than four hundred years ago."

"Bravo. Your mathematical skills are impressive."

"I can't expect a man of your limited background to appreciate something so historical."

He ignored her comment and walked to the other side of the tower. "What's that open space over there?"

"Cirencester Park. Lord Bathurst's estate."

That was a name he didn't want to remember. How long had it been since he'd seen that man? Ten—no, fifteen years at least. He was one of his father's cronies, of little interest to a rebellious youth. What would he think if he knew that Jack stood here on the church tower at Cirencester, with a female who had rescued him from the gallows?

He would think him crazy, no doubt, and he wouldn't be far wrong. The mad Miss Sterling and her gentleman thief. A farce in three acts to be performed at Covent Garden Friday next.

Jack felt a light touch on his arm and he saw Honoria at his elbow.

"It is pretty, isn't it?"

"If you like trees and grass. Personally, I prefer being inside, with a comfortable chair and a good glass of wine."

She peered over the railing. "I see Uncle and the others below. We should go down."

"After you, *dear* Cousin."

"A gentleman should precede a lady on such steep stairs. In case she misses a step."

"So both of us can take a tumble? Seems rather foolish to me."

"I'll trust you to maintain your footing."

"Suit yourself." He ducked through the doorway and started down the steps. Halfway to the bottom he realized Honoria lagged far behind him and he halted guiltily.

"Am I going too fast for you?" he called.

"Not at all. It's this dratted dress."

Jack wanted to tell her he wouldn't mind if she hitched it up to her knees. But she'd likely box his ears for that.

"Remember, I'm here to catch you."

"A lot of good it will do when you are two turns ahead of me."

Jack took her hand. "Allow me to assist you, my dear."

Honoria took a step, slipped, and crashed into Jack. Instinctively, he grabbed her, struggling to regain his own balance as he fell back against the wall.

Jack sucked in a deep breath, his heart pounding at the sudden mishap, relieved they hadn't tumbled down the narrow stone steps. He had not cheated the hangman in order to break his neck in a moldy old church. As his panic eased, he grew aware of the soft roundness of Honoria's breasts pressed against his chest, and smelled the light scent of her lavender water.

Last night, when he held her on his lap, he had been more worried about being caught in the study than in enjoying the experience. Now he savored the moment and nuzzled against her hair.

A strangled noise escaped her throat.

"Really, Norry, if you wanted me to hold you in my arms

again, you only needed to ask. You don't have to fling yourself at me."

"Let me go, you oaf!"

"Some thanks I get for rescuing you." Jack dropped his hands from her waist. "Shall we try to descend again? Or do you want to go first this time?"

"I'll follow you."

"If you pulled up your skirts, you'd have an easier time."

"You'd like that, wouldn't you? Unfortunately for you, ladies don't do such things."

"I thought it was a good idea." He reached out and took her arm. "Ready?"

Honoria kept her eyes riveted on her feet as she stepped down each stair. It had been only the briefest instant, but she felt as if he had held her in his arms for ages. It reminded her all too clearly of last night. Both times it had been shockingly pleasant. Which was ridiculous.

Even if he was an attractive, exciting man, he was also a thief and a rogue. He was the symbol of danger and unreliability. Then why had she felt that brief, unfamiliar sense of safety when he had clasped her in his arms?

It had been relief, of course. Relief that she hadn't fallen all the way to the bottom of the stairs. Jack's tall and substantial body had saved her from a nasty fall. No wonder she hadn't minded his arms around her. Any man would have been welcome in that situation.

Then why did she regret that she had forced him to release her? Why did she wish she had lingered a bit longer in his grasp?

The church was empty when they reached the bottom

of the tower and entered the nave. Honoria looked around, puzzled. "Where is everyone?"

"They probably went back to Norcross already."

"Aunt Sophia would not leave without *you*. Perhaps they are out in the churchyard."

Stone grave markers leaned against each other in crowded disorder behind the church. Honoria walked among the narrow paths, reading the inscriptions on the stones. "Look at this one."

"Poor bastard," Jack said. "Dead at twenty."

"This one will make you feel better. He was nearly eighty."

A long-forgotten phrase leaped to his mind and he spoke without thinking. "*Post mortem nihil est, ipsaque mors nihil.* After death nothing is, and nothing, death."

"Isn't that Latin?"

"Something I saw scratched on the wall in prison."

Suspicious, Honoria grabbed his arm. "What other interesting things were carved on the walls? Shakespearean sonnets? Poetry?"

"Plenty of that." He thought for a moment, and then recited:

> *"Fair Chloris in a pigsty lay;*
> *Her tender herd lay by her.*
> *She slept; in murmuring gruntlings they,*
> *complaining of the scorching day,*
> *Her slumbers thus inspire."*

"*That* sounds more like what you would find on a prison wall."

"Would you believe an earl wrote it?"

Honoria was skeptical. "Of course. Earls always write odes to pigs."

"Actually, it was an ode to something else." Jack's grin widened. "But the explanation is tedious."

"Or scurrilous, no doubt." Honoria continued to explore the yard, occasionally glancing over her shoulder at Jack.

Once again, he'd confounded her. A thief who knew Latin and spouted poetry—even if doggerel verse. She began to realize there was much more to him than he admitted. But why was he so unwilling to reveal it?

Halting abruptly, Honoria suddenly wished for the security of the group. Jack Derry had the most unsettling effect on her, particularly when they were alone.

"Let's find the others."

When Jack and Honoria joined the guests in front of the church, Sophia tittered like a giddy young girl at the sight of them together.

"Did you enjoy your explorations?" she asked with a smile.

"I belive Honoria enjoyed herself immensely." Jack patted her hand. "The view from the tower is indescribable."

As was his behavior, Honoria thought to herself. She tried to pull her hand away, but he held it tightly.

"This was so much fun, we'll have to take another day trip," Mrs. Grose said. "A pity it is too far to visit Badminton. My sister says the grounds are lovely."

Sophia sniffed. "They may be vast, but I daresay they aren't nearly as nice as the ones at Houghton."

"Indeed?"

"Oh, yes." Sophia launched into a long discourse on the virtues of her grandson's gardens.

Jack settled back into his seat. It had been an amusing excursion—especially with Honoria's delightful misstep on the stairs. He warranted he would not have another chance to be so close again.

Jack reminded himself that he had sworn off women, but he hadn't sworn off thinking about them. And it did not mean that he was going to give them up completely; it only meant he wasn't going to become entangled with one again. Those were two very different things. Still, it would be interesting to discover if he could get Honoria Sterling to melt in his arms long enough for more than a hasty kiss. The more he thought of it, the more he liked the idea.

Moving with deliberate casualness, Jack shifted on the seat until his thigh pressed against Honoria's. She darted him a startled glance and edged farther toward the corner of the coach.

Chapter 10

In the drawing room after dinner, Sophia eyed Honoria with a sly look. "You're acting mighty mysterious this evening. Planning a late-night assignation with your beau?"

Honoria laughed to cover her discomfort; Sophia's words were very close to the truth. "I hardly need to meet Jack in secret."

"You two spent a good deal of time together today." Sophia's eyes twinkled. "Did he steal a kiss or two?"

Against her wishes, Honoria blushed.

No, he hadn't kissed her today. But that panicked embrace on the stairs had been as intimate as a kiss—and equally unsettling.

"Jack behaved like a perfect gentleman."

Sophia shook her head. "A pity."

Honoria glanced up in relief when the men entered. Jack could occupy Sophia's attention.

Honoria rose and went to meet him. "I think we should search again tonight," she said in a low undertone. "I kept the keys."

"Good girl. I'll come get you as soon as your uncle retires."

"Mr. Barnhill." Sophia's nasal tones rose above the hum of conversation. "I want to have a word with you."

Jack looked at Honoria. "What have I done now?"

"I've no idea." Honoria schooled her features into an innocent expression. "Perhaps Aunt Sophia wishes your opinion on some matter." She gently pushed Jack in her direction. "Hurry, or she will grow impatient."

She walked away and joined Lady Mayflower, leaving Jack to battle her aunt on his own.

Jack's behavior perplexed her.

This evening, for example. Every time she glanced his way, she found him looking at her, a wicked gleam in those warm brown eyes. And when she wasn't looking, she still sensed his eyes on her, watching her at dinner and in the drawing room. And he had acted like a captivated swain in the coach, with his knowing smiles, mischievous winks, and subtle touches. Add to that the incident in the library and it grew puzzling. It was as if he knew how uncomfortable she felt under his flirtatious attention, and he dared her to ignore him.

Honoria wanted to. Wanted to forget everything about him except that he was here to find her necklace. But it was impossible to push Jack from her mind. The more she learned about him, the more she was drawn to him with a strange mix of curiosity and sympathy.

She had discovered a few things about him today, things that puzzled her. He was far more educated than he admitted—that Latin verse had not come from a prison wall. Why, then, was he stooping to a life of crime?

He may have lost his money on horses, but there were other ways for him to earn a living. Didn't he want to? Or hadn't he had the chance?

She feared that once he had his share from the sale of the necklace, he would soon gamble it away and be forced to steal again. The thought of Jack Derry hanging from the end of a rope caused an uneasy twinge in her stomach. He didn't deserve such a drastic end. She would feel better about using him to find her necklace if she knew that he would have some kind of future after they parted.

Not because she wanted to be a part of that future. Jack Derry could never give her the future she wanted. But she wanted him to find the happiness that had eluded him so far; the happiness that she had known in her past, and struggled to find again.

Beneath his cynical mask, there was a man, a real man, who needed the same things she did. Honoria wanted to break through the facade and find the real man behind it. The man whose teasing smile sent shivers down her spine, and whose grinning glances caused her knees to weaken.

The man in whose arms she had felt the first sense of security since her father died. Jack deserved to experience that same type of security. The security of being loved, and loving someone in return.

It just could not be her.

Since he had to wait anyway for Sir Richard to go to bed, Jack agreed eagerly when his host suggested a few hands of whist. Even if no money was involved, a game was better than trying to converse politely with a roomful of old ladies.

He didn't mind drinking the claret either. Jack took another sip of the excellent vintage and glanced at his cards. Not a bad hand. His partner was Grose, the solicitor. He was a decent, if conservative, player and they did well.

A particularly tricky round demanded his total concentration, and when Jack looked up again, he was surprised to find the ladies gone.

Grose clapped him on the back. "Good job, Barnhill. Nice play on that last hand." He rose and stretched. "Time for me to head upstairs."

Latham, Richard's partner, left also.

Sir Richard looked at Jack. "Are you as handy at piquet as whist?"

Jack nodded, and refilled their glasses while Sir Richard shuffled.

"I can't tell you how pleased I am about your engagement to Norry." Richard skillfully dealt the cards. "My brother's death was a terrible blow. I tried to do what I could for her, but it was difficult. It'll be good to see her happy again."

"Her happiness is my paramount concern."

Richard studied his hand "How did you two meet?"

"It was at her cousin's. I rode over one afternoon to find Honoria visiting and, well, I fear it was love at first sight." Jack smiled in a disarming manner. "I fear you think we are being hasty."

"Not at all, not at all. If you're a friend of Norry's cousin, you certainly have my approval." Richard reached over and refilled Jack's glass. "Have you made plans for the wedding yet?"

Shaking his head, Jack struggled to count his cards, but the numbers and shapes kept shifting before his eyes.

"May I suggest that you marry here at Norcross? It is Honoria's home, after all."

Jack glanced up, surprised at the offer. "It's kind of you to offer."

They tallied their points and Richard laid down the first card.

Jack tossed down the response and took another drink of claret. "This is a fine wine."

Sir Richard beamed. "It's quality stuff and it impresses the guests."

"I hear there is a high-placed one arriving soon."

A sly smile crept over Sir Richard's face. "A prince, no less. Course, they are as common in Germany as a baronet is here, but the title sounds impressive."

"How did you strike up an acquaintance with the man?"

"Met him during the celebrations. Did you go to town for them?"

Jack didn't have to fake his regretful look. "No, I missed the whole thing. It sounded exciting."

"Well, one prince isn't much, compared with tsars and kings, but it's something for Norcross." Richard topped Jack's last card. "Does your family hail from Yorkshire?"

Jack frowned at the last move. He could've sworn the ten had been played already. "Sussex," he mumbled, vowing to concentrate harder. After all, piquet was his game.

"Then you were visiting in Yorkshire?"

Realizing his error, Jack sought to cover his discomposure with a hasty play and threw down the eight. "I mean we're originally from Sussex. Moved to Yorkshire some time ago."

"How does Norry's aunt get on? I only met Caroline once, but she has the kind of personality that remains in one's mind."

Confusion gripped Jack. "Caroline?"

"Edmond's mother."

Jack sat up straighter, trying to think. Was that Norry's aunt's name? "Emily. Mrs. Stephenson's given name is Emily."

"Oh, good Lord, you're right." Richard gave an embarrassed smile and tossed down another card. "Been years since I saw her."

Jack frowned as he examined the remaining cards in his hand. He was completely out of hearts and clubs, which meant Sir Richard would continue to trump him. "Looks like I'm all in." Squinting, he tried to bring the wavering figure of Sir Richard into focus. " 'nother hand?"

Richard shrugged. "Why not?"

Jack shuffled the cards with clumsy fingers. What was wrong with his play tonight? Normally, he played a damn fine game of piquet, but his luck was certainly off. He should have taken more tricks on that last hand.

He took another sip of claret, then nearly choked as the realization hit him. The claret. He was getting drunk. Jack almost laughed. Drunk? The man who could drink many a lord under the table was drunk himself?

Of course he was. He hadn't had more than a glass or

two of wine at any one time in months, and he'd certainly consumed more than that tonight. He stifled a grin.

He'd have to pay more attention to his cards. Jack made it a policy never to allow drink to interfere with his gambling, and for the first time, he was glad they weren't playing for money. It'd be embarrassing to rack up debts he couldn't even begin to pay.

Jack looked up and saw Richard eyeing him with a considering gaze.

"Does your family have substantial holdings in Yorkshire?"

"Big enough."

"What type of horses did you say you raised?"

Jack examined his host with a bemused expression. Horses? Norry hadn't said anything about horses. He tried to recall her instructions. Edmond ran sheep . . . Jack was supposed to run sheep, too. "Sheep," he said in a triumphant tone. "Sheep and hay."

"Of course." Richard smiled with chagrin. "Not quite the same thing, is it? Thought about running a few sheep down here, but I'm doing all right with the farm and the dogs. Have you had a chance to see the kennels?"

"Norry showed me around," Jack lied. "Nice animals."

Richard beamed. "Some say it's a fool thing to be involved in. But as long as there's hunting, there's a need for dogs. Do much hunting?"

"Some." Jack frowned as he contemplated his next move.

Richard darted him a fatherly smile. "Glad to hear you're a huntsman, my boy. My brother didn't care for the sport. Now me, I'd be lost without it."

"What I really enjoy"—Jack enunciated his words with deliberate care—"is horse racing."

"Oh, you do? Did you make it to the Derby this year? That was some race." Richard shook his head ruefully. "Had money on Snowdrop."

"Too bad he lost." Had Sterling played the queen? Damn that claret; Jack couldn't remember one thing tonight. Mentally crossing his fingers, he tossed down the ten.

Richard lost the trick, and finally the game. "Looks like my luck's turned."

"Close game." Jack did not bother to disguise his relief. He still had the knack, after all.

Richard gave him a pat on the back. "We'll have to have a rematch."

"Anytime." He stood and placed a steadying hand on the table. "Ought to get to bed."

Richard waved him away. "Thanks for the game."

After crossing the floor with slow, deliberate steps, Jack pushed open the heavy drawing room door. Once in the corridor, he leaned against the wall, grateful for the solid support.

Lord, he was drunk. Wouldn't little miss prim and proper be furious? Shaking his head at the fuss she'd make, he walked unsteadily toward the stairs. Norry would rip him up one side and down the other if she could see him now.

He came to an abrupt halt at the foot of the steps. Oh, God. They were supposed to search tonight.

He could still do it. After Sir Richard fell asleep, Jack

could gather up his tools, and present himself at Norry's door. Everything would be fine.

Stepping up, he stumbled and grabbed the banister railing.

Reaching his room at last, he battled for a few seconds with the doorknob. Swaying slightly when the door finally swung open, he grabbed the frame to hold himself up before he staggered over to the bed. Fumbling with the buttons of his coat, he pulled it off and lay it with exaggerated care across the chair. He sank down on the edge of the bed and struggled to remove his boot. As he leaned over to pull off the other, Jack tumbled to the floor.

He made a feeble attempt to rise, then fell back against the carpet with a thump. Moments later, he was asleep.

Honoria frowned when she entered the morning room for what had to be the tenth time and found only Aunt Sophia eating breakfast. There still was no sign of Jack. Pouring herself a cup of tea, Honoria sat beside Sophia. "Have you seen Jack this morning?"

Sophia cackled. "Lost him already, have you? You ought to keep better track of such an eligible young man."

Honoria ignored her remark. "We planned to go for a drive this morning, but I haven't seen him."

"Might still be abed." Sophia licked a drop of jam off her finger. "Your uncle is."

Norry felt a stab of anxiety. She had left Jack reluctantly last night, reasoning he couldn't get into too much trouble playing whist with Uncle's friends. She'd fallen asleep while waiting for him to come to her room. Had something gone wrong?

Setting her cup down with a clatter, Honoria bolted into the hall. She'd better find out exactly what happened last night.

Mounting the steps two at a time, Honoria fought to control the sinking feeling in her stomach. If Jack had done something foolish, she would have his head.

No one was about when she reached the bedroom floor. Hastening to the end of the corridor, Honoria rapped tentatively on Jack's door.

"Jack? Are you there?"

There was no answer. Glancing over her shoulder to make sure no one was watching, she opened the door. The room was dark, the curtains closed as if he still slept. But the bed was empty.

"Jack?" she whispered.

A deep groan met her ears and she walked around the foot of the bed. Jack lay in a crumpled heap on the floor.

"What's wrong?" she shrieked.

He rolled over onto his back, groaning with every movement. "What time is it?"

"Half past ten."

"In the morning?"

Honoria caught the faint odor of stale wine, and anger surged through her. The man was drunk! She crossed to the windows and jerked the curtains open, letting the blinding sunlight stream into the room.

Jack flung his arm across his eyes. "Good God, woman, close the curtains!"

"I will not. How dare you do this to me? You promised!"

Jack moved his arm and peered at her with one barely open eye. "Promised what?"

"That you wouldn't drink heavily!"

"I lied. Now close the curtains."

"How did this happen?"

"I was playing cards with your uncle."

"With Uncle? Oh, Jack, what have you done?"

Jack grabbed his head, a pained expression on his face. "Nothing, I hope."

"What happened? What did you talk about?"

"Dogs. Horses. Cards."

Honoria sat down on the bed. "Did he say anything about me? Or the necklace?"

"He wants our wedding at Norcross."

"That I doubt. What else did he say?"

"That you needed a husband and he was glad you found one."

Honoria laughed.

Jack clutched his head. "Not so loud, please."

"You deserve to suffer." She studied him with narrowed eyes. "Think, now. Are you certain you didn't make any mistakes?"

"I lost a few hands of piquet. That was a mistake."

"Did he ask about your family? About your history?"

Jack screwed up his brow in concentration. "He wanted to know if my family lived in Yorkshire. And he talked about horses."

"What do horses have to do with anything?"

"He confused them with sheep. I told him I raised sheep."

Honoria bit her lip. Why Uncle Richard's confusion? She had told him Jack ran sheep on his land. Unless . . .

Her hand flew to her mouth. Did Uncle suspect that Jack wasn't who he said he was? Had he been testing him? "What else did he ask you?"

Jack shrugged to a sitting position, then rested his forehead on his legs. "I don't remember. God, my head hurts."

"You've only yourself to blame."

"I knew you'd understand."

"You fool!" Honoria lashed out at him, fear and anger gaining the upper hand. "He was examining you."

"An exam? Did I pass?"

"Oh!" Honoria quivered with frustration. She flung up her hands in disgust and marched to the door. "I expect to see you in the breakfast room in twenty minutes." She shut the door none too gently.

Drinking with Uncle! How dare he make such a stupid mistake! One wrong word could ruin everything. She would have to make certain that Jack didn't get drunk in Uncle Richard's presence again, even if she had to stay up all night watching him. She wasn't going to allow him to ruin things now.

Jack groaned again as he struggled to lift his head.

God, he'd been a fool. He really hadn't drunk that much claret last night, but since he hadn't drunk much of anything for a while, he should have known better.

Gingerly pulling himself to his knees, he peered at his reflection in the mirror. He looked like hell, with his bloodshot eyes, puffy face, and dark stubble.

In fact, he looked exactly like what Honoria Sterling thought he was—a lowborn thief.

Jack turned away from the mirror and poured some water into the basin. Stripping off his shirt, he splashed water on his face and chest. His stomach roiled at every sudden movement and his head throbbed. Jack swore not to be so foolish again.

While he slowly gathered his shaving things, he tried to recall all that had been said the night before. He had been a great deal drunker than he first thought, but still, he couldn't recall saying anything wrong. They'd talked about horse racing, sheep, Edmond's mother . . .

Jack paused in the middle of lathering his face. Sir Richard had asked him about Edmond's mother, but called her by the wrong name. Was Norry right? Had the man been testing him? Jack shuddered at the thought, then dismissed it as another of her wild fantasies. Richard Sterling had no reason to be suspicious of him. He was a man obsessed with hunting dogs and little else.

Still, the first nagging doubt crept into Jack's brain. Had Sir Richard deliberately plied him with claret last night, thinking to loosen his tongue? Maybe he should show a little more caution the next time they drank claret together.

Jack wiped the last bit of shaving soap from his face and rummaged around in the wardrobe for a clean shirt. He had a pounding headache and the very thought of eating breakfast set his teeth on edge. A cup of tea, or even better, a strong cup of coffee, was the only thing he wanted.

He gave his hair a quick brushing and pulled on his

coat. Squaring his shoulders, he marched toward the door, careening against the door frame before he lurched into the hall.

It was going to be a long day.

Honoria sat alone in the morning room when Jack came down. He breathed a sigh of relief, which he instantly regretted. With no witnesses, she would be able to tear into him without restraint.

Jack sat and poured himself a cup of tea. It was tepid but he drank several cups of it anyway, since there wasn't any coffee. The tea had been in the pot for some time, and tasted bitter, but it distracted his stomach from the lingering odor of kippers from someone's earlier breakfast.

Honoria glanced at him, her blue eyes cool. "Feeling better?"

"A little." Jack reached for a piece of toast. It was cold but he forced it down.

"I assume you didn't search last night?" Her tone dripped acid.

He shook his head, wincing at the pain that shot through his skull.

"You're not here for a carouse."

"How could I forget."

"What do you propose to do now?"

"Is your uncle home today?"

She nodded.

"Well, then I can't search his room. What else do you suggest I try?"

"Use your imagination." She stood. "I'll talk to you later."

That demure smile hid the soul of a witch, Jack

thought sourly as he watched her leave. Perhaps he would hide in the library, nursing his aching head, and getting a few more winks of sleep.

To his delight, he found the library deserted. It would be the perfect place for a nap. He settled down into one of the high-backed chairs and closed his weary eyes.

Before he had the chance to fall asleep, he heard the door open and a light footstep crossed the room. Jack stifled a groan. She was back to torment him already.

"There you are!" Honoria looked disgustingly cheerful. "I've been looking all over for you. Edmond promised to take Uncle Richard riding. You can search his room while he's gone."

"How much time do I have?" he asked.

"Several hours, at least. I'll help you and it will go twice as fast."

That's all he needed, Jack thought grimly. Norry hanging over his shoulder like a officious tutor.

"I'd rather you acted as lookout," Jack said. "It wouldn't do for a servant to come in and surprise me."

"You're right."

"I want to make certain he's left the grounds before I go in," Jack said, rising. "We can watch from my room."

They hastened up the stairs. Jack pushed Norry ahead of him and closed the door. "Come on, we can see the stables from my window."

"Can you see him yet?"

"Which way are they going?" Jack asked.

"Toward the Grange—to the left."

Jack peered toward the trees. "Is that them?"

"Where?"

"There."

Norry pressed her forehead against the window glass. "I don't see anything."

"Over here." Jack clamped his hands on her shoulders and turned her slightly, pointing. "See?"

"I think so."

His lips were close to her ear and he fought the urge to kiss it. He didn't want to frighten her by moving too quickly. Instead, he took a deep breath of her lavender scent and dropped his hands about her waist, pulling her back against him, tucking her head under his chin. "We'll wait a few minutes," he said.

"Here?"

Honoria's voice came out in a high-pitched squeak and Jack smiled as he tightened his hold.

"Are you uncomfortable?"

"No—yes."

Jack laughed. "Just like a woman, always changing her mind."

"Let go of me."

Immediately, Jack released her, and Norry quickly stepped away. "I'll check the corridor."

Skittish as a new colt, Jack thought. He had barely touched her and she reacted as if he had launched a full-scale assault. Even worse, her innocent reactions had a disastrous effect on his own control. Desire flooded him at the remembrance of her body pressed close to his.

Honoria stuck her head through the doorway, beckoning to him. With resignation, he followed her down the hall. With Plummer's keys, she unlocked the door to Sir Richard's room, then pushed Jack inside. "Good luck!"

Smiling grimly, Jack surveyed the room. Besides the expected bed and chairs, Sir Richard had crammed nearly every conceivable piece of bedroom furniture into the room. All with drawers everywhere. He hoped Edmond planned to take Sir Richard Sterling for a nice, long ride.

The man had expensive tastes, Jack discovered. His stockings were silk, his gloves made to order, his hats from Lock's. No expense spared in that area. Jack looked through each item of clothing, checking pockets, folds, and pleats but found nothing more than a few spare coins and scraps of paper.

He froze suddenly when he heard a tap on the door. Honoria's head appeared around the edge. "How are you doing?"

"I *was* doing fine until you nearly scared me to death."

"Have you found anything interesting?"

"Of course. A complete written confession in which he admits he stole your inheritance and plans to sell you to the Barbary pirates."

"Honestly, Jack, you act as if this is a game."

He looked at her, wearily. "As near as I can tell, your uncle leads a boring, mundane life, likes well-made clothing, and keeps his pockets clean."

Honoria's face fell. "You haven't found it."

"No. I doubt it's here."

Her eyes drifted to the dressing table. "Have you searched there?"

"Not yet. I was about to start when you burst in on me."

"You need to hurry. If you can't finish today there's no telling how long it will be before you can try again."

Jack saluted. "Yes, ma'am."

"Just find the necklace," she said as she stomped out the door.

Jack grinned. She looked so enticing when she was angry.

As soon as she left, he redoubled his efforts. Every minute made him more certain that Sir Richard wasn't hiding the necklace here, but Jack wanted to make sure. That necklace was worth too damn much; he didn't want to make a mistake.

Finally, he admitted defeat and make a last quick survey of the room, making certain there was no sign of disturbance. He peered quickly into the corridor but didn't see Norry. Jack slipped out the door, and hastened down the back stairs.

Once in the library, Jack poured himself a generous brandy, sat down in one of the comfortable chairs, and tried to think of anything besides Norry, Richard Sterling, and the damned necklace. The more he thought about them, the more worried he became.

Chapter 11

Honoria accepted Jack's lack of success with resignation. Being held in Jack's arms was far more disturbing to her peace of mind than not finding the necklace. Yesterday, she could argue that fear had elevated her reaction on the stairs at Cirencester. But she had no such excuse today. She had reacted to *him,* and nothing else. And before she had asked him to release her, she had enjoyed the feeling. *That* she could not do. Being attracted to Jack was all wrong.

Yet when Jack strolled into the drawing room before dinner, her pulses quickened.

He bowed elegantly before her. "And how is my fair Norry this evening?"

"Quite well."

Having spotted Jack, Sophia made a direct line for him, her arrival preceded by the overpowering scent of violets. She tapped Jack on the arm with her fan.

"I have not seen you all day. Do you think you can neglect me with impunity?"

Jack took her hand, bringing it to his lips. "An unfortunate conflict on my part, Lady Hampton. I promise you my undivided attention for the remainder of the evening."

"You may start by taking me into dinner." She held out her arm and Jack placed it on his.

Honoria would never have guessed he'd play his gentleman role so well. Looking at him now, seated across the table from her, she saw no trace of the weary, despairing man she'd saved from the gallows at Gorton. Instead, she saw an elegant, witty gentleman who looked as if he belonged at this table more than some of Uncle's guests.

That was what she wanted, wasn't it? So why did she still feel this nagging unease? There was something about him, something she could not quite put her finger on, that unsettled her.

No, it wasn't Jack who unsettled her; it was her reaction to him. And his devil-may-care attitude that frightened her as much as it enticed her.

Honoria determined to find out more about him. In a way, she hoped it might explain her growing fascination with a man who could be both a convicted thief and a person well versed in poetry.

What was he hiding? And from whom?

After following Sir Richard and the others into the drawing room after dinner, Jack sprawled on the sofa next to Lady Hampton.

Sophia wagged a critical finger at him. "You haven't been paying much attention to Norry today."

Jack tried to look aghast. "I haven't? How thoughtless of me."

"She pretends not to notice, but I see her looking in

your direction." Sophia leaned forward in a confiding manner. "Don't let her missish airs put you off."

"I think you misunderstand the situation."

"Bosh." Sophia peered at him through her quizzing glass. "You don't look like a Yorkshireman to me. Remind me of one of my old beaux. Led him on a merry dance, I did, before I wed another."

"I imagine the poor man was heartbroken."

"Turned around and married some pandy-faced earl's daughter within the year. I always thought he took her sight unseen, just for spite."

"Amazing."

"I never wanted to be a duchess, anyhow. Too dull a life." Sophia looked at him again through the glass. "You certainly do have his eyes."

"Whose eyes, Aunt?" Honoria came up beside her.

"Oh, one of those young men from my better days. Long before your time." She pulled her shawl closer around her and stood. "This side of the room is too drafty. I'm going to sit by Mrs. Mayflower." She directed a broad wink at Jack as she left.

Honoria glanced at him with suspicion. "What did you say to her?"

Jack held up his hand in a defensive gesture. "I didn't say anything. She thinks I should be showing you more attention." He grinned at the faint color that rose in Honoria's cheeks. "She wanted us to have time alone."

"I want to look in the study again tonight. I can't believe Uncle Richard would hide the thing anywhere else."

"I agree. I'll come to your room after the household is asleep." He grinned and took her hand. "And now I will pay you my most devoted attention so you can reassure your aunt that my heart is in the right place."

Honoria pulled her hand away. "Then perhaps you will get me a cup of tea."

Her nerves played havoc with her confidence when Jack finally appeared at her door.

"It took you long enough," she complained as she followed him down the rear stairs.

"I waited until I was sure everyone was asleep. Pardon me for being so cautious."

He opened the study door. While Honoria lit the candles and set them atop the desk, Jack took his lock-picking tools from his pocket. This time, it only took him a few minutes to breach the lock.

"Look at *everything*," he told her. "If he doesn't have it here, there might be some reference to where it is. It can't still be in the bank vault in London."

While Honoria searched the smaller drawers, Jack pawed through the mass of paperwork in the bottom one. Breeding records for the dogs. Just what he wanted to find.

"It isn't here!" Honoria shut the last drawer with a slam, her dismay palpable. She sat back on her heels. "What are we going to do now? It isn't in his room; it isn't here. Where else would he hide it?"

Jack considered. "Let's search this room again," he said. "We might have missed something the other night."

"Like a loose floorboard?" Honoria darted him a scathing look. "We went over every inch of this room."

Ignoring her, Jack bent to inspect the Sheraton side

cabinet. Honoria dutifully felt the chair upholstery and Jack inspected the backing of each and every painting.

With growing frustration, Jack turned around and scanned the room. The only thing left was the curio cabinet, and the necklace certainly wasn't sitting on any of the shelves. "Did you check all the drawers there?"

Honoria looked up. "Of course."

Jack decided to look anyway. When he pulled open the bottom one, he paused. "What's in the long box?"

Honoria came to his side. "What long box?"

Jack pointed to the wooden case in the drawer.

Honoria looked at him, her blue eyes dancing with excitement. "That wasn't there the other night, I swear."

Jack lifted the box carefully. "This time, I think a hairpin might do the trick." Honoria handed him one. Jack inserted it in the lock and jiggled it back and forth, giving a smile of satisfaction when the lock sprung open.

"Now that's a cooperative lock," he said, lifting the lid.

Honoria reached out a trembling hand and touched the dazzle of stones nestling in the box, then looked at Jack. "Is this the real one?"

Jack grabbed the necklace and took it over to the candle. "Next time, remind me to search during the day; the light's better."

Honoria fidgeted while Jack scrutinized the necklace.

"It's very nice work," he said at last. "No question that a master jeweler had a hand in it. But"—he paused, watching the tension grow in her eyes—"it's a very clever fake."

Honoria sank down into a chair. "I don't know if I should be thrilled or disappointed."

"It supports your idea that Sir Richard plans to cheat the prince."

"But that still doesn't help us. We have to find the real one."

Jack looked thoughtful. "I'm more curious as to how this got here—when it wasn't here two nights ago."

She flushed. "I swear it wasn't there when I looked before. Uncle must have put it here in the last two days."

"But why? It's almost as if he knew we'd already searched here." He looked suspiciously at Honoria.

"I certainly didn't tell him."

"Who else knew what we were up to?"

"Edmond?" Honoria frowned. "That's ridiculous. Why would he tell Richard?"

"I don't know." Jack carefully set the necklace back in the box. "But I don't think you should tell him what we found tonight."

"Aren't you being overly suspicious?"

"Just remember whose neck is on the line." Jack put the box back into the drawer.

He walked over to the cabinet and took out the brandy, along with two glasses.

"I don't want any," Honoria said.

"Have some anyway." Jack handed her a glass. "After all, it's a celebration of sorts. We've succeeded in part of your quest."

"The unimportant part," she said dolefully.

"Not necessarily. We know for certain there is a copy." He stretched his feet out before him. "Have you thought about what will happen if we don't find the real necklace?"

Jack laughed. "You most certainly would. You should be thankful I took the matter out of your hands. Now you won't have to throw yourself at me in a contrived manner."

"This is nonsense. Let me go."

"Another kiss first."

"All right, one kiss." She sat frozen, her eyes clamped shut. "Well?"

"I'm not going to kiss you. You have to kiss me."

"What?"

"That's the deal." He squeezed her waist. "Kiss me once, and I'll let you go up to bed. Unless, of course, you'd like me to accompany you there as well."

"I would not."

"Then kiss me quickly."

Norry leaned forward and touched her lips to his for the briefest second.

Jack gave her a skeptical look. "You call that a kiss?"

"Yes."

He shook his head sadly. "My dear Norry, you have a long way to go." He stood suddenly and pulled her to her feet. Cradling the back of her head with one hand, he drew her against him so tightly she could scarcely breathe. Tenderly, he brought his lips down on hers, moving, teasing, his tongue ever so softly tickling the outline of her mouth. Honoria drew in her breath in a surprised "oh," and he plunged his tongue into her mouth, tasting the mingled flavors of her and the brandy. Jack felt her knees weaken and a delicious warmth crept along his spine.

Suddenly he drew back and released her.

"Now that," he said, "was a kiss." He grabbed her by

the shoulders and turned her toward the door. "Now off to bed with you, before I decide you need another lesson."

Honoria didn't stop to take a candle but fled into the corridor.

Jack laughed wryly. Now he knew that she and Edmond weren't lovers; she couldn't be that good an actress. Her inexperience was obvious. She was innocent, yet . . . awakening.

Which meant he should leave her alone. He had no business getting involved with her. Honoria wasn't a bored wife looking for a bit of excitement. Even though her innocence acted like a powerful aphrodisiac, it also frightened him.

Jack hated complications. And Norry was a very big complication—or would be, if he allowed it. His paramount concern was saving his neck and earning his money. Anything—anyone—diverting him from those twin goals posed a danger.

Even one as sweetly enticing as Honoria Sterling.

Still, what harm would come from a mere flirtation? If she wanted to set up her own household, she needed to learn a little bit more about life—and men. In fact, by favoring her with his attentions, he might be doing her a favor.

Edmond would be the only one who might object, but as long as he didn't have any designs on his cousin, it was doubtful that he would say a word. Jack thought he was safe in that direction; there was nothing to hold him back.

Nothing, except the last remnants of his tattered honor, which told him that seducing an innocent virgin was not the proper thing to do.

But when had Jack ever done the right thing?

* * *

Honoria's heart still thudded wildly in her chest when she climbed into bed. Jack's kisses had the most unsettling effect on her.

Her intellect, her reason, told her that she was being foolish, stupid, even. She knew the type of man he was. Even if he had once been part of a respectable family, he was now a scapegrace of the worst sort. She should be horrified at the very thought of kissing him. But she wasn't.

He was right about the attraction of a rogue. Weren't history and novels filled with stories of women who were drawn to just his type of rascal? It only meant that she was no different from other women.

That was all it was—a rather perverted interest in a man who was outside her world. She had allowed her rash impulses to get the better of her intellect tonight, but it would not happen again.

She had now satisfied her curiosity; she knew exactly what it was like to kiss Jack Derry. Honoria told herself firmly that she had no need to do it again.

Even if she knew she wanted to.

Because that path led to danger. And no one would rescue her if she made the wrong choice. Only her own strength of will could protect her from Jack, and she feared that the time would come when she might not be strong enough.

The safest course was to avoid being alone with him. Which only complicated the search for the necklace. She would have to include Edmond in the future.

How silly she was. As long as she kept Jack at arm's

length, he posed no threat. Certainly, she had enough sense for that. There would be no more brandy in the library—and no more stolen kisses.

Honoria dreaded going downstairs in the morning. It was much easier to think about ignoring Jack in the privacy of her room than in actual practice. She would take one look at him and her cheeks would flame scarlet at the memory of her wantonness last night.

She sighed with relief when he wasn't in the morning room. Hastily eating her breakfast, she made her plans for the day. Keeping away from Jack was paramount. Perhaps Aunt Sophia might like to go for a drive. As soon as she finished eating, Honoria dashed off to find her great-aunt.

She met her in the hall, hanging on to Jack's arm.

His eyes lit with a deep glow of approval when he saw her, and Honoria felt the heat rise in her cheeks.

"Honoria! There you are. Sleeping late this morning?" He patted Sophia's hand. "Lady Hampton assures me you are normally an early riser."

Honoria swallowed hard. Somehow, she must learn how to act normally around him again; after what had happened last night, it wasn't going to be easy. If she talked to him, let him know that his teasing remarks and wicked smiles were not easy on her . . .

She turned to Sophia. "May I borrow Jack for a bit, Auntie? We have a few matters to discuss."

Sophia winked broadly at Jack and gave him a poke in the ribs. "Talk about setting that date."

Honoria led him to the library. Shutting the door, she turned to speak, but before she could open her mouth he swept her into his arms and kissed her.

After a moment of stunned surprise, Honoria felt herself melting in his arms, leaning into the kiss, responding to the insistent demand of his lips and tongue. And as swiftly as she realized what she was doing, she struggled to pull away.

"Stop that!"

"Isn't that why you wanted to get me alone?"

"No!" Honoria took a wobbly step backward, reaching for the edge of a chair to steady herself. "I wanted to talk with you about last night. About . . . about us."

He leaned back against a table, arms folded across his chest. "Yes?"

"You make me uncomfortable."

"*I* make you uncomfortable? Or is it that you're not comfortable with yourself? With what you feel, and what you want?"

"The only thing I want is my necklace," she said, with a firmness that she did not feel.

Jack smiled, and the sight sent shivers up her spine.

"You frighten me," she said.

"I am a very frightening fellow." He reached out a hand and caressed her cheek. "You are very right to fear me, Norry. I am a very bad person."

Jack leaned closer, his breath a whisper against her ear. "But there are some things I'm very, very good at." His lips brushed the side of her neck. "I'd like to show you just how good I can be."

Honoria fled into the hall.

Chapter 12

She nearly collided with Edmond. He reached out to steady her.

"Is something wrong?"

She shook her head.

"Come with me for a minute." He took her by the elbow and led her into the deserted morning room. "Have you found it yet?"

Jack had told her to keep their discovery quiet. "We didn't find anything in Uncle's room yesterday."

"I still think you are putting an enormous amount of trust in a fellow you barely know."

"I can rely on him."

"All the same, I suggest we keep a close eye on him. Who's to say he won't run if he finds the necklace."

"Jack wouldn't do that."

"Now, Norry." Edmond's tone was chiding. "You, of all people, should be less trusting. Look what your uncle did to you."

"I am not a child, Edmond. I am capable of knowing if someone is trustworthy or not. I feel as comfortable trusting Jack as I do you."

"I only hope he lives up to your confidence in him."

"He will."

"Is there anything more I can do to help? Do you need me to lure Sir Richard away again?"

Honoria shook her head. "I'm beginning to think the necklace might not even be here yet. We may have to wait until the prince arrives to find it."

"You know I'll do whatever I can to help. I'm as eager as you to right this wrong."

Honoria gave him a light kiss on the cheek. "I'm so glad you're here. I know we will find it eventually."

After he'd gone, Honoria reflected on his words. Was she foolish to trust Jack? Was she allowing a roguish flirt to trample on her common sense?

But the person who told her about Jack said he could be trusted. And they'd made their agreement before she had been gripped by this attraction. Jack would not betray her with the necklace.

Still, there were other ways he could betray her. She wanted security—he scoffed at it. She wanted a future—he didn't think beyond the next morning. She wanted a man who would love and cherish her—and Jack merely wanted her in his bed.

Yet her mind was consumed with thoughts of a roguish thief with a wicked grin and enticing kisses. A man for whom her resistance wavered further with each new encounter.

She must avoid him. With that thought firmly in mind, she went to the drawing room.

To her surprise, Jack was there, surrounded by a circle

of doting ladies. Honoria thought he looked like a sultan with a rather ragtag harem.

He jumped to his feet when he saw her. "There you are. Are you ready to go for that ride we planned?"

Before she could respond, he turned to the other ladies. "I do not mean to slight you lovely ladies. Would any of you like to accompany us?"

Mrs. Grose tittered. "No, thank you." She nodded knowingly at Lady Bolton. "Riding's for youngsters like you."

"Why, surely you don't consider yourself old?" Jack grinned. "Not an attractive woman like yourself?"

Honoria bit her lip. The man was an incorrigible flirt—particularly with older ladies. And they loved it.

Even as her instinct told her she shouldn't go riding with him alone, she went to her room to change into her habit.

He sat a horse well, Honoria noted as they rode across the lawn. "Did you grow up in the country?" she asked with feigned innocence.

"No ma'am. I'm a city boy, born and bred. Right in the heart of the Seven Dials."

"And I'm Princess Caroline," Honoria retorted. "You don't come from the rookeries any more than I do."

"How can you be so sure?"

"You aren't anything like that."

"Have you even seen the Dials? Or the Holy Land?"

"No."

"I have," he said, and his voice turned harsh. "They're no laughing matter." Then his rigid bearing relaxed. "I was born in the country, Norry. That's why I headed for London the first chance I had."

"Was it the country you didn't like—or your home?"

"The country was all right—for a time. But I'll take the city over it any day."

"I don't think I'd ever like to live in a city." She gestured at their surroundings. "It is so peaceful here. The city is too noisy and crowded."

"That's what makes it exciting. There are so many things to see, so many things to do. Look at us here—we had to visit Cirencester for entertainment. Everyone is sitting around waiting for the prince to arrive. In London, we would be too busy to even worry about his visit."

"Then what were you doing in Shropshire? I thought that was the country."

"A repairing excursion."

Honoria frowned in puzzlement. "Repairing excursion?"

"That's a polite way of saying one is hiding from someone or something—usually the debt collectors."

"Were you?"

"I was fleeing someone else."

"A woman?"

"Her husband."

Honoria gazed straight ahead. She did not want to hear another reminder of Jack's misspent past, or how imperfect a gentleman he was. Theft, women, and gambling. Were there any vices he hadn't practiced?

Angrily, she urged her horse into a canter.

Jack's mount followed and the two horses raced across the field. For just a moment, Honoria forced herself to think of nothing but the breeze on her face and the powerful horse beneath her. If only she could spend her days like this, without a care or concern. But as she reined in her mount at the far hedgerow, all her worries came back in an instant. Jack. The necklace. And Jack again.

"What do you think of Norcross?" she asked, when they slowed the horses to a walk again.

"It's a pleasant setting—if you like the country."

"What do you think of Uncle Richard?"

"He acts like a typical country squire. I would never guess that he was bent on cheating you."

"That only goes to show what a good judge of character you are."

"If I were, I would never have been arrested in the first place. Don't worry. Just because I don't hate the man, it doesn't mean I'm not going to look for your necklace. Besides, if he tries to talk about those blasted dogs with me one more time, I would do it just for spite."

"Why don't you like dogs?"

"My father had dogs."

"What was it like for you, growing up?"

"Like a fairy tale." His voice dripped with sarcasm. "I was the pampered, cosseted darling. The baby of the family, surrounded by adoring brothers and sisters and doting parents."

"I never had any brothers and sisters."

"Be glad you didn't," he said.

Then, after a few moments' pause, he continued: "I fear you've been taking lessons from your great-aunt. Is all this snooping about one's background a family trait?"

"Oh, yes," said Honoria. "We're incurably curious."

His words had been teasing, but she knew he was warning her off. Jack didn't want to talk about his past.

She tried to imagine him as a child, without the layers of cynicism and world-weariness that he wrapped himself in now. Had his father hurt him—either physically, or through neglect? To never know that your father loved you . . . She could not imagine such a thing.

She wondered if, buried under those layers of hurt and age, a little boy still lurked—a little boy who only wanted to be loved and cherished for what he was, who he was.

After seeing Honoria into the house, Jack remained outside.

He didn't like her asking so many questions. He didn't want to answer them, didn't want her to know any more about him. More than ever, he feared that if she knew the truth, she would be shocked and disillusioned.

And he didn't want that reaction from her. Let her think he was only a well-mannered thief. That way, he wouldn't disappoint her. And she wouldn't disappoint him.

"There you are, Barnhill. Honoria said you might be out here."

Tensing, Jack turned around. Edmond had a knack for sneaking up on him. "Yes, here I am."

"Did you two enjoy your ride?"

Was this a flare of jealousy after all? "Your cousin is a skilled rider."

Edmond nodded and pointed toward the garden. "Let's take a walk, shall we?"

"What do you want?" Jack asked bluntly.

Glancing around, as if fearing they would be overheard, Edmond took a step closer.

"It's about Norry."

"What about her?"

"Well, Sir Richard has been asking me a lot of questions about you two."

"Such as?"

"Oh, most have been the usual things: how long have I known you, are you a decent fellow, can you provide for her. But only today, he commented on how you didn't seem like the most lover-like couple. I'm afraid he might be developing suspicions."

Jack grinned. "We can't have that, can we?"

"No." Edmond looked down at the grass, then back at Jack. "I think you need to take the initiative here. Lord knows, Norry's a born schemer, but I don't think she quite has the talent to carry this off."

"What should I do?"

"Act more like the swain. You certainly looked as if you knew what to do the other night."

"A pity it was you instead of Sir Richard who found us, or we wouldn't have to worry."

"That would be the ideal thing—contrive for him to find you in a similar situation."

Jack eyed him with mock reproof. "You aren't worried about your cousin's reputation?"

"Good God, man, she's supposed to be engaged to you. No one cares about that anymore."

"It's too bad Sir Richard's rooms are in the other wing; if he caught me leaving Norry's room in the wee hours of the morning he wouldn't have any more questions."

Edmond stared at him for a second, then laughed and clapped him on the back. "And you might find yourself leg-shackled in that case. I think a few kisses in a dark corridor would suffice."

"Of course, if Sir Richard sees you leaving Norry's room at night, he might wonder again. As I did."

Edmond grinned. "Caught out, was I? You don't have to worry, Barnhill, I have no designs on my cousin. I merely think it's safer to talk about our plans in the privacy of her room."

Jack slapped Edmond heartily on the back. "Don't worry, I'll handle the late-night visits from now on."

"That suits me. Anything to keep Sir Richard in the dark. Norry said you didn't have any luck yesterday with her uncle's room."

Jack tried to look disappointed, but secretly he was pleased. Honoria had not told her cousin about the paste.

"I appreciate you taking Sir Richard away. It's a pity I couldn't find anything."

"Let me know if I can help again."

"I'll be glad to," said Jack with false enthusiasm.

Jack watched Edmond until he entered the house.

How interesting. Last night, he had decided to pursue Norry with more vigor, and now Edmond practically ordered him to. At least Jack was certain they weren't lovers. No man would push his lover into another's arms, no matter how devious the plan.

Besides, Norry was not a talented enough actress to feign her skittishness when she was with him.

If Sir Richard was suspicious, it was critical that he and

Norry worked harder at playing the loving couple. He grinned. That wouldn't be too difficult a task.

He still didn't trust Edmond, not completely. The magically appearing paste necklace still bothered him. He wanted to trust Norry, and thought he did. But he had trusted Rachel, too, and nearly died for his misjudgment. He didn't want to make that same mistake again.

He would follow Edmond's advice and see what happened. And keep a very close watch on his back at the same time.

Jack played the attentive beau before and during dinner. Honoria seemed nonplussed by his attentions, but Sophia gave him nodding glances of approval. When the men rejoined the ladies in the drawing room, Sophia beckoned them both to her side.

"I've been thinking about your wedding," she said, a delighted gleam in her eye. "It would be lovely to have it at Houghton."

Jack caught the quick flash of dismay on Norry's face.

"I'm not sure—"

"We appreciate your gracious offer," Jack said, patting Honoria's hand. "But I fear my family would be devastated if we married anywhere except at home."

"A Yorkshire wedding?" Sophia snorted. "What kind of event is that? No one will want to come."

"We only plan a small ceremony," Honoria said hastily.

"Well, then the least you can do is have a decent set of bride clothes. We'll go up to town this fall and take care of that."

Honoria smiled wanly and looked to Jack for help.

"I think it's a marvelous idea. Norry needs a new wardrobe suitable to her new status."

"What new status?" she murmured in an undertone.

"Married lady," he shot back. "You don't think I want my wife looking like a dowd?"

Sophia nodded her head vigorously. "Exactly. The poor child has been dressing herself for years." She looked fondly at Honoria. "Not that there's anything wrong with your clothing, my dear, but you could use a little more style."

Jack nodded his head in agreement.

"It's a wonder you asked me to marry you if you thought so poorly of my style," Honoria said.

"Let's say that I was able to see the diamond in the rough." He reached out and tweaked one of her curls.

"Perhaps it would be best to worry about such things after the wedding," she said. "You could take me to London yourself. I would love to see all your favorite places."

He leaned over and whispered in her ear. "I don't think they would allow you past the door."

She jabbed him lightly with her elbow.

Oblivious to their byplay, Sophia sat with a faraway look in her eyes. "A wedding dress," she said dreamily. "One fit for a princess."

"Look what you've done," Honoria said to Jack. "She'll talk of nothing else for days now."

A look of innocence crossed his face. "Should I have offended her by refusing?"

"Yes!"

"I was only trying to play my part. I thought it would be

good to talk about wedding plans. Isn't that what engaged couples do?"

"Not with Sophia," said Honoria. "I don't want to deceive her more than I have to."

Jack took Honoria's hand and brought it to his lips. "I hate to be the cause of your distress, love. Please forgive me."

"What are you doing?"

"Being your worshipful servant."

"Stop it, then. Everyone is staring."

Jack looked around the room, his grin widening as he saw she spoke the truth. "They will only think we are deeply in love. What's the harm in that?"

"It's not true."

He squeezed her hand. "But it could be, don't you think?"

She flushed and looked away.

Smothering a grin, Jack excused himself and ambled over to share anecdotes with Reginald Grose.

The house, like the guests, was wrapped in late-night silence when Edmond tapped lightly on the study door. Sir Richard appeared and ushered him in.

"Port? Claret? Brandy?"

"Port's fine."

Richard poured him a glass, picked up his own, and took his seat.

"Anything new to report?"

"They searched your room, as you know, but Honoria hasn't said anything more about the study. Either they didn't find it, or they haven't looked yet."

"I'll give them a few more days to try," Richard said. "If they don't take the bait, I'll try a new tack."

Edmond sipped his port. "Isn't it dangerous to let them find the copy? What if the fool can't tell the difference? They could take it and what would you give to the prince?"

"I don't think they will try to take anything until the prince arrives. Norry is no fool; she'll wait until she is sure the prince has the paste."

"Don't you fear someone discovering the switch?"

Richard laughed. "That buffoon won't be able to tell the difference. And in case someone else can, I'll be sure he only sees the real one."

"Then you'll hand the prince the paste when he leaves. A good plan."

Sir Richard held up his glass in mock salute. "And then I'll ask my dear niece to remove herself from my house."

"Will you send her back to her nurse?"

"She can go to hell for all I care," said Sir Richard in a chilling voice.

"She has a champion in Lady Hampton . . ."

"That old crone?" Sir Richard snorted. "She doesn't know with whom she is speaking half the time. She's no threat."

"My mother expressed concern . . ."

Sir Richard smiled thinly. "Then by all means, take her home with you. Or get this Barnhill fellow to take her off your hands."

"That might not be a bad plan. They certainly deserve each other."

Sir Richard walked over to the side table and refilled

his glass. "The trick is to let Norry think she is on the verge of succeeding."

"And I will surely commiserate with her over her failure—since it's my loss as well."

Sir Richard nodded. "You're doing a good job, Stephenson. I plan to double what I said I'd pay you."

"You are too kind."

Too kind, indeed. Edmond kept a smile on his face, but inside he regarded Sir Richard with silent contempt. He was doing all the work. But would Sir Richard reward him appropriately? No. His miserly payment was nothing compared to the value of the necklace.

It would serve the man right when Edmond walked off with it.

"More port?"

With a smile, Edmond held out his glass.

Jack slipped quietly down the back stairs. He had grown accustomed to these late-night forays. Too bad he didn't have Norry with him tonight. But he wanted to get another look at the study.

He still felt uneasy about finding that paste necklace last night. It had appeared too conveniently, and he didn't believe they had missed it the first time. Someone had moved it to the study within the last two days.

The question was: why?

There were only two answers—pure coincidence or Richard Sterling knew what was going on.

The latter caused his stomach to churn uncomfortably. Jack's main goal was to stay alive. If Sir Richard knew that he and Norry were after the necklace, Jack could be in grave danger.

His stocking feet made no noise in the empty hall as he passed the library door and headed toward the study.

And halted. A thin band of light showed under the door. Stepping closer, Jack heard the low rumble of voices. Quickly he backstepped. He didn't want Sir Richard to find him wandering about at this hour; he retreated up the main stairs and positioned himself at the top, keeping out of sight behind the railing. Jack wanted to know who shared this late-night rendezvous with Sir Richard.

His head drooped more than once before he jumped alertly at the soft click of the door opening. He heard footsteps cross the hall and start up the stairs.

"Thanks for the port."

At the sound of Edmond's voice, Jack almost swore out loud. Regaining his senses, he returned quietly to his room.

Sir Richard and Edmond, together in the study at this hour? Was Edmond betraying Norry—and Jack as well?

If Edmond was conspiring with Sir Richard, Jack knew he must protect himself. The safest course, the wisest choice, would be to leave Norcross at once.

But he couldn't leave Norry to the scheming machinations of her uncle, and her cousin. He owed her something for saving his life. He prayed that returning the favor wouldn't put him back into danger.

Chapter 13

When Honoria joined Sophia in the drawing room the following morning, all her great-aunt could talk about was the upcoming shopping excursion to London.

"I think we should take you first to Madame Fourchet." Sophia nodded her head for emphasis. "For the wedding gown, at least. She is the best modiste."

"I don't need a London modiste for a private family wedding."

"Nonsense. You heard what your young man said; it's what he wants. You don't want him to be ashamed of you, do you?"

"Who is going to pay for all this? Jack cannot afford it and I certainly have no money."

Sophia patted her hand. "You leave that to me. I'll have a word with your uncle. He owes you that much after that disgraceful will of your father's."

"You cannot blame Papa for *that*."

Sophia looked at her with a curious glint in her eyes. "Oh?"

The door to the corridor opened and Honoria turned around, hoping it would be Jack. This was all his fault;

she would make him talk to Sophia and straighten things out.

But instead of Jack, a beautiful blond woman stepped into the room. "I hope I am in the right place." She eyed them eagerly. "Is this the drawing room?"

Honoria nodded, wondering who she was. She certainly didn't look like one of Uncle's usual guests.

"Oh good, then I didn't get lost. You are Sir Richard's niece, I believe? I am Lady Milburn."

Honoria instantly recognized the name from her uncle's guest list. "It is a pleasure to meet you. May I present my great-aunt, Sophia, Dowager Lady Hampton."

Lady Milburn sank into a chair, striking a languishing pose. "I hope you don't mind me intruding. My husband went to look at the dogs and your uncle suggested I might join you."

Sophia squinted at her. "Your husband is Viscount Milburn?"

Lady Milburn nodded.

"Good Lord, you mean old Toddy's dead?" Sophia shook her head. "Now why didn't anyone tell me?"

Lady Milburn flushed crimson. "Toddy is my husband."

Sophia stared at her. "Good God, you must be forty years younger than he."

Honoria was mortified. "Sophia!" She turned toward Lady Milburn. "Please excuse my aunt."

Lady Milburn waved a dismissive hand. "I am accustomed to it by now; after all, we've been married for five years."

"Children?" Sophia asked.

Lady Milburn shook her head.

Sophia smiled. "Good. Never held with having children of second marriages. Makes things too confusing. Establish the succession and be done with it, that's what I say."

Cringing inwardly at her aunt's tactless words, Honoria asked the new guest, "Would you like some tea? We were just about to have some."

Lady Milburn smiled, showing a set of even, white teeth. "That would be very nice."

After ringing for tea, Honoria settled back in her chair, trading awkward glances with Lady Milburn.

Honoria thought the new guest was one of the loveliest ladies she had ever seen. Her silvery blond hair was arranged in a deceptively simple manner that probably took her maid hours to achieve; her clothes looked as if they had been copied from the pages of the latest fashion magazines. Honoria experienced a sharp pang of envy. She had never dressed so well, even when her father was alive.

Not that she minded, of course, but sitting here next to this elegant beauty, Honoria felt dowdy and countrified in her plain gown. She looked up in relief when the tea cart arrived, with Jack right behind.

"I see I'm just in time for some refreshment, sweetling," he said.

"Jack, this is Lady Milburn, a guest of Uncle's. My friend, Jack Barnhill."

Lady Milburn turned to welcome him and seemed to freeze in her chair. Her face turned a ghastly shade of white and for a moment Honoria thought the lady might faint. Jumping up, Honoria grabbed Lady Milburn's hand, which felt like ice.

"Lady Milburn?" she asked anxiously. "Are you all right? Jack, get the brandy. Hurry."

Jack was out the door like a shot. Honoria chafed Lady Milburn's hands, making soothing noises. Should she send for the doctor?

"Looks as if she's seen a ghost," Sophia observed.

Plummer appeared in the doorway. "You requested brandy, miss?"

Honoria nodded absently, her attention focused on the woman before her. Sophia poured a few drops of brandy into a cup of tea, and a large dollop in her own cup.

"Drink this." Honoria handed the brew to Lady Milburn, who took a sip or two, choking slightly. Gradually, the color returned to her cheeks.

"I feel such a fool." Lady Milburn laughed uneasily. "I don't know what happened; a slight touch of dizziness. Perhaps I am more tired from the journey than I thought."

"Let me take you to your room." Honoria stood and offered her arm. "I'm sure you'll feel better after you rest."

"Thank you."

"Breeding, most likely," Sophia muttered under her breath as the two women left the room. Honoria darted a dampening look over her shoulder at her aunt as the two women left the room.

After telling Plummer to bring the brandy, Jack went out the side door and ran across the lawn, fighting his panic. He had to find someplace to hide.

Of all the rotten chances! He had been foolish to think that his luck would hold; it never did. Once again, everything was about to blow up in his face, and he was helpless to prevent it. He already felt the iron shackles rubbing against his ankles, the rope binding his wrists.

Lady Milburn—Lord, he couldn't even remember her first name. He hadn't used it much—theirs had been a short if passionate liaison at one of the numerous house parties he had once frequented. She'd been married to a gouty, overindulgent husband over twice her age and had been ripe for a tumble.

Now she was here at Norcross and all his subterfuge was about to be destroyed. He had to find her and talk with her, before it was too late. Now that the first shock of recognition had worn off, he cursed himself for running from the house, but his immediate instincts had been to flee. Now, he wished he was back inside, where he could contrive some way to get her alone for a few minutes, and ask—no beg—her to remain quiet. She knew him as Jack Derry, and if that name ever came out, he was sunk.

Jack stared at the house, torn between returning and remaining in the safety of the park. In the house, if they tipped to him, he would be hard-pressed to escape. Here, outside, he had a fighting chance to get away.

He would stay outside. Honoria had showed him the unused summer house yesterday; he could keep watch from there. At the first signs of a chase, he would be off into the woods. He would stay well away from the house until he knew for certain that he was safe. Tonight, he'd find a way to contact Honoria and find out if he could return.

By the time Honoria had settled Lady Milburn into her

room and made certain that she felt better, Aunt Sophia had fallen asleep.

Honoria did not mind. She didn't want to talk any more about bride clothes and shopping trips for her nonexistent wedding. Finding Jack was more important. Honoria would tell him in no uncertain terms that he was to stop encouraging Sophia by talking about this wedding nonsense.

She looked everywhere she thought he might be, but there was no sign of him. He had spoken to Plummer about the brandy, then disappeared without a trace. He wasn't hiding in the library; Honoria even looked behind all the curtains to make certain he hadn't concealed himself there. Where could he be?

Honoria's frustration grew as the day wore on. She couldn't find him anywhere. He hadn't even shown up for lunch, which was very odd. Jack usually availed himself of every opportunity to eat. Honoria worried that something might have happened to him—but she suspected that, like a cat, Jack had nine lives.

Of course, there was no way to tell how many he had already used up.

By late afternoon, her worries had grown. She tried to shrug off her apprehensions. Jack had no reason to run away. He hadn't taken anything from his room—she'd checked it several times during the day. He only had the clothes he was wearing, and no money. He hadn't taken a horse from the stable either—Honoria checked.

By the time she dressed for dinner, Honoria was barely able to restrain her panic. Had he gone for a walk, stepped in a rabbit hole, and broken his leg? Fallen into the pond and drowned? Been attacked by gypsies in the woods? All the possibilities seemed ludicrous, but she could not fight her fear.

When she joined the guests in the drawing room before dinner, Jack wasn't there. Lady Milburn hastened to her side.

"Isn't Mr. Barnhill planning to join us for dinner? I hope nothing is wrong?"

Sophia clumped over, leaning heavily on her cane. "Yes, where is that rascal? He promised to read to me this afternoon and he never did! I've a good mind to whack him over the head with my cane."

Honoria pressed fingers to her temples. "I believe he was feeling poorly earlier. Perhaps he decided to dine in his room."

"You said Mr. Barnhill is from Yorkshire?" Lady Milburn asked Honoria. "Has he lived there long?"

Before she could answer, Edmond moved to her side, eyeing Lady Milburn with an appreciative glance. "Honoria, dear, who is this lovely lady?"

"Lady Milburn, my cousin, Edmond Stephenson. My mother's sister's son."

"The right side of the family," Sophia noted with an arch look. "Daughters of the Sixth Earl of Bolton, you know. But from his second wife, alas, so the new earl is only a distant relation. One of the reasons it's always best not to have a second family."

Lady Milburn flushed.

Taking her hand, Edmond bowed low, filling the awkward pause. "A pleasure, Lady Milburn."

"Toddy." Sophia raised her hand in greeting, then

limped toward the elderly man who entered the room. "What a surprise to find you here."

Honoria watched a tiny, stooped gentleman take her hand. "Sophia. What a pleasure to see you again."

Sophia poked a bony finger at his chest. "What do you think you're doing with a schoolgirl for a wife?"

He guffawed, his face suffused with pride. "She's a looker, isn't she? Havenhurst's youngest."

Honoria took sympathy on Lady Milburn and drew her to the far corner of the room. "Sophia is not mean-spirited. She only has a deplorable tendency to speak her mind."

Lady Milburn looked at Honoria with tear-filled eyes. "Please don't tell my husband that I asked after Mr. Barnhill."

"Do you know him?"

"We met—two years ago. Although he was not calling himself Barnhill then. I was visiting in the country, Toddy's gout flared up so he spent most of the time in his room and we . . . I . . ."

Honoria was too stunned to respond.

Lady Milburn knew Jack? How could he? She was the wife of an earl, and earls, as a rule, didn't associate with men like Jack.

But what kind of man was he? A thief? A rogue? An educated man who was hiding behind the label of thief? The kind of man who could have been included in the company kept by Lady Milburn? The kind of man who wasn't what he claimed to be?

It all made perfect sense. He might have been a down-and-out thief when she met him, but he hadn't started life at that level. He had fallen there—and his acquaintance with Lady Milburn indicated just how far he had fallen.

Uncle Richard brushed past and held out his arm. "Lady Milburn . . . ?"

Dinner lasted an excruciatingly long time. Honoria could hardly control her relief when the ladies retreated to the drawing room. Once she settled Sophia, she would search in earnest for Jack. And when she found him . . .

"That gal is breeding, mark my words." Sophia nodded toward the pale-faced Lady Milburn.

"Perhaps it is merely indigestion," Honoria retorted waspishly. She was dying to get close to Lady Milburn, to find out more about the story, and to plead with her not to reveal the truth about Jack's identity, but Mrs. Mayflower sat beside her and showed no signs of leaving soon.

"Wonder if Toddy knows?" Sophia mused.

"Of course he would know; he's her husband, isn't he?"

Sophia gave her a knowing look. Honoria glared back at her. "Are you saying—?"

"Won't be the first young wife to cuckold her husband. Why, I remember when old Lord Warburton married that Walton girl . . ."

Honoria did her best to ignore Sophia's ramblings. Lady Milburn was suffering from shock and confusion at seeing Jack, not pregnancy.

Lady Mayflower stood at last. Honoria started across the floor, but before she could reach the settee, the men joined them. Lord Milburn walked with a trembling gait to his lady's side and spoke a few words. She rose, and he leaned on her arm while they made for the door.

Honoria gnawed her lip in frustration. Now she would not be able to talk to the lady until morning—if then. She had to find Jack.

She searched every room in the house, but there was no sign of him. Was he hiding in the stables? Honoria didn't relish the task of looking for him in the dark, but she didn't know what else to do.

Finally, Honoria went to her room to change into a more suitable dress. After taking a lantern from the kitchen, she stepped out into the darkened garden, her cloak wrapped about her.

Jack crept closer to the house, watching the lights first flare and then dim in the upstairs windows. The guests were going to bed. Good.

There had been no sign of excitement or surprise coming from the house. Maybe the lady had kept her mouth shut. He would slip back inside and see if he could talk with Honoria. Maybe they could find some way to persuade Lady Milburn to keep silent.

Cautiously, he made his way up the servants' stairs. Would it be smarter to go straight to Honoria's room?

His door was shut, and by crouching down on the third step he couldn't see light seeping under it. He turned the knob and pushed the door inward.

The room was pitch black and Jack swore under his breath. He groped for the candle on the table and went out into the hall, lighting it from the wall sconce. Finally, he reentered his room and shut the door.

"Where have you been?" Lady Milburn sprang from the chair. "I have been in a panic all day. We must talk."

Jack set the candle on the table and perched on the edge of the bed. "Talk."

Lady Milburn turned pleading eyes on him. "Promise me that you won't say anything to my husband."

"Why would I want to say anything to your husband?"

"I have heard that some men like to . . . to brag about their conquests."

"You're afraid of your husband finding out about us?"

She nodded vigorously.

Jack roared with laughter. "This is rich."

"What is so funny?"

"I've been hiding in the garden all day, worried about what *you* would say. Don't you wonder why I'm being called Barnhill?"

She shrugged. "Derry, Barnhill, whatever name you wish. It's your business." She looked at him from lowered lashes. "Unless, of course, you want to tell me?"

"Let's leave the mystery be. Suffice it to say I have no desire to reveal our—uh—relationship to your husband. As far as I am concerned, madam, we never set eyes on each other until today."

A look of relief flashed over her face. "Oh, thank you! I am ever so grateful." She flung her arms around him.

"A touching scene."

Jack glanced over Lady Milburn's head to see Honoria standing in the doorway. Lady Milburn moved away from Jack.

"It's not what you think," she said. "I was merely thanking your . . . friend. He has done me an enormous favor."

Jack took Lady Milburn's hand and kissed it lightly. "Go

back to your husband," he said softly. "You have nothing to fear from me."

Honoria stood impassively, while Lady Milburn left.

Jack sank down on the bed again, heaving an enormous sigh of relief. "God, I need a drink."

Honoria turned to him. "Would you mind telling me what is going on?"

"I know her."

"So I gathered. Intimately?"

"Intimately enough. We were visiting at the same house a year or so ago. Her husband was ill, she was bored . . . you know the type of thing that goes on."

"Not really." Her eyes glittered ominously. "Enlighten me."

"Oh, leave off, Honoria. The important thing is that she knew me as Jack Derry. I've been living in terror ever since this morning and I don't have the energy to argue with you. She won't cause any trouble—she is more worried her husband will find out the story."

"How, exactly, did you meet her? I didn't realize you kept company with earls."

"You'd be surprised at the elevated company I've kept. How else was Gentleman Jack to ply his trade?"

"How many other of your ex-mistresses can I expect to find among the guests?"

Jack shook his head. "I swear, I didn't recognize her name on the list you showed me."

"Are you sure you even knew it?"

Jack grinned, his old spirit salvaged. "Probably not."

Honoria fought the urge to slap his face. She had spent most of the day gripped with fear, frantically searching the grounds, ruining her good slippers in the process. Only to find that Jack had indulged in a sordid liaison with a married woman whose name he didn't even know.

Jack brushed past Honoria on the way to the door.

"Where are you going?"

"As I said, I need a drink. Care to join me?"

"Absolutely not."

"Suit yourself, darling." Hands crammed into his pockets, he left the room.

Honoria fumed. How dare he make light of her concern? He acted as if the whole thing was a joke, rather than a crisis that had nearly brought her plan to a crushing end.

Chapter 14

Flinging her muddy slippers into the corner, Honoria uttered a few choice words on the character of Jack Derry. Instead of traipsing outside looking for him, she should have gone to bed. To think she had actually been *worried* about him.

Her fingers trembled as she struggled with the fastenings of her gown. She had seen the way he and Lady Milburn were embracing before she had entered into his room. No doubt they planned to resume their relationship. The nerve of her. And him.

Flinging her dress onto the bed, Honoria uttered an unladylike expression. After all that she'd done for Jack, this was how he repaid her? Reaching for her brush, she dragged it through her tangled curls. He did not deserve her help. He would probably gamble away every penny he earned, or spend it on spirits, or women.

Lady Milburn, beautiful and worldly-wise, elegantly dressed and experienced was everything that Honoria wasn't.

Honoria shouldn't care. Jack was a thief, a man with low morals and even lower ambitions. But with a sharp pang, Honoria realized just how much she wished he were not; wished that he was the kind of man she could turn to, could love.

She caught a glimpse of herself in the mirror and scowled back at her reflection. She wasn't going to let this episode ruin her plans now. Things had gone too far to turn back.

With determination, she hastily refastened the gown she'd had so much trouble untying. She would let Jack know how she expected him to behave around Lady Milburn. With circumspection and restraint.

Honoria hurried down the stairs. He was in the library, most likely, since there was always a decanter of brandy there. She winced as her bare feet hit the cold wooden planks in the hall. The library door was ajar and she saw a light within. She had found her quarry.

Silently, she pushed the door open farther and slipped into the room. Jack sat with his back to her, his feet propped up on a table, a glass in his hand.

Honoria crossed the floor with a light step, halting behind his chair. "I hope you're not going to drink yourself into a stupor again."

Jack lowered his feet and swiveled about in his chair. "I just might. Would you like to join me?"

"Of course not. I came her to discuss your behavior."

"Have I done something wrong?"

"Everything." Honoria paced to the bookcases. "I don't think you're taking your job seriously."

Jack took a long swallow of brandy, studying her carefully over the rim of his glass. She looked different with her hair down. Less arrogant. Softer. More feminine. Most feminine, in fact.

Honoria whirled about. "Are you listening?"

Jack leaned back in the chair, cradling the glass in his lap. He smothered a smile at the sight of her bare toes peeping out from beneath the hem of her gown. "What do you want me to do?"

"Find the necklace. It is the only hope for us both. Look at you." She cast a scathing glance at his glass. "You spend more time drinking brandy than searching."

"An honorable occupation." Jack held up his glass, twirling it slowly so the candlelight glinted off the facets.

"As honorable as that of thief."

Jack placed a hand over his heart. "You wound me, Norry. I thought you were beginning to like me."

"You are here for one thing, and one thing only. Find me that necklace."

He reached for the decanter at his elbow and refilled his glass. "Are you sure you don't want any? You'd feel much better after a sip or two."

"I didn't come down here to drink with you."

"Pity. I rather enjoyed the last time we shared the brandy."

Honoria stamped her foot in frustration. "You are the most insolent, insensitive man I have ever met."

"I am?"

"Yes, you are. Not to mention a libertine."

"Ah, you refer to the matter of Lady Milburn."

She angrily paced the floor, her skirts swishing with her irritation. "Do you always go about doing whatever you wish, without regard for the consequences? Did you ever think of the trouble you might inflict upon her?"

"And I thought it was *my* tender hide you were worried about."

"You deserve everything you get."

"Oh, hardly that. I don't think I deserved a lot of what has been handed to me. But I manage to go on anyway."

"Spare me the sad stories." Honoria pointed an accusing finger at him. "You never once think about the results of your actions."

"Strong words coming from someone who is asking me to steal. Or do you exclude yourself from your condemnation?"

"I am only taking back that which is rightfully mine," she said heatedly. "You take what was never yours in the first place. You've been here days now, and have barely accomplished anything."

"I taught you how to kiss, for one thing."

"You are not supposed to be kissing me."

"Yes, but whenever did I do what I was supposed to?" Jack set his glass down with a plunk. In two long steps he crossed the room and took Honoria's arm. He looked down into her blue eyes. "It's so boring."

She tried to pull away. "Stop this."

"All in good time." He slipped one arm around her waist, pulling her against his body. "I think it's time you treated me with more respect."

"I can't give respect where it hasn't been earned."

"Then perhaps I'll earn it." Jack brushed his lips against her forehead. "So soft," he murmured as he trailed kisses across her cheek. "Just a little kiss, Norry," he whispered, pressing his mouth to hers.

His tongue nudged her lips apart, plunging into her mouth, seeking her, tasting her.

Tentatively, she touched her own tongue to his. Jack groaned, and he buried his hand in her curls, pulling her closer. Honoria awkwardly ran her hands over his shirt, and with a woman's instinctive knowledge, she pressed herself against him.

His kisses deepened, demanding her response while his hands moved across the silken fabric of her dress. Jack's hand curved over her softly rounded bottom, and her surprised cry jolted him back to reality. Tearing his mouth away, he looked down at her.

A range of emotions flitted across her face—budding passion replaced by confusion, then embarrassment. He pressed his forehead to hers.

"Ah, Norry, you don't know the temptation you pose."

She drew away, her cheeks flaming. He saw the dawning apprehension in her eyes, knew she feared the strange new feelings coursing through her.

"Please, Jack, no more."

"I'm only a common thief, after all. Stealing a kiss is part of my nature."

She darted him a stricken glance. "I can't expect you to behave when I . . ."

Reaching down, Jack picked up his glass and saluted her with it. "If you don't want to be the recipient of unwanted advances, I suggest you put on some shoes and pin up your hair before you indulge in late-night meetings with a gentleman. Otherwise, it gives a man all sorts of improper ideas."

Honoria stared down at her bare feet and her face flushed crimson. "Good night," she cried as she fled out the door.

Jack drained his glass. Skittish as a new colt. But what could he expect from a blasted virgin?

For a few minutes, she had melted into his arms as if she knew what she was doing. He'd actually felt dizzy with delight when she'd responded. She was innocent as hell, but beneath that innocence there was passion. A passion that begged to be unleashed.

Should he be the one to do it? The honorable side of him—what was left of it—said no. But that other side—the wild, rebellious, devil-may-care side—urged him to pursue her. It wouldn't take much now, he was certain.

He poured himself another brandy. He was going to get drunk tonight, but he didn't care. Right now, he needed the drink to make him forget the softness of Norry's lips, the feel of her breasts pressed against his chest . . .

This was something he hadn't anticipated when he had agreed to help her. He never imagined that he would be filled with desire for Honoria Sterling. She was a sharp-tongued, managing, manipulative woman. And he wanted to bed her so badly he physically hurt just to think about it.

She had sounded downright jealous when she harped on him about Lady Milburn. Could he somehow use that to his advantage? He could engage in a subtle flirtation with Lady Milburn whenever Honoria was near, to test her reaction. If he goaded her enough, would she melt in his arms? Jealousy could spur women to do all sorts of things.

Jack smiled. It would be a far greater challenge without the spur of jealousy to urge her on. But he had never played by the rules before, and he wasn't planning to now. He wanted Honoria badly enough to make success certain. He would make use of every advantage he could.

At first he had only thought to steal a few kisses from her. But now, he wanted more. She had no idea of the picture she'd presented when she appeared before him, barefoot, with that long, chestnut hair streaming down her back. Seducing Honoria Sterling sounded like a marvelous plan.

Besides, any woman who would stoop to the lies she'd expounded in her cause couldn't have too many scruples. Honoria just needed someone to show her how much fun she could have when she quit worrying about being respectable.

He thought Honoria Sterling would be very good at being unrespectable, if given half the chance. And it would be a delight to teach her. Lord knew, it was the one thing he was good at.

Jack faced the morning with bleary eyes. He'd slept poorly; not because of the brandy, but because of Honoria Sterling. She had filled his dreams, the kind of dreams he'd never had before. Dreams in which she mocked and belittled him while he sat silent and seething; dreams in which he'd swept her into his arms and into his bed, and then had finally thrust himself into her body.

Why in the hell had Lady Milburn shown up here? He

felt nothing for her—affection or lust—but she was a reminder of what he had been before, what he had done before. He wanted that life again, wanted every part of it—fine clothes, fine wines, friends, fun, and willing women.

Instead, he wore secondhand clothes and his dreams were tormented by an angel-faced virgin who thought of him only as a rogue.

Slamming the door to his room, Jack trooped down the back stairs and hastened across the yard to the stables. He waited impatiently for a horse to be saddled, then took off across the lawn at a breakneck pace. If a good, hard ride didn't ease the ache in his body, he would find something else that did. It had been a long time since he'd worked himself to physical exhaustion, but it was just what he needed right now.

A part of him wanted to turn the horse toward the lane and keep riding until he reached London. Only danger awaited him at Norcross. Danger in the form of Miss Honoria Sterling. He had to find that damn necklace and get out of here—fast.

If he left now, he would not be tempted into seducing her. He could make his way to Paris easily enough. Jack Derry would be all but forgotten. He would never use the name again.

But at the same time, he wanted to stay. Wanted to see this crazy drama played out for a bit longer. Wanted to see if he could melt Norry's cool, virginal exterior and release the passionate woman who lay underneath.

Of course, stealing her virtue might prove as dangerous as stealing the necklace. Jack might find his neck in another kind of noose—a lifelong one.

He laughed at the thought. He was the last person on earth Honoria Sterling wanted to trap into marriage. And she was certainly the last woman on earth who could.

If Honoria had been nervous about facing Jack the other morning, the thought petrified her today. She lay in her bed, watching the morning sunlight steal across the ceiling. She was torn between fear and longing and a gnawing ache that she didn't want to think about.

He had kissed her again. Pressed his lips to her forehead, her cheeks, her lips . . . Placed his tongue in her mouth . . . And she had responded like a wanton, pressing herself against him, her own tongue seeking his.

Honoria blushed hotly at the thought. He'd been both tender and gentle. He didn't frighten her at all. It was her own reaction that terrified her. She'd enjoyed his kisses far too much.

Her cheeks flushed with heat; not from mortification, but from the shocking realization that she wanted to repeat the whole experience.

She should not want to have anything to do with him. Jack Derry wasn't an honorable man; Honoria knew that. He was a thief, a womanizer, an *adulterer*. A man who had no honor; the type of man she had no business thinking about, or longing after.

Yet she did. Her body was filled with new, unfamiliar sensations. Wild, yearning feelings for something. *Someone*. A man who was totally wrong for her. And Honoria realized with a cold sweep of fear that she was beginning not to care. Jack's past, Jack's future grew less important to her with each kiss.

She was almost disappointed when she found the morning room deserted. Eating quickly, she headed for the drawing room. Once again, Jack presided over the coterie of female guests. Honoria examined him with suspicion. Usually, he disdained the company of the ladies. Why was he here now? Did he plan to torment her again?

Her glance drifted across the room to Lady Milburn, sitting in front of the tall windows in a pose calculated to show off her form to the best effect. Honoria stifled an irritated gasp as she watched Jack walk with casual determination toward the window.

Honoria felt Sophia's bony elbow in her side. "You better keep an eye on that one," she said. "Men flock to her like bees to honey."

Shrugging, Honoria tried to adopt a look of supreme unconcern and picked up her sewing. "What Jack does is his own business."

"Only if you don't want his business to be yours."

Honoria stabbed her embroidery needle into the handkerchief and took another stitch. Jack's business *was* hers—particularly if he did something that put her whole plan in danger. Renewing his acquaintance with Lady Milburn certainly fell into that category. How long would it be before she grew confused about Jack's changing identities? One slip and they were all sunk. She had to trust Lady Milburn would keep Jack at arm's length—although Honoria found it difficult to envision Toddy playing the role of the enraged husband no matter what his wife did.

Lady Milburn laughed, and Honoria glanced in her direction. Annoyance shot through her at the sight of Jack's head bent close, whispering some private observation. Lady Milburn's hand went over her mouth to stifle another laugh.

Standing so quickly several of her threads fell, Honoria crossed to the bell rope and rang for a fresh pot of tea. There was more than one way to break up their cozy tête-à-tête.

When the tea tray arrived, Honoria asked Lady Milburn to do the honors, effectively disengaging her from Jack. With a smug smile, Honoria sat beside Sophia again.

"Honoria, dear, would you mind getting my paisley shawl?" Sophia looked pointedly at Jack. "Perhaps Mr. Barnhill would be so kind as to help you."

"I think I can manage a shawl on my own."

Jack was right beside her. "Allow me."

He shut the door behind them and leaned against it, arms folded across his chest. "That was a most skillful maneuver. Your great-aunt is more up to the mark then she pretends."

"Obvious is a more apt description."

"Either way, she arranged for us to be alone. You must be pleased."

"You have far too high an opinion of yourself if you think that."

"I've learned enough about ladies over the years to know what I see. You're jealous, aren't you?"

Honoria looked at him with puzzlement. "Jealous? Of whom?"

Jack pushed himself off the door and sauntered toward her. "I'm not blind, Honoria. I saw those dark glances you cast in my direction."

"If I was casting you any glances this morning, it was probably because I was so pleased with your behavior. You are behaving like a regular drawing-room denizen."

"You're irritated because I was talking with Lady Milburn."

"Ordinarily, I think it's good for you to consort with your betters. But with your past history, I am not certain Lady Milburn is the best company for you."

Jack took a step closer. "You are only afraid that I might want her again."

"That would imply that I cared about your dalliances—which I do not. Now, I need to fetch that shawl."

"You are worried that she's the one I want in my bed." Jack took her hand and brought it to his lips. "I assure you, you have nothing to worry about. You're the one I want."

Honoria's heart thumped in her chest. "Don't be ridiculous."

Jack curled a wisp of her hair around his finger. "You can't deny what went on last night, Norry. You want me as badly as I want you."

Shivering at the touch of his fingers, Honoria fought the urge to turn and run. "The only thing I want you for is to find my necklace."

Laughing lightly, Jack chucked her under the chin. "We both know that for a lie. But if you want to maintain the illusion for a while longer, I will let you."

Deliberately, she turned her back and walked up the stairs.

Chapter 15

When Honoria came down the stairs with Sophia's shawl, Jack had disappeared and Edmond stood waiting for her in the hall.

"Lady Hampton isn't making things easy for you, is she?"

Honoria sighed. "I can't blame her after the lies I've spun. She'll be heartbroken when she discovers I'm not getting married."

"He seems to enjoy annoying you."

"Jack?"

"You were uncomfortable this morning."

Only because he kissed me last night. She laughed lightly. "Jack is only trying to soothe Aunt Sophia. I think he's doing a better job than I."

"I hope he won't allow himself to be distracted from his true task. I thought he paid too much attention to our newest guest this morning."

"You mean Lady Milburn?"

Edmond nodded. "That kind of attention isn't appropriate for an engaged man. People might wonder at it."

"They are old friends," Honoria explained. "Naturally they wish to talk."

"Indeed?" Edmond hid his surprise. "I find that of some relief. Lady Milburn can vouch for his character, then?"

"I know Jack's character," she insisted. "As I told you before, I trust him."

Edmond bowed. "As you wish."

They returned to the drawing room and Honoria placed the shawl around her great-aunt's shoulders.

Sophia laughed. "That's a neat trick. Leaving with one man and returning with another. What did you do with Jack?"

"I believe he went for a walk," Honoria lied.

"A capital idea," Edmond said. He shot an inviting glance at Lady Milburn. "Perhaps some of the ladies would like to do the same. It is such a beautiful day."

"Not these old bones," Sophia said. "I don't plan to do any more walking than I have to."

"Are the gardens here nice?" Lady Milburn asked.

"Most attractive," said Edmond. "I could show them to you, if you would like."

She stood. "I would be delighted."

Edmond looked at Honoria. "Cousin?"

She shook her head. "You go ahead. I want to untangle my threads."

"Is this your first visit to Norcross?" Edmond asked as he escorted Lady Milburn from the house.

"Yes, it is a lovely country home. Do you visit often?"

"Not until recently. My cousin's father fancied himself a scholar and did not entertain widely. Sir Richard is a more amiable host."

"Your cousin seems a very sweet girl. I am told she is planning her wedding."

Edmond nodded. "I understand you are a friend of Jack's."

She looked at him with surprise. "Where did you hear that?"

"My cousin mentioned it. Have you known Jack long?"

"We met some years ago; I have not seen him in an age. I understand he lives in Yorkshire now?"

"Close to my own holdings. He must have still been in Surrey when you met him."

"Surrey? Jack lived in London."

"Well, of course, I meant the family home. Is that where you became acquainted, in London?"

"It was in the country, actually. At a party much like this."

"I hope it was a more interesting gathering. The company here has been sadly flat. Until your arrival, that is."

"You flatter me, Mr. Stephenson."

"Edmond. I cannot help but think you are speaking of my dear-departed father when you call me by that name."

"My given name is Daphne," she said, with a flirtatious gleam to her eyes. "And you may call me that—unless my husband is nearby. He can be a trifle jealous."

"I will be most careful to call you Lady Milburn in public," Edmond said, guiding her down the pathway. "It must be difficult at times, to be married to an elderly man. Life with him cannot be lively."

"There are compensations," she said. "He does tend to retire early—and dislikes sharing a bed."

"You must find yourself lonely at night."

"Sometimes," she replied, with a coquettish smile. "But what of you, Edmond? You are not married; you sleep alone. Don't you find it lonely?"

"Often."

"Perhaps your cousin will introduce you to one of her friends. You could have a double wedding."

"I am not so certain there will be a wedding for her."

"Are you predicting unhappiness for your cousin?"

"Let's say I will be surprised if she is married within the year."

Lady Milburn eyed him doubtfully. "You think Mr. Barnhill will withdraw?"

"Things are not always what they seem—and people's plans can change."

From the lawn, Jack saw Edmond walking with Lady Milburn. What was the man up to? Jack hurried toward the garden. Of all the people here, they were the two he did not wish to see together. Lady Milburn could tell Honoria's cousin more about Jack's past than he wanted Edmond to know. Jack quickened his steps until he was within hearing.

"Plans certainly can change," he said, strolling up behind them.

"Jack!" Lady Milburn smiled. "We were just talking about you."

"Oh?"

"Yes. I think Edmond is worried about the seriousness of your intentions toward his cousin."

"And what did you tell him?"

"I am not sure what I should say." She gave him a meaningful look.

Jack smiled blandly at Edmond. "You know I have Honoria's best interests at heart."

"Of course," said Edmond. "I never meant to suggest otherwise. How interesting that you two are acquainted."

Jack shrugged. "One is bound to meet old friends again."

Lady Milburn slapped him lightly on the arm. "How dare you call me old!" She pouted prettily. "I should refuse to acknowledge you after such a belittling remark."

Grinning, Jack took her hand and bowed. "You must forgive me, my lady. I should have said 'good' friends. Will you forgive me?"

"I shall consider it. Will you be bringing your bride to town for the Season? As your *friend,* I would love to give a dinner party for you."

"Our plans are indefinite right now. But should we decide to come, I will be certain to let you know."

"I shall like that . . . immensely." She took Edmond's arm and held out her hand to Jack. "Shall we go back to the house? I do not want to be out in the sun too long."

Jack frowned. He didn't want Edmond talking with Lady Milburn. Honoria's cousin already displayed too much curiosity about Jack's past. If he ever learned the true story about Lady Milburn . . . What had Honoria told Edmond? He and Lady Milburn had sworn each other to silence.

Honoria knew the danger of questions about Jack's past. If Sir Richard ever thought Jack was anything but what he claimed, the situation could turn into a disaster.

Assuming Edmond hadn't already told him that Jack was really here to help Norry find the necklace. If Lady Milburn ever revealed that she'd known Jack under another name, his masquerade could be in significant danger; questions would be asked. And once they were asked, there was no telling what truths would come out.

Jack himself wanted to know a great deal more about Edmond. There were too many suspicious actions on his part—that late-night visit with Sir Richard, and his blatant curiosity about Jack's past. Things that made Jack uneasy.

Perhaps he should do a bit of searching on his own, for information about Edmond.

And soon. He wanted to know exactly whose side Edmond was on before the prince arrived, while there was still time to run, if Jack needed to.

But first, he would have a little talk with Miss Honoria Sterling about the value of discretion.

He found her finally in the morning room, surrounded by a table full of silver plate. She was scribbling furiously on a piece of paper.

"Planning on stealing the family silver now?" he asked.

She shot him a dampening look. "I am *helping* Uncle. He asked me to count the place settings."

Jack picked up one of the heavy forks and twirled it in his hands. "The silver would be bulkier than the necklace, but it's a hell of a lot easier to steal. You might think about taking it instead."

"The plate was never meant to be mine; the necklace was."

God forbid that she would take something that wasn't

hers. "Did you tell your cousin that I knew Lady Milburn?"

She nodded, not lifting her eyes from her notes. "He thought you were showing her too much attention in the drawing room. I think he wanted to make me angry. I explained you were merely old friends."

"Good God, Norry, don't you have a brain in your head? No one should know that. Particularly Edmond. We don't want him learning anything about my past."

"Does Lady Milburn know you as 'Gentleman Jack'?"

"No, thank God."

"Then don't worry. Edmond already distrusts you. If I'd expressed a lack of concern over your behavior, he might have wondered. You were spending far too much time with her."

Jack grinned. "So you are jealous after all?"

"I am not jealous."

He flicked a finger across her cheek. "That's one of the things I like about you, Norry. You can be so determined in the face of all reason. I like stubborn ladies."

"Is Lady Milburn stubborn?"

"No," he said slowly. "I don't believe she is. So, you have nothing to worry about."

"I am not worried."

"Oh, you are so sure of me, then? Remember, we are only engaged. Anything can happen between today and the wedding."

"I need to remind you, *Mr. Derry,* that you are merely playing the role of my betrothed. You don't have to act the part when we're alone."

"But this is no act, Norry." He lifted her chin with a finge: and looked down into her blue eyes. "Believe me, I do this willingly." He bent his head and brushed her lips with his. "You're the most damnably attractive woman I've met in a long time."

She looked away. "For all of five months, perhaps?"

"No, it isn't prison that's affecting my mind. It's you. But I don't mind if you play coy, Norry. I like a little shyness in my women as well."

He shut the door behind him and went to his room. She looked almost as adorable angry as she did after she'd been thoroughly kissed. And since he didn't have time for the latter, the former would do for now.

No, she hadn't deliberately told her cousin any of Jack's secrets, and now he'd warned her to be more careful in the future. Sometimes, Norry could be too innocent for her own good.

But *innocent* was not a word he would apply to Edmond Stephenson. Jack wanted to have a good look at his room tonight. Just because Honoria trusted Edmond didn't mean he had to.

Jack excused himself when the port was brought out after dinner. His complaint of indigestion had been easily accepted. While the others sat and drank their port, he'd have ample time to search Edmond's room.

Jack went first to his own rooms and removed his shoes and coat. He retrieved his bundle of "tools" from under the mattress and slipped them into his pocket. Edmond was the type of man who would keep things under lock and key.

Creeping silently down the hall, he tried Edmond's

door. Finding it locked only bolstered Jack's suspicions. Edmond *must* have something to hide. No one locked his door in a setting like this. He easily opened the door with the key Honoria had obtained for him and stepped inside, locking the door behind him.

Setting his candle on the table, he surveyed the room. On the surface, nothing looked out of the ordinary. But then, in this house, it wasn't what was on the surface that counted, but what lay beneath.

With a sigh, he began a methodical search.

He was reaching into the pocket of Edmond's riding coat when Jack heard a noise and froze. Footsteps echoed in the corridor, coming closer.

In one swift movement he shut the wardrobe door, then grabbed the candle and snuffed out the flame with his fingers. He dove underneath the bed as the sharp click of a key sounded in the lock.

Of all the damnable luck! Why on earth had Edmond come upstairs now? Jack envisioned himself stretched out on the cold dusty floor for the entire night. He should have enlisted Norry's help to stand watch.

Jack listened as Edmond crossed and recrossed the room. What was the blasted man doing? He was tempted to lift the edge of the counterpane a fraction and peer out, but caution stayed his hand. He musn't do anything to attract Edmond's attention.

Jack guessed that Edmond stood in front of the dressing table. He walked to the wardrobe, and back to the dressing table again. Jack heard the soft creak of a chair as Edmond sat.

Oh God. This wasn't going to be a short stay.

A faint scratching noise reached his ears and Jack wrinkled his brow as he tried to identify the source. A pen! The blasted idiot was writing a letter. Jack would very much like to know who was so important that Edmond sought the privacy of his room to write. A friend? A lover? Sir Richard?

The thought that Edmond might be preparing written reports for Sir Richard sent a chilled shiver down Jack's spine, then he grinned. More likely, Edmond was writing to his mother.

Jack hoped Edmond was a terse correspondent, because the floor felt harder each minute. He tried to ease the cramp in his right calf, wishing he could stretch his leg out, but he didn't dare move. His left arm, cradling his face, grew numb.

The sound of rustling paper told Jack that Edmond was folding his letter. Now, if he would only deliver it!

As if to torment him, Edmond roamed about the room for several more minutes. Jack tried to shift his aching body, but the faint squeak of the floorboards stilled his movement.

Just when he thought he could endure it no longer, Jack heard the door open and close and the room was once again in darkness.

He lay there for a count of one hundred, then gingerly slid out from under the bed and crawled to the door. He pressed his ear against the wood, but heard nothing. Cautiously, he pulled the door open, and slipped out into the hall to relight the candle. More determined than ever, Jack went back to finish his search.

Edmond's writing box sat on the table and Jack examined it carefully. Taking one of Norry's hairpins from his pocket, Jack worked at the lock on the drawer. Inside, there was no sign of the letter Edmond had written, but there were plenty of letters addressed to him. Jack opened them and scanned their contents. Letters from merchants, asking for payment for the new riding coat, and the new pair of boots, and several pairs of gloves. Most interesting. And another note, reminding Edmond of a "gentleman's obligation" that was due.

Edmond owed money. A considerable sum, if these letters were any indication. Just how prosperous was the farm in Yorkshire? If he didn't have the money to cover his bills, Edmond was in very deep trouble.

Deep enough that he'd be eager to help his cousin steal a valuable necklace.

Deep enough that he'd go to Sir Richard, and offer a deal? Or deep enough that he planned to take the necklace for himself?

Jack relocked the box and left the room. After the rest of the house was asleep, he wanted to have a chat with Honoria about his discoveries.

Leaving his door ajar, Jack listened to the guests come upstairs to bed, but every time he tried to make a dash to Honoria's room, new footsteps sounded on the stairs and he hastily beat a retreat. He feared that by the time he went to her, she'd be fast asleep.

Finally, quiet reigned for several minutes. Jack hurried down the corridor and stepped into her room. She sat at her dressing table, braiding her hair, but whirled about when he entered the room.

"What are you doing here?" Honoria clutched the front of her robe in a protective gesture.

Jack shut the door. "I hoped you were still awake."

She clasped the neck of her robe tighter and Jack grinned. "Obviously, you weren't expecting me. Although I must say, that is a fetching ensemble."

"Oh, do go away. If someone finds you here . . ."

"You are expecting company?"

"No!"

"Then we should be all right." He sauntered over to the bed and perched on the edge of the mattress.

"Where were you this evening? Uncle said you were ill."

"I was—frozen with terror, to be exact."

She looked at him with alarm. "What happened?"

"I was searching your cousin's room when he nearly caught me."

"What were you doing in Edmond's room?"

"I thought it warranted an investigation. He's been asking a lot of questions about me today; I had a few about him I wanted answered."

"Why didn't you ask him, then?"

"Sometimes the answers are better found in a more subtle way."

Honoria played with her braid. "Did you find anything?"

"Only that your cousin is heavily in debt."

"Edmond?

"It appears he is not the virtuous Yorkshire farmer that he pretends."

"What type of debts?"

"Clothiers, mostly. And gambling debts."

Relief crossed her face. "In other words, the normal thing for a gentleman."

"Perhaps. But I intend to keep a close eye on him, just in case. Desperate men can do desperate things."

Jack leaned forward, taking the braid from her hand. "You really shouldn't do this to your hair. I like it much better hanging loose—as it was the other night in the library."

Honoria snatched her braid away. "*I* prefer to wear it this way." She pushed back her chair and stood. "Now, I think you should leave."

"You don't want to do any more searching tonight?"

"I cannot imagine any other place where the necklace could be. I think you're right, Uncle won't bring it here from the vault until the prince arrives. You may as well go to bed."

Jack nodded and stepped closer. "Is that an invitation?"

"No!"

"A pity." He reached out and twitched the folded lace collar of her robe. "I like to see a lady in white lace."

"Please. Go."

Ignoring her words, he reached out, pulling her into his arms. She smelled his warm, claret-scented breath, felt the buttons of his waistcoat through the thin fabric of her night rail. In an instant, Honoria realized how dangerous her situation was, here, in her bedroom, with the house asleep around them. And the danger wasn't from Jack himself, but her reaction to him.

Then his lips were on hers, his tongue pressed into her mouth, and she forgot her worries as pleasurable sensation flooded her body. Her hands gripped his shoulders and she drew him close.

"Nice," Jack mumbled as he trailed kisses across her cheek and down her neck.

His hand was rubbing magical patterns across her back that made her feel both hot and cold. One part of her brain screamed a warning, telling her this was unbelievable folly. Another part grew weak and unresisting, reveling in the feel of his mouth and tongue, his hands on her back and—

His fingers caught at her braid again.

"This has to go," he mumbled, struggling with the ribbon while he continued to kiss her. "No braids for Norry."

Deftly, he unwove her hair and ran his fingers through it until it hung down her back in loose tendrils. "Much better," he whispered against her ear, the tiny breaths of air sending shivers up her spine.

He didn't kiss her again but clasped her tightly against him, one hand wrapped in her hair, the other stroking her back. Honoria buried her face in his neck, afraid to meet his eyes. He'd instantly know how much she enjoyed this.

Suddenly his hands stilled and he merely held her, his chin resting atop her head. Neither of them spoke a word. Honoria's heart sounded like a booming drum in her chest. She felt Jack's heart beating its own rapid pattern as she clung to him.

He finally released her and took a step back, cradling her face in his hands. After dropping a gentle kiss on her lips, Jack's hands fell to his side.

"Sweet dreams, Norry." Slipping out the door, he left as quietly as he'd come.

Honoria sank into the chair, shaken by the encounter.

It was difficult to comprehend this unfamiliar feeling of desire. It was as if her body had a mind of its own, and nothing she could think or say could change the way she felt when Jack held her in his arms. And every time he did, she gave a little more of herself to him. She was playing with fire, but she wanted to be burned, wanted to feel more of the scorching heat. Wanted to bind him to her so he'd take her with him when he left.

There. She'd admitted it. She wanted to go with him, wanted to stay with him, wherever he went. Even if the thought terrified her.

Why had he left her so quickly? As Jack sat in his room, staring into the darkness, the question rolled through his head. Closing his eyes, he conjured up the vivid image of Honoria in her night rail, her hair in a jumbled mass after he'd unwoven her braid. It was a pretty picture. One that he would like to see again . . . and again . . . and again . . .

She'd been willing and pliant in his arms, and if he couldn't have achieved her complete capitulation tonight, he could have pushed her a good way toward it. So why didn't he? Why had he dropped his arms, virtually pushing her away, and fled to his room?

He was afraid of her. Afraid of what he felt for her. And afraid of what she wanted from him, knowing he could never give it to her.

Honoria wanted everything that he disdained—security, respectability, stability. He'd fought against them all his life. And if he didn't relish the depths to which he'd ultimately sunk, he wasn't going to embrace those qualities now either. Especially not for any woman—even Norry.

Yet he wanted her. When he compared her to Lady Milburn, Jack wondered how he could ever have bedded the other woman. It wasn't Norry's virginal freshness that drew him, but her courage, her determination to fight for what she wanted. She had all the enthusiasm for life he'd lost over the years. When he was with her, he almost thought he could get it back. She could show him how.

But the price she demanded was too high. Better to slake his desire for her warm, willing body, then leave, before she tried to convince him he really could change. Because Jack knew that he couldn't.

Chapter 16

After a solitary breakfast, Jack retreated again to the library. He'd turn into a damn scholar if he spent any more time here. But it was one of the few places in the house where he could escape the other guests. Honoria was the only other person who ever came in here—and he wasn't averse to seeing her.

Jack picked up a two-day-old copy of *The Times* and began reading. He'd barely reached the second column of adverts when the library door flew open. Honoria dashed into the room, a look of utter panic on her face.

"He's here!"

"Who's here?"

"The prince."

Jack jumped to his feet. "Here? Now? I thought he wasn't due for two more days."

"Well, he just arrived." Honoria wrung her hands. "Oh, Jack, what are we going to do?"

"There's no need to worry," he said, with more conviction than he felt. "We have plenty of time to think and plan. He's going to be here for a fortnight, isn't he?"

"Yes, but—"

"Not another word," Jack said, taking her hand. "Leave everything to me. Things will be fine."

"Do you really think so?"

"Of course." Jack planted a soft kiss on her brow. "Now, calm down. Everything will turn out all right."

She flashed him a radiant smile and left the room.

Jack frowned. He didn't like this. The prince was here and the game was going to go forward in earnest now. The prince's arrival meant that the real necklace would soon turn up as well.

The question was where and when.

In less than an hour a footman appeared, bearing a summons for Jack to join his host and his "most distinguished guest" in the drawing room. Jack glanced at his modest garb and grinned. Court dress wasn't required for such an august presence?

The other guests were already in the drawing room, being presented to the royal guest, when Jack entered. He struggled to hide his mirth at the sight of the prince. The man was short and plump, with florid cheeks and a laughably old-fashioned powdered wig.

"Ah, Barnhill, there you are." Sir Richard gestured for Jack to join them. "Your Highness, may I present Jack Barnhill. He is a particular friend of my niece's."

Jack bowed to the seated prince. Despite the gold-trimmed uniform dripping in medals, the prince was even more unimpressive up close.

"His Most Royal Highness, the Prince of Rinsdorf-Rödgen." Sir Richard beamed as if he were somehow responsible for the man's exalted title.

"Your niece is a most charming *Fräulein,*" the prince said to Sir Richard, directing an appreciative look at Honoria. He motioned her to come forward and he took her hand in his. "Most charming."

Instantly, Jack bristled at the prince's actions. "Miss Sterling," he said coldly, "is the very essence of English womanhood."

"Ja, ja." The prince nodded vigorously, causing his chins to jiggle.

Sir Richard coughed. "I must tell you, Your Highness, that there is an understanding between my niece and Mr. Barnhill."

"Ach!" He pinched Honoria's cheek. "I offer you my felicitations, *liebchen.*"

Jack knew that if he really was engaged to Honoria, he would plant the prince a facer. Instead, he smiled grimly and withdrew. Lady Milburn came up beside him.

"A round little thing, isn't he?" she whispered. "Not at all like those Prussian Hussars I saw in London . . ."

"Sir Richard doesn't seem to mind," Jack observed. "And Lord knows, the Prince of Wales doesn't cut a better picture himself."

Lady Milburn stifled a giggle behind her hand.

Frowning, Jack watched Honoria's uncle hover about the prince. Sir Richard was a parvenu—it was obvious in the way he fawned over his royal guest. German princelings were as common as pheasants in September, but Sir Richard acted as if he was entertaining the king himself. The prince accepted it as his due.

Edmond appeared at Jack's elbow. "I fear you may have

a rival for Honoria's affections," he said, glancing pointedly at the prince. "He seems quite taken with her."

Jack's eyes narrowed as he stared at the prince and Honoria, whose right hand was still in the prince's clutches. His admiring glances were rapidly developing into leers, and a spurt of anger shot through Jack. Enough was enough. He didn't like the idea of any man looking at her like that—particularly a fat German prince.

Honoria glanced at Jack and he saw the silent plea in her eyes. She wanted him to rescue her.

She *needed* him to rescue her.

The thought gave him a strange stab of pleasure, until the implications of that need triggered his deeper fears. He didn't want to be needed by anyone, least of all her.

Yet he had to rescue her from the prince all the same.

Taking Lady Milburn's arm, Jack drew her toward the prince's side. Bowing, he looked sternly at Honoria. "Really, my dear, how unfair of you to monopolize the prince's time. Lady Milburn is most anxious to speak with His Highness about his homeland."

Honoria curtseyed. "Please excuse me, Your Highness, but Mr. Barnhill is right. I have been most selfish."

The prince's beady eyes gleamed as he scrutinized Lady Milburn. He patted the sofa beside him. "Sit, sit, my lady."

Taking Honoria's arm, Jack guided her across the room.

"Oh, Jack, I am in your debt," she said when they were out of earshot. "What an odious little man! I don't care if he is a prince. And he is to be here for a fortnight. Whatever am I to do?"

"Play your cards right and maybe he'll take you home with him," Jack teased.

She laughed but then her face grew anxious. "Stay close to me, please? I don't want to be alone with him."

"I will stand guard over you day and night. Particularly at night—that's when you'll be in the most danger."

A smile teased at her lips. "From the prince or you?"

Jack took her elbow and steered her toward the window. "That depends on how dangerous you find me," he said in a low undertone. "I don't think you looked terribly frightened last night." Briefly, he touched his hand to the side of her neck. "Or was it fear that caused your pulse to throb there when I kissed you?"

She blushed.

Jack's eyes lingered on her, leaving her no doubt of what he was thinking—their wanton embrace in her room last night.

She held his gaze for a minute, then she turned away.

Dinner was a drawn-out, interminable affair in which Sir Richard sought to impress his royal guest with every dish imaginable. Jack was sated after the first course, yet more food kept coming. No wonder the prince was as fat as a pig—the rest of them would be, too, if they ate like this at every meal.

The prince, to Jack's relief, was not fond of port, so the gentlemen spent only a short time together after the meal before they followed the ladies into the drawing room.

Jack hastened to Honoria's side. Her eyes lit up in welcome at the sight of him, and for a moment Jack thought how beautiful she was. She was the type of woman who would draw admiring looks from every man in a room.

Then he deliberately chastised himself. There were

other good-looking women in the world. Safer ones. Ones who didn't expect anything of him.

"The prince isn't a port drinker, thank God. Is there any way we can—?"

"Honoria." Sir Richard beckoned to his niece.

"Your royal admirer awaits," Jack whispered. He placed his hand in the small of her back and gently pushed her forward. "Do not stay *too* long. His devoted attention might provoke my jealousy."

"Believe me, you have no cause for concern."

Jack scowled as he caught a glimpse of the prince, leaning toward Honoria in a possessive manner. This time, she could count on Jack to extricate her from the royal clutches. But who would rescue her from other grasping men in the future? Not Sir Richard, that was certain. He would probably serve up his niece on a silver platter if it pleased the prince.

Hearing the door open, Jack glanced up to see Lady Hampton enter, leaning heavily on her cane. She had dined in her room tonight and Honoria had worried that she wasn't well. Jack moved to assist her and Honoria joined him.

"Thank goodness Aunt Sophia's here!" Honoria reached for Jack's hand. "I was able to get away from his royal fatness."

Sophia's eyes brightened when she saw Honoria, but then they narrowed as she scanned the room and her face grew puzzled.

Jack escorted her to her usual chair. "How is my favorite lady this evening?"

Sophia gave him a bewildered look. "When did you arrive? I don't remember you being here."

Jack darted an uneasy glance at Honoria.

"Would you like Jack to get you a cup of tea, Auntie?"

"Jack? Who's Jack?"

"Mr. Barnhill," Honoria said gently, pointing to Jack.

"You forget me so easily, my lady?" Jack asked, feigning despair. "My heart is wounded."

"I know you. You're the spitting image of your father." Sophia's expression grew confused. "But you can't be his son, can you? He married the Thornton chit. You must be his grandson."

Honoria glanced at Jack and was shocked at the deathlike pallor of his face. "Are you all right?"

"Quite."

Honoria turned back to her aunt and her heart sank. Sophia had been lucid for so long that she had almost forgotten how great a fuss her great-aunt could make when confusion set in.

"This has been an exciting day," Honoria said quietly. "Would you like me to take you back upstairs now?"

Sophia thumped her cane. "I want to know more about this young man."

Honoria glanced around, noting with dismay that several people were looking in their direction. She directed a pleading glance at Jack. "Could you help me . . . ?"

"Lady Hampton, I believe the moon is starting to rise. Shall we go for a stroll in the garden?" Jack took her hand but Sophia snatched it away.

"I don't know what game you're playing, but I don't want to have any of it," she said. "Just like your grandfather, you are. I knew it the moment I laid eyes on you. That namby-pamby miss he married didn't weaken the bloodlines, not at all."

Jack hardly dared to move. Had Sophia really made the connection, or was this just more of her confused ramblings? He didn't wait to find out.

"Let's go," he mouthed to Honoria and together they both stood and nearly dragged Lady Hampton from her chair. "It's time for bed, Aunt."

Sir Richard hastened to their side. "Is anything amiss?"

"Auntie's had a bit too much excitement today," Honoria said. "I'm sure she'll be better after a good night's rest."

Sir Richard darted an apprehensive look at the German prince, but he appeared oblivious to the disruption. "Get her out of here then."

The resistance suddenly went out of Sophia, and Honoria and Jack easily guided her out in the hall. She leaned heavily on Jack's arm as they climbed the stairs.

At the top, she turned, and looked at Jack again. "You are sure you're not his grandson?"

"I'm adopted," Jack said.

"Oh, dear," said Sophia, then she brightened. "That must be why you look so familiar. You must be one of those 'misty' ones." She patted Jack on the arm. "You look just like him, you know. It's a pity I'm not a few years younger. I daresay we could have had a grand time together."

Honoria nearly wilted with relief when they reached Sophia's room. Jack waited in the hall until Josie, the maid, arrived to help with her mistress.

"Is she all right?" he asked Honoria when she came out of the room.

"I hope she will be better in the morning. It's remarkable that she's been so clear all this time." She glanced at him. "Do you really look like your grandfather?"

"It's hard to say; I never met the man. He was dead long before I was born."

"Aunt Sophia certainly thinks you look familiar."

"Your aunt thinks everyone looks familiar."

"True. When she gets an idea in her head, however wrong, it's difficult to convince her otherwise. By tomorrow, she'll probably remember you're Jack."

"I hope so." He took her hand. "We should return to the drawing room."

"I know."

Jack bent to kiss her, wrapping his arms about her as he drew her close.

"Oh, Jack," she said, leaning against him and kissing him with a passion that both surprised and delighted him.

It must be his miserable fate, thought Jack, to have a willing woman in his arms when at any moment another guest might come across them, and with her uncle waiting for them downstairs.

He used to be more skilled at staging his seductions. But Honoria could make his calculated resolve flee when she pressed herself against him. If he wasn't careful, she'd cause him to lose all control.

And control was one thing that Jack needed to maintain. With a wry grin at his sacrifice, he disengaged her hands from around his neck.

"We'd better report back to your uncle," he said.

Honoria stepped away. "You're right."

Jack tucked an errant wisp of hair behind her ear. "Although you might want to wait a minute or two. Right now, I don't think there's anyone in the drawing room who wouldn't immediately know what you'd been doing."

He tapped her lightly on the nose. "Except Toddy, perhaps, but I don't think he notices much of anything. I'll go down and you follow when you're ready."

She nodded and Jack squeezed her fingers. "Don't worry, your aunt will be better tomorrow. Either that, or she'll have convinced herself that I'm Napoleon and then we will really be in trouble."

Honoria's soft laugh lingered in his ears as he returned to the drawing room.

Not long after he went back downstairs, Sir Richard invited Jack to join the prince in a game of whist. Jack's enthusiasm mounted when the others opted to play for money this time.

Feigning nonchalance, Jack paid strict attention to each hand. This might be a friendly game to the others, but for him, even a few pounds would make an enormous difference. Deeply engrossed in the first hand, he gave Honoria only a passing nod when she returned.

Jack won steadily, but not spectacularly, which suited him fine. He didn't want to draw too much attention to his card-playing skills. But when the last hand was played out, Jack found himself forty pounds richer.

Sir Richard congratulated him. "Nice play, Barnhill. You've a good head for whist."

Latham smiled. "I'd like to take you to my club, when

you're in town. There's a few men I'd like to see you challenge. They've taken enough off me over the years; it'd give me great satisfaction to see you do the same to them."

"I was lucky tonight," said Jack.

"Luck, hah!" said Grose. "I'll have you for my partner anytime."

The prince smiled. "A good head for cards you haf."

As soon as he could, Jack excused himself. Let them linger over their brandy; he wanted to contemplate his good fortune.

Forty pounds. He hadn't seen that much money in a long, long time.

And once he found the necklace, he'd have a great deal more.

When she went to Aunt Sophia's room in the morning, Honoria was stunned by the scene of chaos.

"Put those scarves in the traveling case." Sophia sat propped up against the pillows, drinking her morning tea and ordering her maid.

"What are you doing, Auntie?" Honoria demanded.

"Going home."

"But you can't!"

Sophia looked imperiously at her niece. "And why ever not?"

"There's Uncle . . . and the prince . . ."

"I don't want to spend time with some overweening German prince. I've been away from home quite long enough. No, Josie," she told the maid, "put those slippers in the big trunk."

Honoria looked wistfully at her aunt. "Can't I persuade you to stay? Who will I talk with after you're gone?"

"Maybe you'll start to pay more attention to that young man of yours." Sophia nodded her head for emphasis.

"He doesn't want me hanging on his arm."

"No, but you could do a better job all the same. Men like to think they're the center of your world. My leaving will give you a chance to do that."

Honoria opened her mouth to protest, but Sophia patted her hand.

"Now I want your promise to visit me this fall, girl. Bring Jack with you; my grandson would like him, I think. We will plan our trip to London." She leaned forward. "I think you ought to talk privately with the boy's mother when you can. If he's not the spitting image of old Mornington, I don't know who is. There might be a scandal lurking in the past." Sophia's eyes gleamed. "You know how I love a scandal."

"Who is Mornington?"

Sophia preened herself. "One of my old beaux. In his day, of course, that dark hair would have been powdered, but there's no mistaking the eyes." She sighed. "I almost hated to give up those eyes."

Honoria sympathized. A single glance from Jack could send shivers up her spine.

Giving her aunt a hug, Honoria stood. "I shall miss you. And I will come to Hampton this fall."

Sadness tugged at her when she finally bundled Sophia into the coach. Honoria would have to leave England once she had the necklace and she did not know how long she would have to stay away—or even if she could ever return. And even though Sophia's confused ramblings about Jack had frightened her last night, the thought of losing the irascible old woman brought Honoria deep distress and sadness.

There was only one person who could dispel the gloom.

Honoria found Jack in the library.

"Sophia has left for home," she said. "She was completely lucid this morning. As far as she's concerned, you're Jack again." She looked closely at Jack. "Do you know anyone named Mornington?"

Sitting very still, Jack tried to control his pounding heart. "I don't think so," he said finally, slowly. "Should I?"

"Sophia says you remind her of someone named Mornington. She hinted that your mother might have had an illicit liaison with the man. It was your eyes, she said."

"I've been told they're my best feature." He searched her face for a reaction. "What do you think?"

She met his glance for a moment, then looked away. "I think you've had far too many women whispering sweet things to you."

The corners of his mouth quivered. "Jealous?"

"No!"

Jack sighed. "Then I will have to find another way to pique your interest."

"Please, Jack, you must think about the necklace. Surely Uncle has it in the house, now that the prince is here."

"You want to search the entire house?"

"Unless you'd rather spend the day in the drawing room talking with the prince."

"Let's start with the attic."

At the sight of the dusty jumble of furniture, trunks, and oddments in the attic, Honoria shuddered. "I'd forgotten how many things were up here."

"It should only take us three or four days to look through everything."

"It was never this bad before. Standards have certainly declined since Uncle has been here."

"You don't have to tell me that. I was covered in dust after crawling under Edmond's bed the other night."

Jack set the candle down and inspected the floor. "Someone has been up here recently—you can see footprints. I'll look over here."

Honoria moved in the opposite direction. She brushed past tables layered with dust, an ancient birdcage, and stacks of hat boxes before she spotted a small trunk in the corner. Bending down to examine it, her excitement rose when she saw the smudges in the dust.

"Jack! Come look at this."

In his haste to reach her, he bumped against a stack of chairs, which fell over with a clatter and a billowing cloud of dust. Coughing, Jack moved with greater caution.

"Look how the dust is disturbed on the lid of the trunk."

"Let's see what's inside."

Eagerly, Jack peered over her shoulder, then burst out laughing when he saw the contents.

"Ladies' undergarments! How exciting."

Jack reached past her and drew out a heavily stitched, lace-up corset. "It's a pity your aunt left this morning. This would probably bring back all kinds of memories for her."

Honoria snatched it from his hand.

After rummaging through the contents of the trunk, he sat back on his heels, a puzzled look on his face. "It's all clothing—from your grandmother's day. Why would anyone be interested in those?"

"Could Uncle have been hiding the necklace here?"

Jack shrugged. "Maybe. But it isn't there now, so it doesn't matter." He stood and resumed his prowling.

Honoria continued searching. Hearing Jack's sudden gasp, she turned to look but there was no sign of him in the gloom.

"Jack? Where are you?"

"Over here."

She found him perched on the arm of a chair, staring at a well-worn, faded rocking horse.

"What is wrong?"

Jack pushed his toe against the horse's leg, setting it rocking.

"There was a horse like this at home. I remember spending hours galloping across the nursery floor in search of evil knights and dragons."

Honoria sat down beside him. "You are not the baseborn man you pretend."

"It's not the manner of my birth that is important; it is the way I've lived my life. I'm not proud of it."

"But you could be," she said as she followed him to the attic door.

Pulling out a handkerchief, he wiped her cheek. "You had a smudge of dirt," he said, then turned and fled down the attic stairs.

Chapter 17

Jack spent the rest of the afternoon roaming through the house, searching through anything—everything—that might hide a necklace. When the time came to dress for dinner, he'd looked in more drawers, behind enough pictures, and under so many pieces of furniture that he never wanted to do anything like this again.

The situation was rapidly becoming a damned nuisance. Forty pounds wasn't much, but it was enough to get him to London. If he only had himself to think about, he'd be tempted to depart and the necklace be damned. But he couldn't leave Norry to the mercy of her uncle.

When Jack entered the drawing room before dinner, the guests were clustered around the prince.

"Did you earn all those medals fighting against Napoleon?" Mrs. Grose asked, eyeing the glittering jewels on the prince's chest.

"Oh, *ja, ja*. This is the Order of Maria Katharina, and the Franz Friedrich medal, and the Great Cross of the *Fürstentum* Rinsdorf-Rödgen."

"Very impressive," said Jack, with an impish grin. He

nodded toward the portrait over the mantel. "Almost as impressive as those jewels."

"*Ach, das Rubens*. They are most exquisite, are they not?"

"Particularly when worn around the neck of a lovely lady. Are you buying them for a princess at home?"

The prince glanced at Honoria and his eyes lit up. He turned to his host. "Sir Richard, let us see this necklace we have traveled so far to find."

Sir Richard looked surprised by his request. "Your Highness, the necklace is being stored in a safe place. I am more than willing to get it for you, but it cannot be done on such short notice."

The prince frowned. "I understand. But you will have it for the ball, *ja*?"

Sir Richard bowed. "Of course."

The prince's eyes lit on Honoria. "And perhaps this lovely lady would be willing to wear it for us. You do not mind, *liebchen*?"

"Not at all, Your Highness. We all wish you to enjoy your stay at Norcross."

"*Ja,* I think I will."

After dinner, Jack realized that he missed Lady Hampton's presence. Until she'd accused him of having the Mornington eyes, he'd appreciated her insistence that he stay at her side in the drawing room—she was certainly the most interesting guest there. Now, if he wasn't careful, he'd have to talk with either the prince or Sir Richard's other guests. Both prospects made him shudder.

He could flirt with Lady Milburn, he supposed, if only

because it would annoy Edmond and infuriate Honoria. But the idea didn't sound particularly appealing. Somehow, when he compared the two women, Lady Milburn didn't seem as alluring as she once did.

Still, he decided that he would direct his attentions at Lady Milburn, if only to ease the tedium.

He mumbled a few parting words to Sir Richard, and edged his way across the room until he was behind Lady Milburn.

"You look as bored as I," he said.

Lady Milburn laughed lightly. "Am I that transparent? I thought I was hiding it well."

"Anyone under the age of fifty would be bored to tears."

She nodded in Honoria's direction. "Miss Sterling looks as if she's enjoying herself."

"She doesn't have a choice. She's Sir Richard's niece."

"I own, it strikes me odd to find you here. This doesn't seem like your usual type of gathering."

"I felt it my duty to accompany Honoria."

"And, of course, there is the opportunity to meet the prince."

"Is that why you're here?"

"I'm here because Toddy wished it."

"A devoted wife."

"Indeed."

Jack observed Honoria. She was pretending to listen attentively to Mrs. Mayflower, but the nervous nibbling of her lower lip belied her calm. She glanced in his direction, and he quickly turned back to Lady Milburn, who was fanning herself.

"Allow me," he said, taking the fan from her. He waved it before her face in slow, languid movements. "Better?"

"Much."

"Of course, a stroll in the garden would be even more cooling."

"It sounds like just the thing. These warm August nights can be so . . . exhilarating."

Jack settled Lady Milburn's shawl around her shoulders and led her out to the terrace.

"The night air is most refreshing," she said, looking up at him with an inviting smile.

"Indeed."

Sitting down, Lady Milburn patted the bench beside her. "Do sit. I will develop a crick in my neck from staring up at you. Poor Toddy's gout has been bothering him again. He's taking laudanum to help him sleep better."

Trying to look sympathetic, Jack's gaze drifted toward the terrace doors. How long would it take before Honoria came looking for him? He felt Lady Milburn's fingers on his arm.

"One of the unfortunate side-effects is that he sleeps so soundly, he wouldn't notice if Napoleon's troops invaded the house."

"Laudanum can have that effect," Jack agreed.

Her fingers tightened on his arm. "He'd never notice if I . . . slipped away for a while."

Jack had half a mind to ask her where she intended to go in the middle of the night, but he caught himself in time. It was obvious she wanted it to be Jack's room. And as quickly as he realized that, he also realized that he didn't want her there. Not now. Not ever.

"I'm not sure . . . ," he began.

"Worried that your charming young lady will find out?"

Lady Milburn's voice was teasing, but Jack heard her undertone of sarcasm.

"She might construe it as an unmannerly act. You know how young, unmarried ladies are."

"Dull and boring?" Lady Milburn asked.

This time there was no mistaking the edge to her voice.

Jack couldn't recall having turned down a lady before and he realized he wasn't doing a very good job of it. He could play along with her, and make sure his door was locked when he retired. But bluntness might be the best course after all.

"I've made it a practice to never resume an affair once it's ended."

She moved her hand to his thigh. "Never?"

Jack took her hand and placed it back in her lap. "Never."

Honoria watched Jack escort Lady Milburn from the drawing room with angry disbelief. What did he think he was doing? He'd drawn the curious looks of every person in the room—everyone, except the sleeping Toddy. People would think the worst of Jack—and they were probably right.

"Excuse me," she said to Mrs. Mayflower, and fled into the hall. Where were those two?

Suddenly, she remembered Jack's last action—fanning Lady Milburn. Of course. They were outside in the cool night air.

Was the man incorrigible? Last night he'd been kissing

her; now, he was probably doing the same thing with Lady Milburn. Wasn't one woman enough? Or weren't a few simple kisses enough?

The very thought of Jack sharing kisses with Lady Milburn made Honoria's blood boil. That woman had no right to him.

Jack belonged to *her*.

Jack nearly sagged with relief when he saw Honoria sail through the terrace doors like an avenging angel.

"Lovely night," he said, jumping to his feet.

"Isn't it?"

"The drawing room was so warm," said Lady Milburn. "Mr. Barnhill kindly brought me out here for a breath of fresh air."

"I believe I heard Toddy asking for you," Honoria told her in an icy tone.

Lady Milburn rose and held out her hand to Jack, while she glanced with amusement at Honoria. "Pray just remember," she said, " 'never' can be a very, very long time."

Jack leaned back against the balustrade, arms crossed over his chest, watching Lady Milburn reenter the house. "Is Toddy even awake?"

"Everyone saw you two leave."

"So? It was as the lady said, I escorted her outside for a breath of fresh air. Lord, you could probably slow-roast an ox in that room."

"You told me you were going to keep away from her. Yet every time I see you, you're at her side."

"Watching me carefully, are you?"

"No!"

Jack pulled her against him, kissing her with a hard, demanding mouth.

"You *were* afraid," he said, looking into her eyes. "You thought you'd find me out here doing exactly that with Lady Milburn."

"I did not."

"Yes, you did. Admit it. You were wondering if I might be kissing her, and if I liked her kisses better than yours."

"Of all the egotistical—"

Jack lowered his mouth to hers again. "If it makes you feel any better, I do prefer yours. Although my basis for comparison is rather slim, as I don't exactly recall the experience with her."

"But—"

"Hush. Kiss me, Norry."

His mouth came down on hers before she could say anything. He kissed her softly, then more fiercely, his tongue slipping into her mouth, tasting her soft warmth. Her hands crept up his chest and wrapped themselves around his neck; her tongue touched against his.

Her innocent response filled Jack with dizzying desire. He wanted this woman. He wanted to awaken her, wanted to watch her learn the secrets of her body and his.

Norry's pained moan brought him to his senses. He tore his mouth away, gulping air while he gently pushed her away.

"I swear, Norry, if you don't go back into the house this minute, I won't be responsible for what happens next. Go, please."

She looked at him with wide eyes, then fled into the house.

Jack felt a twinge of shame. Seducing a virgin—at least a lady like Honoria—was no small business. It would have an impact on the rest of her life. Did he want to take responsibility for that?

He shook his head wryly. This was a new twist. When had he ever worried about the consequences of anything he'd done?

Since you nearly died, that small voice told him. Since the day that demure little scamp had plucked him off the gallows and given him a new life.

He owed her something more than a quick tumble in the sheets for that.

Jack didn't return to the drawing room; he didn't want to risk another confrontation with Lady Milburn. He'd be safe enough in his room. It was only when he passed Honoria's bedroom door that he halted, and debated.

He wanted her so badly. Why couldn't she be a bored matron like Lady Milburn? He wouldn't think twice about bedding her then. No complications, no regrets, just a few evenings of pleasure.

But Norry was different—and not just because she was a virgin. For the first time in his life, he'd met a woman he didn't want to walk away from. And that frightened him far more than the gallows at Gorton.

She wanted security, protection, reliability. All things he knew little about, and was woefully unprepared to offer anyone, least of all himself. There was no place for

Norry—for any woman—in his life. And knowing that, he should leave her alone.

Instead, he opened the door and entered her room.

Jack moved the chair so she wouldn't see him when she first walked in, wishing he'd thought to bring a glass of brandy with him. He hoped he wouldn't have a long wait.

When Uncle Richard and the prince sat down to cards, Honoria realized it was time to go to bed. Jack obviously wasn't coming back to the drawing room; she'd wasted the last hour waiting for him.

If he wasn't asleep, she wanted to have a word with him. But what was she going to say? That she was confused, uncertain, afraid; elated, excited, expectant?

She could actually believe, after their words on the terrace, that he did want her, and not Lady Milburn. Jack Derry wanted *her*. As badly as she wanted him. For Honoria was now able to put a name on what she felt, and she knew it was desire. Desire for the man she loved.

Hesitating outside his door, she tapped lightly. Hearing no response, she pushed it open. The room was dark, and she took several halting steps toward the bed.

It was empty.

Honoria had enough confidence now to know that he wasn't with Lady Milburn. The dark glances that lady had cast her way told Honoria all she needed to know about what had transpired on the terrace. Jack had spoken the truth—he didn't want Lady Milburn anymore. He was probably looking for the necklace.

Entering her own room, she set the candle on the table and kicked off her slippers.

"Where have you been?" Jack demanded.

Honoria whirled about. "What are you doing here?"

"Waiting for you. I thought you'd decided to sleep in the drawing room."

"And I was waiting down there for you!"

Jack stretched and rubbed his neck. "I nearly fell asleep."

"Why were you waiting?"

"I wanted to talk with you."

"About what?"

"About what happened on the terrace tonight."

Honoria regarded him steadily. "Why did you send me away?"

Jack took her hand and rubbed his thumb over her palm. "It was for your own good, Norry. If you had an ounce of sense in your pretty little head, you'd tell me to get out of your room this minute."

She smiled. "And if I don't?"

"I'm not what you need, Norry, or think you want. Forget about your necklace and send me away. It's the safest thing."

"For you or me?"

A shadow crossed his eyes. "For both of us. This is very dangerous, Norry. Very dangerous. You're becoming most damaging to my self-control."

Instead of retreating, Honoria stepped closer and glanced at him with faint amusement. "How awkward for you."

Jack took a deep breath, then cradled her face in his hands. Slowly, deliberately, he kissed her. He made it insistent, demanding, prodding her lips apart with his tongue and then plunging into her mouth.

He feathered one hand down her neck, along her shoulder, tangling it in her hair. With the other, he groped along the neckline of her gown, curving his hand over her breast. She tensed in his arms but didn't pull away.

He cupped the curve of her buttock, drawing her hard against him, pressing his arousal against her, waiting for her to recoil with horror.

Instead, she pulled his head even closer, matching him kiss for kiss.

Jack struggled out of his coat while Honoria fumbled with the buttons on his waistcoat. Brushing his hands aside, she pushed both garments off, then tugged at his shirt, pulling it from the waistband of his pantaloons. Every time her fingers brushed against him, his breathing grew more erratic.

She slipped her hands under his shirt and ran them up his chest, her fingers traced scorching patterns over his skin. He sucked in his breath at the pleasure.

Untying the fastenings at the back of her gown, Jack slid the dress off her shoulders, down her arms, and onto the floor until she stood before him, clad only in her chemise. Her breasts swelled against the fabric, begging to be kissed.

Quickly, he lifted Norry and set her on the high bed, then stripped off his shirt and unfastened his pantaloons. In an instant, he faced her, clad only in his drawers. They did nothing to hide his desire.

Sitting beside her on the bed, he pulled the pins from

her hair, flinging them across the floor. He used his fingers as a comb, fluffing out her hair.

"I love the color of your hair in the candlelight."

Then he drew her chemise down, over the first swell of her breasts, lower and lower, until they were exposed, erect and firm.

"Ah, Norry, you are so lovely." He cupped them lightly with his hands as his head dipped lower and he laved a nipple with his tongue. Kneading one breast with his hand, he drew the nipple of the other into his mouth, sucking, nipping, teasing.

She moved restlessly beneath him, her hands and her innocent motions doing more to fire him than the actions of the most experienced courtesan.

His hand caressed her belly in spiraling circles, stroking down her leg, teasing up her thigh. Brushing against her mound of tight curls, his fingers inched closer, ever closer, tickling the inside of her thighs, forcing her legs open. His hand dipped lower, seeking, probing.

He groaned at her wetness. It was the final sign of her capitulation, the signal that her desire burned as strongly as his. Slowly, he stroked her, reveling at her response as she arched against his hand.

Fumbling with the ties to his drawers, Jack frantically pushed them down over his hips.

"You are a witch, Norry, a witch," he whispered hoarsely, barely able to control the throbbing agony of his body. "What kind of spell have you put on me?" He reached down and guided himself to her.

Oh God. Remember she's a virgin.

He raised up onto his knees and groped through the tangle of sheets for his drawers. "Raise your hips," he commanded, and slid the cloth under her.

He must go slowly, carefully, to make sure he didn't hurt her.

"It will be good, I promise," he whispered in her ear, taking tiny nips at her earlobe. "Trust me, Norry."

He guided himself into her again, pressing into the soft flesh, feeling her part around him.

Slowly, he moved inside her, watching her carefully, seeing the expression on her face flicker between surprise and desire. With every thrust, his restraint weakened. Reaching the barrier, he pushed against it gently, then harder and harder until he broke through. Norry gasped but his mouth was on hers instantly, kissing, murmuring reassurances. He pulled her with him, rocking them against the mattress. He heard his breath coming in ragged gasps and felt a trickle of sweat drip down his cheek. Slickened with moisture, their bodies moved in rhythmic unison, faster and faster until she arched beneath him with a moan and he called her name, over and over, as he released himself into her.

Honoria brushed back the damp strands of hair from Jack's forehead, cradling him against her breasts. A tingling lassitude crept over her; she couldn't even think about what she'd just done. The physical sensations had been overwhelming, racing from burning desire to discomfort to an ecstasy that was indescribable.

Jack stirred and raised his head, grinning at her crookedly. He kissed the tip of her nose, then her eyes, her cheeks, her chin. With a contented groan, he settled down beside her.

"Ah, Norry."

Her named sounded soft as a caress. She snuggled close to him, finding a secure happiness in his arms.

Honoria awoke several times during the night. Once, she rolled to her side and watched Jack as he slept. He was restless, until she curled up beside him again and he stilled immediately.

When she woke again, he was leaning on one elbow, looking at her. Her cheeks reddened at the intimacy of his gaze, but she reached out her arms to him and pulled him close.

"Easy," he said. "I don't want to hurt you."

"You can never hurt me."

With a groan, his mouth traced a pattern of fire down her throat.

Moving beneath him, her hands stroked down his back to reassure him of her need.

Later, as she drifted lazily in a golden haze of near-sleep, a jarring motion disturbed her.

"Norry?"

Her eyes flickered open. Jack, dressed now, looked down at her, shaking her shoulder gently.

"It's morning," he said. "I need to return to my room before the house is awake."

She struggled to sit up, and he came into her arms, rocking slightly as they clung together.

"Go back to sleep, Norry. I'll talk with you later."

"I love you," she whispered, tightening her grasp. "Oh, Jack, how I love you."

In a determined effort to disguise his sudden terror, Jack swept his mouth over hers. "Sleep well," he murmured, then pulled the covers over her before slipping from the room.

Chapter 18

Jack sat in his room, staring out the window.

He'd known, of course. It had been obvious for days. But he'd continued to lie to himself, pretending he wasn't aware. Now she'd told him she loved him, and he was saddled with a load of guilt he didn't want or need.

Jack couldn't rid his mind of images from last night, her expression as she'd moaned out her pleasure and called his name. She'd looked utterly trusting, safe, secure. Yet what she wanted from him—commitment, stability, security—he couldn't give. He didn't know the first thing about any of them.

He wished he could snap his fingers and instantly make her hate him. But he couldn't and he'd have to find some way to make it up to her . . .

The necklace. She wanted that more than anything—even him. He had to find it for her. If she had the necklace, she wouldn't need him anymore.

Honoria's only regret when she awoke was that Jack wasn't there beside her. Now, alone with her thoughts, she had to face what had happened.

She caught a glimpse of herself in the mirror. Was this what a fallen woman looked like? A jumble of hair, reddened cheeks, and a self-satisfied expression on her face?

Words couldn't describe what she felt. She was different, yet the same; confident, yet frightened. Frightened, because even though she knew the type of man Jack was, she didn't care, was willing to overlook everything because she loved him.

Did he love her? She didn't know, but realized that it didn't matter, either. He cared for her, and care could grow into love over time. For now, it was enough that he wanted and desired her.

Eventually, they could have more. Once they had the necklace, they could go anywhere, do anything. They could be together without fear or shame.

Honoria could hardly wait.

She felt a twinge of apprehension when she went downstairs at last. What was she going to say to him? She did not think she could even look at him without blushing. But she had to face him eventually; the sooner the better. Guessing Jack would be in the library, she went directly there.

He glanced up when she entered the room and he came toward her with an eager step. Grasping both her hands, he leaned over and kissed her cheek. "You look well rested."

Honoria blushed.

"I've been thinking about you all morning, wondering how you were, what you were feeling." He drew back and searched her face. "Are you all right?"

"I—I feel . . . strange and wonderful at the same time," Honoria stammered. "Is that good?"

Jack chuckled and pulled her close. "Whatever you feel is right, Norry. Although if you continue to wear that cat-who-swallowed-the-cream smile, people might grow suspicious."

Her cheeks reddened again. "Do I really look that way?"

"You look like a woman who's been thoroughly pleasured," he said, running a finger along her jawline. "Beautiful."

Honoria's hands flew to her cheeks. "You make me feel as if I should hide in my room for a week."

"Only if I can be there with you." Jack grinned at her look of surprise. "God, you're adorable." He leaned over and kissed her swiftly, fiercely.

In one night she'd undergone the transformation from girl to woman. And that one night had done nothing to slake his desire for her. Having tasted her passion, he wanted to experience it again and again.

"Jack?" Her soft voice broke into his thoughts. "We have to find the necklace."

He sat back in his chair. "I know. The ball is only three days away. Sir Richard will have to bring the necklace here by then."

"I will talk with the prince," Honoria declared. "Maybe I can persuade him to ask Uncle to bring it out sooner."

"Good idea," said Jack. Kissing the palm of her hand, he pushed her toward the door. "I think it is best if we stay apart today—or everyone will know that we're now lovers."

She blushed and Jack couldn't resist giving her another hug. "I'll talk with you in the drawing room before dinner."

Letting out a deep sigh, Jack walked over to the window. Already, he regretted what had happened last night—not for his sake, but hers. That was the frightening part. Once he started to think of someone else, instead of himself, he'd open the door to all sorts of problems.

He needed to do what she'd hired him to do—find the necklace and sell it. Then he could take his payment, and disappear. She'd be hurt and angry, but she'd feel that way about him eventually, anyway, once she realized that he couldn't ever be what she wanted.

Then he laughed. There was no point in worrying about things now. As far as he knew, the necklace wasn't even in the house yet. His worries would start only when he found it.

After lunch, Jack returned to his room to change his shirt.

The moment he entered his room, something felt wrong. The skin on the back of his neck prickled, a sure sign that something was amiss. But what?

Slowly, he turned around, scanning the room. Nothing looked out of place. He pulled open the wardrobe doors and surveyed his clothing, but everything looked undisturbed.

Surveying the dresser top, he racked his brain to remember exactly how he'd left the toilet things in the morning. Had the razor been to the left or the right of the brush? He couldn't remember.

What could anyone have been looking for in his room? The money he won at cards the other night?

Jack went back to the wardrobe and pulled out his evening coat. He felt along the bottom seam, uttering a sigh of relief when he felt the crackle of paper beneath the material. His money was still safe.

Then what . . . ?

He returned to the dresser and pulled open the top drawer, running his hands over the orderly piles. Socks, handkerchiefs . . . keys.

Keys! The key ring was gone.

Dashing back to the bed, he lifted the mattress, uncovering the wrapped bundle lying beneath it. At least his collection of tools was still safe.

It was possible Honoria had taken the keys back—she'd borrowed them from the butler after all and he might have wanted them. As he left his room to find her, he prayed that was the explanation, even though he had the unpleasant feeling it wasn't.

The prince had taken up residence in the drawing room, and Honoria was not there. Jack finally found her down in the kitchen trading recipes with Sir Richard's cook.

"I thought you might like to take a stroll around the grounds," he said, with deliberate casualness.

She looked at him with such blinding adoration that Jack felt a further stab of regret for what he'd done last night. *Don't look at me like that, Norry. I don't deserve it.*

They went down the front steps and crossed the lawn, walking toward the lane.

"I thought you were going to keep away from me," she said, with a teasing smile.

Jack's face was grim. "I think someone was in my room earlier today," he said.

"How do you know? Were your things disturbed?"

"The ring of keys is gone. Did you take them?"

She halted suddenly, staring at him. "No," she whispered.

He took her arm and drew her along. "I didn't think you did. Which means someone else is responsible."

"Uncle?"

"I think there is a likelier culprit."

"Who?"

"Edmond."

She stopped again. "Why would Edmond want to do such a thing?"

"Because I think Edmond is working with your uncle."

"Jack, you're crazy. Edmond's been helping me from the start."

"I didn't say anything earlier because I didn't want to alarm you. But I found those two having a cozy, late-night chat in the study a few nights ago. They were on quite friendly terms."

"That doesn't mean a thing."

"Think about it, Norry. The paste necklace showed up after we'd searched the study—*after* we told Edmond we hadn't found anything. Two nights later, I find him in secret conversation with your uncle. Now, someone's searched my room and taken those keys. There's too much going on here for it to be coincidence, Norry."

Norry scuffed at the gravel with the tip of her shoe. "I

can't believe Edmond would be working with Richard. I'm paying him to help me."

"Perhaps Sir Richard offered a higher amount. I told you Edmond has debts. He may have sold his services to a higher bidder."

She shook her head. "I cannot believe it. Edmond is my *cousin*. Uncle Richard is nothing to him."

Jack shrugged. "I think it would be wise to be very careful around him in the future. He must not learn any of our plans. If I'm caught with the necklace—"

Honoria wrapped her arms about him. "I won't let that happen."

Jack gathered her against him. "We have to be very, very careful from now on. And not another word to Edmond."

"I won't tell him a thing."

"Did you have your talk with the prince?"

She gave a mock shudder. "I did—and I think I convinced him to talk with Uncle."

He kissed her brow. "Good girl."

They strolled back toward the house. When they came within view of the house, he reluctantly dropped his arm from her waist. He didn't want Edmond knowing about their more intimate relationship, either.

Honoria's words with the prince bore fruit that night after dinner. Shortly after the men joined the ladies in the drawing room, Sir Richard slipped out. When he returned, he set a silken bag before the prince. "Here you are, Your Highness."

The prince untied the string and everyone crowded around to watch as he upended the bag into his hand.

"Good God," said Grose, eying the glittering gems. "The thing must be worth a king's ransom."

"Isn't it exquisite?"

"Surprised Prinny didn't try to buy it."

The prince beamed like a proud parent. Then his eyes lit on Honoria. "*Liebchen,* come here. I should like to see how it looks on you."

Honoria's hand rose to her throat. "Right now?"

"I insist." The prince picked up the necklace and moved toward her. She turned quickly and allowed him to fasten it around her neck.

"Lovely, lovely." The prince took her hand and pressed kisses on her fingers. "I did not think it was possible to improve your beauty, *blümchen,* but with this, you are unsurpassed."

Feigning nonchalance, Jack inched closer. He wanted to get a damn good look at this necklace. If it was the real one, he wanted to know.

"A pity I won't be able to outfit you in such jewels," said Jack, stepping up beside her. "You might wish to find yourself a richer match."

Her radiant smile scorched him to the depths of his toes. "I do not need jewels from you."

Jack reached out and fingered the necklace, then turned to the prince. "It is a masterpiece. You will be the envy of collectors everywhere."

"*Ja, Ja.*"

Honoria glanced at Jack and winked. She unfastened the necklace and handed it back to the prince. "Thank you for letting me wear it." She shot a challenging look at her uncle. "I had forgotten how lovely it was."

"As are you, *Fräulein*."

Sir Richard put the necklace back in the bag. "If you will excuse me, Your Highness, I must return this to a safe place."

The prince nodded and Jack surreptitiously pulled out Honoria's father's watch and checked the time. He should be able to get a better idea of where Sir Richard's "safe place" was by timing his absence.

That was the real necklace and Jack felt a shiver of anticipation at the knowledge that it was now in the house. All they had to do was find it—and not get caught.

Richard returned in less than six minutes. Just enough time to get to the study and back. Jack smiled to himself. He was going to be busy tonight.

It took some time before Honoria was able to talk privately with Jack.

"Was that it?"

"Oh, it's real enough," he said.

"We have to look tonight."

Jack smiled at her enthusiasm. "I will look. You need to keep an eye on Edmond and Richard. I don't want either one sneaking up on me. I'll come to your room later."

"I can hardly believe it is over, at last."

"Believe it," said Jack, with an easy grin. "The fun is just beginning."

The prince wanted to play "vhist" again and Jack was prevailed upon to join the game. He didn't mind; he might earn more. He had to wait until everyone went to bed before he could dare search the study.

He succeeded in his first goal, increasing his winnings

with each hand, but he wondered if he would ever see the end of the game. Every time he tried to quit, someone insisted he continue play. It was long past midnight when the gathering finally broke up.

"Good game tonight," Edmond said in a companionable tone as they climbed the stairs together.

"I can't complain," said Jack.

"What did you think of the necklace?"

Jack shrugged. "It's worth a great deal of money, that's for certain. If it's the real one."

"Couldn't you tell?"

"I'd have to spend more time with it, in better lighting to know for certain."

"You don't think the prince would know the difference?"

"I doubt it. In fact, it might be impossible for me to tell unless I see the two together."

"How do you plan to do that?"

"That's up to Honoria. I follow her lead."

"Well, this scheme can't end too soon for me. I don't need any more high stakes game like tonight."

Jack clapped him on the shoulder. "I'll partner you next time—you'll do better. Good night."

"Good night."

Jack went to his room, intending to make certain everyone was asleep, particularly Edmond, before he stuck his nose out the door.

He prowled his room anxiously, the disappearance of those keys still bothering him. Finally, he pulled off his boots, letting them fall to the floor with a thud. Splashing water on his face to keep awake, Jack counted out his winnings from the night. Another thirty pounds. A few more nights of this and he wouldn't even need Norry's money.

But he knew that it wasn't the promise of money that was keeping him here. It was the chance to help Norry, to provide a future for her. Even if he wasn't going to be part of it.

After another hour of restless yawning, Jack decided that the household must finally be asleep. He pulled on a thick pair of socks and reached for the door latch.

The door was locked. Jack jiggled the handle, but it would not budge.

He didn't need to guess *why* someone had locked him in his room—it was the *who* that worried him.

It would be easy enough to pick the lock, but Jack thought it might be a bit smarter—and safer—if he put off his plans to search tonight. If someone was concerned enough to lock him in, that was incentive enough for him to stay here. If Honoria came to his room, he would have her let him out. Otherwise, he was going to get a good night's sleep.

Chapter 19

Honoria confronted Jack while he was eating breakfast. "Why didn't you come to my room last night? Did you look for the necklace?"

"I had a minor problem. Someone locked me in my room."

"What?"

"The whist game broke up late; I walked upstairs with your cousin and planned to wait in my room until I thought everyone was asleep. When I tried to leave, I found out my door was locked."

"Was it Edmond, do you think?"

"I certainly would like to know."

"This can't go on. We have to find the necklace as soon as possible."

"I agree with that. The sooner I can get away from here, the safer I'll feel."

"I want to come with you when you go to London."

Jack looked at her, dismayed. "I don't think that's a good idea, Norry."

"Why not?"

He fumbled for an excuse. "I don't know where I'll have

to go, or who I'll have to deal with to get the necklace sold. I might have to take the stones out and sell them one by one."

"How long will that take?"

"I don't know." He played with his fork. "That's why it's better for you to stay here until I have your money."

"But what if Uncle discovers that it is missing right away?"

"If you don't have it, what can he do?"

"I don't want to stay here any longer than I have to."

Jack took her hand. "Go back to Nursey's then, or have Edmond take you to his home."

"But how will you find me when you've sold the necklace?"

"You'll have to let me know where you are. I'll give you an address in London—you can contact me there."

"I still think it would be so much easier if I went with you in the first place."

Jack shook his head. "All that will do is increase your uncle's suspicions. We don't want him chasing after you."

"But I don't want him going after you, either. Jack, he could have you jailed."

"Once I leave here, he'll never find me. London is a very big city and I know my way around."

"Do you have to sell the whole necklace right away? Why not sell enough stones to get us to Paris and sell the rest there?"

"Paris may be awash with jewels for all I know. I'll find out when I reach London. You might get a better deal there." He squeezed her fingers. "It's not a bad idea, though. It will arouse less suspicion."

"I'll do whatever you think best."

Jack almost shouted at her in frustration. "This isn't *my* life we're talking about Norry, it's yours."

"You don't want to take me to France with you, do you?"

He cringed inwardly. How could he tell her the truth—that he couldn't bring himself to take her with him? "Of course I do. But, Norry, I can't promise that it will be 'happily ever after,' either. I will not make you any promises that I cannot keep, and I want to make sure that you don't make any decisions thinking that I will."

She looked away. "I understand. You will stay with me only as long as you want to. I'm not asking you for more, Jack. That is enough."

"You are a fool, Honoria Sterling. A darling, adorable fool." He kissed her fiercely. "I don't want to ruin your life."

"You can't," she said simply.

"I already have. I only hope you won't grow to hate me for it."

"I could never hate you, Jack. No matter what you do or what you say."

Jack held her close, but his face was pale. God, why had he allowed such an innocent to fall in love with him? He'd ruined her life already and the longer he allowed her to think there was some future for them, the more damage he caused. Yet he didn't want to give her up, didn't want to let her go. He'd hold onto her until he'd ruined everything for both of them, until he knew that she'd hate him for the rest of her life. Because everything in his life had always ended in disaster.

He stood abruptly. "Let's go outside. We need to make our plans for the ball."

Edmond's eyes narrowed as he stood in the window, watching Honoria and Jack stroll through the gardens. There was something in the way they stood, the light touch of her hand on his arm, the way she glanced up at him when he spoke . . .

They were lovers, he suddenly realized, and a slow smile crossed his face. This was a perfect opportunity. For lovers could easily have a falling out—and the resulting suspicion would only aid him in his own quest for the necklace.

It was time to talk with Sir Richard again.

Edmond found him at his desk in the study. Sir Richard looked up with undisguised impatience.

"What is it?"

"Some interesting news. I think your niece may be contemplating a real marriage after all."

"Oh?"

"I think they're lovers."

Sir Richard looked unimpressed. "You know this for a fact?"

"You only have to watch them for a short while to notice."

"How is this going to help me?"

Edmond sat down. " 'Hell hath no fury like a woman scorned.' I suggest we drive a wedge between them. One might be willing to betray the other."

Sir Richard considered. "You think this Barnhill fellow might turn against her?"

"We can find out. He claims he's merely working for her." Edmond leaned forward eagerly. "See if he's willing to work for you instead."

"This damn scheme is going to cost me money," Sir Richard grumbled.

"I saw that necklace," Edmond said. "You can afford it."

"True, true. I'll have a talk with the man. It'll give me great pleasure to stop that little schemer."

"She's a determined chit."

Sir Richard sneered. "Spoiled is more like it. She thinks she's entitled to everything her foolish father promised her. Where would that have left me, I ask you?"

Edmond smiled. "Women have no understanding of money matters."

"Damn right. And I intend to teach her a lesson she won't forget."

Jack was suspicious and not a little worried when Sir Richard approached him that afternoon and suggested they have a "friendly chat" in the study.

"I'll get right to the point, Barnhill. I'm not convinced that this marriage is the best thing for my niece."

"According to Honoria, you have little to say about the matter."

"Legally, that is true. But since her father did not see fit to appoint a guardian for her, I feel it is my duty to play that role. I feel an obligation to look out for her interests."

Yours or hers? Jack thought. "I admit I am disappointed to hear of your concern. What can I do to reassure you?"

"The only thing that would reassure me is your removal from her life."

"That's a rather harsh suggestion," Jack said, watching Sir Richard closely. Did he know why Jack was here?

"But one that I feel is necessary."

Richard drew out a sheaf of papers and Jack felt a trickle of sweat drip down his back. Good God, what had the man discovered?

"I am prepared to make a sizable . . . deposit to your bank account if you consent to break this engagement with my niece."

Jack stared at him, incredulous. "You wish to pay me to leave Honoria alone?"

Sir Richard coughed. "If you want to put it that way, yes."

Struggling mightily not to laugh, Jack attempted to look interested. "Just how much are you prepared to . . . deposit?"

"A thousand pounds."

A thousand pounds. Nearly twice what Norry had offered him. And money that brought him no danger, would require no effort to earn. Only a fool would say no.

"What conditions do you impose?" Jack asked.

"They are simple. Merely communicate to my niece—in writing, if you please—that you no longer wish to maintain your engagement."

"Do you wish a public announcement as well?"

"I should like to spare the girl the humiliation of that," Sir Richard said. "We can devise some story to explain your sudden absence."

Jack's brain whirled at this turn of events. "Why now? Why didn't you express your concerns earlier?"

"Frankly, Mr. Barnhill, I did not think my niece had any

other option. She is dowerless and not many men would be willing to take such a woman." He darted Jack a pointed glance. "And although I can commend you for your sacrifice, I think it is worth your while to change your mind."

"What will happen to Honoria?"

"You need not worry about that. I will see that she is taken care of."

"This is all rather sudden." Jack tried to look doubtful. "I don't know what to say."

"I'll give you time to think on the matter." He held out his hand. "I don't think I need to remind you not to say a word about this to Honoria. I don't think she would understand."

Jack nodded and left the study, heading directly for the stables. He needed to think and the back of a horse was a good place to do that.

What had prompted this turn of events? Did Richard suspect that the engagement was false to begin with—that Jack was really here to help Honoria find the necklace?

Or, worse, did he know Jack's identity, and figured the easiest way to get rid of him was to pay him off? It avoided the awkward problem of dragging in the authorities. If Gentleman Jack was apprehended at Norcross, the scandal would be enormous.

Either way, Jack didn't like it.

But a thousand pounds. That would last him a long time. He'd be able to set himself up in Paris on that amount. If he could be sure that Sir Richard would really look out for Honoria, Jack would be tempted. It would be the best thing for her—and himself.

For no amount of money could erase the fact that he was still a thief. Norry deserved better than that. If she had searched the entire island, she couldn't have come up with a worse man. Yet the foolish girl was in love with him and Jack didn't know what to do.

A gentleman would do the honorable thing and withdraw. Of course, a gentleman would never have gotten involved with her in the first place.

But there was that nagging doubt about Sir Richard's motive. Did he want to get rid of Jack so he could deal with Norry without witnesses? Did he want to catch Honoria with the necklace?

Either way, she was at risk. And Jack couldn't let her come to harm. He owed her his life, after all.

Still, he would give a great deal to know just what lay behind Sir Richard's offer. The wrong choice might be a life-or-death matter for both Jack and Honoria.

He rode for a long time, but he was no closer to a decision when he returned to the house. He had to do what he thought was best for Norry.

The evening in the drawing room passed in a blur to Honoria. She found it difficult to concentrate on anything now that she knew they were so close to success. Tomorrow night was the ball; the necklace would be there, and if all went well, it would soon be hers.

She could hardly believe that the struggle was almost over. Or that so much had changed. Once she had wanted the necklace so she could live life on her own; now, she wanted it for both her and Jack, for their life together. The little cottage that she once longed for now seemed silly, childish.

How could she have guessed that the bedraggled prisoner she saved from the gallows in Gorton would change her life so dramatically? Or that she would fall top-over-tails in love with him?

Glancing at Jack, she felt a fluttery sensation in her stomach at the very sight of him. As if sensing her gaze, he glanced up and his dark eyes caressed her from across the room. Honoria ducked her head to hide the pink flush that crept over her cheeks. Her body tingled with the memory of how he had touched her, how she had responded to his ardent caresses.

She would go to him tonight, letting him know that she wanted him, needed him. Simply because he was Jack. He needed one person in his life who accepted him for what he was, what he had been. She did not care about the past; it was over and gone. Only the future mattered—their future, together.

The one that started tomorrow night, when they had the necklace.

When he left the drawing room that night, Jack stationed himself at the top of the stairs. He wasn't going to be locked into his room tonight, and he wanted to make sure both Sir Richard and Edmond were in bed before he did any searching. He would rather wait out here than play cards until all hours of the morning.

He saw Grose leave the drawing room, which meant Mayflower and the prince were still at the gaming table.

Jack yawned and leaned back against the wall. This whole evening might be an exercise in futility, but there was too much at stake to ignore the opportunity.

Somewhere, somehow, one of them was going to make a mistake. Jack had to make sure he was there when it happened.

He heard the drawing room door open again and voices echoed in the hall. Cautiously, he stepped back into the shadows. Edmond and Mayflower came up the stairs; Sir Richard chatted with the prince for some time while Jack danced with impatience. Finally, the sound of ponderous steps told Jack the prince was coming up the stairs.

Jack slipped around the corner and waited for the prince to enter his room, then he moved silently down the stairs. He had to find Sir Richard.

A faint breeze brushed against his cheek and he saw that the terrace door was ajar. Jack stepped out of the house. The nearly full moon cast enough light that he didn't need a lantern, but it also meant that Sir Richard could see him if he looked. Jack stayed close to the shrubbery as he searched for Sir Richard.

He saw him at last, striding across the rear lawn. There could be only two possible destinations—the stables or the kennels. Jack prayed it wasn't the latter.

Skulking in the shadows, he kept his quarry in sight. Jack groaned silently when he saw Sir Richard veer right at the stables. He was going to see those damn dogs. Yet Jack felt a thrill of anticipation at the knowledge; Sir Richard wasn't in the habit of paying them a late-night visit.

He heard the dogs' joyous barking when Sir Richard entered their lair. Jack crept around to the back. He couldn't hear a thing above the noise, but it didn't matter.

What was Sir Richard doing at the kennels at two in the morning? Hiding the necklace, perhaps?

In the din from the dogs, Jack almost missed his departure. Suddenly realizing that the yelping had subsided, Jack saw Sir Richard hastening back to the house.

Damn! Jack took off at a lope.

Sir Richard hadn't been in the kennels for long. But it was long enough to retrieve something—or else hide it again.

Jack couldn't get close enough to Sir Richard to see if he was carrying anything, yet he didn't dare search the kennels either; the dogs would wake the dead with their barking. He'd find some excuse to look in the morning.

Once again, Jack sensed that he was operating one step behind Sir Richard. First, there was the paste necklace that showed up *after* he searched the study, then the disturbed trunk in the attic with nothing but underclothing in it. Were the kennels another false lead?

He wouldn't know until he looked.

He waited outside until he saw the flicker of candlelight in Sir Richard's window. Jack wanted to make damn sure the paste necklace was still in the study. It only took him scant minutes to verify that the box was still there.

Back in his room, he set his own candle down on the table and stripped off his clothes, then froze at the faint sound of breathing. Slowly, Jack turned around and scanned the room, letting out a relieved sigh when he saw a shadowy shape beneath the bedcovers.

It had been a long time since a woman had come to *his*

room. And he was torn between sending her away, and taking advantage of her. Again.

Maybe she wouldn't wake, if he just lay next to her, but he would find that sheer torture. He sat down on the edge of the bed.

"Jack?" Honoria whispered sleepily.

"Did you expect someone else?"

Her eyes flickered open and she smiled at him. "I didn't want you to be locked in your room alone tonight."

Even the most honorable man couldn't be expected to walk away now, Jack thought. And he was less honorable than most.

So why did he plan to send her back to her room?

He gave her a quick hug then stood. "Time for you to go back to your room, Norry."

She looked at him, disappointed. Bending over, he kissed the tip of her nose.

"I think you're a bad influence on me," he said, with a wry laugh. "I'm starting to think like a gentleman. And no gentleman entertains a young lady of quality in his room."

"Are you angry?" she asked, her eyes wide.

"Angry?" Jack laughed. "Stupid maybe, but not angry." He wrapped a lock of her hair about his finger. "Humor me, Norry. Let me act like a gentleman now. It's probably the first time I ever have."

He walked her to the door and checked to make sure no one was outside. Then he pulled her into his arms and kissed her again.

"Tomorrow, I want to take a look at the kennels."

"I thought you hated dogs," she murmured.

"I want to know why your uncle went out there in the middle of the night."

She gave him a startled look. "He did?"

Jack nodded. "I followed him tonight."

"Do you think he's hiding the necklace in the kennel? Jack, we must go look."

"And have the dogs wake the entire household with their barking? We'll look during the day. Tell your uncle we want one of the pups as a wedding present."

She hugged him, and slipped away to her room.

If he wasn't careful, he'd end up doing something foolish. She was the kind of woman who could innocently lure him into folly. Now, when he was more than half infatuated with her, Norry could convince him to do anything.

Half infatuated. Jack didn't want to be a half, or a third, or a quarter infatuated with anybody. He didn't want to need her, or care for her.

He had learned long ago that it was better not to care at all than to care too much.

Except it was already too late.

Chapter 20

In the morning, Honoria waited for Jack with barely contained excitement. She tried to pay attention to Mrs. Mayflower, but all she could think about was the kennels, and the possibility that the necklace might be there. If Jack was willing to brave the dogs, he must think they would find it there.

Secretly, she was pleased he'd sent her away last night. That simple act showed he cared for her more than she dared to hope. Jack *was* a gentleman.

When Jack entered the morning room, his face was set in a grim line and Honoria knew he wasn't looking forward to this venture at all.

"Are you ready?" he asked.

She nodded and followed him out of the house.

"What exactly did Uncle do last night?" she asked as they walked across the grass.

"He came out here, ducked inside the kennel for only a minute or two, then went back into the house. He didn't look as if he was carrying anything either time."

Her face fell. "You don't think he hid the necklace out here?"

"I don't know what the hell he was up to." Jack said. "But it looks damn suspicious when it's at two in the morning."

The kennels were a newly constructed building of brick, built after Sir Richard took possession of Norcross. The dogs sent up a rapturous clamor as soon as they spotted Jack and Honoria. She reached over the gate of the first pen and scratched the ears of Sir Richard's prime bitch.

Jack steeled himself to their presence and scanned the interior. If Sir Richard had hidden anything out here, it had to be easily accessible.

There were no trunks of tack or equipment hanging on the walls. In fact, the interior was spare, without any boxes or cabinets. Unless there was a recess behind one of the bricks, Jack couldn't imagine where anyone could hide anything.

Jack ran his hands over the walls, checking for missing mortar or a loose stone. In the corner, at the base of the wall, he found one. Eagerly, he pulled out the brick and stuck his hand into the recess.

Empty.

Jack glanced over at Norry. She knelt in the far stall, cuddling the newest litter of puppies. They crawled all over her skirts, licking her hands and nuzzling her legs. She lifted one and held it up to her face, touching her nose to his.

Jack couldn't tear his eyes away. She looked so happy, so carefree as she played with the boisterous pups. The sight caused a sharp pain in his chest.

This was the kind of life Honoria needed—a placid estate in the country, with nothing more important to worry about than what to serve the guests for dinner, or whether or not she should replace the hangings in the drawing room. She needed a loving husband, adoring children, and even a kennel full of stupid dogs.

She didn't need a dissolute thief who could only offer her a life of exile, insecurity, and hurt.

Honoria looked up, her expression now serious. "Did you find anything?"

"A loose brick—and an empty hole. I can't tell if anything was ever in there."

She stood, brushing the straw off her skirt. "We shall have to keep searching, then."

Jack looked around. "Where?"

"It could be in one of the dog pens."

"Oh, wonderful."

"I'll check the puppies."

Scowling, Jack looked doubtfully at the nearest dog. He held out his hand. "Nice doggie."

The dog sniffed his fingers suspiciously, then sat down, tail wagging. Cautiously, Jack scratched the beast between the ears as he stepped over the railing.

Keeping a wary eye on the dog, Jack kicked at the straw but found nothing more than some well-chewed bones. He moved to the next pen, half-heartedly scuffing his boot in the straw until his toe connected with something hard. Dropping to his knees, Jack pushed away the straw and uncovered a small metal box.

"Norry," he called hoarsely.

"What is it? Did you—oh!"

Jack handed her the box.

"Can you open it?"

"I hope so." He fished in his pocket and drew out a thin piece of metal, which he stuck in the lock, opening it with ease.

Inside lay the same silken pouch Sir Richard had handed the prince last night.

"You open it," Norry said. "I'm too nervous."

She wasn't the only one. With trembling fingers, Jack untied the strings and pulled out the glittering necklace.

"You've done it!" Honoria dropped the box and flung her arms around Jack. "Oh, Jack, you found it."

"Let's make sure," he said and stepped closer to the door. He examined it closely under Honoria's watchful gaze.

Finally, he shook his head. "This is the copy."

He saw her eyes cloud with disappointment. Putting the necklace back in the bag, he relocked the box.

"I find that interesting, since I checked the study last night and saw that the other box we found was still there." He laughed suddenly.

"What is so amusing?"

"What if Sir Richard switched the real necklace with the paste, knowing that we probably wouldn't pay any more attention to the copy?" He shook his head at his folly. "Clever bastard. I should have actually looked at it."

Honoria grabbed his arm. "Let's go now."

Jack stuck the box back under the straw and they struck out toward the house.

"I want you to find out where your uncle is, first," Jack said. He ducked into the morning room to wait for her, and she was back in moments.

"He's in the drawing room with the prince," she announced in a breathless whisper.

"Don't let him leave."

"Jack?"

He turned.

"Good luck."

He grinned. "If I don't turn up in the drawing room in twenty minutes, it's because I'm on my way to London."

"You'll need money." She started to the door. "Let me get some."

Jack patted his pocket. "Your uncle's friends have been making generous donations at the whist table."

He kissed her quickly and headed for the study.

Honoria bit down on her lip in frustration when Jack strolled into the drawing room. He hadn't found it. She hastily excused herself, hoping Jack would follow her upstairs. They needed to plan their next move.

They would have to wait until tonight, now, when Uncle brought out the necklace for the ball. Thank goodness the prince had insisted that she wear it. Somehow, some way, she would get it safely into Jack's hands.

A light tap sounded on her door and she started in surprise at the sight of Edmond.

"I need to speak with you."

"Is anything wrong?"

He paced the room for a few seconds, then turned to look at her. "I don't know how to tell you this . . . Jack Barnhill has made a deal with your uncle."

"What kind of deal?"

"He's not going to help you find the necklace; he's planning to leave Norcross in the morning—with a great deal of money in his pocket."

"Did Uncle tell you this?"

He laughed. "It certainly wasn't Barnhill."

"I don't believe it," she said. "I think Uncle is making the whole thing up."

Edmond took her arm. "Then we must find Jack and ask him."

They found him in the library, engrossed in the paper. Edmond glared at him with undisguised scorn.

"Honoria wants to hear about Sir Richard's offer."

"What offer is that?"

"Don't lie more than you already have, Barnhill," Edmond said. "Tell Honoria what you plan to do."

"What do *you* know about it?" Jack demanded angrily.

"Sir Richard came to me this morning and told me how eager you were to accept his money."

"I'm eager to accept anyone's money," Jack said with a smirking grin. "Tell me, what is he paying me to do?"

"You intend to take his money and leave, don't you?"

Jack laughed.

"Really, Barnhill, I cannot condone this shabby treatment of my cousin." Edmond took a menacing step toward Jack.

"Then why did you tell her about it?" Jack asked.

"Someone had to. You obviously weren't going to say anything."

Jack looked at him coldly. "Stephenson, get out of here, now. I want to speak to Honoria. Alone."

With obvious reluctance, Edmond left the library and Jack locked the door behind him.

"Is it true?" Honoria asked.

"Your uncle offered me a thousand pounds to break our engagement and leave."

She laughed mirthlessly. "Ironic, since we are not really engaged."

"I was more interested in why he thought it necessary to make the offer. Does it mean he knows I'm here to help you find the necklace?"

"How could he?"

"Who's the person who told you about this offer?"

"Edmond." Honoria frowned. "I can't believe he would work against me like that."

"Probably your uncle offered him money, too. We know he needs it."

Norry walked to the window. "If Uncle knows all our plans, there is little point in continuing, is there? We may as well give up."

"I'm disappointed in you, Norry. I never thought you'd want to give up."

"If uncle suspects, you are in terrible danger. I can't let you be caught." Her voice faltered. "Perhaps you should leave."

"You could have a bit more confidence in my abilities."

She looked at him, her blue eyes wide with pleading. "Jack, it's not worth the risk."

"Damn it, Norry, do you think I'll quit now when success is only a few hours away?"

"Uncle won't let you get near the necklace."

"Remember, it's going to be fastened around your pretty neck." Jack ran his fingers lightly across her throat. "All we have to do is switch it for the paste."

"Can we?"

"We only need to divert Sir Richard for a few seconds. Trust me, Norry, the necklace will be yours before the night is over."

Wrapping her arms about his waist, Honoria leaned against him. "I don't want to lose you, Jack—I don't think I could live without you now."

He stroked her hair. "Norry, I can't promise . . ."

She put her fingers over his lips. "I know, Jack. But if I don't ask you for anything, maybe you won't find it so hard to stay with me."

He shut his eyes. It was madness, what she did to him. He lost all his reasoning when he was with her, and he didn't even care. All he knew was that he wanted her more than anything else in his life.

Jack kissed her fiercely, hungrily. While one hand curved around the soft roundness of her breast, the other cupped her bottom, molding her to him. "I need you," he whispered. "God help me, but I do."

Dropping to his knees, he pulled Norry with him, fumbling with the fastenings of her gown as his mouth covered hers. Baring her breast, he lowered his head, mouthing first one nipple and then another as she arched against him.

With their breaths coming in ragged gasps, Jack eased her to the floor, touching her, caressing her. He grabbed her skirt and inched it up her legs, over the tops of her stockings. Stroking up her calf, and her thigh, his hand felt her hot warmth enveloping his fingers as he sought to bring her pleasure.

"Oh, Jack, please," she begged. Her mouth was hot, demanding as she kissed him with fierce intensity.

Fumbling with his pants, he freed himself and nudged her legs apart with his knee and slowly eased himself into her welcoming heat.

"God, Norry, you feel so good." He rained kisses on her face and neck as he thrust into her. She moved with him, challenging his control. He brought his hand between them, hearing her moan at his touch, his own madness growing. He couldn't slow, couldn't restrain himself. She stiffened beneath him and his mouth covered her cry of pleasure as he poured himself into her with long, pleasurable strokes.

Later, he was almost embarrassed to look at her. No other woman had ever had such a devastating impact on his control. He felt as awkward as an untried schoolboy.

He brushed back a damp tendril of hair from her forehead. "I'm sorry, Norry, I couldn't help myself. Did I frighten you?"

She drew his head down for a kiss. "It will take more than that to frighten me, Jack Derry."

He grinned and squeezed her tightly, unwilling to let her go.

Never had he felt this way about a woman. She had woven a spell around him with her innocent ways and now held him fast.

It was going to take every drop of willpower that he possessed to give her up. But somehow, he had to find the strength. Norry needed far more than he could give her.

He almost wished they weren't going to get the necklace tonight; it would give him an excuse to stay with her longer. But the longer he stayed, the harder it would be to leave. He would have to console himself with the thought that once she had the necklace, her future was assured.

"You look so solemn," Honoria said.

Jack laughed uneasily. "I'm merely trying to recover my strength." He gave her a soft kiss and sat up.

Laughing, they straightened each other's clothing and Jack tried in vain to repin her bedraggled hair. At last, Honoria scurried out of the library. Jack waited ten minutes, then he too went upstairs.

While the guests were busy dressing for dinner, Edmond sought out Lady Milburn. She would be a key player in the little drama he and Sir Richard had planned for the night. As long as the necklace was around Honoria's neck, Sir Richard didn't want her out of his sight. Edmond was quite willing to help—it might enable him to get his hands on the necklace himself.

He tapped lightly on her door and she admitted him immediately.

"I need your help," he said.

"Oh?"

"I have come to the sad conclusion that Jack Barnhill is not a suitable match for my cousin."

She laughed lightly. "I didn't need you to tell me that."

"I would like to enlist your aid in proving it to my cousin."

"What can I possibly do to help?"

"Two things. I need to convince Barnhill that Honoria

doesn't care for him—and to show her that he prefers the company of another woman."

"And you wish me to play the role of that other woman?" Her eyes twinkled mischievously.

"If you don't find the idea too distasteful."

She ran a finger down Edmond's shirtfront. "And what benefit will I derive from this little game?"

He grabbed her hand. "The satisfaction of knowing that you've saved a young girl from a terrible marriage."

"And . . . ?"

"The opportunity to lure Barnhill back into your bed."

"It is an interesting proposal. I shall have to think on it."

"I will talk with you again after dinner," Edmond said. "I hope you will want to help."

She will, he thought. As badly as he wanted the necklace, she wanted Jack more. If she diverted Jack tonight, they might both get what they wanted.

Honoria felt like a fairy-tale princess when she floated down the stairs to the drawing room that evening. The rustle of her satin underskirt sounded like music to her. It was going to be a night of magic . . . and triumph. She had pushed all her worries aside. By tomorrow, the necklace would be hers.

Jack's lovemaking this afternoon had taken her breath away. If she had loved him for being gentle and tender the first time. his passionate demands today made her feel desired, a true woman.

Edmond tried to poison her mind against Jack, but she knew him too well, knew that a man who had loved her with such fierce longing could not betray her. Jack would take care of her.

The excited voices from the drawing room drew her attention. Honoria uttered a quick prayer. *Please, let everything go all right.*

When her uncle brought out the necklace, Jack would retrieve the copy from the kennels. Then all she had to do was get away from Sir Richard long enough to make the switch. As long as there was a necklace around her neck, Sir Richard would never suspect they'd try something so audacious.

By tomorrow, it would all be over.

And just beginning, as well.

In the drawing room, the prince beckoned her to join him.

She curtseyed before him. "How are you tonight, Your Majesty?"

"*Gut, gut.*"

His beady eyes roamed over her form and Honoria wished she could flee.

"You will allow me the first dance tonight, *liebchen, ja?*"

"Yes, Your Majesty. It would be an honor."

He leaned forward and whispered, "I know how to dance the *waltzer* that you English find so shocking."

"I regret that I do not. But I am sure Lady Milburn does. You two could demonstrate for us all."

"What? You do not know how to waltz?" Jack had came up behind her and put a possessive hand on her shoulder. "We shall have to remedy that before we go to town in the spring, darling."

With a curt bow to the prince, he guided her away.

She looked at him curiously. "Do you know how to waltz?"

"I've never seen the dance in my life," he said, grinning wickedly. "But if it's as scandalous as they say, I'm sure I'll enjoy it."

Edmond approached them, a disapproving look on his face. "Don't you think you are acting in an overly familiar manner, Barnhill?" He looked pointedly at Jack's arm, which was still draped over Honoria's shoulder.

"After all, we are engaged," Jack said. "I think people will allow us a few signs of affection."

"But *I* know it is only a ruse," Edmond said, in a low undertone. "You are seeking to take advantage of the situation—and my cousin."

"I am?" He looked down at Norry, a smile on his lips. "Do my attentions discompose you, sweetling?"

Norry smiled up at him. "Not at all."

Edmond glowered. "I'm going to keep a close eye on you, Barnhill. I mean to protect my cousin." Edmond stomped off.

"Interesting," said Jack. "He almost sounds jealous."

Then Jack remembered what Sir Richard had told him yesterday: "I will see that she is taken care of." Did he mean that Edmond wanted her?

The thought seemed unlikely, given Edmond's indifference toward his cousin, but Jack couldn't forget those first days at Norcross, when Edmond had acted like a jealous lover.

It didn't matter. Jack knew whom Honoria truly loved. And he felt a surprising sense of smugness in knowing that she had chosen him over her more respectable cousin.

Only the Norcross house guests and a few select neighbors sat down to dinner; the others from the neighborhood would only be attending the ball. Jack wished the preliminaries could be dispensed with so they could get on to the important event of the night—switching the two necklaces.

There was no lingering over the after-dinner port tonight, with more guests arriving. Jack stood back and watched as Sir Richard greeted them, Norry at his side. These had been her neighbors, after all.

Each guest was in turn introduced to the prince. To Jack's amusement, they all seemed visibly impressed by the royal presence.

He wandered about the ground floor rooms that were set up for the guests. The drawing room was as bright as day and awash with a moving rainbow of color from the ladies' gowns. There were enough jewels in the room to satisfy the greediest thief. But there was only one piece Jack wanted; only one piece he had to have.

Stepping back into the hall, Jack felt the familiar surge of energy that preceded a job. He was on edge, his senses heightened. Voices sounded loudly in his ears, the swirls of color blended before his eyes and the candlelight flared. He felt the strange, sickening tightening in his stomach.

He was ready.

Standing beside her uncle, Honoria strove to mask her

impatience. Even greeting her old neighbors did not calm her. All she could think about was the necklace . . . and Jack. Tonight was the night. They would succeed, she knew it; she felt it in her heart.

It would take exact timing to accomplish the switch; if anyone saw, she and Jack were sunk. But because she trusted him, believed in him, she knew he would find a way.

A footman handed her a tall flute of champagne and she took a few nervous sips. Nearly all the guests had arrived; the musicians tuned their instruments. At any moment, Uncle Richard would fasten the necklace around her neck. He could not know how that would please her.

Chapter 21

At last, Sir Richard broke away from greeting guests and disappeared toward the back of the house. Nervously, Jack licked his lips. It was starting.

He lingered in the hall, chatting with one of Sir Richard's neighbors, waiting for Norry's uncle to return. If, as he suspected, Sir Richard wanted to keep a close eye on him tonight, Jack wanted to keep an even closer eye on Sir Richard.

The sound of steps on the stairs startled Jack, and he turned to see Sir Richard descending. Jack greeted him with an amiable smile.

"Your party already looks to be a success," Jack said. "My congratulations."

"Thank you. Have you thought more about that matter we discussed?" he asked casually.

"I am interested in your offer, Sir Richard."

"Good." He held out his hand. "I'm glad you've decided to see things my way, Barnhill."

"One more thing"—Jack stepped in front of Sir Richard—"I want to know your plans for Honoria."

"You don't need to worry about her; I'll see that she is taken care of."

"Shall we finalize things tomorrow, then?" Jack asked. "I want to get this over with quickly."

"I will meet with you in my study at—say—nine?"

"That will be fine."

Jack followed Sir Richard into the drawing room, watching avidly as he strode over to the prince. Sir Richard murmured something to the honored guest and handed him a small bundle.

The necklace.

The prince beckoned to Honoria and she walked to his side, standing calm and steady as he fastened the gems around her neck. Jack admired her cool aplomb. She acted as if wearing a fortune around her neck was an everyday occurrence. When the musicians struck up a rousing country dance, the prince led Honoria onto the dance floor.

Jack edged toward the door. Crossing the hall with studied nonchalance, he stepped outside into the refreshingly cool night air. Halting for a moment, he allowed his eyes to adjust to the dim light before he rummaged in the shrubbery for the meat scraps he had wheedled out of the kitchen maid. Then he hurried toward the kennels.

The dogs sent up a tremendous roar of barking when he entered the kennels. Reaching into the bag of scraps, he flung them as quickly as he could into each pen until the barking subsided. Taking a deep breath, Jack held out a mutton bone as further enticement and stepped into the pen where he'd found the paste necklace that morning. Squatting, he rummaged through the straw, breathing a deep sigh of relief when he found the box. He quickly picked the lock, then lifted the lid, uttering a swift prayer as he did so.

Thank God it was still here.

He dumped the necklace out of the bag and quickly stuffed a few bones inside to replace the weight. Slamming the lid shut, Jack locked the box, and replaced it under the straw. Seconds later, he strolled casually toward the house, the paste necklace in his pocket.

Now, to find Norry.

He entered the hall again and grabbed a welcome glass of wine from a serving table.

Lady Milburn stepped beside him and touched his arm. "You are not among the dancers?"

"I'm afraid not."

"Won't Miss Sterling be disappointed?"

Jack smiled. "I plan to dance with her eventually. But what of you? You will not lack for partners."

"These boring country squires? I have no desire to have my toes trod upon."

"Ah, but there is always the prince."

"Or you."

Jack saw the blatant invitation in her eyes. "How can you be so certain I won't step on your toes?"

"I seem to recall dancing with you when we last met. It was not . . . unpleasant."

Jack bowed and held out his arm. Since she wouldn't go away, he might as well dance with her.

Edmond now partnered Norry and Jack gave her a brief wink as they came down the set. He saw the answering delight in her eyes that told him she was as excited as he.

The set with Lady Milburn lasted an interminable time. He wanted Honoria for his partner, wanted it to be her hand he clasped, her face he smiled at. Jack breathed a sigh of relief when he finally joined Norry.

He made a formal bow before her. "May I have this dance, Miss Sterling?"

She held out her hand. "Of course, Mr. Barnhill." They took their place among the other couples.

"You look exquisite tonight," he said, when the steps of the dance brought them together. Never had she looked more beautiful to him. Her blue eyes sparkled with anticipation and her cheeks were flushed with heat and excitement.

"Thank you. You are quite handsome, as well."

Jack grinned. "That is a lovely necklace you are wearing."

"It is, isn't it?" She fingered it lightly. "A family heirloom, you might say."

"I have it," he whispered softly.

Honoria missed a step and Jack reached out a hand to steady her. "Easy now."

She darted him an apologetic smile. "I fear one of my slippers has come untied."

"Then by all means, you must retie it." Jack led her off the floor to one of the chairs ringing the room. He knelt before her and fumbled with her shoe with one hand, palming the necklace with the other.

"Quickly, Uncle's coming over."

"Bend over."

She did so and Jack stuffed the paste necklace into the bodice of her gown.

Jack barely had time to unfasten her laces when Sir Richard came up behind him. "Is anything wrong?"

"My slipper came untied," Honoria said. "I didn't want to trip while I was dancing."

He nodded. "Good idea." He stood by patiently while Jack retied the laces.

"Perhaps you will honor your uncle with a dance?"

"Of course." Rising, she smiled apologetically at Jack and followed her uncle.

If only he could get her away from Sir Richard for a few minutes. Then the necklace would be theirs.

Edmond watched the interplay with narrowed eyes. There was no question Honoria and Jack were up to something. Despite her surface air of calm, Honoria was agitated. And even Barnhill lacked his usual devil-may-care attitude.

He couldn't believe they would try to steal the necklace in plain view of everyone at the ball. No, they would wait, and make their move later. Then Edmond would relieve his insipid cousin of the prize.

Still, he wanted to make certain Honoria and Jack were kept apart, just in case they had something audacious planned. Smiling slyly, he went looking for Lady Milburn. It was time to enlist that lady's help once more.

Jack darted an infuriated glance at Lady Milburn as she approached him again. Couldn't the infernal woman take no for an answer?

She clamped her hand on his arm. "I think it is time for a breath of fresh air. Join me for a stroll outside."

Remembering what had happened last time, Jack tried to disengage her hand, but she resisted his efforts. Reluctantly, he allowed her to lead him onto the terrace and into the darkened garden.

"This has been an interesting visit," she said. "So many things going on, and many of them not what they seem."

"Oh?"

"Yes. Take your engagement, for example."

"My engagement?" Jack feigned innocence.

"I've been told it is a sham; a story devised to please Sir Richard."

"Why would I wish to perpetrate such a scheme?"

"Money, perhaps."

Jack had to laugh. *Everyone* thought he could be bought. "Whoever told you a thing like that?"

"Oh, the story has been bandied about."

"Stephenson?"

"He might have mentioned it."

Jack frowned at this bit of news. Everything always came back to Edmond. "Why should he think that would be of any interest to you?"

"He might have intended it as a measure of comfort. To let me know that my hopes were not completely impractical."

"Your hopes? What are those?"

"That we could see each other again. You will be in town this fall, will you not?"

She stopped suddenly and wrapped her arms about his neck. "Kiss me, Jack." Without waiting for his answer, she rose on tiptoe and pressed her mouth to his.

* * *

When the dance ended, Sir Richard led Honoria from the drawing room.

"I have something I wish to discuss with you," he said. "Let's go to the study where we won't be overheard."

"I really don't think—"

He took her arm. "Now, Honoria."

Unwilling to create a scene, Honoria meekly complied, acutely conscious of the heavy necklace lying between her breasts.

"I own, Honoria, that I have not been easy these last days. I've been worried about you."

Honoria tried to quell her stab of panic. "Worried?"

"Yes, worried." He frowned. "I do not think that Jack Barnhill is the right man for you."

She laughed. "I don't see where you have any right to an opinion about it."

"I am the head of the family, and I know my brother, bless his soul, would never forgive me if I let you come to harm."

Honoria stifled a bitter laugh. "I am in no danger, Uncle. And I do not see a long line of men waiting to court me."

"There is *one* man I know who would make you a fine husband."

Honoria looked at him skeptically. "Surely, you don't mean that German buffoon?"

Sir Richard smiled. "I imagine he might be brought around if that's what you wish. But no, I was thinking of someone with closer ties to the family. Your cousin, Edmond."

"Edmond?"

He nodded. "He was utterly shocked when you announced your engagement to this Barnhill fellow. And if a man's friend cannot approve of the marriage, what does that tell you about the prospective groom?"

Her eyes narrowed suspiciously. "When did Edmond ever express any reservations about Jack?"

"Oh, he spoke of his concerns when you first arrived. I urged him to be patient until I could take the measure of the man myself. But alas, I fear I have to agree. He is not the kind of man for you, Honoria."

"Don't you think I'm the best judge of that?"

He patted her hand in a patronizing manner. "Women do not always act in their best interests. That is why it falls to the men of the family to make arrangements for them."

"This is ridiculous."

She started toward the door, but Sir Richard grabbed her arm. "The man's a gambler, Honoria. I've seen it in his eyes when he plays cards. He'll always be in trouble."

"Perhaps I'm a gambler also."

"Does it interest you to know that I offered him money to break your engagement?"

She looked at him coldly. "He told me."

"Did he also tell you that he accepted? And he will be leaving Norcross in the morning?" Sir Richard's expression softened. "I know it is hard to believe that of a man you've trusted, Honoria. But you have to accept the truth."

"I really don't care what you think about Jack. I choose to trust him." She turned to go.

"This is your last chance, my dear. If you throw in your lot with him, I won't come to your rescue later."

As if he ever would. Honoria gave him a brittle smile. "I will remember not to appeal to you for help."

She almost collapsed with relief when she stepped into the hall. Uncle hadn't suspected what she carried; now she only had to switch the necklaces. And find Jack.

Honoria darted across the hall to the deserted morning room. It would only take her a few seconds to change necklaces. But before she could even reach up to undo the clasp, Edmond appeared at her side.

"There's a rather sordid encounter occurring in the garden that I thought you might take an interest in."

"Oh?" She eyed him coldly. "And why do you think I would be interested?"

"Mr. Barnhill is one of the participants."

Honoria didn't need to guess the lady's identity. Or why Edmond wanted her to know about it.

She gave an indifferent shrug. "I really don't care."

Edmond followed her back into the drawing room, but she deliberately turned her back on him. Honoria had nothing more to say to her cousin.

Jack had been right about Edmond—he was definitely trying to cause trouble. It had taken all her willpower not to slap Edmond across the face. If Jack was in the garden with Lady Milburn, he either had a very good reason, or he'd been lured out there as part of Edmond's machinations. Why else had her cousin been so eager to tell her?

Honoria had no doubts about Jack's feelings toward her, and nothing Edmond or her uncle said would make any difference. She loved him, and trusted him, and that was all that mattered.

* * *

Jack reached up and gently disengaged Lady Milburn's hands from his shoulders. "Tell me, are you doing this on your own initiative, or were you encouraged?"

He heard her sharp intake of breath. "How can you prefer her to me? What can she possibly offer a man like you? She knows nothing of the world."

"Perhaps I have developed a preference for innocence in my old age."

"She also has no money. Need I remind you of the *generous* allowance Toddy gives me?" She laid a gloved hand on his arm. "I don't want you to throw yourself away on some starry-eyed chit who cannot give you one-tenth of what I can."

She pressed her lush curves against him. "Take me, Jack, now."

"Some other time." Jack pushed her roughly away and stalked off toward the house.

Something very strange was going on. He wanted to talk with Honoria, to warn her that Edmond was up to something. Pushing his way through the crowd in the hall, he entered the drawing room.

Honoria was there, dancing again. Jack's eyes darted to the necklace around her neck. Was it the real one—or the paste? Had she managed the switch?

Jack leaned back against the wall, arms folded across his chest, and watched her and her partner circle the floor. The moment the music ended, he stepped up to her side.

"I believe this is my dance?" He took her hand and led her away.

She smiled with relief. "Where were you? I was terrified. Uncle Richard dragged me into the study and I thought for certain he knew what was going on."

"What did he want?"

"To tell me what a poor match you are for me."

Jack laughed to cover his consternation. "Your uncle and I do think alike on some things."

"Jack!"

"We need to switch the necklaces."

"I've noticed that either Uncle Richard or Edmond is constantly at my side. They aren't going to leave us alone together."

"I'll deal with them," Jack said. "As soon as you have the chance, switch the necklaces."

"What do I do with the real one?"

"Put it where the other one is now." He grinned wickedly. "It will be a joy to retrieve."

When the dance ended, Jack handed Norry over to her next partner and hastened off to set his plan in motion.

He found a red-faced and angry Lady Milburn in the morning room, picking at some sweetmeats.

"I know someone put you up to that scene outside," he said. "How would you like to turn the tables on him?"

Lady Milburn looked at him, suspicious.

"Look," said Jack, "Stephenson has been sticking his oar into everyone's business the entire time he's been here. I think it's time he had a taste of his own medicine."

"What did you have in mind?"

"A little note would be appropriate, inviting him up to

your room for a chat. All I need you to do is keep him there for ten or fifteen minutes."

"How?"

Jack grinned. "I think you could find a suitable excuse—and a willing partner."

Lady Milburn licked a smudge of sugar from her finger. "Very well," she declared.

Jack grinned. "There is paper in the library. Write your note and I'll see that it is delivered."

"With pleasure."

Once the note was in his pocket, Jack looked around for a footman. He found one at the supper table and handed him the note, then sauntered back into the drawing room, casually approaching Honoria, who was sitting out the set.

"About five minutes after your cousin leaves, I'm going to create a diversion." He nodded a greeting to Mrs. Mayflower. "For God's sake, switch the necklaces as fast as you can. I don't know how long I can keep Sir Richard away."

She nodded.

"I'll worry about how to get it from you later." He watched as the footman came in and handed the note to Edmond. Jack nudged Honoria and they both watched Edmond read the note, then head for the door.

"Five minutes," Jack reminded her, then walked boldly to where Sir Richard stood chatting with one of the guests. Positioning himself so that Sir Richard could not get a clear view of Honoria, Jack smiled warmly.

"I've been thinking that I'd like to have one or two of

your pups to take back to Yorkshire," Jack said. "What kind of prices are you asking for them?"

Sir Richard stared at him. "You want some of my dogs?"

Jack nodded. "I'm not real keen on dogs, I'll admit, but I know a good investment when I see it. I imagine there's a few packs back home that would be interested in bringing in some new blood."

"Well, to tell you the truth, Barnhill, I hadn't planned on selling any of the new litter."

Jack squirmed with frustration. Would he be too obvious if he glanced over his shoulder to see if Honoria had managed to get out? "Oh? Why is that? Don't you think they'll be good breeding stock?"

"They are excellent animals," Sir Richard said, sputtering with indignation. "That's one of the reasons I want to keep them. Thought I might try to put together another pack of my own."

"I'm sorry to hear that. I was looking forward to having those dogs. Now that I have the money to afford them." Jack chuckled and managed to catch a glimpse of Norry's empty chair. Good girl!

Sir Richard smiled thinly. "Perhaps you'd be interested in some of the yearlings? They're green, of course, but that's no different than a pup. This way, you'd have a better idea of what you're buying."

Jack nodded agreeably. "That's acceptable." He darted a quick glance at the door, praying Lady Milburn still detained Edmond. "Why don't we go look them over?"

"Now? Good God, man, I can't leave now. We'll do it tomorrow."

Smiling sheepishly, Jack shifted slightly, putting the door in better view. Shouldn't Norry be back by now? "What about preparing them for travel? I suppose they need some sort of crate."

"If you hire a post coach, they won't need to be crated," Sir Richard said acidly.

Jack grinned. "Guess I can afford to do that too, can't I? But what about—uh—you know, the mess?"

Sir Richard gave him a scornful look. "I have found that newspapers work quite well."

"Oh, yes, I hadn't thought of that. Good idea." Jack felt the sweat trickling down his back as he struggled to prolong the conversation. He had to give Norry enough time. "What do you recommend for feeding?"

"Mr. Barnhill, I do have other guests here tonight. Perhaps we could continue this discussion tomorrow?"

Jack bobbed his head. "Certainly, certainly. Just one more thing—have you named them yet?"

Sir Richard appeared dumbfounded. "Of course they have names! How could I call them, otherwise?"

"Would the dogs be too confused if I changed them? I would rather name my own dogs, you know. It's, well, a personal thing. I'm sure you understand."

"You can call them by any goddamned name you want," Sir Richard said in a low, menacing tone. "Just get the hell out of here and leave me alone."

Jack backed away with an abashed expression, inwardly roaring with laughter.

The sudden look of alarm on Sir Richard's face as he scanned the room cause Jack's grin to fade. *Hurry up,*

Norry. Sir Richard stormed toward the door, but just as he opened it, Norry came in with Edmond beside her.

The moment Jack stepped up to Sir Richard, blocking his sight of the room, Honoria dashed for the door. She must work quickly.

Frustrated by the number of guests milling about the hall, she darted into the dining room, but it too was full of people. Frantically, knowing that time was running out, she pulled open the door to the library. It was dark, and deserted.

Leaving the door ajar, she fumbled with the clasp to the necklace, her trembling fingers making it all but impossible. At last, the catch opened and she practically jerked the necklace from her neck. Setting it on the floor, she pulled the paste copy from her bodice and hastily fastened it around her neck.

She almost slipped the real necklace back into her bodice, then hesitated, realizing it would be far simpler for Jack to dash in here and retrieve it. Lunging for the nearest chair, she slipped it under the cushion. Then, patting her hair as if she had merely stepped into the library to adjust her coiffure, she walked back into the hall.

Edmond nearly collided with her at the drawing room door. His face was red and he was out of breath as if he had been running.

"Goodness, Cousin, what is the matter?"

He stared at her as if disbelieving her presence. "You're here."

"Where else would I be?" She wrapped her arm

around his. "I think it is time for you to dance with me again."

Jack sucked in his breath at the sight of Edmond with Norry. Did that mean Lady Milburn hadn't kept him upstairs long enough? Had Norry been able to make the switch? She had to have done it. He didn't know how he was going to divert Sir Richard again unless he set the house on fire.

As if he wished to deliberately heighten Jack's anxiety, Edmond led his cousin out onto the floor. Jack watched them with narrowed eyes, knowing full well that he couldn't tell which necklace she was wearing, but irrationally hoping he could.

Glancing across the room, he saw the smug expression on Sir Richard's face. Jack prayed that it was a false smugness and that he and Norry would have the last laugh tonight.

The moment the dance ended, Jack was at Norry's side, pulling her into the new set that was forming.

The minute she squeezed his hand, he knew that she had done it. He wanted to sweep her up in a crushing hug right there in the middle of the drawing room. Instead, he maintained a serene composure.

"Your uncle is going to sell me two of his dogs," he announced brightly.

"What?" Norry looked at him in puzzlement. "Oh, that is what you were talking to him about. How clever."

He twirled her around. "Perhaps after this dance, you will let me take you in to supper."

"I am not particularly hungry. If you wish to sit down,

I suggest you go to the library, instead. The chairs there are much more comfortable."

"Are they, now?" Jack looked at her with frank approval. They would not have to risk an exchange, now. "I shall have to try them for myself. Thank you for the suggestion."

She gave him a radiant smile. "I think you will be well pleased."

"No more than I am now," he said, clasping her hand as she circled him again.

Lingering in the drawing room after their dance, Jack tried to appear the very picture of casual ease, even though his heart pounded in his chest. He was only seconds away from success and he was not going to do anything to jeopardize his next move.

Seeing Lady Milburn come back into the room, Jack walked to her side. "May I take you in to supper?"

"Why, thank you, Mr. Barnhill."

"What happened?" he asked her in a low undertone.

"He seemed suspicious from the first. I did what I could."

Jack smiled at her. "You did just fine."

He filled plates for both of them and they joined the Mayflowers at one of the small tables in the morning room.

After eating a few bites, Jack stood. "If you will excuse me for a moment, I have a little matter to take care of."

Lady Milburn waved him away.

Checking carefully that no one paid him any attention, Jack walked into the library. After waiting a few moments to make sure no one followed him, he stuck his hand under the nearest chair cushion.

It was almost too easy, he thought, as he pulled out the gems, but he wasn't going to complain. He dropped the necklace in his pocket and went back to the morning room, taking his chair beside Lady Milburn again.

He couldn't leave Norcross yet; it was too early and Sir Richard might notice if he left the ball too soon. He'd hide the necklace in a safe place for the next few hours, then retrieve it when he was ready to go. If Sir Richard realized what had happened, Norry would be in real danger. Jack wanted to make sure she was safe before he left.

Stifling a yawn behind her gloved hand, Honoria struggled to keep her eyes open as the clock struck three. As nominal hostess, it was her duty to remain downstairs until the last guest left, but she did not think she would last that long.

Silently, she willed the guests to leave. Despite her protestations, Jack wouldn't leave until he knew that Sir Richard had accepted the paste copy as real. He had made no move to take it from her and Honoria feared it would be dawn before he allowed her to go to bed.

Finally, she decided to take the initiative. Screwing up her courage, she approached her uncle.

"It has been a lovely party, but I cannot stay awake for another minute," she said. "I know you want to have the necklace back before I go upstairs to bed."

Sir Richard held out his hand. Unfastening the necklace, Honoria handed it to her uncle with icy calm, hardly daring to breathe when he slipped it into his pocket.

"I should like to have another chat with you tomorrow, after Mr. Barnhill leaves," he said.

Honoria nodded and kissed his cheek. "Good night."

She winked at Jack as she left the drawing room.

Chapter 22

Hastening to his room, Jack quickly changed out of his evening clothes, pulled out his portmanteau, and began stuffing his possessions into it. The mail coach left Cirencester at half past six and he intended to be on it. He'd be halfway to London before anyone realized he was gone.

At the soft click of the door latch, Jack whirled about. Edmond stood in the doorway, a pistol in his hand.

"Planning a journey?"

Jack continued to cram his clothes into the bag. "I told Sir Richard I would go. I'm keeping up my end of the bargain."

"Did he already pay you? How providential." He raised his pistol. "Empty the bag."

"Afraid that I'm taking the family silver?"

"I'm not worried about the silver. I want the necklace."

Jack calmly folded a shirt. "I think you'll have to talk with Sir Richard about that. It's his, after all."

"Don't play the fool with me, Barnhill. I know you have it."

Jack laughed. "You have a better appreciation for my talents than I do. All I was able to find was the copy."

Motioning with the gun, Edmond took a step closer. "Empty the bag, man."

"Are you planning to give it to Norry? How very thoughtful of you."

Edmond laughed harshly. "I've no intention of giving it to her. I'm going to take it."

"Maybe I should stay, then," said Jack. "Sir Richard promised me that she'd be taken care of."

"Oh, I'll take care of her all right. She might prove to be an amusing companion—for a while. What do you think? Will I enjoy her?"

Jack's fists clenched.

"I must admit, that surprised me," Edmond continued. "You don't strike me as the kind of man with a taste for virgins. Or weren't you the first?"

"You'll never know," Jack said evenly, itching to smash Edmond's face.

Ed smiled maliciously. "I'm eager to discover if you broke her in properly. Empty the bag."

With an indifferent shrug, Jack dumped it out onto the bed. Edmond stepped forward eagerly and Jack swung the empty bag at him, knocking the pistol to the floor, and swiftly kicking it under the bed.

"Now we're even," he said, and they circled each other warily.

Jack leaped forward, plowing his fist into Edmond's stomach. He doubled over, grabbing his middle and gasping in pain. Jack's fist connected with his jaw and

Edmond slumped to his knees. Another blow knocked him to the carpet.

Grabbing a shirt, Jack knelt beside the dazed Edmond and hastily bound his hands together and then stuffed a sock in his mouth.

"You really need to spend some time in a boxing saloon," Jack told him. "That was a pretty pitiful performance."

Edmond glared at him, then kicked out with his foot and smashed Jack on the shin.

Swearing, Jack landed a swift kick of his own to Edmond's knee and the man grunted in pain. Jack took a cravat and tied his legs together.

"There." He stood and admired his handiwork. Then he hastily repacked his clothes and shut the bag.

"I imagine they'll find you eventually," he said, and started for the door. He stopped suddenly. "I almost forgot." Bending down, Jack retrieved the pistol from under the bed.

"It's a pity there are so many guests about tonight," Jack said. "I'd take great delight in shooting you." Seeing the fear in Edmond's eyes, he laughed. "Yes, you're really a prime specimen of English respectability, aren't you? Trying to steal from your cousin and her uncle at the same time."

Sticking the pistol in his bag, he left the room, carefully locking the door behind him.

Slipping out onto the dewy grass, Jack squinted into the darkness, then struck out toward the stables. Even the stable lads weren't awake at this hour, which was just as well. Working silently but quickly, Jack hastily bridled and saddled one of Sir Richard's prime hunters.

He led the horse through the stable yard, wincing at the sounds of the hoofs striking against stone, then across the lawn, and well down the drive. Jack stopped and looked back at the house, picking out Norry's window. Regret tore at him; regret for what might have been, regret for what could have been, if he wasn't the kind of man he was.

"Good-bye, Norry," he whispered to the night. Then he mounted and urged the horse forward without taking a backward glance.

He arrived in Cirencester with enough time to eat a hearty breakfast before the Mail arrived. He'd been able to buy an inside ticket, and apart from the unpleasantness of being cooped up in a coach for hours, he looked forward to the journey. For the first time, he felt a twinge of doubt about the wisdom of leaving Honoria behind. Would she have been safer with him? He missed her already and he tried to convince himself that he was doing what was best for both of them. The break was easier this way.

Who was he kidding? It was easiest for him. Walking away without saying good-bye was a cowardly act.

Just the type of thing Gentleman Jack would do.

When the coachman's horn played out its merry tune, Jack was already in the yard, standing to one side while the hostler waited with the horses. The Mail swung in, the spent horses were quickly unhitched from the traces, the new ones brought to the poles, and Jack climbed inside. He took his seat, the coach lurched forward, and they were out of the yard and on their way.

He patted the comforting weight of the necklace in his pocket. There was one thing he could do for Honoria.

Honoria was awakened at eight by a loud pounding on her door. "Who is it?" she called, eagerly.

"Your uncle."

Norry pulled on a wrapper over her nightclothes and opened the door.

"Where's Barnhill?" he demanded.

"I assume he's asleep in his room."

Sir Richard frowned. "Someone took one of my best horses this morning before the stable hands were up."

"I thought you wanted him to leave. Weren't you going to pay him to do so?"

"Not with one of my horses. And I haven't paid him yet."

"Then no doubt he will return. I can't imagine anyone turning down a thousand pounds."

Sir Richard's eyes narrowed. "He told you?"

"Edmond did."

"I can't find your cousin either," Sir Richard muttered.

Honoria tried to look concerned. "Perhaps it was he who took the horse. Could he have met with an accident?"

"I'll look into it," Sir Richard grumbled.

Once awake, Honoria could not go back to sleep. She paced her room restlessly, knowing that with every passing moment, Jack traveled farther away from her uncle's grasp.

Finally, she dressed and went outside, welcoming the cool morning breeze on her flushed face. It was too hard to contain her excitement in the confines of the house. She wanted to run, and laugh, and dance for joy.

Instead, she contented herself with a brisk walk to the stables. She couldn't help but look at the kennels. Already, finding the paste there yesterday seemed like a lifetime away.

Which in a way, it was. Now that Jack had the necklace, her new life had begun.

She hugged herself. As soon as he sold the necklace—or enough of the stones to give them plenty of money—he would send for her. From London, they would go to Paris and then the whole world was open to them.

Honoria met Uncle Richard in the hall when she entered the house. His face was red with anger.

"What's wrong?" she asked, the first stabs of fear licking at her.

"He took the horse all the way to Cirencester!"

"Who?"

"Barnhill."

"Jack is a skilled horseman. I'm sure your horse is fine."

"I know he is," her uncle grumbled. "He's back in the stables now."

"Jack?"

"No," Sir Richard said with exasperation. "The horse."

"I don't know why you are complaining to me. Talk with Jack."

Sir Richard halted at the foot of the stairs. "He's gone."

"Gone?" Honoria tried to look puzzled.

"He sent back the horse, with a note extending his

apologies for abusing my hospitality. And he didn't even ask for his money." He paused. "Something is not right here."

Honoria followed him up the stairs. "What do you mean?"

"Barnhill's gone and your cousin hasn't been seen all day."

"Maybe they eloped."

"Don't be flippant, Honoria." Sir Richard strode down the hall and knocked on Jack's door. Getting no answer, he tried the knob. "It's locked. Honoria, ring for Plummer. Have him bring his keys."

Honoria complied, praying that she was doing the right thing.

Sir Richard stormed the corridor with mounting impatience. "Where is that man?"

Plummer arrived at last. "Sorry to take so long, sir," he said with an apologetic smile. "I had to find the spare set."

Sir Richard jerked the ring from his hands, inserting the key in the lock. Pushing open the door, he stepped into the darkened room and stumbled over Edmond's bound form.

"Good God, man, what happened?" Sir Richard pulled out the gag and Edmond sucked in several lungfuls of air.

"That bastard! He tricked us all."

Richard knelt and untied Edmond's hands and feet, then helped him up. Edmond staggered to the bed.

Sir Richard handed him a glass of water. "Tell me what happened."

"I kept my eye on Barnhill all night. I followed him up here and found him packing his bags."

"Isn't that what you wanted him to do?" Honoria asked her uncle.

"I tried to stop him . . . He fought like a madman. It's a miracle he didn't kill me."

"Why would Jack want to kill you?"

"He has the necklace," Edmond said bitterly.

"Are you sure?" Sir Richard asked. "Did you see it?"

"No," Edmond admitted. "But why else would he be in such a hurry to run out of here?"

With a stricken look, Sir Richard dashed out of the room.

Honoria could hardly conceal her glee. Their plan had worked and Jack was safely gone. Smart, clever, wonderful Jack.

She gave Edmond a scornful look. "Jack was too much for you, was he?"

Edmond jerked her toward him. "This is all your fault. You're going to pay for my loss."

"Your loss?" She laughed. "You didn't have anything to lose."

He slapped her across the face. "You stupid bitch. Do you really think I was here to help you? I wanted that necklace as badly as you did."

Her hand flew to her stinging cheek. "You traitor."

Edmond sneered. "I'm not the only one. Do you really think he's planning to come back for you? You'll never see him again, I promise you."

"I trust Jack. Unlike you, he won't cheat me." She glared at her cousin.

Sir Richard came into the room, a bleak expression on his face.

"The necklace is gone." He pulled a silken sack from his pocket. "This is the copy."

"Barnhill took it," Edmond said flatly.

"He seems the most likely candidate," said Sir Richard sourly, then darted Honoria a dark look. "Unless it was you."

"Really, Uncle, I know you're upset, but how could you even suggest such a thing?"

"Don't act stupid, Honoria." Edmond glared at her. "Your uncle knows all about your little plan—and that Barnhill was working for you."

"You have no proof that Jack has the necklace. You want to blame him because he isn't here to defend himself."

"Then why did he knock me down when I tried to stop him?" Edmond demanded.

"What right did you have to be in his room in the first place?"

"Mark my words, he took it." Edmond's expression darkened. "And I'm going to get it back if I have to hunt him all over the island."

"How do we know you don't have it, Edmond?" Honoria demanded. "I think we should search *your* room."

"Stop this wrangling!" Sir Richard shouted. "*I* will decide what to do."

"We should go after him," Edmond said.

"Don't be a fool, Stephenson. He's long gone."

"Then what are we going to do?"

"While the prince is still here, this has to be kept quiet." He looked coldly at Honoria. "I shall tell the company you are indisposed. Edmond, take her to her room."

Edmond jerked her arm and pulled her toward the door.

"Lock her in," Sir Richard added. "I want her to stay put."

When they reached her room, Edmond pushed her roughly down onto the bed. "Give me your room key," he demanded.

"Try and find it."

Edmond appeared to take great delight in pawing through her things, dumping the contents of her drawers on the floor while he searched for the key.

"Aha!" He raised it triumphantly. "See you later, Cousin."

He shut the door behind him and Honoria heard the click of the key in the lock.

Honoria sank into a chair before her knees buckled under her. She really wished she was adept at swooning faints; it would be a welcome relief to collapse. Instead, she buried her face in her hands.

Everything depended on Jack now. She reassured herself that he had taken the necklace for both of them.

But how could she go to him if Uncle Richard kept her a prisoner? She had to get out of here somehow while the guests were still at Norcross.

It was late afternoon when she heard the key turn in the lock.

Sir Richard entered. "You and Barnhill must have made some arrangements to meet. Is he coming back for you or were you to go to him?"

Honoria stared at him, keeping her expression innocent. "Since I didn't know he was leaving, I made no such plans."

"Don't play the fool with me. Your cousin's kept me informed of your plans since the beginning. I know you both came here to steal that necklace."

"Since Edmond claims to know so much, why don't you ask him how to find Jack?"

Sir Richard looked thoughtful. "You will have made some plan . . . Unless he really intends to keep the necklace for himself. That would displease me greatly."

"Perhaps he will contact you. You did promise him that money, after all."

Sir Richard headed for the door. "I'll send your dinner up," Sir Richard told Honoria.

"What, no bread and water?"

"I will talk with you again tomorrow, Honoria. Maybe you will decide to be more cooperative after a night's sleep."

Honoria smiled blandly. She was glad Jack had insisted she memorize his London address. Uncle would never get it from her.

She remained locked in her room all that day and the next. Uncle came twice each day, but she continually claimed she knew nothing. Edmond brought her food and also tried to coerce her, but she refused to even speak with him.

On the third day, Uncle himself brought her breakfast.

"Dress for traveling," he said. "We are leaving in an hour."

"How nice. I look forward to a change of scenery."

"You could make this easier for yourself if you would cooperate."

"I cannot tell you what I don't know."

He shrugged. "As you wish."

In exactly an hour, Edmond came to her room. "Let's go."

"Are you coming with me? How nice. Does Uncle plan to tell everyone that we have eloped?"

"You will wish that we had before the day is over."

He clamped his hand on her arm so hard she knew it would leave bruises, and pulled her down the rear stair.

The coach was drawn up outside the stables. Edmond pushed her inside and climbed up next to her. "Your uncle will be along in a minute."

Honoria deliberately turned her back on him and stared out the window until Edmond snapped the shade down. When Sir Richard arrived, the carriage started down the lane.

Honoria knew it was pointless to ask where they were going. She doubted they would tell her. Perhaps she could guess as the journey progressed.

They drove through Cirencester, which told her they traveled east. Would they be going to London? Surely, they didn't think they could find Jack in that city.

But an hour from Cirencester, the carriage turned off the turnpike and jounced down a smaller lane. After crossing a stream, the road climbed a small hill, then leveled out. They halted at a gatehouse while the iron gates were flung open, then proceeded only a small distance before stopping in front of a gracious manor house.

"Dare I inquire where we are?" Honoria asked.

Edmond snickered.

"A place where you can repent on your sins in private," Sir Richard said.

As they walked toward the house, Honoria examined its facade more carefully. Iron bars covered the windows.

A burly footman opened the door and they stepped into the hall.

"Tell Mrs. Jenkins that Sir Richard Sterling is here."

Honoria surveyed the entry hall with a puzzled expression. It was completely bare of ornamentation or furniture. She looked at her uncle. "Where are we?"

Sir Richard gave her an icy smile. "Welcome to the Spring Meadow asylum, Honoria dear. It is to be your home . . . until you decide to be more cooperative."

Sleep did not come easily to Honoria that night. Although it was not cold, she shivered and drew her blanket closer. Through the undraped window, pale moonlight shone through the bars, casting stripes upon the bare wood floor.

She was not frightened. So far, it was little different than staying at a very inhospitable inn. Twice, they had brought her food, plain, but palatable.

But after being locked in her room for three days at Norcross, the solitude here was wearisome. In her own room, she at least had her sewing and her books. Here, there was nothing to break the monotony. Thinking was her only occupation, but fortunately, that could occupy her for weeks.

Somehow, she had to get word to Jack, to warn him. She feared that when he didn't hear from her, he would go to Norcross, and Uncle would be waiting.

Jack was her only hope of rescue. The irony of the situation amused her. After rescuing Jack, he now had to rescue her. She prayed it would be soon, dreading the endless days of isolation before her.

This was not at all how she thought it would turn out when she'd taken Jack from the gallows. Her easy success there led her to believe the entire adventure would be accomplished with ease. Part of it had. But now it had grown far more complicated than she could ever have anticipated.

Because she had not anticipated falling in love with Jack. And because she had, she had handed her uncle a very potent weapon. But as long as she remained strong, it did not matter. She would never tell him where to find Jack.

All she had to do was wait for Jack to come to her. That he would, she had no doubts. The only question was how long it would take.

Chapter 23

After a week at the asylum, Honoria grew accustomed to the monotonous routine. As a "guest," she was allowed more freedom than the other patients—twice-daily walks outside and a reading period in the library.

But it didn't take the strange, late-night howling from the woman across the hall, or the now-familiar click of the key in her door lock to remind Honoria that she was a prisoner in a mental asylum. And that her uncle was the jailer.

Returning from her afternoon walk in the high-walled garden, the dutiful attendant at her heels, Honoria was surprised to find the matron waiting for her at the door.

"You have a visitor."

Honoria's heart quickened. Could it be Jack? Had he discovered what Uncle had done and was here to rescue her?

Her hopes came crashing down when she saw Uncle Richard waiting in the parlor. He motioned for her to sit.

"Are they treating you well?"

She looked at him coldly. "You have no right to keep me here."

"That situation could be remedied in time." He handed her a letter. "This came for you."

Honoria unfolded the paper and read the note.

Norry—it was an enjoyable time, but all good things must come to an end. A lovely lady like yourself will not be alone for long. Accept these earrings as a gift and wear them in memory of your first lover—Jack.

She looked up and Sir Richard set two earrings in her hand. Honoria didn't have to look closely to see that they were cheap trinkets.

"As you see, my dear, there is no honor among thieves. Your partner has cheated you."

A roaring sound filled Honoria's ears. She felt strangely light-headed and there was a rolling, queasy sensation in her stomach. She looked again at the words on the paper, but she could no longer make them out as her vision blurred. It was as if they were written in a strange foreign language, one that she could not understand.

Jack had taken her necklace. He'd betrayed her. She had trusted him, relied on him, and he'd failed her.

Just like everyone else.

She sank her head into her hands and wept. Not for herself, but for what might have been. For all her shattered dreams and plans. And she wept for Jack. He'd stolen more than the necklace, and her innocence. He'd also taken her heart—and smashed it to pieces. Deliberately, callously, thoroughly.

Uncle Richard was right. There was no honor among thieves.

"When did this arrive?" she asked hoarsely.

"Yesterday." Sir Richard formed a steeple with his fingers. "Now that you have seen how he betrayed you, do you still wish to keep his whereabouts a secret?"

"No."

"Good. I will go after him. When I have my necklace back, you may go free. Now tell me where he is."

Dully, Honoria recited the address she had committed to memory.

Sir Richard jumped to his feet. "I'm glad you have finally seen reason." He started toward the door, then halted. "I hope you continue to enjoy your stay here. I will do what I can to make it short."

In a daze, Honoria followed the attendant back to her room.

How could she have been so wrong about Jack? How could she have been so incredibly, laughably, unbearably foolish to think she could trust a man who was nothing more than an elegant thief?

Honoria had prided herself on the cleverness of her plan, while all the time Jack had been laughing at her naivete, plotting his theft while he cozened her into thinking he cared. When in reality, Jack Derry cared about no one but himself.

She still had the power to destroy him. If she told Uncle who Jack really was . . . But even now, knowing what he'd done to her, Honoria couldn't bring herself to sentence him to death. Losing the necklace would be punishment enough for Jack.

Jack sat hunched over the wobbly table in his shabby

room, his night's gambling winnings spread out over the scarred surface.

He'd done well—again. His bank account grew daily, and it wouldn't be long before he could leave for Paris.

Two weeks, he decided. He didn't want to stay in London any longer than necessary. After all, there was gambling in Paris as well, and for even higher stakes, if the stories were true. It was time he sold Honoria's necklace and left.

He hadn't tried to sell it yet—either individual stones or as a whole. Instead, he'd taken it to the bank his first day in town. It had taken longer than he'd planned to decide how to dispose of it properly. But he thought he'd found the right man at last.

Yawning, he scooped the money off the table and stuffed it into a leather pouch. Placing it under his pillow, he sat down on the edge of the bed and pulled off his boots. He'd have another nice deposit for his bank account tomorrow. Enough, in fact, that he could afford to dine in elegance tomorrow night. That thought cheered him as he climbed into his narrow bed.

It was past noon when he awoke. Throwing on his clothes, Jack ambled down the street toward the tavern where he ate most of his meals. The food was decent, for the price. He could do worse. After eating he'd pick up his new coat from the tailor. No more secondhand clothes for him.

Jack winked brightly at the barmaid when he entered and sat down at his usual table in the corner. She knew what he wanted.

Someone had left a day-old copy of the *Chronicle*. Jack

passed over the advertisements and scanned the "Scenes From High Life" column, looking for any familiar names. But with the Allied celebrations over, everyone had left for the country—or Paris.

The barmaid returned, with a brimming mug of ale and a cold meat pie. Jack nodded absently, engrossed in reading the articles from the Paris papers. He needed to cross the Channel, quickly, before the opportunities vanished.

While he ate, Jack continued reading. During his first days in London, he'd devoured the papers, starved for news of the city. But once he'd learned what had changed, and what was still the same, his interest waned. He wasn't going to be here long, after all. Paris was the place that concerned him now.

Skipping past the shipping column, Jack skimmed the rest of the news, looking for any interesting tidbits.

" 'ere's a letter arrived for you."

The barmaid tossed it onto the table.

Jack took it eagerly. It had to be from Honoria; no one else would write to him here. He tore it open and scanned the contents.

The page fell from his trembling fingers. Something had gone wrong. Terribly, horribly wrong, and it was all his fault.

Picking up the letter, he read it again, more slowly this time. He could barely believe her words. Honoria, locked in an asylum as if she were a madwoman. Jack trembled with rage. It was Sir Richard who should be locked up for what he had done to her.

Never once had Jack thought that she'd be trapped in her own web. That was the reason she'd hired him—to make sure suspicion fell outside herself. But by leaving her behind, he'd caused her to become tangled in the net set for him. While he sat in the Thorn and Bush in London, free to come and go as he pleased, Norry remained locked in some provincial hellhole.

Jack froze.

Or was that what Sir Richard wanted him to think? If she really was in an asylum, Honoria never could have sent this letter on her own. Had Sir Richard forced her to write this?

If so, that meant Sir Richard had this address and could be looking for Jack right now.

With an oath, Jack grabbed the letter, scattered a handful of coins on the table, and raced out into the street, nearly colliding with a crossing sweeper. Reaching his rundown building, he mounted the steps to his room three at a time, and didn't stop until he pulled the door shut behind him.

He had to get out of here. Now.

Pulling open a drawer, he scooped up the contents and flung them onto the bed, turning back to empty another just as quickly.

He needed something to put everything in. Sticking his head out the door, Jack whistled loudly. In a few minutes, the youngest son of the landlady peered up the stairs.

"I need a valise," Jack shouted at him. "Can you find one for me?"

"How far's yer rent paid up?" the urchin demanded.

Damned sod was as greedy as his parent.

"Through Friday," Jack retorted. "Go ask your mother if you don't believe me."

"I'm supposed to ask," the lad said, climbing the stairs. "How big you want?"

Jack looked the boy over doubtfully. "The biggest you can carry," he said at last and gave the boy some money.

Thank God he'd decided to wait until he arrived in Paris to get more than the mere necessities of a new wardrobe. He could cram what little he had into a plain traveling valise. When the brat returned, he'd send him down to get a ticket on the Dover Mail. With luck, Jack could be out of the city by late afternoon.

As soon as that damn boy returned, and went for the Mail ticket, Jack would have to go to the bank and withdraw most of his money. He'd leave some behind, for emergencies. He could have the rest sent to him, in Paris.

And the necklace. He had to get the necklace.

No, he thought, he'd leave the necklace where it was. No one would ever find it there—Richard Sterling didn't know Jack's real name and he'd be safer traveling without it. Without a necklace, there was no proof of what he'd done. No proof at all.

Except a completely sane woman locked up in a madhouse in Gloucester.

Jack could not leave her there.

He pulled out his watch. Norry's father's watch, the one she'd given him the day after their arrival at Norcross.

If it hadn't been for Norry, he'd be lying in a pauper's grave in Shropshire, surrounded by the eternal blackness that awaited him. Jack didn't think there was a heaven, and he'd already spent his time in hell.

Which was what he'd consigned her to.

He shuddered to think what would happen—what

might have already happened—to her. He had barely kept his own sanity in the common room of a prison. How would Honoria ever keep hers?

Jack sank down onto the bed, burying his face in his hands. He couldn't let her stay in an asylum. It was his fault she was there, and it was his responsibility to get her out.

At least he had the means to do so. He had a bargaining piece that Sir Richard definitely wanted. Jack would make him a trade—the necklace for Honoria's freedom. He didn't think Sir Richard would object to that.

He might try to have Jack arrested. But that would be part of the deal—Sir Richard would get the necklace only if he agreed not to pursue either of them.

Jack didn't want to go to Gloucestershire. He wanted to take the Mail to Dover, climb aboard a ship, and sail across the Channel to France, forgetting England, Sir Richard, the necklace, and Honoria. But he knew that it was impossible. He'd never be able to forget Honoria now if he didn't help her.

Instead, he'd buy a ticket on the Gloucester Mail, hire a horse when he arrived in Cirencester, and confront Sir Richard Sterling at Norcross. Jack had to, for Norry's sake, or he'd never be able to live with himself.

The Mail left at half past five in the morning, but Jack awoke at three, unable to sleep any longer. He didn't mind; the nightmares that had invaded his brain made waking a relief. The thought of Norry in trouble tore at his soul.

There was no sleeping on the trip; he'd had to settle for

an outside seat. The weather was mild but it could have poured rain for all Jack cared. Each milepost rolled by with excruciating slowness; every change of horses seemed to take hours.

He felt he'd been traveling for a week when the coach finally slowed on the approach to Cirencester. Jack scrambled down the moment it halted at the inn yard, and dashed inside. Within minutes, he'd made arrangements to hire a horse, deposited his gear with the landlord, and downed a quick mug of ale and a slab of bread and cheese.

It was shortly after five when he rode out of town in the direction of Norcross. If all went well, Honoria could be free soon—tomorrow, even.

If all went well. Things could still go wrong. Sir Richard could have him arrested and there wasn't much Jack could do to save Norry from inside a jail. He laughed wryly. This time, she wouldn't be able to come to his rescue.

His only leverage was the necklace. As long as Sir Richard didn't have it, Jack had a chance. He'd make damn certain Honoria was free before he handed it over.

As he drew closer to Norcross, Jack's agitation increased—along with his guilt. If he had taken Norry with him, as she had asked, this never would have happened. As a result, he was going to have to give the necklace back to Sir Richard.

But that task would be easy compared to facing Honoria. She would say it was all his fault, and she would be right. She'd hired him to save her future, and he'd failed miserably.

A conscience was a damnable thing to have; it meant one wasn't free to do what came easiest. The easy route for Jack led toward Paris. The tough road lay ahead. A year ago—even two months ago—he wouldn't have given it a moment's thought. Now he was trapped by his guilt.

Guilt that by leaving Honoria behind, he'd implicated her in the theft. Guilt that he'd allowed her to fall in love with him, when he knew he didn't deserve her love.

The shadows were lengthening when he reined in the horse at the top of the drive. Some instinct for preservation made him dismount there, and tie the horse to the hedge. If he had to leave Norcross quickly, he didn't want the dratted animal in the stable.

Steeling himself for the ordeal, Jack walked across the lawn and up the front stairs. His knock on the door brought a loud yelping and howling from inside the house.

The dogs. The damn dogs were inside the house this time. The door opened and they rushed past the footman, sniffing at Jack's boots and nuzzling at his hands.

"I need to see Sir Richard," Jack said, trying to control his urge to run.

The footman nodded and led him into the hall. In a few minutes he returned, and silently escorted Jack to the study.

"Ah, Mr. Barnhill." Sir Richard stood behind the desk. "I wondered if I would see you again."

"I have a proposition for you," Jack said.

"Indeed?" Sir Richard pointed to a chair. "Please be seated. I should dearly love to hear your proposal, Mr.—

ah—Barnhill. I assume that is the name you are going by?"

"Where is Honoria?"

"Such a touching display of concern. I didn't know there was such honor among thieves."

"Honoria has not stolen anything."

Sir Richard sighed. "Not in the technical sense, no. But the law draws no distinction between the perpetrator and the instigator. My necklace is gone; she hired you to steal it. Therefore, she is guilty."

"I'm sure the law also takes a dim view of passing off fake gems for real."

"Do not be tiresome, Mr. Barnhill. Do you think anyone cares about the frivolous purchase of some obscure German prince?"

"Is she in an asylum?"

"What else was I to do with her? I didn't want the public scandal of having her arrested, but I certainly didn't want her in this house any longer."

"Send her to her great-aunt, then."

"Lady Hampton?" Sir Richard laughed. "It would be more appropriate for her to join my niece in that asylum."

Jack knew Sir Richard wasn't going to make it easy for him. "What if your missing necklace is returned? There would be no reason to punish your niece further."

Richard's eyes gleamed. "I'm afraid it's not so simple as that. The whole incident has caused me a great deal of distress, not to mention expense. The facilities at Spring Meadow are not inexpensive." His eyes gleamed. "I would hate to have to transfer her to a public asylum for lack of funds."

"If you release her, the necklace will be returned to you."

"The handsome thief comes gallantly to her rescue? It sounds very much like a fairy tale."

"One that could have a happy ending for all parties."

Richard eyed him with a speculative look. "I would have to have the necklace in my possession before I could even think about arranging Honoria's release."

Jack shook his head. "When Honoria is taken out of the asylum, the necklace will be returned."

"You admit then that you have it?"

Jack shrugged. "I may know the person who does."

Richard stood and leaned over the desk, his palms on the surface. "Then I suggest you tell him that if the necklace is not in my hands by six tomorrow evening, I'll make absolutely certain that my niece doesn't set foot out of that house—unless it's on the way to Bedlam."

Jack stared at him coldly, although he wanted to wrap his hands around Richard Sterling's neck. "When Honoria is free, the necklace is yours."

Sterling nodded his head in agreement. "I'm glad you've decided to be sensible, Barnhill."

Chapter 24

They quickly settled the arrangements and Jack slipped out of the house. He didn't relish riding to Cirencester in the dark, but he had no choice. He wasn't going to spend the night at Norcross. Somehow, he didn't think Richard Sterling would invite him to stay. Besides, Jack had to make arrangements for Honoria.

He would be lucky if she even spared a word for him, after what he had put her through. Would she ever believe that he had meant it for the best? That he had left her behind in order to protect her, not betray her? Jack cursed himself thoroughly for having dragged her into this. He would spend the rest of his days regretting that choice.

It wouldn't take long to ride to Gloucester tomorrow, but Jack wanted to be there as early as he could. He needed to find a place to make the exchange on the following day. Sir Richard had agreed to let Jack choose, and he wanted to do it carefully. He didn't want to walk into a trap; Richard Sterling wasn't a man to be trusted.

Despite his weariness, Jack slept poorly. He couldn't stop imagining Norry in the asylum, what she must be feeling, thinking.

How she must hate him.

He would leave for Paris as soon as this was over. It was more important now than ever that he left the country. There wasn't anything left for him in England now.

Once again, he wished he could turn back the clock to that fateful day in Gorton. And pray that she arrived too late this time.

Jack was up before the hostler, and waited impatiently in his room until he heard sounds from the stable. Without waiting for breakfast, he departed.

Upon reaching Gloucester, Jack slowly rode through the streets of the ancient city, looking first for the inn where he was to leave his messages for Sir Richard. He found it easily enough. Now, Jack only needed to decide on a meeting place. At first, he thought to use a small, out-of-the-way hostelry, but the more he considered it, the more he realized that a bustling posting house would better suit their notions of privacy.

It would be better for Honoria, too. Jack had no illusions that she'd be willing to come with him, but he knew he had to keep her someplace safe. Nursey's was the ideal location, and he'd be able to make the arrangements for Honoria's journey at the inn.

Only for a moment did he dare to hope that she would agree to go with him to Paris, and the idea fled from his mind as quickly as it came. He was not that much of a fool to pin his hopes on the impossible—or the ridiculous. Norry didn't want the kind of life he could offer her. He'd only bring her further grief.

After locating a suitable inn, Jack dispatched a note to

Sir Richard and continued looking until he came to a smaller, simpler place a short distance away. Here, he stabled his horse and tried to eat something. It was not an easy task with his insides churning with apprehension and anticipation.

If it wasn't for Honoria, he could have handed the necklace over to Sir Richard last night and his troubles would be over. But from the moment he'd read those awful words in that letter, Jack knew he had to rescue her. She might never thank him for it, but he couldn't live with himself if he walked away.

Pushing his chair back from the table, Jack rose and strode out of the taproom, leaving most of his meal uneaten. He wandered aimlessly about the streets of Gloucester. At another time, he might have even appreciated his ancient surroundings, but all he felt now was an overwhelming sense of impatience and gloom.

Honoria looked up in surprise when she heard the matron's key in the lock. Her eyes widened at the sight of her uncle, standing in the doorway.

"It appears there is some honor among thieves after all," Sir Richard said. "Your friend is back."

Jack? Jack had come back? Her first leap of joy was replaced by a dull pain. For what? To make her humiliation all the more painful with the reminder of what a fool she'd been?

"You're coming with me," he said.

"Why?"

"Think of yourself as a bargaining chip," he said as he motioned for her to follow him. "He has something I want and you're my means of obtaining it. We've arranged a trade."

"You're going to let me go?"

Her uncle nodded. "Once I have the necklace back, there's no more reason to keep you in here. You're free to leave with your thieving friend."

Honoria halted suddenly. "I will not be going anywhere with him."

Richard smirked. "You may decide that issue among yourselves. My objective is to regain my property."

My property, she thought dully. But now, she no longer cared. When Jack had betrayed her, taking the necklace for himself, he'd ripped away all her cares and desires. Nothing mattered anymore. Not the asylum, not the necklace, not Jack.

Blinking against the bright glare outside, Honoria followed her uncle to the waiting carriage. Uncle climbed inside, refusing to help her. Honoria scrambled up the steps and the jailer slammed the door shut. The coach lurched forward, flinging her onto the seat.

Honoria stared in bewilderment at the cloaked woman sitting next to her uncle. Who was she?

Then comprehension dawned. The woman's chestnut-colored hair explained the entire situation. She looked coldly at her uncle. "You're going to trick him, aren't you?"

Sir Richard smiled. "How observant of you, my dear. Yes, two can play this game of deception and lies."

Honoria laughed bitterly. "It's only what he deserves."

Sir Richard lifted a brow. "What, no words of sympathy for your lover?"

"No."

"A pity you didn't think so clearly before. You could have avoided this entire, sordid mess."

Honoria lapsed into silence. Hadn't she already told herself that a hundred times over? But she couldn't go back and undo what had been done. She would live with her mistake for the rest of her life. The only bright spot was that it probably wouldn't be very long.

"Are you sending me back to the asylum?" she asked dully.

Her uncle nodded. "I had to remove you—in case he had someone checking. But my friend here"—he patted the hand of the lady beside him—"she will play your part in this little drama."

"You don't think he'll notice?"

Shrugging, Sir Richard drew a pistol out of the compartment in the door and tucked it in his pocket. "It won't matter. I firmly intend to take back my necklace."

In a way, Honoria was relieved. It mattered little if Uncle Richard let her go. With no money, no home, and no hope for either, her life outside prison wouldn't be lengthy. She could swallow her pride, go down on her knees, and beg her distant relatives to help her. They might be willing to offer her some assistance. Enough to keep her alive, for a time. Otherwise, she had very little hope. Stealing or selling her body were her only choices, and neither would keep her alive for long.

Was this how Jack felt in Gorton? she wondered listlessly. Knowing that there was no hope ahead, had he welcomed death on the gallows as a way to end the pain?

No, she thought suddenly. She wouldn't allow him to

defeat her, too. She'd survive—because she had to. Because she wanted to. If only to show him that she could.

Jack paced anxiously across the inn's yard, darting glances at the entrance, waiting for a glimpse of Sir Richard and Honoria.

If the necklace had felt like a lead weight in his pocket earlier, it now felt like a ship's anchor. If he didn't need to rescue Norry, he would gladly have left it on the table at Norcross. But to save her, he had to play this out to the end.

He glanced again at his watch. Five more minutes.

He wished he had the funds to hire a coach to take her to Nursey's. Instead, she'd have to do with a seat on the Mail. She could make most of the journey today; he'd send along money to pay for a night's lodging, and renting a gig to get to Nursey's. He'd see her safely away before he left for London.

He'd already reserved her a room at this inn. He didn't know what condition she would be in. True, it was a private asylum, but that might not mean much. Surely she would want—and need—a bath and a change of clothes. He'd found her a plain but serviceable dress at one of the secondhand clothiers. He hoped Sir Richard would send the rest of her things to her.

A carriage pulled into the yard and Jack shrank back against the wall. But the man who stepped down was a stranger and he relaxed for another moment.

He tensed again when another carriage pulled up in front of the inn. Peering around the entry pillar, Jack held his breath as he saw Richard Sterling step down, then turn to assist a woman from the carriage. She was wrapped in a hooded cloak, and Jack couldn't see her face, but the wisp of chestnut hair that strayed from the hood told him who it was.

His heart pounding in his chest, Jack stepped back behind the post and watched as they approached the inn. He'd left a note inside telling Sir Richard to meet him in the private parlor. Jack wanted to make certain Sterling hadn't brought along additional men.

But he and Honoria were quite alone. Jack watched as they both disappeared through the side door. He deliberately restrained himself and counted slowly to two hundred before he made his way across the yard.

A trickle of sweat rolled down his back as he stepped through the entryway. They were in the third private parlor, as one walked toward the back of the inn. Jack scanned the corridor for any suspicious loiterers, but only a maid with an armload of sheets was in sight. Taking a deep breath, he walked down the hall and opened the door to the parlor.

Sir Richard stood before the window, looking out onto the street. Norry sat slumped in a chair, her face hidden in the shadows of the hooded cloak she still wore. Jack ached to reach out and pull her into his arms, and knowing that he couldn't caused an even deeper ache.

Sir Richard turned slowly. "So," he said, "you're here at last."

Jack nodded and shut the door behind him.

Richard gestured toward Honoria. "You see my niece, free from jail. I've carried out my part of the bargain. How about yours?"

Jack glanced at Honoria, wishing she'd look at him, finding it maddening not to be able to meet her eyes. Yet it was for the best, he told himself. He wouldn't want to see the hatred and condemnation in those blue depths when she confronted him.

"First, sign this." Jack thrust a folded piece of paper at Sir Richard.

"What is this?" Richard scanned the paper with a frown. "This wasn't part of the agreement."

"Sign it, or there is no agreement." Jack gestured impatiently. "I don't want to take the chance of you changing your mind."

Sir Richard shrugged. "Whatever you say." He reached for the pen on the table, dipped it into the ink, and signed the paper, whereby he admitted that Honoria Sterling wasn't involved in the theft. He handed it back to Jack.

"Satisfied?" he sneered.

"Norry?" Jack walked over and extended the paper. "This is for you. Your uncle can't put you into prison again."

Wordlessly, she took it from him.

"The necklace?" There was an edge of impatience to Sir Richard's voice.

Jack untied the waist pouch hidden under his coat. Pulling it free, he turned toward Sir Richard, only to find a pistol pointing in his face.

"Very slowly," Sir Richard said. "These damned hair triggers, you know."

Jack straightened. Sir Richard reached out his free hand and grabbed the pouch, then tossed it to Honoria. "See that it's there," he said harshly.

Jack stared in wonder as the woman slipped back her

hood. The hair was the exact shade, but the face wasn't Norry's. He whirled on Sir Richard. "What have you done with her? Where is she?"

"Back at Spring Meadow by this time, no doubt," he said with a smirk.

"You bastard."

"Oh no, I assure you, I'm quite legitimate. And ready to apprehend the notorious thief who conspired with my niece to rob me. Just think of the excitement a double hanging will bring. The merchants of Gloucester will thank me."

Jack struggled to control his breathing. He had to get out of here—and he had to let Sir Richard think he didn't care. "You've certainly got the advantage," he said, in mocking tones. "I salute you for your cleverness."

"The necklace's 'ere," said the woman.

"Thank you for your assistance, my dear. Put it on the table and you're free to go."

Eying him warily, she crept to the table, set the necklace down, and slipped out the door.

"Does the magistrate meet us here, or are you taking me to his doorstep?" Jack asked.

"He'll be meeting us at the jail," Sir Richard said. "I wanted to take care of this quietly."

"One more thing." Jack strove to keep his voice light. "Did Honoria's father really leave her the necklace?"

"Do you accuse me of stealing from my own niece?" Sterling laughed. "A foolish girl has no need for a necklace as valuable as this. My brother was a fool."

Jack smiled grimly. Norry had been right. It made him angrier than ever that he had to give the thing back. He'd like to take the jewels and cram them down Sir Richard's throat.

Frantically, he tried to remember the layout of the inn. The corridor outside led to the rear stairs, he knew. Was there a rear door as well? And would Richard Sterling dare a shot inside the inn? Jack didn't know the answer to either question, but he would have to take the chance.

With the gun, Sir Richard gestured toward the door. "You first, my friend."

Jack reached for the door handle. All depended on surprise, speed, and luck. It was the latter he needed most, and luck was the one thing he'd always seemed short of.

But it didn't matter. The worst thing that could happen was Richard Sterling would kill him. After spending five months in prison, Jack knew that being dead could have its advantages.

The door swung inward and Edmond stepped into the room, clutching a pistol. He held out his hand to Sir Richard. "I'll take that necklace now, if you don't mind."

"What?"

Edmond sneered. "You don't think I'm going to let it get away from me this time?"

"How dare you, Stephenson!" Sir Richard started toward the door.

Edmond cocked his pistol. "The necklace, Sir Richard."

Eying him warily, Jack edged closer to the door.

Edmond swung around, training his pistol on Jack. "Don't move, Barnhill. You still have a part to play here."

Jack held up his hands defensively. "I don't want any trouble. I brought the necklace back; you two can fight over it."

"No," Edmond said, a cunning look in his eyes. "You and Sir Richard are going to fight over it. A fight to the death, I may add."

"Open the door, Barnhill," Sir Richard commanded.

"Don't move," Edmond said.

This is ridiculous, Jack thought. Tensing suddenly, he flung back the door and bolted to the left. A pistol shot echoed in the hall as Jack sprinted down the back corridor. He was at the stairs now and dodged to the right. Booted steps sounded behind him and Jack knew if there wasn't a door, he was done for.

Loud footfalls sounded on the stairs. "Eh, wot's goin' on? You can't make a fuss like this in my inn."

Jack drew up short in dismay. He'd reached the rear wall and there wasn't a door. With a cry of anguish he frantically scanned right and left—and saw the door, beneath the stair.

He pushed thorough it and found himself in a narrow passageway between the inn and its neighbor Without hesitating, he darted right and raced toward the rear of the stables. He had a better chance there than on the main street.

Voices sounded behind him but Jack didn't stop. He rounded the corner of the stables and took off at a dead run toward the mouth of the mews.

He thanked whatever god had given him the idea of leaving his horse at another inn. It was a race against time, but Jack thought he could get out of town before Sterling rounded up enough officials to come looking for him.

Panting hard, he leaned for a moment against a wall,

struggling to catch his breath. If he remembered rightly, the other inn was two roads to the left. He'd have to cross the main street, but Sterling would probably concentrate his search on the side streets. Jack hoped so.

By the time he reached the stables, a deep, searing pain tore at his chest. Yelling for a stable boy, Jack grabbed the saddle off the rack and headed down the stable aisle, looking for his horse.

"It's an emergency," Jack gasped when the boy appeared. "A shilling if you can get me out of here within the minute."

The stable lad raced to comply. Although every second seemed more like hours, the boy completed his task with lightning speed, and grinned excitedly at the shiny shilling Jack tossed his way. Leaping into the saddle, Jack headed his horse toward the street.

Quickly, he tried to orient himself. He needed to head for the Westgate Bridge; it was the least likely escape route. He dared not race his horse down the street, or he'd attract attention, but Jack urged him into as sprightly a trot as he dared. More quickly than he hoped, he reached the edge of town. He gave the horse his head and they galloped down the road toward Herefordshire.

Jack finally slowed his mount to a walk, the animal's heaving sides too reminiscent of his own labored breathing as he had run for his life in Gloucester. The only way Sir Richard could catch him now was if he was directly behind him, and with other roads heading west and south from Gloucester, it seemed unlikely.

God. That had been a close escape.

Even so, he'd failed. Sir Richard had the necklace and Honoria was still in the asylum.

Had she even known of his efforts to free her? Probably not, but he wished she did. Wished she knew that he'd tried to rectify his wrong, had tried to save her. Now she'd never know, and he'd never have another chance. The necklace had been his only hold over Sir Richard; there was nothing more he could do to save Norry. The necklace hadn't been enough; her uncle wanted to punish her as well. Jack was helpless in the face of such vindictiveness.

He didn't regret the mess he'd made of his own life, but he had no business ruining Norry's. Guilt and fear gnawed at him. There must be some way, some person who could prevail over Sir Richard.

As quickly as the answer came, he tried to shove it away. *Anything but that. There had to be another way.* But the more he looked at the problem, the more Jack realized he had one last option. It was a slim chance at best—the man had never done anything for him in the past—but maybe, because it was for Norry and not Jack, he might be persuaded to help. And if any man in England had the power to persuade Sir Richard, it was he.

With an anguished groan, Jack admitted he had no choice. He would have to go to his father, and beg his help.

Chapter 25

Despair washed over Honoria as she huddled in the corner of her room. Ever since she'd been escorted back through the gates, she feared that this time she would never come out again.

She clung to one small spark of happiness. Jack had given up the necklace. He hadn't betrayed her, but instead gave up everything he had in his futile attempt to save her.

Thank God he had escaped.

It was her fault that he was left with nothing. She'd succumbed to Uncle's treacherous lies and betrayed Jack to him. What must he think of her now? That she was a foolish, silly girl, and he was right.

Her only consolation was that he was alive—and free. She only hoped he valued that enough to keep himself safe.

Honoria did not know what would happen to her now. Maybe, since Uncle had the necklace back, he would release her when his anger subsided, or when he tired of paying her keep here.

But where would she go then? She had no relatives

who could help her now. In fact, she rather hoped Edmond died from his wound, but she didn't think a ball in the arm was usually fatal. A pity Uncle had not taken better aim. At least she had the small satisfaction of having Edmond's treachery revealed to her uncle.

Yet that did nothing to help her.

If only she could go to Jack. But she did not know where to find him, or if he would even speak to her. What need did he have for an impoverished lady who'd stupidly caused him to toss away a fortune? Even if she fell down on her knees and begged, he would never relent.

She would be better off if Uncle kept her here forever.

Jack reined in his horse and stared down the sloping hill to the house below. The weathered stone facade, castellated roof, and forest of chimney stacks gave it a grim and forbidding appearance.

How he hated this place. Memories of the miserable fifteen years he'd spent here welled up in him and for a moment, he almost turned his horse around. He had ridden hard for two days and he was exhausted. The thought of confronting his father made him cringe. But he had to continue, for Honoria's sake, if not for his.

Urging his horse into a slow trot, Jack rode down the drive. As expected, a liveried footman meet him at the base of the stairs. Jack handed him the reins and climbed the wide marble steps.

Another footman waited outside the heavy oak doors.

"I'm here to see His Grace," Jack said curtly.

"Do you have a card?" the servant asked with a barely concealed sneer at Jack's disheveled appearance.

"He'll see me," said Jack grimly. "Tell him the prodigal son has returned."

The footman's eyes widened. "Wait here. I shall see if His Grace is receiving callers."

At least he didn't slam the door in my face, Jack thought. Although he'd been gone so long, he doubted anyone ever thought he'd be coming back.

The footman returned in a few minutes. "His Grace will be with you shortly. Kindly follow me to the library."

"I know where it is."

Jack crossed the hall and stepped through the library doors, scanning the room's interior. Nothing seemed altered. The same expensive, leather-bound books neatly filled the shelves, the same valuable Italian paintings, collected on some long-ago Grand Tour, hung on the walls. He walked to the far end of the long, narrow room and gazed out the window onto the manicured front lawn.

The sameness of it all shocked him. Somehow, he'd expected this place to have changed as much as he had. Instead, it looked frighteningly unaltered. It was almost as if time had stopped—or reversed itself by eleven years.

He walked over to the long, oaken library table and ran his fingers along the side, feeling the indentations in the wood. He bent down and peered at the marks.

JDH. His initials, carved in the wood when he'd been incarcerated here for some infraction or other. Instead of reading his Latin, he'd defaced the furniture and earned himself another whipping. At the time, he hadn't cared.

Nor did he now. The past couldn't be changed. All he could hope now was that his father would be willing to help him this time. Just once.

Jack heard a muffled cough and turned. The footman smiled apologetically. "His Grace will see you in the study."

Jack nodded and followed him into the hall. Their footsteps echoed loudly in the high-ceilinged entry and Jack shivered at the chill sound. The marble grandeur of the hall was designed to impress, but Jack had always found it coldly depressing.

The footman pulled open the door to the study, then stepped aside to allow Jack to enter, closing the door quietly behind him.

The Duke of Mornington stood staring out the window, hands clasped behind his back.

Despite himself, Jack felt the old, familiar mix of fear and rebellion. How many times had he been sent here, to explain his transgression and to await his punishment? He was doing very much the same thing now, but instead of punishment, he was asking for a favor. From a man who rarely granted them.

The duke turned and Jack stood stiffly under his scrutinizing gaze.

A low growl reached Jack's ears, and from the corner of his eye he glimpsed a giant black mastiff standing before the fireplace, eyeing him with suspicion.

At last, the duke broke the heavy silence. "You are still alive, I see."

Jack shrugged. He could say the same of his father. His hair was whiter, his face more lined, but he was as imposing as ever.

The duke's eyes narrowed sharply. "I assume this is not a casual visit. What sort of difficulty are you in?"

Jack flinched at the words, but held his ground. "It's not me . . ." He hesitated. "A friend of mine is in some trouble. I'm responsible and I need you—ask you—to do what you can help."

"What sort of trouble?"

Jack swallowed hard. "Robbery. But the charge is false—it was all a family dispute," he added quickly. "And the item's been returned to the owner, but the man won't relent."

The duke walked over to his desk and sat down, directing Jack to a nearby chair. "Tell me the whole of it," he said wearily.

Jack hesitated. He didn't dare tell the entire story. Glancing at his father, he sighed and began.

"I was asked by a lady to *retrieve* a necklace that should have come to her as part of her inheritance," Jack said.

"Who held this necklace?"

"Her uncle."

"And the necklace really is hers?"

"Yes." Jack dared a faint smile. "Her father told her it would be hers at his death."

"Go on."

"I found it for her, but before I could hand it over, her uncle discovered it missing. In retribution, he locked her up in an asylum for the insane."

"Where were you at the time?"

Jack ignored the question. "As soon as I learned what had happened, I stepped forward and returned it to her uncle, in return for his promise to set her free. But she is still locked in that hellhole."

"How can I help?"

"You know that the right word, whispered in the right ear, would gain her freedom."

"You want me to use my influence to free a woman who enlisted your help to steal a necklace for her?"

"Yes." Jack met the duke's hard eyes without flinching.

The duke shook his head sadly. "Jack, Jack. It was always thus with you. Getting yourself and others into scrapes."

"I never before asked you to help," Jack said coldly.

"Why now?"

"She's being punished for no reason," he said. "I can't let her pay for my crime."

"You wish to take her place?"

"No." Jack's voice was even. "But if that's what it will take to free her, I am willing."

"Who is this uncle?"

"Minor gentry in Gloucester. Sir Richard Sterling."

"Sterling, Sterling," the duke mused. "Can't say that I can place the name. The girl says this necklace is rightfully hers?"

"When her father died, the uncle produced a will, naming him as sole heir and guardian. She says she'd seen a different document, that left a portion of the estate, and the necklace, to her. Sir Richard virtually admitted it to me."

The duke made a steeple of his fingers. "So she took matters into her own hands, eh?" He looked sharply at Jack. "Why did she light on you as her accomplice?"

Jack flushed. The less he said about Gentleman Jack, the better. "Sheer chance," he lied.

"Is she in Gloucester?"

Jack nodded. "At a private establishment."

"Should be an easy enough matter to take care of," the duke said. "There are ways to persuade this uncle to drop his complaint."

"I'm sure that—"

The duke cut him off. "The question is, what is to be done with you?" He glared at Jack with barely disguised disgust. "From the sound of things, you've turned out exactly as I would have expected. I'm rather surprised to find you even alive—or in England."

"I've been lucky," Jack said flippantly.

The duke stood, indicating the interview was over. "Your mother is in the drawing room. You may pay your respects to her."

Jack rose and darted an apprehensive glance at the duke. "Will you help?"

"I'll think on it," the duke said evenly.

Jack could only bow and withdraw.

In the hall, he leaned his cheek against the wall. Its cool surface felt good on his flushed skin.

God, it had been as miserable an ordeal as he'd anticipated. The only good thing was that he'd been able to avoid a full recounting of his activities over the years. Although he doubted he would get away with that, in the end. The duke would want to know just how low his son had fallen, would take pleasure from knowing all his predictions had been correct. There was nothing the duke liked better than having his opinions confirmed.

But he'd agreed to think about helping Honoria and that was what mattered. Jack would go through any form of hell to free her from jail. He knew the duke would come up with his own special form of torture.

Jack straightened and brushed back his hair. It needed cutting and in an instant he was transported back to the kitchen of Nursey's cottage, where Honoria had snipped away his long, lank prison locks. How he wished he could turn the clock back, and start over. He'd do everything differently.

Everything. Starting from the moment she'd spirited him away from Gorton. He'd jump out of the carriage and run forever.

He started down the corridor toward the drawing room. The thought of seeing his mother filled him with about as much pleasure as seeing his father. In some ways, he blamed her more for all that had happened here. Never once had she interfered in the battles between father and son, absenting herself in her rooms when the tension grew too high.

A footman was stationed outside the door and he hastily swung it open when Jack appeared. He strode into the room with a nonchalance he didn't feel, his eyes scrutinizing the gray-haired woman sitting by the window. Like his father, she didn't look to have changed.

"Hello, Mother."

The Duchess of Mornington turned in her chair, and gave a cry of surprise at the sight of him. "Jonathan! Whatever are you doing here?"

"Like the proverbial bad penny, I always turn up."

The duchess eyed him critically. "Goodness, you look a disgrace. Your hair's too long, and those clothes . . ." She shuddered. "Does the duke know you're here?"

"We had a cordial conversation in the study."

"Why are you here?" she asked bluntly.

His lips twisted wryly. "To see my wonderful family again, of course."

The duchess's eyes glittered with a dangerous light. "If you truly had a concern for your family, you would have returned years ago."

"I'm here now," said Jack wearily.

The duchess gestured to a chair. "Sit." Jack obeyed, feeling like a chastened child.

"I don't suppose you've found a respectable existence for yourself."

Jack shrugged. "I've managed to stay alive."

"Where are you residing now?"

"I spent a lot of time in Shropshire."

"I believe you saw the marquess at Newmarket a few years back."

Jack stifled a grin at the remembrance of his brother's surprise at that encounter. "We exchanged a few words. I understand he has a large family."

"As do Sophia and Catherine."

"And do they scare the children into good behavior with tales of their wicked uncle Jack?"

The duchess pierced him with a dampening look. "I see you have not lost your unfortunate predilection for levity."

Jack remained silent. It was apparent that neither parent cared that he was here—and alive.

He shouldn't be surprised. After all, they hadn't cared about him when he lived here. Why should their feelings change when they hadn't seen him in eleven years?

But deep inside, he wished they had. Wished they

would reach out to him with open arms, welcoming him back into the family. Wished that someone, outside of his own worthless self, cared what happened to him.

There would be no fatted calf for this prodigal son.

"You will be pleased to know that George survived the Peninsula unscathed."

"How many children does he have?" Jack asked.

"George has not yet married."

"What? I am not the only disgrace to the family?"

The duchess glowered at him. "It was hardly fit for him to take a wife with the war." She leaned forward. "*Why* are you here?"

"A friend of mine is in difficulty. I appealed to His Grace for help."

A swift look of disgust crossed the duchess's face. "I should have known you'd find yourself in a scrape. Is your father going to assist you?"

"He said he'll consider the matter."

The duchess sighed. "I suppose I should let Mrs. Benson know you'll be joining us for dinner." She eyed his clothing with dismay. "I don't imagine you have anything suitable to wear."

"I was in a hurry and didn't have time to pack my evening rig," Jack said with sarcasm. "I'll be certain to bring it next time."

The duchess stood and Jack scrambled to his feet.

"It is time for my nap," she declared. "Dinner is at seven." With regal elegance, she swept from the room.

Jack looked around with indecision. Since he wasn't going to get a warm welcome, he wished he could be on his way. But Norry's fate depended on his father's cooperation, and Jack was determined to wait as long as he needed to.

He only hoped the duke would arrive at a decision soon.

Jack left the drawing room and started down the corridor. A maid scurried past, glancing at him curiously, but he ignored her.

His long stride soon brought him to the end of the corridor and he turned left toward the western—Elizabethan—wing. He counted the doors—one, two, three, four. Hesitating, he stopped outside the last one, then, with a grimace, he opened the door.

There was still a bed, and a dressing table in place. But any other sign of its former occupant was gone. The wall hangings and curtains had all been changed. Even the prints on the wall were different. Misty, pastoral scenes.

He shrugged and shut the door. They'd probably cleared it out the day he left.

Restlessly, he continued to prowl the corridors, poking into nooks and crannies he remembered from days long ago. Some spots seemed frozen in time—the library, the entry hall, the old nursery. Others, like his room, had been changed nearly beyond recognition. All the public rooms sported new hangings and furniture, the cast-off items no doubt crammed into the attic. A woman like Norry could maintain an easy life selling his mother's discards.

Norry. Jack felt the sharp pain of guilt and shame at the thought of her—of what she thought of him. He'd dashed all her dreams. But he was here, at the house he'd sworn never to set foot in again, in a last, desperate attempt to set things right again.

She might never forgive him, but at least her life wouldn't be completely ruined. He'd find some way to get her money, to give her the independence she craved. He couldn't bear the thought of Norry suffering more than she already had.

God, he wished he'd never met her, wished she'd never read of Gentleman Jack and conceived this wild scheme. She'd be safe now if she hadn't. Safe from the one person who'd done her the most harm.

It was still an hour before dinner when Jack returned to the drawing room. He was too restless to sit, but prowled the room like a caged beast, seeking an exit but knowing there was no escape from this house.

Jack's nervousness increased throughout the uncomfortable meal. He was loath to bring up the subject of Norry's release, fearing his father's refusal. But the food he ate, the wine he drank, made no impression on his senses. He could only wait, and worry.

Surreptitiously, he studied his father, looking for some hint of the duke's decision. But Mornington remained impassive, only speaking to criticize the sauce on the carrots, praise the perfect doneness of the beef, and to comment on Her Grace's delicate appetite. He didn't speak a word to Jack.

To her credit, the duchess tried to create some conversation. She rattled on about Jack's brothers and sisters, nieces and nephews. But as Jack cared little about them, he didn't express much interest.

He suspected his father was toying with him, as he'd

loved to do all those years ago, making him wait and wonder until the suspense was murderous. Jack struggled to keep his voice impassive, his demeanor relaxed, to show the man that his tactics no longer rankled.

After an interminable time, the cloth was removed and dessert brought. At last, with a nod from the duke, the duchess rose and retreated to the drawing room. Mornington sat silently while the butler poured the port. But when he left, Jack could no longer contain himself. With mingled dread and hope, he turned to his father.

"What do you—"

"I've decided to help you," the duke said suddenly.

Jack shut his eyes, uttering a silent prayer of thanks. *You may hate me forever, Norry, but I can at least give you back your freedom.*

"However"—the duke gazed into his port—"there are some conditions I ask of you in return."

Jack nodded impatiently. He wanted to be gone, to start setting into motion the process for Honoria's freedom. He could be back in Gloucester by late tomorrow, if he rode hard and fast.

"First, I want you to come back into the family."

Jack's laugh was tinged with bitterness. "It's a little late to prepare me for the church. Not that they'd ever take me."

The duke's expression remained impassive. "I was thinking more of sending you to Longmead."

Jack stared at him. "Longmead? I'm no farmer."

"No, but you don't seem to have an aptitude for any other calling." The duke frowned. "Except gambling, I hear."

Jack's face was set in sullen lines. He'd expected the duke to exact some payment, but this . . . ? Exile on a Norfolk farm?

"The estate turns a tidy profit," the duke said. "The man there knows his business."

"Then why send me there?" Jack asked. "I would have to rely on him to manage the place."

"You need something to do. I'm not going to turn you loose in London and watch you make a fool of yourself again."

Jack flushed at the setdown. He'd like to tell His Grace to take Longmead and be damned. But Honoria's freedom was paramount. Jack would agree to anything to help her. Later . . . well, he didn't think a promise elicited under duress was binding.

"I'll go to Longmead," he said with calculated reluctance. "But don't expect me to become an expert on turnips or pigs. I don't give a damn about the day-to-day running of a farm."

"That's acceptable." The duke refilled his glass. "You needn't look so glum. I don't intend for you to be there alone. Even with your unfortunate past, it shouldn't be too difficult a matter to arrange. Your mother will find you a suitable girl to wed."

"Marry!" Jack jumped up so quickly that he knocked his chair over. "I'm not going to be forced into any kind of marriage. Particularly with anyone who meets with your approval."

The duke calmly sipped his port. "It's your decision, of course. But don't expect my help otherwise."

Trembling with rage, Jack turned away. He clenched his fists, biting back the angry words that he longed to utter.

He had to think of Norry. Norry, alone and frightened in that miserable asylum. Norry, alone and defenseless, slipping into real madness with no one but him to care.

He had to agree—and the duke knew it. There was no other way; he had no other choice. From the moment Sir Richard had laughed in his face, Jack had known it would come down to this. The only question had been how high a price his father would demand.

And he'd demanded a high one. Restoration to a family he despised. A wife he didn't want. What went unsaid was all that went with those things—a conformable, settled existence, with obligations, restrictions, rules. The things he'd run from all his life, hemming him in forever. He'd never be free again.

Jack unclenched his fists. He hoped that someday Norry would appreciate what he was about to do for her. This was a worse sacrifice than taking her place in jail. At least there was an eventual end to that torture. This would last the remainder of his life.

Slowly, he turned back toward his father. "I'll do whatever you want," he said firmly.

The duke smiled in triumph. "Good. Now, as to your problem. What do you think would be most effective—putting in a word with the magistrate or dealing directly with the uncle?"

Jack remembered his last meeting with Sir Richard. "Dealing with the uncle would be quickest," he said, with a malicious pleasure. Sterling was no match for the duke. Jack only wished he could be there to see him crumble.

"What's the real reason behind Sir Richard's actions?"

"I believe he's in need of money. He tricked a German prince into buying a paste copy of the necklace."

The duke waved a hand. "Please, spare me the sordid details. This entire family sounds like a den of thieves. I'll prepare a letter to send in the morning. You can take it to him and begin the negotiations. I suppose I'll have to go to Gloucester and have a little chat with him."

"I think someone else should take the letter," Jack said hastily. Even with the power of the duke behind him, Sir Richard would not be pleased to see Jack again.

"I'll send my secretary, then," mused the duke. "While we wait, you can take the time to inspect Longmead."

Exile already, thought Jack. Not yet. He had one more thing he wanted to do before the walls closed in on him. "I want to go to Gloucester." Jack dared his father to say no. "To see Nor—Miss Sterling."

The duke's expression was guarded. "Do you think that wise?"

"It's my fault that she's in that asylum. I want her to know that I also helped to free her."

The duke nodded. "Well enough. Longmead will be awaiting you when you return. You can meet me in Cirencester. I assume you want to be there when I speak with Sterling."

Jack didn't know what his father would say to Sir Richard, but he knew that Norry was as good as free. No one had ever stood up to the Duke of Mornington and won. Not even Jack.

Swallowing hard, the words nearly sticking in his throat, Jack turned to the duke. "Thank you, Your Grace."

Raising his glass to his lips, the duke accepted the thanks as his due.

Chapter 26

With a perverse sense of justice, Jack insisted on sleeping in his old room.

As he lay in bed, listening to the ancient house creak and groan around him, he struggled with his conflicting emotions. Norry would be free, soon. The duke spoke of "negotiations," but Jack knew he would really send an ultimatum. Honoria could be free within days if all went well.

He wanted to be there when it happened, wanted to be the one to give her the news, to stand there as they unlocked the door, and led her from the room. It was the only way he could show her that he regretted what he'd done. If she'd even talk with him at all.

He'd need to make all the arrangements to send her to Nursey's again. Jack winced, knowing he'd be out of money, but it couldn't be helped. He had to take care of Norry.

And in Norfolk, what need did he have of money?

After a restless night, Jack rose with the dawn. He downed a hasty meal in the kitchen, left a polite note for the duke, and was on the road while the dew still lay heavy on the grass. Gloucester was a very long ride away.

It was hard to believe that a few short weeks ago he'd been at Norcross, laughing and teasing Norry. It came as a shock to realize just how much he missed that—and her.

Yet he shouldn't be surprised. From that night on the terrace, when he'd begun to doubt his carefree ways, he'd been trapped in her spell. And when he'd bedded her, it wasn't because he was trying to take advantage of her innocence, but because he wanted to, needed to.

Just as her adoring glances and innocent plans for the future frightened him, they'd encircled him as well. He'd spent so much time telling himself he was free, he'd not noticed that he'd given up his freedom a long time ago—maybe from the first moment he'd agreed to go along with her plan. He'd fought, struggled, complained, and argued, but his fate was sealed from the first.

He'd fallen in love with her. It wasn't an emotion Jack was familiar with, but he knew that it was the only thing that could make him feel this miserable, and willing to sacrifice everything that was important to him to win her freedom, and maybe her forgiveness.

She'd find it amusing that he thought it a sacrifice. What person didn't want a settled existence, with security, a future, and stability? It was what she wanted more than everything. But to Jack it had always meant bars, cages, and locks. He wasn't free to be himself, but always had to be what someone else wanted.

Even Norry had wanted to change him. She wanted him to have a goal, a plan, a future. All the things that signified security to her. When she'd talked of cottages, children, a future, he'd run like a frightened rabbit.

But he'd already admitted to himself that he was tired of the life he'd been leading. He wanted to start again, to do things right this time. Too much freedom could be as stifling as none; absolute freedom gave one absolute power to destroy oneself. Why else had he been standing on the gallows in Gorton, not caring whether he lived or died?

At least now he cared whether he lived. All because of Norry. She'd given him a second chance and it made him realize just how precious life was. Too precious to throw away with the roll of a dice or the turn of a card. Precious enough to make the effort to hold on to it, to do something with it.

He couldn't picture himself at Longmead forever. Farming wasn't in his blood any more than the church. But it would give him a base, a place to call home. A place he could make into a home of his own.

With a wife of his mother's choosing.

The solution was so obvious that Jack laughed at the simplicity of it. There was only one person who could make his life bearable; only one person he could imagine spending his life with. Deep down he knew it was the only way he could survive; the only way he could still conform and remain the person he was.

He only had the monumental task of convincing her that it was what she needed—and wanted—as well.

He could employ bribery and threats. She'd used those tricks enough times on him. But it was time for all the tricks and deceptions to end. There could only be honesty between them from now on. He'd tell her why he wanted her, why he needed her.

Because she was the only person who really knew him. Better, even, than he knew himself. And she was the only person who'd ever loved him for what he was, not for what they wanted him to be.

At the next crossroad, he took the southern turn. It was only a small detour; he'd still arrive in Cirencester in plenty of time to join his father. But he needed to make sure the matter was dealt with quickly, before he became too frightened and changed his mind.

Before his parents had time to weave plans of their own for him.

It would be his final act of rebellion before he settled down into the kind of life that everyone wanted him to live. The kind of life that would be a joy only if he had Norry at his side.

Jack paced the stable yard in Cirencester, anxiously glancing toward the entry at the sound of each approaching carriage. Where was the duke? Had he changed his mind?

He consulted his watch. It was already half-past twelve. If the duke didn't arrive soon, they'd have to postpone going to Spring Meadow until tomorrow. One more day that Norry would have to remain locked in.

At the familiar sound of jingling harness, clopping hooves, and creaking wheels, Jack looked up again, just as the elegant traveling coach of the Duke of Mornington swept into the yard. Jack breathed a sigh of relief.

The duke's secretary, waiting beside Jack, ran up and

lowered the steps and the duke climbed down. "Are all the arrangements made?"

The secretary nodded.

"Good." Mornington turned to Jack. "You still wish to go along?"

Jack nodded. More than ever. He wanted to see the look on Sir Richard's face.

"Allow me to rest for a few moments and we can be on our way."

The duke's rest was as hasty as he'd promised, and it was less than thirty minutes later when the carriage, with its ornate coat of arms emblazoned on the side, left for Norcross.

The duke turned toward the secretary, Foxton. "Does the man have any inkling of what I'm about?"

Foxton shook his head. "I merely said you wished to discuss a financial matter with him. He's puzzled, but I answered none of his questions."

"Good, good." He looked at Jack. "Have you spoken with the girl yet?"

"I'll wait until she's free to leave," he said quietly.

The duke nodded and lapsed into silence.

The footman at Norcross looked surprised to see Jack, but his expression changed to amazement when the duke announced himself. With a great deal of bowing, the footman escorted the three men to the study, where Sir Richard awaited them.

Sir Richard stepped forward, his hand extended, when the duke entered the room. Catching sight of Jack, Sterling started and stared. "You!" He looked obsequiously at the duke. "Excuse me, Your Grace, but are you aware of the identity of this man?"

"Unfortunately," the duke replied. "It is on his behalf that I am here to see you."

"But—" Sir Richard stammered—"your man said—"

"My man said what I told him to say." The duke stripped off his gloves and took a chair. "Please, Sir Richard, be seated. My time is valuable and I do not wish to spend any more of it here than I have to."

Jack smiled at the stunned look on Sir Richard's face.

"I am here," began the duke, "to ask you to free your niece—Honoria, I believe her name is—from the Spring Meadow asylum."

"She—and that scoundrel—conspired to steal some valuable jewelry from me," Sir Richard growled. "I'm only serving the cause of justice."

The duke waved his hand. "We will discuss justice later. Right now, I wish you to write a letter to the matron, ordering her to release your niece."

"I don't know what this felon has told you, but he's as guilty as she. More so, for he's the one who actually stole it."

"And as I understand things, you now have it back. Therefore, I see no need for your niece to remain incarcerated."

Sir Richard bristled. "I fail to see your interest in this matter."

"I am very interested," the duke said. "As would be the authorities, if they ever knew why it was in your possession."

"As sole heir of my brother—"

"You took the opportunity to deprive your niece of her share of the estate," the duke finished flatly. "And that is something I do not think you wish to become common knowledge."

Sir Richard glared at Jack. "Has this fool been filling your head with his ridiculous tales? He's no more than a common thief; you can't believe a word he says."

"While my *son's* behavior has often been in question, his veracity never has been," said the duke.

Richard stared. "Your son?"

Jack bowed. "Lord Jonathan Derrington Howard, at your service, Sir Richard."

Sterling jumped to his feet, looking from Jack to the duke and back again. "By God, what kind of game are you two running?"

The duke signaled to Foxton. "The papers."

His secretary produced a set of documents, which were set on the desk before Sir Richard.

"If you would be so kind as to sign these . . ." The duke coughed hesitatingly.

Richard stabbed an angry finger at Jack. "I want you off my land this instant!"

The duke looked to Jack. "Perhaps it's best if you wait outside," he suggested. "I'm sure that Sir Richard and I can come to an agreement more quickly if we are left alone."

Jack was willing to leave. He'd already seen all he wanted to—the look on Sir Richard's face was adequate compensation. All he wanted was to get the matter over and get Norry out.

"Be careful," he said, in warning, as he headed for the

door. "The last time I tried to bargain with him, he pulled a pistol on me." He shut the study door with a firm thud.

Waiting in the hall, he heard the upraised, angry voice of Sir Richard coming from the room, but he couldn't make out his words. After years of fighting with his father, Jack knew Sir Richard had no chance. The duke would get what he wanted.

No more than twenty minutes passed before the duke and his secretary emerged. The duke darted a glance at Jack. "We can free your friend now. I have everything we need."

Jack eagerly headed for the door.

Honoria paid no attention to the increasingly raucous cries of the other inmates down the hall. No doubt a new "guest" was coming to join them. She sat back on her bed, arms clasped about her knees, and stared at the wall.

It wasn't an utterly unpleasant place. No one bothered her; she spent her days in solitude. Boredom was the real danger here. Boredom and despair.

Was this what had worn Jack down, in his long months of imprisonment? It was a wonder he'd survived at all. She feared she would be utterly mad before the year was over. As strong as she was, she knew she couldn't last much longer.

"Norry?"

See? This only proves I am losing my mind. Now I'm hearing Jack's voice as clearly as if he were in the room with me.

"Norry, I've come to take you out. You're being released."

She kept her eyes downcast, staring at the booted feet of the man before her. It was easier to preserve the illusion that way. Even if it was madness, she'd rather believe it than the miserable reality surrounding her.

"Your uncle has given in. You can leave."

Slowly, she lifted her eyes, past the boots, the stained breeches, and the dark coat until she looked into the wary brown eyes.

Jack's expression was apprehensive. "I had to give him back the necklace. He was supposed to have released you then, but—"

"I know," she said quietly. "He tricked you. I'm sorry."

Jack held out his hand. "Come, Norry. It's time to leave."

"And where am I to go?" she demanded bitterly. "I'm certain Uncle Richard will welcome me with open arms at Norcross."

"I've arranged a room for you at one of the inns in Cirencester. I thought you might want to go to Nursey's tomorrow, after you've rested."

Slowly she stood, despair pressing down on her shoulders. "I suppose that is the only place I can go. I'm sure the rest of my family has disowned me."

"Come home with me, then," Jack said.

Norry smiled sadly. "Home? Where is that? A cow barn? A clearing under a tree?"

"There's a farm in Norfolk," he said quietly. "My father has given it to me to manage."

She stared at him. "Your father? I thought he'd disowned you long ago."

He flushed. "We have reached an accommodation of sorts."

"How nice."

Jack reached over and took her hand. She flinched at his touch but didn't pull away.

"There is a meal waiting for you at the inn in Cirencester. And a bath." He grinned. "I even brought you some clean clothes. And lavender water."

Honoria looked at him. "Why, Jack? Why are you doing this?"

He shifted uncomfortably. "I had to," he said at last. "I . . . I never meant for this to happen to you, Norry. I thought I was protecting you by leaving as I did. There would be nothing to implicate you . . . I thought you would be safe."

"I asked you to take me with you."

"Norry, I swear I thought it best. How was I to know your uncle would do something like this? I came back as soon as I got your letter." He squeezed her fingers. "I am sorry about the necklace, but I couldn't let him do this to you."

He met her gaze and the pain in his eyes surprised her.

"All my life, I've done what I wanted, without thinking of anyone else's needs or wants. But I swear, Norry, that I would have taken your place here if it meant you'd have your freedom. For the first time, I wanted to put someone else's needs above my own."

He drew in a breath. "It took me so long to contact you because I was waiting to sell the necklace in London. It took some time to arrange because I wanted you to get as much money as you could for it."

"You planned to come back for me?"

He bowed his head. "No. I was going to send you the money and go to Paris. Not because I wanted to, but because I thought it would be better for you."

"Why?"

"You're the only person who's made me ashamed of what I am, and what I've done—and who thought I could do something more." He laughed bitterly. "You almost convinced me I could change."

She searched his face. "Can you?"

"Not by myself. But if I had the right person to encourage me . . ." Jack took her other hand. "I know you want a house in the country, a settled existence, security. I fought against that all my life because that's what everyone wanted for me. Now . . . well, it doesn't sound quite so terrifying, if you're there."

"I don't care, Jack, I fell in love with you as you are, as you will be." She struggled to blink back tears. "Don't change yourself into someone I don't even know."

"I'm tired of being selfish and arrogant and thinking only of myself. Norry, I started to rescue you out of guilt. But the more I thought about it, the more I realized I wanted to free you for my own sake. Because it meant I was doing something for someone else, taking care of you, looking out for you. I've never cared enough about anybody to do that before." A wry grin crossed his face. "I want to keep caring for you."

He reached into his coat and pulled out a wrinkled paper, his face breaking into a smile. "It's a special license, Norry. If you want to walk out of here and never set eyes on me again, I'll understand. But if you'll let me, I promise to adore you, take care of you, love you, and need you. Because I do."

In that instance, Honoria realized that she'd been quite as selfish as Jack. For she, too, had only been thinking of herself and what she wanted. And it was surprising and heartwarming to think that Jack needed her, that she could actually do something for him.

"I love you, Jack. I think I have from the first moment in Gorton, when they took that hood from your head and I looked into your eyes."

"Ah, Norry." Jack pulled her into his arms.

There was a discreet cough at the door. "Excuse me, sir, but are you and the lady ready?"

Jack released her and Norry caught sight of the man standing near the door.

"I brought a minister along," Jack said. "In case you said yes."

Honoria smiled fondly at him. "The typical arrogance of Jack Derry."

"Please," Jack said. "If we could begin the ceremony."

The minister looked about doubtfully. "Witnesses?"

Jack beckoned to the matron in the hall. "Grab one of your assistants, quick."

He turned back to Honoria and looked down. "You don't mind? I know it's not exactly a proper wedding, but—"

"It is fine," Honoria said.

"Dearly beloved . . ." intoned the minister.

" . . . to love, honor, cherish, and obey . . ."

"Good God, this place is appalling."

Jack jumped at the voice and looked anxiously over his

shoulder. "Quickly," he whispered to the minister. "Get on with it. I do. I will. She will too."

Honoria looked at him in confusion. Jack nudged her gently. "Answer the man."

"I do."

"By the powers vested . . ."

"Haven't you got that dratted girl out of here yet? What's taking so long?" The Duke of Mornington stood in the doorway, peering into the common room.

Honoria turned a puzzled face to Jack.

"My father," he explained weakly.

She peered over her shoulder at the elegantly dressed gentleman standing in the corridor.

"He's a rather intimidating-looking person," she whispered. "I can see why you two did not get along."

Jack face formed a lopsided smile. "Wait until he finds out what we've just done."

He took Norry's hand and led her to the door, stopping in front of his father, who stared with blatant curiosity at Norry.

"Norry, I should like you to meet my father. His Grace, the Duke of Mornington."

Honoria's mouth gaped. "Your father's a duke?"

The duke's lips quivered. "You must be Miss Sterling."

"Lady Jonathan Howard," Jack said hastily. "We were just married."

Honoria took a step backward and stared at Jack. "Who, exactly, are you?"

"They named me Jonathan Derrington Howard at birth," he said with a sheepish smile. "But I've always been known as 'Jack.' "

Honoria wrapped her arms around him, burying her face in his chest. Jack was not sure if she was shaking with laughter, or relief. He darted an apprehensive glance at his father.

"Well," said the duke, looking remarkably unperturbed, "I think then that this might be considered a wedding present of sorts." He reached into his pocket and pulled out a glittering mass of diamonds and rubies. "Sir Richard decided that his niece had a right to this after all."

Jack took it from him and handed it to Norry. "It's yours, now," he said, his voice husky. "To do with as you please."

"Then I should like to have the most glorious honeymoon in Paris."

Jack whooped with laughter and picked her up, twirling her about in dizzying circles in the narrow corridor.

Epilogue

Jack put another log on the fire and stirred the coals with the poker until it burst into flames. With a satisfied smile, he took his seat on the sofa. Outside, the wind from the North Sea howled, but inside the small parlor, it was snug and warm.

He put his arm around Honoria and she rested her head against his shoulder.

"Only two more hours," he said. "Do you think you can stay awake?"

"I slept all afternoon in anticipation. I am determined to see the new year in."

Jack placed his hand over her softly rounded belly. "And how is the guest of honor doing tonight?"

"Sleepy. Like his mother."

Jack laughed. "We could wait upstairs. In bed."

"Then I will fall asleep. No, I will do better here."

They lapsed into a comfortable silence.

"Jack?"

"Yes, love?"

"Christmas wasn't really as bad as we feared, was it?"

"No," he admitted slowly. "I think . . . well, it seemed

that all the things I hated so much before were not so bad now."

"That's because you were coming back as a man. You know they can't do anything to you now." Honoria darted him a sideways glance. "Did he really intend to make you a clergyman?"

"That's the role of the third son. Just think, if I'd been born before George, I could have gone into the army. Now that would have been exciting."

"And I never would have met you."

He hugged her. "True. At least I can thank my father for something."

"Are you ever going to tell him about Gentleman Jack?"

"Norry, there are some things that parents do not ever wish to know."

"I think the duke was pleased when you told him about the baby."

"Only because he thinks it is a sign that I am going to settle down."

"Will you?"

Jack opened his mouth to defend himself until he saw the teasing look in her eyes. He took her hand.

"I never thought I could be so content as I am right now."

"Really?"

"Really. Right now, I can imagine nothing more pleasurable than sitting here watching you grow rounder and rounder for the next five months."

Honoria made a face. "I am glad we went to Paris. Sophia is so disappointed that we will not be going to town for the Season."

"I'll take you next year." Jack nuzzled at her neck. "That is, if you aren't pregnant again by then."

"I should hope not!"

"It won't be for lack of trying." He brought his mouth down on hers in a kiss that sent her blood boiling.

"Maybe we *should* welcome the new year upstairs," she whispered. "If you promise to do your best to keep me awake."

"Oh, I will," Jack said. "I most certainly will."